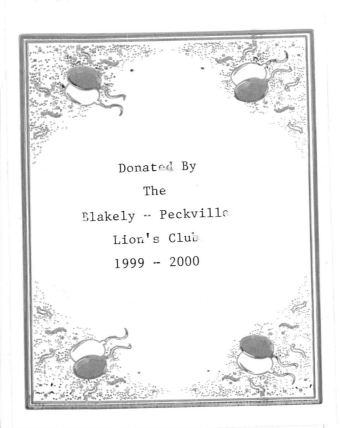

Donated By
The
Blakely -- Peckville
Lion's Club
1999 -- 2000

FOUR
CORNERS
of NIGHT

FOUR CORNERS of NIGHT

Craig Holden

Thorndike Press • Chivers Press
Thorndike, Maine USA   Bath, England

This Large Print edition is published by Thorndike Press, USA and by Chivers Press, England.

Published in 1999 in the U.S. by arrangement with Delacorte Press, an imprint of Dell Publishing, a division of Random House, Inc.

Published in 1999 in the U.K. by arrangement with Macmillan Publishers Ltd.

U.S. Hardcover 0-7862-1883-5 (Mystery Series Edition)
U.K. Hardcover 0-7540-1301-4 (Windsor Large Print)
U.K. Softcover 0-7540-2225-0 (Paragon Large Print)

The text of this Large Print edition is unabridged.
Other aspects of the book may vary from the original edition.

Set in 16 pt. Plantin by Rick Gundberg.

Printed in the United States on permanent paper.

Library of Congress Cataloging in Publication Data

Holden, Craig.
  Four corners of night : a novel / by Craig Holden.
    p. cm.
  ISBN 0-7862-1883-5 (lg. print : hc. : alk. paper)
  1. Large type books. I. Title.
  [PS3558.O347747F6 1999b]
  813'.54—dc21   99-17845

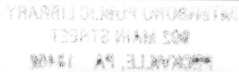

For Emma,
a book of daughters,

and

for Tom Barden,
who gave me the first glimpse
and then named it

The whole of the wideness of night is for you,
A self that touches all edges . . .

— WALLACE STEVENS

ONE

1

The call comes over on a Sunday morning. It comes while we sit in this old Denny's restaurant, now kind of weather beaten with a couple of broken, boarded-over windows, out toward the western part of the city, and wait for our Grand Slams.

"Buck ninety-nine," Bank says. "Who can afford not to eat this shit at that price?" He's said this over the years maybe fifty times in this restaurant with me.

The place has grown suddenly crowded with the church people. I remember that this is Palm Sunday for the Christians.

Neither Bank nor I say much anymore. We've been talking for nearly thirty years and have pretty well said what we have to say to each other. So we listen to the radio that Bank has carried in. Even here, off shift, after a long night of hammering, he can't let it go, cannot step out of the flow of garbage and pain. And when we hear an "All units" come over on channel four, we both sort of freeze and wait for it, although it is not our responsibility, because that's what we've been conditioned to do.

I do not know why this particular moment strikes me so vividly, the moment these words come over. I have no reason to think it is significant. But for some reason, a premonition perhaps, a detective's instinct — which is a thing worth trusting, I learned long ago — my brain chooses this tick out of the millions of the day to freeze. The way the sunlight slants through the wide window and strikes the table, warming my arms. The way smoke drifts over from the next booth, blue-white and languid, hanging in the sunlit air. The rubbery pink burn scars that mar Bank's throat and forehead and the sides of his face, and the fingerless gloves he still wears over his damaged hands. The angle of his head, the same look of concentration in his eyes I saw for the first time in 1967, three quarters of our lifetimes ago.

I cannot call it, in itself, a remarkable moment but I recognize it for what it is: a deceiver, a moment which tries to disguise itself as just another beat in the continuum when in fact it is something more than that. What, exactly, of course, I do not know.

The night before, from eleven to seven, we rode: the North End, directly above the downtown, what was once the old Polish and Hungarian towns but has become a cracked-out wasteland; Central-North, to the west, which is still working class, small bungalows and narrow two-stories built in the factory neighborhoods of the forties, still held together by nurses and guys who drive local trucks or work at the PO; and the East Side, which is a land unto itself.

I wasn't working, exactly, just riding along with Bank, which I try to do whenever I'm on call. I work days out of the Personal Crimes Section of the newly formed Investigative Services Division, but cruising with Bank keeps my toes in the muddy water of the late-night city, keeps me tapped into a side of its business that rolls up and goes away with the rising of the sun. Since the restructuring of our force, though, a year or so back, when the new Command did away with the old squad system, my on-call time has dropped dramatically, so that now I end up working only a night or two each month.

Old Bank, though, who at various times was my official partner, and who before that became my best friend the year we turned nine years old, has for years now worked a graveyard felony car alone except for those few nights I ride along with him.

Bank has some seniority. He has a rep. He has plenty of admiration on the force and in the city at large, and everyone knows he could

11

walk the sergeant's exam. Bank is also, to a fair degree, famous in our city and even beyond. He's been the subject of local and regional television and newspaper profiles, a slick magazine article or two, and has even appeared on a couple of those nationally syndicated cop shows. The press loves him, and the public does too. More than once he has been asked to make an appearance at a school or some ceremony. And he does it, wearing a turtleneck to cover the worst of his scarred neck. But always, then, it's back out into the night. He won't give it up. He's a maverick. That's just the word. A cowboy riding around crack town all night, stirring up the dogies whenever he can, saying hey to all his dealer snitches, his buddies, ruffling the crack whores with his bright twelve-volt spotlight plugged into the car's cigarette lighter. Them holding their hands up over their eyes and clucking like hens in their house — "Mm. Ah. Wha'choo want?" "Who izzat?" Cluck, cluck, cluck.

"*Girl,*" Bank always says, and it was no different on this night, "it's the *po*-lice."

"Shit. Bank? That you? Shit. S'Bank."

"Cold out here tonight, girl," he said. "Only a couple more days." Meaning they'd be getting their government checks after the first of the month, which would buy their dope for maybe two weeks, so they could take a break from selling it. The second half of the month was their busy time.

"Mm-hm," the one said, a tall, ugly big-thighed girl in a dirty fake-fur jacket and tights. "Boyfriend gone snatch it up anyway. Don't matter."

"You need yourself a new boyfriend."

"Shit," she said. "No shit on that, Mister Po-lice."

Bank said, "Don't *even* let me catch you doing nothing ee-legal out here. You got it?"

"Us? We jus' takin' the night air," she said, and they all cackled.

"I'll be back by in an hour," said Bank, meaning if they were still here he might consider them to be loitering, if not soliciting as well.

"Hey, Bank," the whore said. "You know what?"

"What?"

"You my hero."

The girls broke up into laughter, and Bank laughed, and I laughed, and he killed the bright light and we drove on.

The streets at night are covered by squad cars, uniformed patrolmen. In addition, the city requires there to be a detective present at the scene of any felony arrest. Our city is not terribly large — something like four hundred

13

thousand, double that for the metro area — so these late nights are left to a handful of felony-car dicks who handle anything that comes up, except homicides and cases requiring long-term investigations: arsons, complex robberies, that sort of thing. An on-call day-shift detective is dragged out for these. But otherwise, f-cars manage the nights. This is their job, just to be there.

Most other f-car men I know wait for the phone, riding their desks except when they can't help it, when the phone rings and they have to jump out to a scene. Then it's back in to the Public Safety Building, process the collar, call a squad for a transport, snag some coffee, and start picking away at that stack of paperwork. Until the phone rings again.

But Bank, he stays out, prowling, working the city, watching the buys and the bars and the whores. He carries four different radios with him, to monitor all the bands of the city, and he responds to every call he can, often arriving on scenes before the first squad cars. And when there are no calls, he goes out and finds one:

A kid, say, black, white, Hispanic, walking down the street at 1:00 A.M., hands in pockets. Bank will shine him with the big light, hit him in the face and blind him. If the kid stops, closes his eyes, and cocks his head

14

off to one side, pulls his hands out of the pockets, he's okay. Bank lowers the light and rides on. If he bolts, though, Bank is off after him, out of the car and hauling ass through the ghetto, chasing a boy who an observer might think probably did nothing but got scared.

But it's never that way. They've always done something or got something or know something that allows Bank to bring them downtown and process them. Carrying a crack pipe or a rock, a BB gun, or a real one for that matter, some cash they can't explain. Even if it's only that they're wearing red or green shoelaces, which are gang signs, he'll run them in for violating the city's curfew. And the thing about Bank is, half the time he finds a way to drum up a felony charge where any other cop would see a misdemeanor, or even nothing. Take the BB-gun example. Bank might view that as "possession of tools to commit a felony." He'll figure the kid was out perping robberies with what looks, in the dark, like a real gun. So he'll make the bust, do the paperwork, and go to court to see it through. Often as not these cases get thrown out either by the prosecuting attorneys or the judges, but Bank keeps right on running them in, making everybody work harder than they want to.

Bank's willing to do more paperwork than any other cop I've ever met, and in the end, I suppose, that is one of the secrets of his success. He suffers endless bullshit and red tape to make his version of the system work the way it's supposed to.

The radios crackled and spoke in cop talk, two in the backseat, one on the dash, and one, tuned to Band 4, for the North End and the East Side, the hot one, stuck between Bank's legs, so he could get to it in an instant, without any fumbling in the dark.

Our Saturday night filled with small-time busts — robberies, assaults, dope buys, one aggravated burglary stopped in progress on a dispatch call that we beat the squads to (a kid carrying a TV set from a building in the Lloyd DuShane Homes, a huge East Side housing project), and so on. It didn't faze Bank at all that five of our perps were fifteen years old. Fifteen seems to be the high age of crime. Though I came up through the old Juvenile Squad, I still stop and wonder about this sometimes but Bank just presses on.

Bank likes it when I work a night with him. I not only ride along while he cruises, but then help him pull up the jackets, type the reports and requests for juvenile transfers and so forth, even run the collars around to the Juvie Hall or County, wherever they're headed. So, although he was officially off shift at seven, it was only after nine that we finally landed in the Denny's and ordered our food.

And so the call comes: "Available units, respond to the report of a child missing at 230 King's Court." Dispatch is Carla this morning. Her voice sounds cool and uninflected. Bank raises his ruined eyebrows at me as we listen to the patrols talking it over on the air, to the first descriptions of the scene. I wait to see his reaction.

"Three oh six. What d'you got goin'?"

Dispatch: "Three oh six, a woman says her daughter disappeared. Twelve-year-old daughter."

A young missing almost-teenager on a Sunday morning is surely either a runaway or, more likely, the result of a long Saturday-night party. The girls especially, when they show up at home, finally, with suck marks on the neck and dirty, rumpled clothing, they tell a good story about how they were abducted and violated all night long. Happens every weekend.

Bank and I are kind of smirking at each other when the radio pops again: "Three twenty to three oh six, we're here, ah, at the scene. She's pretty hysterical, the mother. This girl's out riding a bike a few minutes ago, they, ah, find the bike, no girl. Reports of, ah

. . . might be that a car drove by shortly beforehand with two black males in the front seat. Followed the girl around a corner."

So this is something different. I watch Bank, again waiting for his reaction.

Dispatch: "Three two oh, code seven three. Investigative Services has been notified." This means very high priority. The only thing higher is a code seven one, officer in need of assistance, or a seven one red, an officer down.

"Three oh six responding, code seven three."

The airwaves fill with the chatter as more squads and the first detectives arrive at the scene, as it becomes apparent that this is maybe the real thing, a kid missing from a possible drive-by grab, a relatively rare crime, a potentially huge situation. And one that dredges up for us both, but especially for Bank, echoes of the soundless pleas of another child gone missing, echoes of the worst moments either of us has ever known.

And yet Bank has this look on his face, of a kind of horrified rapture. He has already lifted the radio, in preparation of our leaving.

"We're there, buddy," he says.

But I am no longer on call; Bank's off duty. We have no business at this scene. And more than that, to be honest, I feel some trepida-

18

tion: at facing this situation again, at feeling that utter helplessness, the lack of any control, any ability to affect the outcome. Of standing in the river of some mother's grief and feeling my own worthlessness.

The Grand Slams have just arrived: two eggs over, toast, bacon, pancakes, and coffee. I feel starved and exhausted after the long night. I imagine, I long for, that rich sensation of crawling into my cool morning bed, narcotized with heavy food, to wake only after noon into the glare and disorientation of high daylight. There is no way we can scarf all this down. But Bank looks like he'll die on me right here if we don't respond.

I shake my head.

He nods.

"Mack," he says, in the same voice he has used to cajole me for twenty-nine years.

I had actually wondered if he'd feel up to it, if he could face it. Up to it? No force, least of all me, can keep him from that scene.

He leaves me no choice in the end except to surrender. But then, that has always been the way.

In hindsight, in history, perhaps I will come to understand the place of this moment, its meaning, what makes it remarkable, why I have frozen it in this way, so that it will remain preserved in my mind, where it can perpetually happen. Or perhaps not. In any case, I cannot foresee what is coming, but I sense something in its nascence, and it frightens me.

A missing girl. She is an essential part of our story, of Bank's and mine, the heart of it, really. And now here is another who has cried out to us in some way that Bank hears more clearly than I.

We all, I suppose, reenact our lives over and over again, each moment an echo, a mimicking of some other. And the sums of these moments, the hours and months, are echoes as well, of patterns we set before we could ever have understood such things.

I roll my bacon up in the pancakes, lay the toast on top, wrap it all in a napkin, and take a good swig of the coffee, which burns my mouth. Bank does the same. We'll live longer without the eggs, anyway. Bank points a finger at the waitress, meaning we'll catch up to her later and pay the bill, and we're gone, out into the sunlight of a new holy day.

2

In 1985, eleven years ago, Bank and I each got our shield. I was twenty-six and Bank was twenty-seven. (We were born in the same year, but at opposite ends, early for him, late for me.) Bank had been on the force for over five years, since shortly after his return from a stint as a Marine MP at Guantánamo. I'd been on not quite four, since I dropped out after my first year of law school at Libbey University in our city, also my undergraduate alma mater. My joining the force in the first place was Bank's doing, his solution to a dual crisis in my life, his rationale for pulling me along behind him to a place I didn't neces-sarily belong.

For him, the move up to what was then called the Detectives' Bureau was a natural step in the progression of a career that had been natural for him from the start, from before the start, from the very beginning, from the time we were kids. For me the bump was a move of desperation. First on the part of the Command, which knew I was a pretty lousy patrol cop and had been saved largely by the fact I'd been partnered with Bank, and which hoped I'd work out better investigating. (The fact of my degree and my facility with exams made it easier for them to move me up so soon.) And on my own part. I was not happy riding the city, being the symbol and the fact of the law, standing up. I thought about it all too much. Think long think wrong, Bank would say, as a joke between us, because, although he didn't really understand my problem, he knew that for him the Job, his life, action itself, was unconscious, automatic, but that for me it was simply not and had never been.

Bank was big at six three and maybe 225 pounds, most of it pretty solid. He lifted weights in his basement on a good CalGym free-weight system that had been confiscated by the department in a drug raid and bought by Bank at a police auction. His wheat-colored Marine crew-cut had grown out and begun to darken a bit since his discharge, but not too much. He brushed it straight back from his broad, open, blue-eyed face.

In any case, life was better in the Bureau. We both applied to Violent Crimes, didn't get in, got assigned apart from each other, I to an initial six-month stint on a Missing Persons desk. Missing was okay for me, taking calls, making calls, going out to interviews, keeping records, FBI contacts. Okay, but ultimately uneventful and six months of it was plenty. Then my bid for a newly opened spot on the Juvenile Squad was accepted. Juvenile was better. Instead of just shagging runaways and listening to stories of malcontentment, I'd be dealing with practically every manner of crime. Kids, as I've suggested, compose a surprisingly large portion of the lawbreakers of any city, far more, I think, than the average citizen realizes. So the job hopped. Out to the schools, working with the principals and deans, searching lockers for weapons and drugs. Interrogating fourteen-year-olds. Casing the neighborhoods for the gangs that formed and disbanded, for the kids who had been cut loose from any normal tie to society and who just wandered, not even necessarily looking for trouble but always finding it.

Bank went first to the Narcotics Task Force, where he worked in his glory alongside the Tactical Squad boys in their jeans and T-shirts and leather jackets, busting in the doors of dope houses, posing on the street to make buys, getting in on car chases and gunfire. Bank took a bullet even, that year, through the outside of his thigh. Nothing too dramatic — it happened during a raid as a group of them went in through a broken-out window on the ground floor of a project apartment and a Tac officer tripped and fell, accidentally discharging his weapon. But it was a battle wound. Bank was known to drop his trousers around the Bureau at the merest mention of the injury to show people the fibrous plum-colored scar that had formed there. Same color as a fucking purple heart, he'd tell them.

After that Bank was assigned to the Gang Squad, where he began to lay the foundation for his genius as a detective: his contacts. Bank could talk to anybody, from a command officer down to the lowest clocker in one of the loosely structured gangs of our city, make them love him and yet fear him at once. Love and fear, the formula for making confidants. I knew how these people felt.

"Yo, yo, Bank, where you get that *name* from, man?" one of them would ask him.

And the answer, which became a chorus on the street, would come back from someone else, " 'Cause he big as a motherfuckin' bank vault and he *lock* yo' ass up."

And they'd laugh, Bank right along with them. It wasn't true, by the way. He'd had the name since he was a little kid, but it was a good story on the street and we helped promote it.

My own name, by the way, is Max, but I was, and am still, called Mack, on the force and off, and have been since I was nine. In the usual manner of these things my street name — because I am small, a good five inches shorter and fifty pounds lighter than Bank — became Big Mack.

Anyway, with Bank on Gangs and me on Juvenile, our paths crossed frequently. Our clientele were often the same people.

Another line we began to hear, as a typical kind of ironic street wisecrack, was: "Hey, Bank, man, you my hero." This, say, from a dealer-informant who Bank had just half cajoled, half threatened into giving someone up, or from some scrawny smoked-up pipehead as Bank simultaneously mashed his face into the trunk of a car and yanked his arms behind his back to cuff him. It was a dis, and of course Bank knew that, but he always let it slide except for maybe a quick roll of his eyes.

It would not be until after the fallout of the events of the summer of 1989 that people would begin to say that line to Bank and more or less mean it.

I lived at that time with a woman named Gloria Harris, whom I had impregnated in the spring of 1981, at the end of my second semester of law school. We were not, I think, in love anymore, if we had ever really been. The pregnancy panicked me, of course. I did not have it in me to abandon her. The fact that Gloria would not even discuss an abortion (she was, like Bank, a Catholic) angered me, and yet I knew, in my own private moments, that I did not want her to, that I secretly applauded her obstinance even as I argued against it. Having to at least postpone law school, however, was a kind of blessing. My desire to practice law had been waning from the time of my acceptance. I had been, I had to admit in honest moments, looking for a reason not to continue.

Gloria, our seven-year-old daughter, Naomi, and I lived in a tired sixties-era subdivision, a polyglot of working-class white Christians and what I referred to as the exotic minorities: immigrant families of Arab Moslems, Asian Buddhists, and Indian Hindus, and me, an agnostic Jewish-Lutheran with my lapsed Catholic partner. The sort of place designed to offer any man the chance to buy into a planned and organized community. With its three alternating styles of assembly-line three-bedroom house, its little landscaped lawns and poured concrete streets, it looked nothing like where Bank and I had grown up, although it lay only a few miles to the north of that place.

In fact, I had almost taken an apartment at one point, after Gloria and I had had a series of especially nasty battles. She had never asked or expected me to marry her, and did not, I believed, want me to. If she had, earlier on, I probably would have. She was a perfectly pragmatic woman, not hung up at all on protocol or appearance. It was enough if I helped her support the child, paid half of the mortgage and food and clothing bills and so forth, and spent enough time around the house to seem like a father figure to the girl.

Thrown into the bargain was the fact that, as two normal twenty-something-year-olds, we'd have bursts of the urgent need for passion, and Gloria didn't mind our giving in to that as well. It was not, as I've said, love between us. Not romantic love, in any case. Not as I saw it. But it was a thing that came from human need and from the sharing of a child, and though it didn't work all the time, and although Gloria and I each saw other people on occasion, I had, in some real sense of the word, a family.

On the day that changed us all, a still and densely humid Monday in July, I left our neighborhood early and drove east on Brentcroft Road, a major thoroughfare. Farther into the city, near the college, I turned off into the pleasant, wealthy urban village of Heron Hills, where Bank lived with his pretty wife, Sarah, and their daughter, Jamie, who was eleven and who had her fearsome, hard-ass father stuffed firmly into her pocket.

I stopped at the curb in front of the Bank Arbaugh house and tapped the horn once, lightly. Bank and Jamie appeared immediately from around back, Bank's shirt sweated through under the arms already, Jamie panting and red. Bank waved me up to the house.

"Hey, Uncle Mack," Jamie said.

"Glove practice," Bank said, panting a little himself. "Grounders."

"At seven A.M.," I said.

"Gotta fit it in before the real heat," said Bank. "Right?" This directed at Jamie, who loved softball and wanted to be a pro when she was older. Bank used to tell her he wasn't sure they had women's professional softball leagues, yet, but this didn't dampen her enthusiasm. Maybe she'd just go into baseball, she said. The bigs.

"Yep," Jamie said. She wore a baseball cap, navy blue with a red bill and a red cardinal above that, a blue tank top, and red nylon shorts with white stars on them. "I need batting, too, but I got my regular team practice at nine." Jamie was dark haired, like her mother, but her gray eyes actually looked more like Bank's, which was funny because Bank was

28

not Jamie's blood father. Jamie had been a year old when Bank and Sarah met. He had adopted her in the year after they were married.

I said, "Batting's tough."

"Yeah," she said. She plucked at her shirt. Tiny sweat beads dotted her nose. She smiled up at me, revealing her braces, which I still hadn't gotten used to, though she'd had them for a year.

Bank lifted his seersucker blazer from a chair on the front porch and said, "Let's ride."

Sarah had stepped out onto the porch in her bathrobe, wearing no makeup, her hair pulled back. This emphasized all the more her rich dark eyes and her soft and expressive countenance. How beautiful she was amazed me sometimes, at odd, stray moments like this, and how unlikely she and Bank were together. She came from a little money in circles where a little money was more than I ever dreamed of seeing.

I saw it as just another irony in our relationship that Bank turned out to be the one who ended up having some wealth. The fact that he had accomplished this by marriage was beside the point. It was in no way a sore spot between us, although Gloria mentioned it often enough. Honestly, I found it amusing, and though it was one of those details that continued to surprise me when I thought about it, I knew that it shouldn't. Bank had been given his nickname, after all, even before I met him, which was a very long time ago.

Jamie walked onto the porch, where her mother put her hands over her shoulders as they watched us leave. It was my turn to drive that day. We both waved, Bank and I.

Bank said, "Hit it, Professor." My degree was in psychology and English with a concentration in prelaw. The law degree, I had realized by then, at the seasoned age of thirty, I would probably never finish. I had not been meant by the Fates to be an urban cop. I knew it, and Bank, who was utterly responsible for my being there, knew it. But I had accepted it and had even, in my own odd manner, I think, come to enjoy it.

We'd left early so we'd have time for breakfast at the Denny's on Alcore Road, just before the on-ramp to the expressway that would take us downtown. Alcore was a heavily developed commercial stretch that formed the heart of what we called the New West End, which lay between the partially regentrified Old West End, farther into the city, and the far west corridor, where the city was still growing, and where we'd grown up.

Bank and I ate along that stretch often, as did any number of the city's cops.

We finished by seven-forty. When we stepped back out into the parking lot, the heat struck us both. The temperature had already hit ninety and no breeze had lifted its head. The air was dead and stale. This was the sort of day on which bodies rotted almost as fast as we could get to them, the sort of day that drove to a boil the percolating madness of some of our more unstable citizens.

We drove east, into the sun which was obscured in a haze of smog and mist and high distant clouds, into the city.

The elevators on the fourth floor of the Public Safety Building opened onto a narrow, claustrophobic hallway painted a governmental shade of pale green, dark enough to be ugly but light enough still to show the signs of the thousands of dirty bodies that had rubbed against it. Along the central stretch of this hallway, which extended to the left or right from the elevators, stood a series of closed, windowless wooden doors, each bearing a small plastic name plate: CRIME SCENE UNIT; HOMICIDE; BURGLARY/AUTO; ROBBERY/ASSAULT; METRO-NARCOTICS; and so on. The entire Detectives' Bureau on one floor, all off one long dingy hallway.

All the way to the right, forming the north end of the hallway, was an identical door with a rectangle in its center that said JUVENILE/ MISSING PERSONS. The open room beyond that door, the largest of all the squad rooms, was jammed with desks, a small lieutenant's office built into one corner, and a tiny windowless interrogation room built into another. This interrogation room, which we called the Crypt and which was used by some of the other units, too, had its own reputation in the legend of the city. I'd heard hardened bad guys call it the scariest place they had ever been. We sent up cheers every time one of the city's more creative defense attorneys would move for an acquittal based on the contention that the effect of the room was the equivalent of torturing a suspect into confessing. We loved that room. Even now, years later, I'll be somewhere in the city, in an old flophouse or in the jail, maybe, and a mixture of mustiness and sweat and flatulence and smoke in just the right combination strikes me and I'm back there for a moment, in the Crypt, leaning over some poor kid we have cuffed to the chair.

That morning I said seeya to Bank at the elevators. We each went our way, he to the Narco squad room, about midway up the hall near the elevators, where the Gang Squad had its desks, and I to Juvenile, at the end of the hallway.

Most day-shift detectives typically had roll call, then did paperwork for an hour or two before heading out. This day, because it was a Monday, I suppose, went a little longer than that. I remember, for some reason, noting that I had been in for two hours and fifteen minutes when I heard Bank start to yell for me. There was a trace of panic I had never heard in his voice, as it echoed down the hallway. "Mack! *Mack!*"

Any call reporting a felony went through our captain's office, then to the appropriate squad lieutenant or sergeant, then to whoever was available to take it or, in a priority situation, where the command officer directed it. This call, however, had come directly to Bank's desk. It did not bring the report of another gang shooting or a tip-off. It was Bank's wife, Sarah. She said something to him, and here, he told me some years later, his memory of the moment had grown fuzzy, or had never existed at all, his mind having gone to a kind of static. He remembered a distinctive consuming buzzing but not her exact words. Just the sense of them, a series of trivial declarative statements that, strung together in a certain order, cascaded into a nightmare: *Jamie wanted to walk to practice today. Roger was going to meet her on the way. Roger just stopped by on his way home, to find out why Jamie never came.*

I could imagine her voice. It would have been tight and controlled, the fear audible but suppressed. I knew just what she would have looked like too — her lips tight and drawn back at the corners, smilelike, eyes wide, her thin, elegant hands trembling as they fluttered about, the one aspect of her exterior self she could not control under stress.

Roger was Jamie's best friend. I'd seen him around a few times when I was over there.

Bank would later say that he remembered standing as he listened. He remembered squeezing the edge of his desk in such a way that he cut himself on a rough piece of the metal trim. The cut was good, he said; it burned through the static in his head and focused him for a few moments.

"Sarah," he said, "come on. It's not even ten-thirty." Jamie had left for practice at a quarter to nine.

"I know," she said. "But she never got there. That's just not like her."

"Her other friends —"

"I've called everyone. And why would she do that? She'd never do that. Bank?" He heard her voice cracking then with the awful fear. She was right, of course. Jamie would not go off and play without letting them know. More than that, she'd never miss practice.

Bank remembered his brain then slipping back into that white noise, the emptiness of the overload of panic. Though he knew it had to be nothing, he remembered all of his training, his nine years of experience as an officer of the law in this city, failing him at that dizzying moment. The rules, the protocols that governed a situation like this, had left him. He remembered being able only to call out for some help, to his old friend, little Maxie Steiner, Big Mack of the Juvenile Squad of the Detectives' Bureau, who was in a room just down the hallway. He called: "Mack! *Mack!*"

One of the Narcotics detectives, Bank does not remember who, stood up across the room and said, "What is it?"

"Get Mack," Bank said. The next thing Bank remembered was my being there. I found him in his chair, gripping the phone. I took it and said, "Who is this?"

"Sarah."

"Sarah, this is Max," I said.

That part Bank remembered, my saying that. He remembered listening numbly as I put Sarah on hold and hit another button on the phone and said something (I called my lieutenant, Stu Marek, who ran both Juvenile and Missing Persons, a man I liked and whose judgment I respected), and that the squad room seemed suddenly jammed with people, detectives, staff, all listening, then just as suddenly breaking up as they ran off. That quickly, because this was a cop's kid, wheels were set in motion. Calls went to Missing and to the patrol watch commander, who immediately dispatched two blue-and-whites to Bank's house.

Then Bank remembered me saying, "You know how these things go. How they *always* go. You know what it is, a nice summer day, frogs in the creek or a boat or something. She's eleven years old. I know she's responsible, but she's still a kid. Kids wander, Bank. We did it. I think of all the heart attacks we gave my folks. This is just the old payback, buddy."

"I have to go there," Bank said.

I drove. Bank remembered that. There was a frame of time then, several minutes or a half an hour, about which he seemed to remember virtually nothing again.

3

On this Palm Sunday, the thirty-first of March, 1996, after our crosstown rush from the Denny's restaurant, we are two of the twenty or so cops at the King's Court address of a poor ADC family on the east side of the river. The East Side, while exhibiting the attributes of the broader city — the old tall working-class houses jammed together, the ethnic mixing, the low gray quality of it all — seems, still, like another place altogether. It was no accident that the oil refineries were all placed over here, away from the rest of the city. The pervasive reek of petroleum, the surreal elevated burn-off flame that licks perpetually at the socked-in Ohio sky, these are not things the rest of us would tolerate. But those who live on the East Side never had a choice.

Six squads and four unmarked cars are parked at haphazard angles along the block, effectively closing off the street. Even a wagon has shown up for some reason. But a child — I consider her a child, still, at twelve — has disappeared, and that, I suppose, justifies anything.

The disappearances of kids are tough to judge, but are almost always the result of strife — a custody grab, a runaway — or an accident. A child slips into the wide brown Ojibwa River that bisects the city, or into an old drainpipe, or gets whacked by a car and launched into some weedy lot to be discovered a day or two later, dead and broken. Almost always. Ninety-nine plus percent. And in the case of a twelve-year-old, the initial response is usually to just have a detective come out and ask some questions. Does she have a boyfriend? Was she allowed to see him? Have they been fighting? Have you been fighting with her?

But this case, as we knew when we had heard the initial reports, looks different. The girl, Tamara Shipley, riding her shitty bike on her shitty street, turns a corner at the end of the block onto a stretch of empty gravel lane, not so much a street itself as a connection between two streets, a kind of open alley. No houses right there. Some Dumpsters. A high wooden privacy fence at the rear of someone's backyard. Little traffic.

A big black car drives down the block. (Or maybe it was dark brown. Or maybe gray. Or purple, one man said. Witnesses always pick their own, individual colors.) Two men inside, one driver, one passenger. (Three witnesses say they were black; the yahoo who saw a purple car insists they were white.) Its tires throw a little gravel as it spins around the corner into the alley. No one thinks a thing of it. But the girl doesn't come back. She wasn't going anywhere, just around the block, testing out the new chain her mother and a neighbor had helped her put on. Ten minutes pass. The mother walks down around the corner and finds the girl's bike lying in a muddy rainwater puddle. But no girl.

Imagine it: the driver braking suddenly, the passenger door opening, a man leaping out and grabbing her by the hair as she rides past, yanking her from her seat. She can't even scream. Her mother is right there, around the corner. She'll do something. She has to. Except that she cannot. Picture the man dragging the girl into the car, the tires scraping for purchase as it accelerates. Just like that, she is gone.

Of course, this is speculation. There are not, to our knowledge, any witnesses to the disappearance. It might turn out that the girl stepped willingly into the car. Maybe she knew these two men; they might have merely offered her a ride somewhere. Or maybe they had nothing to do with it; perhaps she walked off on her own, and will turn up, unhurt, wondering what all the commotion is about. I do not think so. I know, we all know, that the odds say she will at best be traumatized and damaged, that she very well may never be seen alive again by anyone who loves or cares about her in this world.

In any case, Tamara Shipley is shaping up as a remarkable crime, a huge event, really, the daylight stranger abduction of a juvenile. Its report has brought out the troops. A show of force, and force means numbers, speed, anger. A Fed I know named Rick Simms has already shown up. And a PR officer even from the commissioner's office stands a front yard away in the disorienting intensity of television lights — the press has responded already too — giving a statement on behalf of us all expressing outrage and commitment to the firm belief that we will find this girl.

Later, I figure, the mother will be asked to make some pathetic sniffling statement in her bad English about how it ain't fair, how the girl never got in no trouble and if they was watching they should just bring her back. Her appearance will be predictable: greasy, stringy hair the color of a dead field mouse, hollows under her eyes, and fat under her chin. I'm guessing. I haven't seen her yet.

Unlike Bank I have found that I cannot love people like this. I must not, I think, have been granted the requisite dose of humanity. My interest in finding a solution comes from the sickening knowledge of what this young girl must be going through and, to be honest, from the sheer intrigue of it all.

But Bank is inside with the family, and has been since shortly after we arrived. What has always been surprising about him, but especially after the summer of 1989, what to me, who knows him best, is the most remarkable of his many traits, is the depth to which he feels for these victims. In the list of his qualifications as a cop, which has always been much, much longer than my own, this attribute, empathy, rises to the top, above all the more obvious, expected entries.

And so he sits inside this unsteady-looking house with its peeling white clapboard and green shingle roof, leaning forward toward the terror-stricken mother. And he is crying with her. I know it; I know him too well. And I know this: It is not an act. The tears, only a few coursing down the cheeks, are genuine. He grieves with them, these victims, and for this they love him, and they tell him things about themselves they would never admit to anyone else.

I prefer staying out here, in the air, where I can breathe. I feel uncomfortable at this scene, like I don't belong. This is not my case. And echoes of the past haunt me.

I would prefer not to hear what this family has to say.

Our city has undergone some heavy change over the past couple of years, starting with the election of a new mayor, and then the importation of a new police commissioner. Some of the change we see as positive, some less so. Our new mayor, a Republican businessman chosen to head a tired old Democratic city, has, through will and cajoling and the massaging of favors, enticed a host of outside money, from conventions and trade shows to new businesses to state and federal grants. He is not a pleasant man, nor an insightful one, nor, I think, particularly bright, but he has a nose for money, and that stands him in good stead in some wildly disparate circles.

The restructuring of the force, many of us feel, has been less constructive, although, to be sure, economical. The patrol has been broken up into small, neighborhood-anchored teams, many of whom work out of satellite precincts. Meanwhile, the new Command has done away altogether with the old Detectives' Bureau and its squad system in favor of a centralized homogenized Investigative Services Division. Except for a small Missing Persons Unit (mandated by the state) and a Gang Squad, most detectives are now lumped together in one of three major divisions, Personal Crimes, Property Crimes, or Vice, and, unless they're working a special assignment or undercover, take whatever calls they get, whatever felonies are involved. Our city is not huge, and so can no longer, apparently, afford the luxury of specialization.

The practical effect of this is that the detectives at the scene of the Tamara Shipley disappearance are a cross-section of the old Bureau, guys from Assault and Robbery and Juvenile, some of whom have never worked a kidnapping in their careers.

If this victim, this twelve-year-old girl, does not turn up, the case will stay officially with Missing. If the case resolves itself into an assault, sexual or non, a homicide, or a hostage incident, it will be assigned to Personal Crimes. If it goes out of state or becomes a ransom situation, the Feds will pretty much take it over. But this last seems an unlikely scenario here.

The first step is just to cover as much ground and talk to as many people as possible, and that requires numbers more than any specialized training. This is why six two-man patrol squads have responded, as well as the six assigned detectives and Bank and me. Unlike the scene of a routine violent crime, where certain enlightening bits of biological or chemical detritus exist along with a victim, a missing person leaves behind only a vacuum.

Sergeant Googie Kozlowski, head of the Missing Persons Unit, pauses a moment at the top of the unstable molded-concrete steps leading down from the porch of the Tamara Shipley house. He takes in a deep breath and blows it out, then another. Exaggerated, like he's making a nasal spray commercial.

"Hard'a breathe in nare, Mack," he says. "Stuffy."

I stand in the little patch of dirt they call a front yard, making a note. "Yeah?" I say.

"Too many damn people," he says. "Smells like fried burgers."

Googie is a pretty hefty, fleshy guy with once-blue eyes that have faded to a watery gray. He's been after me for years to take the exams and move into the Command. He says I'm a natural, that I could waltz in. I just haven't gotten around to doing it.

"What do you think?" I say.

He shrugged. "The hell," he says. "Nothin' *to* think. She got grabbed. You know what they're doin' to her." He takes one last deep breath, as if he is enjoying the altitude, then comes down the steps. "I seen some show on the cable, you know, *Wild Kingdom* or some

44

shit. *Nature.* These hyenas? You ever seen 'em?"

"Not live or anything."

"Back legs shorter'n the front. You believe that? Talk about your ass draggers. Can't do nothin' but steal. Worthless smelly lazy fuckin' things. Run in a pack, grab what they want, and go. Babies, whatever. Remind you a something, Mack?"

"How's Bank making out?"

"Animals every-fuckin'-where. He's huddled up in nare with 'em. Reaching out, like he does," Googie says. "You know."

I nod.

"Nothing *to* find out," Googie says. "Don't know shit." He walks off toward his car and hocks in the street, as if to cleanse the taste from his mouth.

I can see now some neighbor who knew the missing girl standing in the camera lights, talking, as the PR sergeant and Detective Sergeant Katherine Biasotti look on. Then Katherine turns away and walks back toward the house. I meet her out on the cracked, uneven sidewalk.

"So, what?" I say.

The elimination of the Juvenile Sex Crimes Unit she had helped establish in the eighties is, I feel, the single most egregious fault of the new system. An assault dick can work a homi-

45

cide if he has to, but to let just anyone, trained or not, handle a sex crime, especially a kid, is a sad and harmful thing. Stu Marek, who's now our captain in Personal Crimes, still runs all the juvie sex cases past her, at least for her opinion.

"So, what, what?" she says.

"Assuming this is what it looks like, you're the ace here."

She shakes her head. "It's frustrating for you, Mack, isn't it?" she asks me. "Nothing to touch and turn," she says. "No one to ask. It must make you chafe."

"I never much liked Missing. And I don't like this," I say. "Just being here."

"I know," she says. "I understand."

"What's all the gabbing?" I nod down toward the lights and the news vans. "What're they putting out?"

"Just that it's a dark late-model sedan, at least two men, black, leaving this area. We've got a hot line cleared already. They're putting out the number. Bank inside?"

I nod.

"Good," she says. "That's good."

Katherine continues on past me, then, toward the group of witnesses — an older couple, a young pretty Hispanic woman, and a crippled man in a motorized wheelchair, who holds his body parts at odd and dis-

46

turbing angles and who saw white guys in a purple car. The four of them wait like a chorus in the yard next door.

Around the far side of the house my feet sink into patches of mud showing through the sparse yellow grass. April rains. I've been planning on buying a pair of those waterproof Gore-Tex–lined jobs that look like regular walking shoes, but they run something like a hundred and twenty bucks a pair and my wife, Peggy, just gives me a look whenever I mention it.

As I think about shoes, though, weird how these things go, I see one: a shoe, the toe anyway, protruding from under a bush. I wonder about things like this. You see a pair of underwear hanging on a fence, a child's coat lying in the street, someone's shoe under a bush. How do these things get there?

In a weed bed I find a good-sized rock, balance myself on it, and peer up over the window frame, which still holds a few flakes of peeled white paint. Mostly, though, it is gray and weathered. From here I have a view into the tiny living room with its new La-Z-Boy recliner, tags still attached, and a thirty-two-inch Panasonic TV set. Probably two grand wrapped up in these items, and what does this family subsist on — maybe ten

G's a year? Maybe less? Now they can spend the rest of their lives fighting to make that minimum payment on the Visa bill.

Bank leans forward, elbows on his knees. The family looks frightened, of course, and in shock. I try to imagine the blow of a thing like this but of course I really cannot, although I was very close to it once. It is Bank who knows, and Bank who can talk to these people and say the things that mean something to them. The family has already answered questions from other detectives before Bank; more will follow: questions about associates, affiliations, friends, acquaintances, strangers they'd recently met, groups Tamara belonged to, teachers; looking, prying, searching for any fingerhold, any odd bump in the texture of their lives that can be peeled back to reveal the rot beneath. But Bank will not press them on these fronts. He'll leave that to others.

Farther into the house, down a hallway, a team from the Crime Scene Unit collects impressions of latent fingerprints from various items in the house, especially from Tamara's room. They'll print the other family members and so by a process of elimination they'll develop a set of Tamara's own prints. They'll also collect hairs and scalp cells from her brush for possible use in tying her to certain locations later on — car trunks, beds, floors — or in identifying her remains.

The family has seen me now and Bank, following their gaze, looks around and into my eyes. He gestures, waving for me to come inside. I shake my head, and motion at him to come out. I do not want to go in. I do not want to meet them. This is not my case.

I shake my head slightly, trying to send him the message without them picking up on it. But he's having none of it. He points hard at me, and then at the floor of the living room, meaning for me to get my ass in there. I wait a moment too long, though, and then next thing I know he's up and striding out through the back door and around the corner of the house. He just looks at me until I follow him up onto the rickety porch, through the tiny kitchen, which is clean enough but does, as Googie said, smell like fried meat, and into that living room, where I do not want to be.

The scrawny fifteen-year-old boy named Emilio Salano, with his nut-brown skin and black eyes and the dark V formed by his hair at the center of his forehead, sits at one end of the couch, opposite the mother, Rochelle, and her remaining daughter, nine-year-old Geena Shipley, who are both particularly white and pale-eyed. The father of the two girls, who was never married to Rochelle, is dead. The boy is from a different liaison and so has a different name. On the street, I'm told, he came long ago to be called Eddie Munster because of his almost freakishly pronounced widow's peak, and that even his family now calls him Eddie.

I am given the La-Z-Boy, the seat of honor. Bank pulls around a straight-backed dinette chair and straddles it. Bank, as I thought, has not really questioned them. He's mostly been commiserating. The mother, of course, would know who he is, what he himself has lived through.

And I don't think the point of my being here is to question them now either.

"Go on," says Bank. And the wan mother says, "She really *was* a good girl."

"Is —" Bank corrects her. Cops, especially those dealing with the missing, learn early on to be careful about verb tenses. I expect her to cover her mouth in horror at this slip, or to look suddenly stricken, as if she has jinxed her daughter's chances of survival. But she does neither. Instead she tightens her jaw and flares her nostrils, which I take as a sign of strength, of control. And to my surprise I find myself feeling a kind of admiration for her.

She does not look like what I anticipated either. She has a hardness about her, a steeliness that comes through her eyes, and she looks savvy in a way I did not expect her to. She is thin, too, gaunt really, through the cheeks and neck. All of this lends her an air of resolve. I meet her eyes, and she holds me there, in her gaze, imploring me, it feels like.

Find her, she seems to be saying. Whatever it takes, *you,* you go out and do it.

4

Our old neighborhood, Bank's and mine, was a semirural township on what was, in the sixties, the farthest western fringes of the city, a hodge-podgy conglomeration of patches of small ranch-style houses and cinder-block cabins that had sprouted between the old farmhouses. Even the smallest, though, had large yards, and the whole area was interspersed with littered tracts of fallow land that served as rough and dangerous but irresistible playgrounds. The layout of the streets had not been designed so much as it had grown, like a web or the tentacles of a tumor, between the larger roads extending westward from the edge of the city. It had few right angles or straight lines and no organization that I could see to any of it.

By the time my family moved in, in August of 1967, when I still had four months left of being eight, the area had just been annexed, and the old township school was now part of the city system. I remember my father, on some of those deep summer evenings, standing with other men, the ones who were not bothered by talking to someone so exotic as an actual Jew, and drinking beer from a sweating steel can. He would just listen, mostly, and nod as the others swore at the city council bastards and the weak-willed county commissioners who had conspired to see this place absorbed.

We had moved here because my father got a job supervising a line in one of the auto glass plants in the south city. He was from Brooklyn, New York, but had spent his adult life migrating gradually westward, following the work. When he was twenty-two and home from his service in the Korean War, he'd taken a job with one of the railroads, working the switching yards up in the Bronx. Perhaps it was a natural consequence of daily contact with the rails that he migrated along them, northward to Poughkeepsie, then to Albany, then west across the middle of the state. Somehow he made the shift from trains to factories and landed in Corning, where he began to learn the glass business. This would have been 1953. He stayed in Corning only two years, but in that time met and married my mother, a Pennsylvania Dutch Lutheran, and fathered a daughter, before moving on to a plant in Buffalo, where he worked for a dozen years. At the end of that span he had become something of an expert, I guess, in certain technical matters connected with the synthesis of rolled flat-glass. My mother used to say that college-educated engineers would come to him at times to run questions, to hear his opinion of changes or innovations they were considering. And so it happened that someone from one of the big glass outfits in west-central Ohio offered him a supervisory job, at a good raise, and with all moving expenses paid. I don't think he cared to move from Buffalo, necessarily, but he was flattered and proud and felt, too, that a man who refused the offer of a step up in the world was a man who taunted the Fates. My father believed very much in fate.

As to why we settled where we did, in the neighborhood I have described, it was the idea of owning so much land that appealed to him, a boy from Brooklyn where, I understand, a few hundred square feet can be a homestead. In Corning my parents had lived in an apartment and in Buffalo we lived in a tight working-class neighborhood, in a gray shake-sided bungalow on a tiny city lot. There were, of course, endless identical neighborhoods in our new city. But when he found that he could afford, out in the old Liam Township, a big drafty farmhouse on nearly four acres of land with apple and pear trees, an eight-hundred-square-foot tilled garden, and a three-bay garage with room for a full workshop, my father knew that he had found his American dream.

And if a few of the neighbors wanted to throw around the word *kike* and not talk to him, well, then, they could just go straight to hell.

My sister, Judy, three and a half years my senior, had little trouble melding into this new place and school. She rode a bus to the big junior high a mile away where the variety of students drawn from all over the southwestern city — a few blacks and Hispanics, Catholic and Lutheran parochial-school kids, musicians and athletes, brains and burnouts, even the retards, as we called them, who attended special classes in a remote wing of the building but who occasionally wandered out into the general student population — formed such an amalgam that it was hard not to fit in somewhere.

But for me, starting fourth grade at the nearer-by elementary school, fitting in was a slow and painful process.

I blamed it in part, and wrongly, on some sort of covert but virulent anti-Semitism. This was confusing because I didn't know if I could even legitimately claim to be a victim of such prejudice since I was only half Jewish by blood, so to speak, and not really at all by training or tradition. (The strong religions of my mother and father essentially canceled each other out, and I do not remember much at all in my childhood in the way of religious practice.) Although there were whispers and pointing and discussions about me — I can still feel the hot stares on my back — in fact, those students didn't know enough to be anti-Semitic. There were some early incidents along these lines in the first month but they were really, I saw later, functions more of curiosity and ignorance, maybe the repetition of some comment they'd heard uttered by their parents, than any hatred. The simple fact was that I was the first Jew, or half-Jew as it were, that most of them had ever met. And after a few weeks I believe most of them didn't think about that fact anymore.

The problem actually was twofold, and the first part of it was really the fault of my own sort of strangeness. I was bright and did not hesitate to demonstrate it. I read insatiably, preferring it to most sorts of play or interaction. I responded to other students' attempts to talk to me with odd, sharp comments or observations, which stemmed from my insecurity and fear but made me sound like a smart-ass. The only person I endeared myself to in the weeks of that September was the teacher, Miss Marcia Marquette, a young, horse-faced woman in her first real job, and the only reason for this was that I was a good student. But endearing oneself to the teacher, of course, is hardly the way to being popular, which I clearly was not. In the classroom kids whispered and laughed and did not talk to me.

On the playground it was even worse, because the second part of the problem was that in addition to being smaller and younger than most of my classmates, I was resolutely antiphysical. I had been asthmatic as a young child and still suffered a range of allergies. And in this strange, hard-edged place, every game, whether played by boys or girls, was a rough and grotesque mutation of the normal games I knew. Red Rover became an ongoing attempt to break a wrist. Pom Pom Pull Away an excuse for all-out full-speed collisions that bloodied noses, left bruises on heads and faces, and even, on one occasion I remember, left a boy with cracked ribs. The object of Tag was not for It to touch someone else, but to knock him down; otherwise, the contact didn't count. And if the knockdown was particularly violent, causing the victim to, say, slide for a distance on his face, then that was rewarded with cheers from the other players. The worst was Gangpile, which was not a game really but a spontaneous event that could happen at any moment, in the middle of any other game. A shout would go up — someone would yell, "Gangpile!" — and by some process I did not understand a victim was chosen and tackled, and everyone else piled on top, fifteen kids, maybe. I ended up on the bottom of more than a few of these piles, and promptly began experiencing suffocation nightmares.

Throughout these first weeks I prayed to some nondenominational god I had never met that my father would be summarily fired and we'd have to move back to our Buffalo neighborhood where, at least, I had the benefit of being familiar.

A slightly built, emaciated-looking kid stood in a chilly drizzle near the corner of Liam Road and Pawtucket Street. The yellow buses had lined up in front of the elementary school, but he was outside, peering one way up Liam, and then turning and peering down the other way. He wore eyeglasses. He was, of course, me. Little Maxie Steiner.

This was on the Monday of the fifth week of school, October, 1967. Nothing had gotten any better. I felt miserable in general, and in particular, since I was wet. I felt the kids on the warm buses watching me, the alien, as I stood alone out in the weather.

Alone until a kid named Gary Urbanowski, with two girls tagging along, walked up the sidewalk and stopped in front of me. My heart leapt and hammered. Gary was older, in fifth grade, and tall for his age, with the longish hair that had become common even in that place, and pretty eyes and a cruel, disingenuous smile.

"You moved on Rutherford Street," he said, as if he were informing me of something I needed to know.

I nodded.

"That big house."

"Uh-huh."

"Your dad rich?"

"Nope," I said.

"Pretty big house."

"It's all right."

"What you standing out here for?" Gary asked.

"My mom," I told him. "She's supposed to pick me up."

"You live on Rutherford. How come you don't take the bus like everyone else?"

"She wants to pick me up." I squinted behind the glass as water ran down my forehead and into my eyes. "Until I get used to things." We'd had this discussion, my mother and I, as recently as the night before. It was I, though, who had begged, crying, for her to

59

keep driving me. I felt safe enough in class or even on the open playground, but panicked about getting into one of those buses.

"So you're a pussy," said Gary.

I remained silent.

He said, "My dad says the Jews killed Jesus."

I looked down then, unsure of where Gary planned to go with this, or of what kind of response was even called for. But I was not then and would never be what you might call rhetorically skilled. The elegant, clever part of my brain, such as it is, goes numb under emotional pressure. So I did what I had learned to do in situations like that, and what I would do, always. I stated blunt facts, as if somehow they could neutralize whatever passions had poisoned the moment.

"It was the Romans."

Gary Urbanowski had not a clue as to what I was talking about or even, of course, what he himself was talking about. And so this flat declaration, especially when it caused one of the girls with him to sort of giggle, succeeded in doing nothing but making him angry.

"What?"

And following my usual form I made it worse by not shutting up.

"The Romans," I told him and the girls.

60

"They did it. They pounded the nails. And Jesus was a Jew, anyway. Don't you even know that?"

Gary had actually reached out and placed his hand on my chest when someone called out from the steps of one of the buses. "Hey! Whatchoo guys doin'?"

I recognized the kid, Charles Arbaugh, from my classroom. Everyone called him by the strange name of Bank. He stood no taller than I, but was much thicker through the chest and neck and arms. A bull of a kid, my father would later call him, with some fondness.

I had actually seen him a couple of times that summer, before school started, riding past our house on his souped-up banana bike with its long welded-on front forks and high arcing handlebars. A kid's low rider, about the coolest thing I could imagine. The sort of bike I knew I did not stand a chance of ever owning. And the kid on it had not so much as glanced in my direction.

On the playground he was just simply tough. He hit hard and fought and went out of his way to get into the situations I ran to avoid. I watched him once pull another kid on top of himself and yell, "Gangpile!" so that he ended up on the bottom.

"He's waitin' for his mommy," Gary said.

To me Bank said, "Don't look like she's coming."

"She'll come."

"He's a pussy," Gary said. "Waiting for his mommy."

"*Shut up,*" Bank told him. He turned to Gary, who had four or five inches on him, and drove a pointed index finger into his chest. I had no idea what caused him to come off the bus and intervene like that. He had not so much as given me a nod in the month we'd been in class together. Grade loyalty, maybe. It was okay for kids in our class to pick on me, but when a fifth grader did it, it became a different thing, a violation of the Bank Arbaugh code of ethics.

Urbanowski squared off and drew back a fist. Bank just stood in front of him, not moving, relaxed, not even raising his hands to defend himself. In this way he dared Urbanowski to hit him. *I'll give you one free shot,* Bank's posture said. *After that we'll just see what happens.* Urbanowski curled his upper lip. Then the tension drained from his posture and he took a half step back. I couldn't believe he'd take this humiliation, but then I got the clear sense that these two had fought before, and that it had not come out in Gary Urbanowski's favor.

"I seen you settin' him up," Bank said. He

grabbed my arm and jerked, pulling me forward a step, then said, "Look."

Behind where I had been standing a boy on his hands and knees grinned up at us. The trick was for Gary to shove me so I'd fall over this kid and go down hard. I'd had it done to me as recently as the day before, and every time it knocked away my wind so completely that I could only lie there and watch the sky go dark.

Bank said, "Whyn't you get the hell outta this rain?" I was by then not only wet but pretty cold as well. I looked once more up Liam, and then followed Bank onto the warm dry bus and past the stares all the way to the very back, outside seat, the choicest seat on any bus, which another boy, Chadwick, from our class had held for him. I could imagine Bank threatening an interloper, his balled fist pressed against the kid's lip, saying, "Seat's mine." He was not a bully, though, I would find, just stronger and faster than most kids in our grade, or even a grade or two ahead, and unafraid to use that advantage when he needed.

Chadwick jumped up when Bank appeared, and then waited so he could sit next to him, but Bank waved him off and motioned for me to sit down instead. Chadwick threw a wounded look and then sulked toward the front to find his own seat.

I drank in the rich sensations, the hot air blowing down from the ceiling-mounted heater, the sounds of children released into freedom, the sense of security, of a kind of acceptance. And guilt. The doors closed. The bus pulled away from the curb. We left. And somewhere behind us my mother was driving slowly past, looking for me. I realized fully at that instant that she would be frantic when she finally parked and went inside and found that I was not there either. And I felt badly about this, and a little frightened of what my father would do when she told him, but something more important had happened, something I could not deny.

"Beats freezing your butt, don't it?" this kid Bank said.

I nodded. It did, I told him. It did.

He said, "So what's your name, again?"

"Max Steiner."

"Mack," he said, because that's the way it sounded. I did not correct him and though I didn't realize it then, I had just been christened, as it were, with my true name in life, the name by which I would henceforth be known to the world.

5

Bank and I wander far from the house where Tamara Shipley lives, through the streets of junk, past houses with sagging, unpainted porches and screen doors that hang from one hinge, dead cars parked on the tiny lawns, cloth and plastic and paper lying in wet heaps in front yards or in the gutters, cracked, collapsing sidewalks, puddles of mud-water that blanket the streets and yards. It is not a ghetto, yet, but is on its way. Once, though, like the north end, it was a strong ethnic place, clean and good and well taken care of. We walk blocks away through residential neighborhoods, knocking, trying to get people to answer and talk.

"*Po*-lice!" Bank hollers, but the doors are all locked and sealed against the world. No one seems to be home. We work the larger thoroughfares, including Moon Street where all the businesses are closed, some because it's Sunday, most because they've gone bust. Moon Street runs north-south, parallel to the river, and is separated from it only by a dead zone of four or five sets of railroad tracks. But we can't see these from the street because of a high dirt embankment that runs upward from behind the low storefront buildings on that side. The gray sky has dropped so low that there seems to be no distance at all between it and the top of the embankment. I could walk across, cut between two empty buildings, climb the muddy hill, and stand with my head in the clouds, a place I have been accused of being more than a few times, usually by Bank.

We stop the few passersby, the folks waiting at a bus stop, all of whom know nothing, saw nothing. The bus comes, exhales, opens up, ingests the people. We are alone. This part of the city, like others, is simply losing its inhabitants. They move away, out into the ever-expanding ring of suburban towns and villages.

Down Moon Street a few blocks we watch a gang of seven or eight kids materialize from between the buildings. They come together in the same manner scattered balls of mercury will attract one another and merge into a single larger mass, fluid and shimmering and unpredictable. They roll toward us with their smooth coffee-and-cream skin, dressed in nearly matching red plaid flannel shirts, buttoned at the collars, high-top sports shoes, saggy baggy acid-washed jeans, some dyed red, red baseball caps all on at the same cockeyed angle, the brims pointing forty-five degrees to the left.

As soon as he spots them, Bank sits down on the bus-stop bench and picks up a damp discarded newspaper to hide his face. I simply stand looking out over the empty, wind-whipped street. The boys amble on, noticing after they've come another block closer these two silly white men lost over here on a dead day, what the fuck. They shuffle onward. They wear grins on their baby faces because Bank and I still wear, of course, our night-shift clothes, casual trousers and jackets, not uniforms or coats and ties. So the boys don't make us for the Man and come right on, grinning, like they're going to at least dole out some commentary, maybe get something concrete out of the bargain, too, who knows?

They roll on up to the bench, then part and flow around, shuffling, dawdling, snickering, signing to each other with chins and eyebrows and hands. I look away from them so they will not recognize me.

Then Bank drops the paper and stands up, plants his hands on his hips, and says, "Morning, boys!" I guess that at least half of them make him instantly, having experienced personally the Bank Arbaugh late-night downtown Public Safety Building shuffle. A fair number of them know me as well. A couple yell "Five-O!" and like roaches under a sudden light now, they scatter, breaking out across the fractured landscape in every direction, flashing their colors and then disappearing between houses and cars, down cracks, back into the sewers. All but one, that is, who Bank holds up off the ground by his collar.

"I know you?" Bank says.

"No, man," says the kid as he struggles and kicks, his face growing pink because the collar has cut off his air.

"You live over in the Lloyd DuShane?"

The kid seems to nod.

"You Mario, ain't you?" Bank says. "Mario Esc-o-bar?"

"No, man," choking, gagging.

"You his brother, man?"

The kid sort of nods.

"What's your name?"

The kid gurgles out something I cannot understand, but Bank says, "Benny. Yeah, Benny fucking Esc-o-bar." Bank looks at me and raises his eyebrows, meaning do I know this one. I shake my head. But I've run into his brother, Mario.

"Well," Bank says, "this little mother's one of the new cocaine kings of the East Side. You're meeting a real celebrity here."

"How do," I say to the kid, who's begun to

68

pass from pink to blue. He is skinny, not much over a hundred pounds. Bank holds him easily.

"You gonna sit and talk to me nice, or I gotta hold you up like this?" says Bank.

"Talk," the kid says. "Talk!"

"You know what I'll do if you run?"

The kid nods, although I myself do not know.

"Okay," says Bank, and pats for weapons, then slaps him down on the bus-stop bench and leans over him. Benny Escobar coughs and rubs his throat with both hands.

"You didn't wear your collar buttoned like that, you might breathe easier," Bank says. "Girl got grabbed over here a little while ago. You know anything about that?"

"No, man," the kid says. "No way." He shines, this boy. His hair is inky black and cut very short and slicked back with some kind of sharply fragrant oil. His skin is clear except for a few blemishes around his hairline and nose and the corners of his mouth. A fine, barely visible mustache of black baby hairs decorates his upper lip. He's shaved off his left eyebrow, and had a red five-pointed star tattooed on the left side of his neck.

"Tamara Shipley," Bank says.

The kid shrugs.

"You doin' much business?"

"What business?"

"What business? You a businessman, ain't you? I want to buy some blow or a couple rocks, I hear you and your brother the place to come."

"No, man," says the kid.

"Who you humping for these days, Benny?"

Benny shakes his head slowly, emphatically.

"What you guys all doin' out here this fine morning?"

"Holdin' down," Benny says.

"Just out patrolling, huh?" says Bank. "Protecting your real estate. What set you claimin'? The Latino *fucking* Brotherhood or some shit like that?"

Benny looks away and continues to shake his head.

"I'm gonna have to run you in, Benny," says Bank.

"What?" says the boy. "Why, man? I ain't done nothin'. *Nothin'*, man."

"Flyin' these colors out here," Bank says. "I tell you guys about that. I call that incitement. You know what *incitement* means? Means you out trying to start something, tryin' to get some other folks caught up. That's a felony. Then we got disorderly conduct." Bank looks at me.

70

"Aggravated rioting," I say.

"Oh, ho, yeah, there you go," says Bank. "This is Big Mack. You know him?"

"Nah."

"Well, you gonna. Come on, stand up." Bank takes some cuffs from his back pocket and jangles them in the air.

"No, *man*," Benny pleads. "Sir, please don't." He has some tears in his eyes.

"Then talk to me, Benny, my man," says Bank. "It's dead over here. Somebody must've seen a car cruisin' around, some hawks looking for a little birdie to snatch up."

"We just come out here. We din' see nothin'. I swear, sir."

"Benny."

"You talk to her brother?" Benny says then. "Her brother's Eddie Munster, ain't he?"

Bank kneels down. "What about Eddie? Is there something going on here?"

This shocks Bank as much as it does me. We didn't really expect to get anything from this kid, except to get him to give up maybe seeing that car in some wild streak of coincidental luck.

"Is Eddie a homie, Benny?"

"A mark," says Benny. "A fuckin' wannabe. He go around false-flagging, you know."

"And what? This some kind of goddamned initiation? His sister has to fuck everyone

71

before they'll let him in?"

"Nah," Benny says. "I don't know nothin' 'bout that. He just been flaggin', that's all."

"Eddie a clocker?"

Benny shrugs.

"He is," Bank says.

Benny doesn't move.

"I'll be go to hell," Bank says. He stands again, looking off, his mouth open, shock roaming across his face. To Benny he says, "Break," and like that Benny flashes and vanishes before us. I look after him, to see where he's gone, but cannot, and when I look back I see Bank sprinting in the opposite direction, back toward the home of Tamara Shipley.

Bank is in the house again when I run up, out of breath. Googie and Katherine and a couple of the patrols stand in the front yard looking in after him, and we can hear him yelling in there.

"Your shoes, goddammit! I want to see your shoes. No! Your *ball* shoes."

Then I remember. I slip around the side of the house again and pull that shoe I saw from beneath the bush. There is another shoe with it under there, of course, and a plastic shopping bag to keep them dry. I see now that they aren't ratty at all, but new and clean and white. High-top Ponies. Hidden there where he can slip them on after he leaves the house. The left shoe, only, has been fitted with crimson laces.

I carry the shoes back around front and hold them up for Bank to see. Bank drags Eddie across the yard to me and snatches the shoes. Then he drags him to a squad car, opens the back door, and sits him down there on the backseat, but facing out. He keeps the door open, and shakes the shoes in the boy's face.

"What does this mean?" Bank asks him.

Eddie does not answer or move.

"I come in to talk to your mother, I see you sitting there, a nice boy wearing nice black shoes, but all the time you were just foolin' me out. Huh? What's this about?"

The kid says nothing.

"You sellin'?"

"Nah."

"Eddie, listen to me. Maybe it's cool to wear the colors and hang out, maybe you're making some money. I don't know. I don't care. I don't give a shit right now. But I gotta know, did something happen that led to your little sister's getting grabbed? You piss somebody off? You being initiated? You got a debt you can't pay? Something like that?"

Eddie looks up at him now, his face dead, expressionless. We're all gathered behind

73

Bank, not crowding him but close enough to listen. Eddie says, "It wasn't no homies."

"Who?" says Bank.

"I dunno. Some niggers. I dunno why."

"You cross 'em up?"

"Some of 'em seen me the other day, I was out taggin' over by the bridge."

"You were painting the bridge."

Eddie nods.

"And some black kids seen you."

"They stop and yell, 'Get the fuck away from there, spic motherfuckas.' We run."

"They shoot?"

"Nah, not then."

"Another time?"

Eddie nods.

"They shot at you?"

"Yeah."

"You were out wearin' colors?"

Eddie nods again.

"When was this?"

"The shooting?"

"No, the bridge."

"Two days."

"How about the shooting?"

The kid shrugs. "Week," he says. "They been comin' around here. I seen 'em comin' around."

Bank looks up at me. His face has gone white with anger, and although he does not

74

say anything, I can see his lips moving, whispering a prayer, maybe, on this day, for little Tamara Shipley.

In the afternoon, tired beyond exhaustion, Bank drives the two of us back through the city to the Denny's on Alcore so we can pay for our breakfasts and I can pick up my car. He does not speak much on the way back. He has that look again on his face I have seen before, of consternation and anger, of bad attitude and calculating thought, the look of his power. The scars on his neck and the sides of his face glow red when he gets like this.

This girl who has turned up gone is the cause, to be sure, and she will be the object of his efforts. But he is thinking, just then, I know, of a different girl.

6

The house Bank and his wife, Sarah, owned in 1989 lay in that section of the city called Heron Hills, after the Heron River, but usually referred to as simply the Hills. The Heron, a small but deep river, twisted like a wounded snake through the area and had cut the valleys and low rises that distinguished this land from the board-flat terrain around it.

The Hills had been founded as an autonomous municipality in the days when the city stopped at what was now called the Old West End (the city's first wealthy neighborhood), when the city's second wave of industrialists and their lawyers and their patent-laden engineers had wanted a new rich place to live which was convenient to, but outside, the city proper. But decades earlier the city had swept westward, around and past the Hills, and eventually the town had been annexed. Still, it remained one of the more exclusive places in the metro area. As a part of the annexation agreement, negotiated in the seventies, the well-off folks who lived there secured guarantees from the city that the school system, among other things, would remain independent — that is to say, it would never be folded into the sprawling and crumbling city system, thus avoiding the possibility of students being bused in or tax revenues drained off. Because of this the property values in Heron Hills remained as high as ever, even as it was surrounded on three sides by regions of the city that were now slipping past their prime.

Bank was, as far as we knew, the only city cop to live in the Hills, civil salaries being what they were. But a couple of years into their marriage Sarah had come into a healthy if not spectacular trust fund, courtesy of her maternal grandfather. It held enough principal to generate a supplement to their yearly income at that time, in the late eighties, of thirty or forty thousand dollars a year. This, combined with Bank and Sarah's salaries (she taught part time at Libbey University, where she'd completed her doctorate in Art History), left them comfortable and able to afford a nice midlevel house here in this nice small town that existed like a bubble in the gut of the rough city which had ingested it.

The actual hills were not much in the way of elevations, but the ground rolled prettily where the waterway cut through them. It was in a shallow, pleasant valley extending out along one of the Heron's feeder creeks that the Arbaughs lived. Certain sections of land directly along the river had been left undeveloped by the village's original planners, communal wooded areas crisscrossed with dirt trails and grassy openings where families strolled and kids played at the water's edge.

From the Arbaughs' brick colonial on Detwiler Place, which was shaded with old oaks, the route to the elementary school led toward the river and then across on either the concrete bridge of the street or over a covered wooden bridge which was part of an alternate walking trail. Both routes came out at Tecumseh Boulevard, across which lay the tended grounds shared by the elementary, middle, and high schools of the Heron Hills system. Tecumseh was one of the busier thoroughfares cutting through the village, and the place Bank and Sarah worried about most. But there was a well-maintained button-activated crossing light. It was here, at the crossing light, three irregular blocks from their house, that Jamie was to have met her friend Roger.

On arriving at his house that morning, Bank immediately launched into a confused and urgent monologue to the patrol cops about what should be done and when and by whom. No one paid particular attention. It ended after thirty seconds when I steered Bank to the front door of his house, where Sarah stood mashing her knuckles into her teeth. The sight of her shut Bank up. I pushed him forward, toward her, in the same manner a schoolboy pushes his friend toward the girl who's waiting to be asked out. And in the same manner, I think, Bank had no idea of what to say to her.

He ended by simply taking her in his arms, which allowed her to cry for the first time since the nightmare began. They stood like this for a long time, allowing me and the others to get to work.

The great hope was that it would only be a matter of time and of canvassing the neighborhood, of questioning neighbors to find someone who had seen the girl, of questioning every friend of Jamie's Sarah and Bank and Roger (who had resolutely declared he was staying until Jamie walked in the door) could name, of searching all the spots where an eleven-year-old girl could lose track of the time. And so that's how we began.

Although it was not formally a Missing Persons case, a newly minted Missing detective named Googie Kozlowski acted as the primary. Googie was forty-two then. His shirts had just begun to grow tight around his neck.

Googie had worked in the Robbery/Assault Unit in Violent Crimes for years but got booted up to Missing the previous year, after the death of his wife, who'd suffered a long illness — a female-type cancer, he called it. They'd been married twenty-three years when she died, and he lost his Robbery cop edge. No one came down on him for it. Command just cycled him out to a calmer backwater, which was Missing. Googie had not yet settled in, and still complained, but that is not to say that he didn't do the job, touching all the bases, turning all the rocks. Still, he talked about the day he'd get to go back to Violent. No way, he said, was he finishing his career in Missing.

Googie began by coordinating the initial ground search, which involved simply looking in as many places and questioning as many people as possible. The patrolmen who had originally responded and conducted the first hurried canvassing of the area all participated in this effort, along with others who came by or were pulled from behind desks downtown and driven out in a caged county wagon usually used to transport convicts. Three more detectives, two from Missing and one from the Homicide Squad in Violent Crimes, had been sent as well. Our lieutenant, Googie's and mine, Stu Marek, would show up an hour or two into the search.

And finally there was Sergeant Katherine Biasotti, the head of the recently formed Juvenile Sex Crimes Unit. Katherine had at least two degrees that I knew of and had been · through specialized training seminars run by the Chicago PD and at Quantico by the FBI. What Katherine did day in, day out, was a thing most detectives I knew could not stomach for long. Homicides, major accidents, assaults were all one thing. But adults raping children was something else. I'd watched weathered cops, who'd witnessed every kind of mutilation imaginable, snap, finally, when confronted with some molester father or roving pedo, and just start in pummeling the person until they were pulled off and restrained. Katherine was not like that. She kept calm almost all of the time. Indignant, perhaps, but calm.

This was not to say that there was any indication that we were involved with a sex crime here, or an abduction at all, for that matter. But Katherine was Bank's friend, and my friend, and she came simply because she wanted to be where she might help.

As word of the crisis spread up and down the street and out through the neighborhood, other folks, neighbors, some friends, some strangers, showed up to help as well. People were given assignments, areas to begin walking, looking for anything they could see that would shed light. This help was welcomed, but also monitored and cataloged — again, although this had not been ruled an abduction, we knew that sometimes, in such cases, the abductor came back to the scene to help with the search. Bank, too, would have been aware of this, but everyone was careful not to give voice yet to this most abhorrent of all possibilities.

At first, Bank stayed inside with Sarah. He told me later he had watched her, trying to feel some anger that would allow him to blame her for not driving the girl to school. But Jamie was eleven, and she'd been riding or walking to school for years. Bank knew that if this was anyone's fault, it was not Sarah's.

Sarah's people were onetime poor folk from the mining hills of southern Ohio, not far from Wheeling, West Virginia, and Sarah still carried in her language a trace of southern accent and phrasing, just enough to beguile. Her maternal grandfather had started out in the Great Depression as a junk man, but had built that humble business, over the next forty or so years, into a chain of steel recycling plants. Her parents had moved to our city ten years earlier so that her father could supervise the launching of three new plants in the western part of the state.

Sarah had been an attractive enough young woman when Bank married her, thin and clean-skinned with that handsome, forthright look of the fortunate. I had noticed, though, as she passed into her later twenties, that she was turning out to be one of those women who grow increasingly beautiful as they age. Until, by her early thirties, she was so striking as to turn heads when she walked through a store or a restaurant. She was as thin as she had ever been, and fit, and naturally refined in a way that Bank never would be.

I had begun to suspect, too, at this time, that some distance had opened between Bank and Sarah. I had my reasons for thinking this, and my avenues of insight into their lives. But now, on this deathly humid morning, none of that mattered. Bank felt desperately close to her at this moment, painfully, frighteningly close, in a way he had not for a long time.

"There's another girl at school, a cheer-leader type, who doesn't like her," Sarah told him. "Michelle something. Jamie said she called her a butch." She dried her eyes with a thumb and middle finger and ended by pinching the bridge of her nose. "The epithets of girls," she said.

Bank knelt on the floor before her and put

his head in her lap. She combed her fingers through his hair and hummed a tune he recognized but could not name.

After a while he said it was time for him to go start looking too. If these good folks were going to help them like this, the least he could do was to help, too. And so he left her sitting, humming, watching out the window for whoever should come walking up the brick pathway to their front door.

The ground search was in full swing by noon. When it did not produce immediate results, when it became apparent that this was more than the case of a girl stopping at a friend's house or losing track of her time in the woods, it was joined by two more MP detectives and additional patrolmen. By two all of the obvious spots had been checked — the secret hiding place beneath the walking bridge Roger had led them to, the backyard of a friend of theirs that had a trampoline and a furnished tree house — and all the residents along and adjacent to Jamie's route had been questioned. So Googie decided upon a new step. Leaving aside the question of foul play, it was possible that Jamie had been hurt, rendered unconscious, unable to respond. The river and its banks were a tomboy's heaven but, as benign and picturesque as they seemed, could snap like a dangerous animal. Bank and Sarah had discussed this, I know, when they first looked at the house six years earlier. Jamie would just have to learn how to act around the water. She had been trained to be a strong enough swimmer and she knew the dangers, but anything might have happened.

And so, at Bank's insistence and his offers to pay for any of the expense (which was roundly refused by both Googie and Lieutenant Marek, who had arrived by then), a team of bloodhounds was called in. We had used this trainer and his dogs on previous occasions, either to look for a body or a missing person or even, a few times, an escapee. We knew the man to be a talented pro and the dogs to be as good as dogs could be at this sort of thing.

By three-thirty the hounds had arrived, been given samples of Jamie's clothing to sniff, and had set off with their croupy, soul-rending baying toward the banks of the Heron River.

July days are long, of course, and this one lasted late, the sun bleeding into the sky and slipping to earth only after nine-thirty. Sarah brought Bank half a roast beef sandwich which he ate while standing on the lawn, looking at the city cars parked all over the street. She told him there'd been a story on the local news stations about Jamie's disappearance. They'd flashed a picture and a telephone number, and the offer of a reward for any good information. The reward was substantial. Jamie's grandparents, Don and Carol Lyell, had immediately put up an initial ten thousand dollars in cash for information leading to the girl's safe recovery, and had pledged up to another fifty thousand in case she didn't turn up in the following day or two.

Bank had begun to realize, with the approach of night, that if his daughter wasn't found by the fall of darkness, we would have a very different situation on our hands. This was simple police knowledge, based on long experience with the canons and probabilities of disaster. The rest of us had discussed this earlier in the day. More detectives, friends of Bank, had shown up after their shifts ended, to help if they could, to pound the street. They seemed uniformly surprised that the situation hadn't resolved itself by then, that the girl hadn't been found one way or the other. The word *freaky* passed between them and they had begun to discuss the increasing odds that an abduction of some sort had occurred. The head of the Bureau, Captain Draves, had stopped by after five to speak with Bank and to offer any additional support the department could give. Even the dogs seemed to sense the urgency of the night pressing in on them. Their baying had changed tones after their handler allowed them a feed and water break at six, ratcheted up a notch in pitch and intensity as their circle widened to the outer reaches of the village, along the banks of the river where it crossed into the wider city and then on to the campus of Libbey University.

Bank was helpless in the end. As helpless to change events, to locate Jamie, as he was to stop the night from coming. Either would have worked, he thought. Either would have amounted to the same thing.

He stopped looking. He stood in the middle of his front lawn and watched the detectives and patrolmen coming and going, checking in and going back out to rerun some tired task. I watched his body drain of any energy, any gumption or desire, except the single, intensely brilliant wish to see his girl step out of one of the cars that pulled up. He stood thus until after nine o'clock.

Don and Carol had arrived earlier, Carol dissolving into tears when she saw all the official cars in front of their home. The three of them were inside now. Bank thought he should be inside, too, with them. But he knew he could not help them at this point.

As dusk fell, though, Bank later told me, he felt a change in himself. The static in his head, which had rendered him an idiot for most of the day, cleared. The panic retreated to a corner of his gut. Now the situation had deteriorated from frightening to desperate. He felt himself grow suddenly capable of acting, as if the fading of hope had taken with it the paralysis of panic.

And he knew why. He had begun to steel himself against his worst fear. Something was desperately wrong, and the result would now almost certainly be bad. Maybe not the worst. Maybe the girl would still be found injured but alive, say, assaulted but not killed, damaged but not irreparable. Or maybe not. The time had come to begin accepting this as a very real possibility. And in so accepting, Bank found that he could function again.

Bank's Cherokee was still downtown in the PS Building garage. So he backed Sarah's new minivan out, then stopped in the driveway and nodded at me. I hopped into the passenger seat, saying nothing. A few of the cops in the street watched us, none waving to stop Bank or ask where he was going. He could not have answered anyway. He headed into the oncoming night and began to drive.

★ ★ ★

We stopped only at a twenty-four-hour service station to fill up. By midnight the odom-
eter registered sixty new miles, most covered
at a rate no faster than thirty miles an hour.
Bank knew he had to drive slowly if we were
to see anything. He'd covered all the streets of
the village many times; he'd covered the surrounding roads of the city, those crossing the
Libbey campus, and had driven farther afield,
out along the major thoroughfares, then ran-
domly turned off, choosing a side street into a
strange neighborhood or, better, an uninhab-
ited place. The van had bounced and rolled
on the rutted dirt under the viaduct on Burns
Road, where seven sets of railroad tracks
spread out in a switching yard, a fine dark
spot to leave a young girl. But we saw
nothing. Bank said little, and I made no
attempt to talk to him.

I know he held no illusion that we had any
real chance of finding anything in this way,
but he knew he could not sleep, and the
thought of sitting in the house with the sniffles
and sobs of others around him made him feel
nauseous, he said. He drove with the window
wide open, so he could breathe. The night
stayed warm and humid throughout. If Jamie
was hurt somewhere, at least she wouldn't die
of exposure.

At twelve-thirty, as we crossed the Detwiler Place bridge over the Heron for the fifteenth time, a new certainty suddenly overcame Bank, forcing him to pull over to the side of the road. He grabbed his gut and leaned forward until his head touched the steering wheel. Jamie was dead. He could never have defended or explained it, but the insight came to him powerfully, in an epiphanic flash, as certain knowledge. I felt it too.

Bank released himself from the van and slid down a steep embankment toward the river, where he vomited until his stomach was empty. And then he began to sob, his body racked with the spasms of his grief.

I followed him down over the hard dirt, through the weeds, and knelt beside him and put my hand on his back. He sagged into me. I held his head against my chest, his face buried in the crook of my arm as he wept. The river babbled in the dark ravine beneath us.

I held him like that until a young patrolman found us after spotting the abandoned van. "Detective Arbaugh, sir," he had said. "Why don't you let us give you a hand." And by then Bank had passed this wave of the grief, as one passes a horribly painful gallstone, and seemed to feel better somehow for having done it, purged at least. He let us help him back up to the road, and accepted my hand-

90

kerchief, which he used to dry his face.

I went home, then, to wash and change and doze if I could. When I walked in the door, I heard the television still on in the family room. It was one o'clock. My own seven-year-old daughter, Naomi, sat in her underpants watching some bad true-crime cop program. The place was a wreck, toys and clothes and particles of food everywhere. I stopped behind Naomi, who did not look up at me, and watched with her, a segment, apparently, on teenaged hitmen. Before I could realize what was being shown, my daughter and I witnessed a quick, shadowy homemade video clip of a young black boy in sweatpants and a baggy Lakers T-shirt walking up to another young black boy on a bus bench and capping him with what looked like a .38 revolver. Just like that, smack, lead in the head. The boy on the bench dropped like ballast as the shooter ran off a few steps, then stopped to look at his handiwork, then turned to the camera and raised a finger skyward. My daughter did not react to this in any visible way. I picked her up and held her to me so she couldn't see the screen, and turned the set off.

Gloria was sitting out on the deck, in the dark, smoking a cigarette, an open can of Bud on the table next to her. There were plenty of empties on the deck around her. She was crying, I could see, and had been for some time. Probably since morning.

"Tough day?" I said, as the emotion I'd been fighting all that day seethed up and out of me. It was unfair, directed at the wrong person, but I could not stop it from coming.

"What?"

"Couldn't get much done around here? This mess?"

Why not just acknowledge the grief we both felt? Why not tell her that I was so afraid I could barely function?

"Fuck you, too, Mack," she said, and justifiably so.

I did not know it then, but it would only be a matter of a few more months before I would lose my own daughter, not to death or disappearance, but to a good job her mother got over in the capital city of Columbus. By the fall of that year I would be alone. I would buy Gloria's share of the house and take over the payments, and take to talking with my daughter once every week or so by phone. As time passed, I would see her less and less often, and our phone calls would spread out to monthly, and eventually even more infrequently than that.

7

After I leave Bank at the Denny's, I drive west on Brentcroft to that same subdivision, that same three-bedroom slapped-together tract house where I lived years ago with Gloria Harris. I don't know why I never sold it.

When I walk in, though, I know something's wrong. It's too quiet. The family room lies immediately to the right from the hallway off the garage, and ahead, past the half-bath, the dining area and kitchen open out. All three rooms look as if they've been wiped by some huge magic hand, every toy picked up, every dish cleared away, every counter scrubbed. Carpets vacuumed and floors swept. Even the island separating the kitchen from the dining area, and the dinette table itself, are free of their usual clutter. Sunday paper nowhere in sight. No TVs and no music. This is not my house. The muscles in the back of my neck tighten.

And then I sniff it. In the same way air smells burned after an electrical charge has passed through it, the house holds the odor of intense emotion, of grief and bitterness and hot anger. The dead remnants of screams and profanity echo from the paint and wallpaper.

My first thought is for the boys, who do not deserve any of this angst and pain. They might be up in their rooms. I hope not because I want to see them first, to have a moment, but if I go upstairs I'll have to confront the situation itself. The family room leads on through the sliding glass door to a small slab of white concrete that makes do as a patio. I stand for a moment, listening, and hear what I hoped I would: a pounding issuing from the walled-in platform built up on one end of the wooden swing set in our backyard. My dad and Bank and I constructed the whole thing using one of those kits that include instructions and the hardware, the nuts and bolts and washers and wood screws, the molded yellow plastic slide, and the blue nylon awning that covers the room. You're supposed to buy the lumber separately, but my dad had enough lying around his shop that I ended up not having to. Because of his and Bank's involvement, the unit ended up so solid that in spite of the natural warpage of the wood, it barely moves even with both boys swinging hard.

From the enclosed platform, a tiny room which the boys immediately recognized as their one true fort, although it measures only three by three feet, the slide emerges and plunges to the earth. I poke my head through this opening and find them sitting next to each other, shoulders pressed together, knees pulled up tight against their chests, feet stomping against the floor as they giggle.

They stop when they see me.

"Dad," says Jack, a raven-haired, pale-skinned boy with a huge gap between his front teeth. Jack's eight. He's my wife, Peggy's, son from her previous marriage, a noisy kid filled with a kind of surging energy that he sometimes needs to blow off by suddenly sprinting or yelling or fidgeting madly. I found it a little disconcerting when we began living together. But I've discovered that if I give him a few minutes outside after dinner, tossing a ball or just walking the neighborhood, it's much easier for him to calm down for the evening. I've come to really look forward to that time. He grins at me.

Ben, newly four, and darker, like me, his blood father, gives me a serious eyebrow-knitted frown until I return it, at which point he, too, smiles. Ben is quieter than Jack, more serious, though he loves a good joke as much as the next guy. Ben's into riddles these days.

I reach into the fort and grab each of them by an ankle.

95

"Gotcha," I say. Then I wait.

"Mom's upstairs," says Jack.

"Bad?"

They nod in unison.

"How bad?"

"The worst."

"The absolute worst?"

"Totally," he says.

"The *really* worst," says Ben.

"Not the really worst," I say.

Jack is serious. "They yelled so much, Dad. We were upstairs. They just kept going. God."

"Mom broke the coffeepot," Ben adds.

"You guys okay?"

They nod.

"You know this doesn't have anything to do with you. Not your fault, not your responsibility. It's just too bad you have to hear it. I feel bad."

"It's all right, Dad," says Jack. He lifts the foot I'm still holding on to and slams it down hard against the floorboards, making them shudder. "It doesn't matter that much." His effort at consolation steels me.

"You want to come inside?"

They nod again, but neither makes a move to follow me.

"Hey, Ben. Why'd the rooster cross the road?"

He looks at me. "The rooster?"

"Yeah."

"Give up."

"To prove he wasn't chicken."

Groans. Laughter. The pounding begins again as I leave.

I find Peggy lying on our bed, the shades drawn and no light on, so that the room is dusky and cool. She holds one arm draped over her eyes. She's pinned her hair up on her head and wears sweatpants and one of my V-neck T-shirts, which fits her actually rather well.

I step into the cool room and over to the closet we share. As I remove my shirt, which is damp across the back and smells slightly, since I've been in it for nearly twenty-four hours, Peggy says, "What time is it?"

"Three-ish."

"Why so late getting home? Why didn't you call?"

"I tried a couple times," I tell her. "It was busy."

"I wasn't on —" she begins, and then bites off her sentence. I wait for her to continue but she just lies there, stock still.

"The phone," I say. "That's it?"

"*No,*" says Peggy. "If you'd let me finish."

"Sorry."

"I'm sorry, Mack. I'm tired. I didn't get much sleep."

"It's okay."

"She was out again, but half the night this time. She went with some friends to the mall. I told her I'd give her this chance, right? But she was to be home by ten. Not a minute later." Peggy pauses and wipes at her nose with a tissue, then continues. "She didn't come in until after two. I was a little bit frantic. I didn't know whether to call you or what, because she pulls this and I don't need you worrying about it, too, but I didn't know if something had happened to her —"

"You should have called me," I say. "Two A.M.?"

"After. So I didn't even get into it with her this morning. I told her she'd have to talk to you. Then this phone thing — she was on almost two hours. I asked her four times to get off in case you were trying to call. She wouldn't even *look* at me, Mack. Like I was not even there." Her voice rises through this until she hits the lower rungs of her shrill register. I can feel those muscles in my neck again.

"I'll take care of the phone," I say. "We'll get call waiting."

"Call waiting is *not* the issue." Peggy sits up abruptly on the bed and slaps the top of her thigh. Like that she is right back into the heart of her fury.

"But it's something I can do."

"You and I talked about that, Mack. We agreed it was an expense we did not need, so we shouldn't get it. But this is not about call waiting or the damn telephone. She wouldn't even *look* at me."

I nod and pull a clean denim work shirt from a hanger and put it on, then drop my trousers, hang them on a hook on the closet wall, and tug on some old soft jeans.

"I'll go down," I tell her.

"You go down," says Peggy. "But I don't know what you're going to say to her, Mack. And I don't know what we're going to do. I just don't know." She lies back and places her arm over her eyes again. "It just can't be like this. No more. It cannot."

And I can tell that she is crying again.

The basement is darker and cooler even than the bedroom. A slight mustiness lingers from a pipe that sprang a leak the previous spring. It was during the cleanup from that mess that we, my dad and Bank and I, began to lay the plans for the room we would build down here for the girl who was coming. By the first of September, in time for the start of the school year, we'd finished the drywall and drop-ceiling and were waiting only for the carpet to be installed. The room was just twelve by ten but encompassed one of the ground-level windows so it had some natural light, and a floorboard heater so it would stay comfortable. In a bad situation, we reasoned, it wasn't such a bad place. A basement room, but nice nonetheless.

We'd misjudged, it turned out, but in the other direction. The room was too nice. Too perfect a place for a teenager: isolated, insulated, effectively soundproof, dark despite the window, cool in the heat of Indian summer and toasty when winter hit. A place, in short, she did not want to leave, a den, a burrow for her hibernation, a cocoon where she could effect her metamorphosis. Peggy and I and the boys look up sometimes, when the basement door opens, expectant despite ourselves, hopeful, yearning to see her changed, suddenly, into someone pleasant, someone who can smile at will, who thinks about the needs of others, who dresses in anything other than grunge. In the seven months of her residence here no such change has transpired.

I knock at the inexpensive hollow-core door, which I helped hang. I knock but can hear the deep thrumming from her headphones and know that she cannot possibly hear the knock. So I open the door a few inches (my father, in his wisdom, cautioned against putting a lock on it), insert my arm, and wave it around. The thrumming stops and the door jerks open.

"Hi, Dad," the girl, Naomi, says. In spite of the tension, the grief I know is coming, it makes me happy to see her.

I lie on the floor, my head back on the seat of a foam cushion chair, the edge pressing into the crease of my neck and on the tightness there, which relaxes me. And the fatigue I've been fighting all day washes over me here in the cool basement of my house. My eyelids close of their own volition and my brain swirls as it fights with itself to stay awake.

"This is not a bad room," I say, the words slurring slightly.

Naomi is nothing if not bright. She has no trouble grasping a situation, discussing, seeming to empathize, some of which is maybe even genuine. But much, I've decided, is cover, the device she uses to get herself out of trouble. She is, in short, a budding ace bullshit artist. I, however, have a very highly tuned bullshit detector. It is, after all, what I get paid for. I cut my teeth on the Juvenile Squad and still hassle with kids her age every day of the week. What's more, Naomi knows this perfectly well. And I, of course, know that she knows. This has led to some interesting conversations between us, dialogues layered in multiple meanings and ambiguities and metaphors.

I force my eyes open. They feel as if they have sand beneath the lids.

"It's great," she says.

"And you like it here."

Naomi pulls her lips into her mouth and tilts her head toward one shoulder, then the other.

"Some of it you like."

She nods. She is an odd-looking girl, but in the manner that many young teenagers are odd looking. Parts of her have developed far along the route toward adulthood, while others have lagged. In time these incongruities will smooth themselves out and she will be as pretty a woman as her mother was, which is to say very pretty, I think. What Naomi has now are the eyes. Doe eyes, we used to call them. Big and wet and expressive, drawn back and rimmed in dark lashes.

These big, wet eyes, though, are embedded in a cute but pudgy face. When Naomi carries extra weight, some of it lands in her cheeks, and she is running a little on the heavy side these days. The weight makes her face look especially young, childlike, but also adds to her breasts as well. A woman's breasts she carries on her fourteen-year-old frame. Full B cups bordering on C's, Peggy has told me, because she's had to order new bras from the Penney's catalog.

"I did *not*," my wife let me know, "have a need for C cups when *I* was fourteen years old."

The weight finds its way to Naomi's posterior too. So she has, I've been led to understand, what is called by her peers, I am told, an awesome booty. I myself have not made this judgment. I cannot look at her in that way. I still see, or want to see, that blubbery little kid I remember, who, for being older, is no less blubbery and no less cute than she was when she was three.

On top of all this, Naomi has just recently dyed her chestnutty hair an inky black and cut it into a kind of ragged cap that spikes down over her ears and forehead, and just covers her collar in the back. The hair is simply ugly, I think, but I do not tell her this.

I force myself to sit up cross-legged on the floor. Otherwise I am going out right there. "The thing is, Naomi," I say, "and I know you know this and we've said it all before and I'm as bored with it as you are, but the thing is, where else is there? We're your family now. Not just me, but us." Facts. "And I have a wife, now, who's about ready to move out on me and take my boys with her."

"She'd kick me out way before that," Naomi says.

"To where?"

"Columbus, I guess."

I laugh out loud. She means to Gloria's parents' house, where she had been living — when she wasn't running away — for the six months before she came to us, since the car accident that killed Gloria.

"What?" she says, and she starts to laugh a little too. After Naomi's third month there her grandmother's chest pains grew so severe, she ended up spending a week in a cardiac care unit. Her grandfather called the police to the house no fewer than seven times in those six months. I drove the sixty miles over there once and talked to those cops, who told me that the girl wasn't breaking any laws, other than a single joint of marijuana the grandfather had confiscated in a floor-to-ceiling search of her room. That and the fact that she'd run away a couple of times, according to the grandfather. They'd make the bust for the reefer if I wanted, they said, shake the girl up a little. Otherwise they were inclined to let it slide. Sooner or later, though, they said, somebody was going to kill somebody in that household.

It wasn't much different, really, from how those two old folks had gotten along with their daughter, Gloria, twenty-five years earlier. And so began a long series of conversations between Peggy and me about moving the girl here.

"I don't know," Naomi says. "To a group home or something."

"And you want that?"

"Mmm, no," she says. "Don't *want* it. Expect it."

"So why not do something about it?"

She shrugs. I have that sudden and disconcerting sense of my own parents speaking from my mouth. The very words.

"I think to start you need to at least apologize to her. She was scared, you know. And for good reason."

Naomi exhales and rolls the eyes.

"You should be thankful," I say. "I've seen plenty, *plenty* of parents who don't give a damn if their kids ever come home. You want that?"

Naomi shakes her head.

"So where were you until two in the morning?"

She shrugs and does not look at me.

"Naomi?"

"Around," she says. "How come you were gone so long?"

"Big case," I say. "That's not the issue. Were you at someone's house?"

"For a while. Mostly just hanging out, you know. I didn't *do* anything bad or anything like that."

"No?"

"No."

"I'm still going to have to ground you again, you know. No more mall; no more friends for a while. You've got to stop doing this. Bad stuff happens at night out there, especially to young girls. You know all this."

She nods.

"And the phone. It's *our* phone, not yours. The family's."

"What was the case?"

"What?"

"The case. Why you were gone all day."

"A girl, almost your age, disappeared."

"For real? God. That's why I was on the phone," she says. "Talking about it. It was on the news. I didn't see you there."

"I was there."

"I got this friend, Zelda. She said she knew that girl. She met her living on the street. Downtown."

"Naomi —"

"You should have heard what Peggy said to me, though, Dad. After I hung up. It was foul."

"Then maybe you should both apologize?"

She shrugs.

I stand up.

"I should just get a phone," Naomi says. She stands up too. "It would solve a lot of problems."

"Then you'd be down here all the time. You hide out too much already. You think we can't get along, so you avoid dealing with it."

She gets quiet then and sits back down on her bed.

"Who's this Zelda?" I ask.

"She lived, you know, around? You know what I mean?"

"Yes, Naomi."

"And she met that girl, Tamara, on the street like a year ago or something."

"Tamara never lived on the street."

"Oh. Really?"

"What kind of people are you hanging out with?"

"I dunno."

"Maybe I should meet some of them."

She shrugs. "You could if you wanted."

"Okay."

"Hey, Dad?"

"Yes?"

"I'll pay for it."

"What?"

"A phone."

"Thirty, thirty-five bucks a month?"

"I could," she says. She leans over and opens a drawer in her bureau, an old thing Peggy picked up at a garage sale and refinished. She removes a diary, unlocks it, and shows me the cash she keeps there. "Two hundred," she says.

"Where's that from?"

"Baby-sitting."

"You baby-sit?"

"You know I do. I did the Vollmers last weekend."

"So maybe once a week you pick up a few bucks."

"I've been doing it since I was eleven. And I don't spend all of it. I put some away every time. For when I need it. Like now. I mean, you said yourself I have no place to go. And this will take care of the problem here. I won't bug Peggy by tying up the phone all the time."

"That's not the whole problem."

"But it is a *lot* of the problem," my wise daughter tells me. "More than you think. It's a woman thing, like a territory thing. It's her phone. I don't *blame* her for being pissed at me. I'd be pissed too."

I do not know what to say, exactly. I nod at what sounds surprisingly like an insight, a bit of common ground discovered, even, I dare to hope, a first step toward these two women identifying with each other.

Or more Naomi bullshit. She will not fight with or confront me in the way she does Peggy. Partly, I suppose, because I am her father, and partly, I like to think, because we have some kind of rapport. But I also think that Naomi just understands that I can't do emotional battle like this, face to face, that I cannot, or will not, tolerate it. And that if she blows up at me, she will force me into taking action. What that would be, neither of us knows, or wants to discover. And so she rolls over, like a dog offering its belly. Only when I am gone do the fangs come out again.

I manage to make it to an early supper. Naomi joins us at the table. She and Peggy murmur their regrets and try to smile at one another, as the boys eat silently, glancing from their mother to Naomi and then at each other. I feel too tired to worry about it anymore. I shovel down my food and crawl upstairs, knowing that I should try to stay up later so as not to throw my clock off too much, but knowing, too, that I cannot.

I lie on our bed and click on the small television we keep on Peggy's dresser. It's news time, and I'm not surprised, I guess, to see that Tamara Shipley has become the lead story, but I am surprised at how vehement the coverage is. I flip the channel and see that it's the same at all three stations, each of which runs a continuous banner giving our hot-line number and the fact that the city is offering a reward for anything useful. Each punctuates the report with frequent close-ups of Tamara's latest school picture. Each repeats the fact that witnesses saw two black men in the neighborhood in a dark, late-model car, the probable kidnap vehicle, in the moments before the disappearance.

Reporters have been all over the East Side, digging up friends and acquaintances, a teacher, an aunt, even her school-bus driver. They all, to the last one, implore her captors to release her unharmed. The mother, Rochelle, makes her requisite appearance, too, as I had predicted, but her English is fine. She speaks softly and does not come across at all as pathetic. I find her plea on her daughter's behalf compelling.

"She's a little girl," Rochelle Shipley says into the camera's lens. "Not an animal. She has a right to be free, to live. Whoever you are who took her, you should think about that, and also this: If anything happens to her, I will spend the rest of my life hunting you down. I swear it to God."

I shut off the set and have just closed my eyes when the phone rings. A moment later

Peggy pokes her head in the door and says, "Mack?"

"Mm," I say.

"Sorry," she says. "It's Stu Marek."

Without opening my eyes I lift the receiver next to the bed and say, "Hey."

"Long night," he says. "You're supposed to go home in the morning."

"Bank," I say, simply.

"Listen," he says. "I know you're beat. But this thing is going apeshit quick. The big chief called me."

"Yeah?"

"Bangers stealing a little girl, raping her, what-the-hell ever. I guess the calls are pouring in. Righteous citizens all outraged. So no limit to the resources, he says. Find these badasses and make us some fast arrests."

"Right," I say.

"So you seen it. What do you think?"

"I think somebody took her."

"Yeah, hey. You really should be in the Command." Stu, like Googie, has been after me for years to take the sergeant's exam and move up.

"I don't know, Stu. It looks like a cold, fast grab. What do you do about that?"

"Shit," he says, then, "There's gonna be a task force."

"Mm-hm."

"You want on it, Mack?"

"Me?" I say, opening my eyes.

"You showed up bright and early. You're on the ground floor. Might as well follow it out, I figure. They can use you."

"Stu —" I start to say, to tell him it was all an accident, my being there. It wasn't like I was gung-ho to go. But he cuts me off.

"Katherine's already on," he says. "Googie'll head it. Simms from Fibbie. Couple others."

"Stu —"

"This is from the top down, Mack. If you're on, anything else pressing you got open, you get the jackets on my desk tomorrow."

"I don't know," I say. "I really don't —"

"Well, get in early, whatever you decide. Preroll. Seven, say. We'll need your notes and all that regardless. You can tell me then. Now get some sleep, kid," he says, and hangs up.

I awake into darkness and the disorientation of irregular sleep, and Tamara Shipley fills my head. She has been waiting for me here in consciousness, where I do not want her to be. I don't remember dreaming about her, or having nightmares, but here she is now, in the night, in reality, right where I left her, not willing to give me even a moment's peace before she sets in.

Where is she, really, at this moment, I

wonder, as I lie beneath our warm comforter. In a field somewhere, dead, her body temperature adjusted now to the ambient air, her skin pallid and mottled with lividity? In a box, buried alive? For a flashing instant, half a breath, I feel the blackness and horror, the protracted suffocation. Or strapped to a cot in the basement of some crack house, her skinny legs spread and bloodied, her eyes half closed in her pain and semiconsciousness, young homeboys sliding into the room to watch her get done for the two-dozenth time, snickering, reaching out to give her a feel?

I sit up and sip from the water glass on my table. Moonlight falls in across our bed. I hear the familiar sounds of my house: the furnace blower kicking on to chase out the chill of night; the front screen door chattering in a stiff westerly breeze — this is what awakened me, I think; my wife, Peggy, breathing heavily in the bed. She lies on her side, her back to me, the position of easiest approach. I relax a little, lie back down, and slide over to her, fit my front to her warmth and curvature.

Sometimes when I do this her breathing pauses, then grows shallower and more rapid, a sign that she's surfacing.

She is a largish woman, but I do not mean by this that she's fat. She is, I tell her, bountifully equipped, and add, in all truthfulness, that I find this deeply attractive. She has a wide, roomy pelvis, a pleasingly broad and padded behind, good muscular legs, a soft milk-white belly and breasts. She is tall, too, at five seven.

On this night, as I lie next to her, her breathing does begin to change. As she shifts and waggles against me, I feel an old familiar charge.

"S'early," she says. "You have to get ready?"

"No," I say. "Not yet." The green Day-Glo numbers on the clock by my bed say it is just four-thirty.

"It's going to be hard, isn't it. Finding that little girl."

That she'd mention this surprises me. She doesn't care to talk much about my work, but the story has pierced people, especially those with kids.

"I don't think we will," I say. "Not in time, I mean."

"S'awful. Horrible. Her mother —"

"Shh," I say, pushing the hair from her face and then running my hand down over her back.

"Mm," she says.

She is a careful and deliberate person, particular about things in ways I am still discovering. But she is grounded, too, solid, and she

114

has that ability to enjoy earthy pleasures in the way they need to be enjoyed, that is, with abandon, with total exposure and release.

We each help the other peel away our night-clothes, and then she pulls me toward her. An image from a few days earlier floats back to me, of her lying facedown with a pillow tucked beneath her hips, pressing her buttocks into the air. The picture of it brings my blood to a pitch.

"How about that pillow thing?" I say into her neck.

"How 'bout it," she says, and laughs in her throat. She flings back the covers.

I float above her then, in the waves of her heat, holding myself up with my arms to watch her moving against me, the rising and falling of her lovely, moon-white ass. "Oh," she says. "Yes."

It is not, I'm convinced, the carnality of the act itself, but its simple life force, that brings the vision forth. Tamara Shipley sits in a stuffed chair in the corner of the room, in moonlight, watching us. I recognize her from the bright-eyed school photo we're circulating. Only, now she has hollows for eyes, dark and sunken and rimmed red. Blood has dried and caked around her cracked lips. Her hair hangs in wet strings. She does not speak or even move. She just sits, waiting for us to finish, and judging us, I feel, as if we are committing some cardinal sin, but forgiving us too. Forgiving us because we are only humans, and adults at that, far past the days of purity to which she so recently belonged, and immeasurably short of the state of grace into which she may well have already passed.

TWO

8

From the elevators the fourth floor of the Public Safety Building looks, in 1996, pretty much as it has since I got my shield eleven years ago. But now the old Juvenile squad room at the south end of the hall lies empty, its linoleum floor torn and peeled back in places, the walls cracked and stained, the stink of decades of detectives and punks still hanging faintly on the air. All the other old squad rooms look this way too.

Now only one door matters, clear at the north end of the hallway, a modern glass door fitted with a hydraulic piston that closes it with an even, efficient *shhh.* This modern glass door opens onto a modular counter with desk and shelves behind it, where the Bureau clerk works at a computer and takes calls on an integrated phone system. Beyond the counter and around a corner the new suite of offices opens out, a huge, bright area decorated in the best kinds of worker colors: tasteful beiges and blues and yellows. Each detective has his or her own cubicle formed by half-height dividers. Each cubicle comes with a built in desktop and drawers, a computer terminal and typewriter and phone, and a standard-issue cork bulletin board. The cubicles were constructed at odd and calculated angles so that, even though they are open, they afford some modicum of privacy.

This is all simply the most overt sign that the old squad system has gone. We're just detectives up here now, few of us considered specialists anymore. We hate this, most of us, and, irrational as we know it is, blame it on the new offices as much as on the new Command.

As I step from the elevator on this Monday morning, I'm met by an unusual sight. A long wooden bench sits inside the glass door to the Bureau. It's common to see one or a few arrestees waiting there, cuffed to the wooden slats, as their paperwork is processed. A few wooden chairs sit outside the door for overflow. But now, not only are the bench and chairs filled, the entire hallway clear back to the elevator is lined with reposing bodies. There must be twenty-five people, most kids, most sitting on the floor, riot-cuffed hands propped on their knees, heads hanging as they doze and wait. They wear the uniform, many of them, ball shoes with red or green or gold laces in the left or right shoe, ball caps turned at the correct angle, plaid flannel shirts, some of them, or T-shirts and jackets, and the usual faded baggy jeans.

Some bleed. One boy holds a cloth up over his eye that has soaked through so that it drips onto the linoleum between his legs. One lies over on his side, a gash in his head open for the world to see. I stop and nod at the two patrol cops who're standing guard, and am about to check the kid myself when the other elevator opens and a couple of paramedics with their gear step out. I continue on.

One older white man wears shorts and a sport coat with no shirt beneath. His right leg has been scraped raw around the knee and the blood has dribbled and dried on the linoleum. I smell his Thunderbird aura as I walk past. A few women sit there, too, crack dolls in jeans and whores wearing cheap knit dresses or shorts, their legs stretched out on the cool floor, their faces all pouty and angry at being dragged in again and kept away from their pipes. One of them wears a short fur jacket. I recognize her from Saturday night on the street with Bank.

"Stab *me* ina back," she says to her friend, just loud enough for me to hear. "Son of a *bitch*."

Some of them look up as I pass. A few recognize me and nod or even call out, asking for my help in processing them or at least in loosening the cuffs. The hallway has filled with the odors of a half dozen aftershaves and colognes and hair grease, and mixed in with it some metabolized alcohol and old dirt and vomit.

Near the glass door to the suite, three particularly young boys sit cuffed together, the one in the middle snoring with his head back against the wall, the ones on either side sleeping, too, their heads resting on the middle boy's shoulders. In sleep they become again what they are: children.

Stu Marek, Captain Marek, now, the head of Personal Crimes, is leaning over the clerk's counter when I walk in. The day clerk, Jeremiah, who's been here since before I got my shield, rolls his eyes when he sees me. His phone lines are all lit up and he's talking furiously into his headset, and ignoring the note Stu keeps shoving in front of his face.

"Morning, Boy Scouts," I say.

Stu grunts. His belly strains a bit at his shirt and belt these days, since he gave up cigarettes; his tie does not quite reach his buckle anymore. But other than that and some grayer hair and full-time glasses, he still looks like the lieutenant I worked for for years, who taught me a good share of what I know about the Job.

I say, "What happened?"

"Bank Arbaugh happened," he says.

"These are *all* Bank's?"

"Every one. A new record. Thirty-seven felony collars in one eight-hour period. He had four squads and a wagon running non-stop all night. Juvie Hall's calling every fifteen minutes wanting to know where they're supposed to put the rest of them. And County's full too."

I lean against the counter. "Where is he?"

"I told him to bag his OT and get out of here, get some sleep," Stu says. He stands upright, but keeps one ear cocked toward Jeremiah's conversation. "So I get to clean up his mess."

I nod, but say nothing.

Stu goes on. "Thinks he's gonna wrap this up all on his lonesome, kickin' ass." He lifts a foam cup of coffee from the counter and sips loudly at it. Then he kind of smiles and says, "Probably could, too, if we let him."

"You're talking about the girl."

"Hell, yes," he says, and sets the cup back down. "Everything's about the girl. Everything's gonna be about the girl. And now, shit, I've had fifty fucking calls already 'cause of Bank — police brutality, civil rights violations — and on top of that I got this mess out here to deal with."

I turn to head back to my cubicle when Stu grabs my arm. "Listen, Mack," he says. "I gotta start pulling this task force together first thing after roll —"

"I don't know —" I begin, but Stu cuts me off.

" 'Listen,' I said," he says. "Something just came up I need somebody to take a look at. I need some judgment here. That's all. It don't commit you. You mind?"

"No," I say.

"Squad out the south end came on an abandoned car, an LHS, about an hour ago, Weikert's Corner area, behind that Food King in Southtown there? You know it?"

"Sure."

"Came up stolen Sunday morning sometime before eight. That's when the owner got up and noticed it gone. And it's clean, Mack. Nothing stripped."

"What color?"

"Dark something or other. If this smells like the real deal, I want to know a-sap. We'll roll the troops and start canvassing. Don't mean you gotta do anything else. I just want someone there I can trust, right now."

I nod.

"Commissioner's gonna drop in at roll, say a few words about this caper," he says. "I'll pass along your regrets at not being there."

"Hey, thanks," I tell him.

Southtown lies roughly on the dividing line between what is called the near-South End, the old, eastern neighborhoods in that part of the city, and the subdivisions in the area known as Weikert's Corner, which then spread away, in ever newer neighborhoods, to the south and west, toward the new malls out at the city's edges. The new part of the campus of the Medical College of Western Ohio and its hospital, built of white concrete and stainless steel and blue glass, lies just to the east.

The paved expanse behind this Food King is a busy place on a Monday morning, semis and smaller trucks waiting to back up to the concrete docks to unload, men pushing wheeled stacks of cardboard cartons or plastic trays in through the opened metal bay doors. But a day earlier, on Palm Sunday, it would have been an unpeopled wasteland of fetid garbage Dumpsters, stained stacks of wooden pallets, and free-floating trash blown up against the high chain-link fence that marks the border with the edge of the medical-college campus. The fence has red and white metal privacy strips woven through its links, which means that only someone watching from up in one of the buildings over there would have seen anything.

The LHS is a nice car, Chrysler's entry in the luxury market: big enough to sleep in, tinted glass, leather upholstery, CD player, six speakers, all the touches. This one stands with the doors open. A detective named Bill Biner, of the Crime Scene Unit, kneels on the asphalt next to it, not touching, just looking in, his latex-gloved hands resting on his thighs.

"They popped the column and turned it with a screwdriver," he tells me when I lean down next to him. "We can pull the whole unit, strip it down, there's a possibility you find the screwdriver, the lab can match it to the scored metal in there."

Biner, the assistant head of the CSU, is a real pro at these things. Anything from arsons to bodies to vehicles, he's meticulous as he combs for evidence. Victims and perps, unless they're dead, play no part in the daily work of these CSU guys. They deal in evidence, everything from prints to fibers to organic debris to chemicals. They secure it, diagram it, collect it, tag it, and get it to the lab. And they testify about it. I think some of them spend half their time in court.

Theirs is a coldly rational, hyperlogical way of looking at the world. What anybody says, what any suspect screams and pisses and moans about, doesn't mean anything next to the facts: here's the physical evidence; physical evidence does not lie. It just is. There's a cleanness to this I must confess I sometimes envy.

"And check this out, Mack," Bill says, as he gets to his feet. He leads me around the opposite side of the car, which is close to the building, so that the open doors nearly touch the walls, and points into the backseat. I lean in next to him and peer inside. It's overcast, and still early, making it dark here in the shadow of the store, so it takes me a moment before I make out the brownish streak on the fine beige leather there.

"Blood?" I say.

"Looks like," says Bill. Where someone might've turned her face and wiped a bloody nose or mouth.

"You're not processing this now?"

"No way," he says. "Flatbed's on the way." Once the car's safely in a specially equipped bay in the garage beneath the PS Building, they'll start taking it apart piece by piece, if they have to, to get at what they need. Until then no one's touching it.

I take a few steps back and look at it again, in the gloom and shadow. "What color is this?" I ask.

"Chrysler calls it Dark Rosewood," he says.

"Wife loves it. She's wanting one of these new Grand Caravans."

"*Rose*wood?"

"Dark Rosewood," he says. "They've had it out for a couple years."

"It's not brown?"

It really does look brown or black or even navy at certain angles, depending on the light, or lack of it. But when Bill pulls out a penlight and aims it at the fender, I can see that it's actually a deep metallic maroon, almost, a kind of reddish-plum color.

"Purple," I say, mostly to myself, and I feel that curious, addictive tingle of the bite of an insight.

"Kind of," Bill says.

I could leave now, make my report to Stu, but instead I follow Bill back to his city car, where he has a full thermos of coffee. He pours each of us a cup and we stand midway between the two vehicles, sipping.

"What do you suppose," I ask him, "leads to a decision by two men to kidnap a girl at nine o'clock on a Sunday morning? I mean, it's an odd time."

Biner shifts his weight from one foot to the other. "You tell me," he says.

"A long Saturday night."

"What, they're out drinking?"

"Drinking. With women. Without women.

Pining away. Eating pills. Smoking dope. I don't know. But Saturday nights can be weird and forever. Why else do it at a time like that? That's the thing here. The timing."

"I don't know," he says.

"The question is," I say, "— guys do a thing like this, say it's a snap decision, does that mean they go in totally unprepared? Empty handed?"

"They worked it out enough to steal a car," Bill says.

"They probably leave their own car stashed behind the store here while they make the grab, then come back and switch afterward. Make sense?"

Bill nods.

I look around at the medical-center campus beyond the fence, at the dozens of far-off windows with a view of the back of this store. Could someone have been at one of them on an early Sunday morning, looking out, by chance, as one guy parked his own car back here, then jumped into another one? Or later, when they showed up again, dragging a girl with them, and transferred her into the car they'd left here earlier? Then, I think, maybe they made the transfer somewhere else and just dropped the hot car here afterward. Who knew? But they were careful, these two. Careful enough that I didn't hold out much

129

hope of Bill and his men lifting any usable prints from the interior.

I continue. "So maybe they worked out a few other things as well, no?"

"Musta," says Bill.

The Food King is tucked into the corner of the L formed by a strip mall of small shops and boutiques. I cruise slowly up one side, then cut across the lot and come back up the other. All these smaller stores would have been closed. And in this area, mostly residential neighborhoods and malls, I can't think of any kind of all-night hardware store or anything like that. That leaves the Food King itself. OPEN 24 HOURS, the sign says in big red letters.

I find the weekend manager in the front office, counting money into cash-register trays. He's a little man with a hard mouth and metal frame glasses with one earpiece held on by masking tape. We chat for a moment, and then I pose the question. Early Sunday morning, before nine o'clock, is there any way to tell what nongrocery items were sold, and who'd been on that register?

The man nods vehemently. He's the expert here. "It's all computers now," he explains. "Bar codes. You ever look at your wife's shopping receipt? Every item, where it used to

130

just say 'grocery' or 'dairy' or whatever, now it says 'low-fat cream cheese' or whatever. Even the brand name." He laughs at this miracle.

"You can't be that busy early on a Sunday."

"Oh, no? Round six you start to get the doughnut-and-newspaper run. It can hop, I'll tell you."

"Yeah? Listen, you got a couple people you can put on those receipts, I call back in a few hours, you got a list for me?"

The man looks at me, calculating time and hourly wages.

I lower my voice and say, "It's about that little girl got kidnapped yesterday. You see that on the news?"

"Yeah," he says, going a little wide eyed.

"You can be a hero, here, buddy."

He sits up straighter and opens his mouth.

"But keep this to yourself," I say, in a near whisper. I glance around, as if someone might be listening. "Confidential. Just between us, right?"

He nods, and he is hooked. Deputized. I've just made his day, his whole week. Everybody wants to be a hero. They just don't know how to go about it, sometimes, until someone shows them the way.

When I radio down to Jeremiah at the PSB,

131

Stu Marek's in a meeting.

"Roll still?" I ask.

"That task force," Jeremiah says.

"Get him out."

"Commissioner's here, you know," he tells me. "In the meeting."

"I don't care. Get him." I'm driving, heading north and east, toward the downtown, but not the PS Building.

"Yeah?" Stu says, irritated, when he radios back a minute later.

"That car looks good," I say. "Blood on the backseat." I tell him my thoughts about the grocery store, and can hear him snapping his fingers on the other end, a thing he does sometimes when he's worked up or thinking hard. "Listen," I say, then. "There may be something else here. I gotta make a stop. I'll get back to you soon."

"Something else what?" he says. "You workin' this caper?"

"That car," I tell him. "Dark Rosewood. A kind of purple, you could say."

"What the hell does that mean?"

"Exactly," I tell him, and flip off the radio.

I catch the on-ramp of the MLK Bridge at the southern edge of the downtown, and drive up and across its great arc, toward the East Side, toward King's Court.

9

On the morning after Jamie Arbaugh vanished, someone delivered six dozen Dunkin' Donuts and several trays of large foam cups of hot coffee to the command center that had been set up in Bank and Sarah's garage. Googie said it had been a couple young ladies, employees in their brown nylon uniforms. They just carried in the boxes and trays and asked where they should put them, did so, and left. We ate and drank and did not ask questions. I would discover months later that the owner of the nearby franchise himself had sent the two girls over with this donation to the cause. When I stopped in to thank him, he waved me off, saying that a man who sold doughnuts could do worse things than to give a few away to tired policemen.

As I sipped black coffee, Stu Marek caught my eye from out in the yard and motioned to me with his head. I walked over to him.

"Antsy?" he said.

I nodded. With the new day renewed efforts were set to begin, and yet a heaviness seemed to overlay everyone. We'd had several dozen tips on the hot-line number that was being broadcast, but they were either obvious cranks or spottings that amounted to nothing. The Feds had come out and talked to Bank about his active cases and about perps he'd put away who were out now, looking for a kidnap angle. But Bank could think of nothing remarkable. There wasn't much the Feds, or any of us for that matter, could do until we knew more about what had happened to Jamie.

And what could we do on this day that we hadn't done yesterday, except widen the ground search out into the city? And how could that really lead to anything? The point of diminishing returns had already appeared out ahead of us. The next step, really, had to be informational: pictures of Jamie posted, stories in the paper and more on the television, notices over the national law-enforcement networks, then wait for a sighting. If none came, then eventually contacts with the national registries. To take these steps, all of us, but especially Bank and Sarah, would have to settle into a new reality, the reality not of a sudden crisis that needed to be addressed, but of a long-term vacuum, the new reality of their lives, of a child who had disappeared and stayed away. A living death, I'd heard someone call it in the past, when we'd witnessed others going through it. It was worse than death, some said, because it had no finality. Just an ongoing, gnawing nothingness.

"Ride?" Stu said. "Not much happening here."

I nodded, grateful to be occupied with something. I had yet to see Bank. He had not come outside since my arrival, largely, I think, because of the phalanx of press vans parked along Detwiler, out beyond the squad and Bureau cars that shielded his house. The city paper had sent a reporter and a photographer, and the three local news stations had sent minicam crews. Crews had even begun to filter in already from other cities, Cleveland and Columbus TV stations, Toledo and Dayton and Cincinnati newspapers, that I knew of. A cop's kid going. Probably a small tragedy, but possibly a big story, one worth sending a crew out to wait for. It was a death watch, actually.

"We'll just look," Stu said. "Coming on twenty-four hours now." It was eight-thirty. Jamie had left for practice at eight forty-five. Things cycle, he meant. Routine events happen at certain regular times, and not again. Mail gets delivered. Someone leaves for work. Someone walks the dog. Same time every day. I felt encouraged by this intelligence. We needed to be out there, watching, when the clock wound past the same point.

Stu Marek, who was then forty-five and who still wore the crew cut he'd been given in the military, slipped behind the wheel of a beige city-issue Chrysler K car and leaned across to unlock the passenger door. I'd come to know him pretty well in the years since he'd taken over our squad. Stu had been, like Googie, in Violent Crimes before that, a field sergeant in the Adult Sex Crimes Unit, what used to be called the Rape Squad. He was moved out, finally, after a few too many complaints from rape victims about this hard-assed detective who made them feel worse instead of better. Guys burned out on things; it was common.

Still, Stu was a rarity, because even with his climb up the command ladder, he'd kept himself out on the street, investigating scenes, keeping tabs, staying known. He had thick sagging bags beneath his eyes and melanotic blotches on the grayish skin of his face, and his mouth had set in permanent reaction to the awful things he knew of the world. I would come to look like this one day, too, I knew, if I stayed out here.

At a quarter till nine, as close to the exact time of Jamie's departure as Sarah could come, we sat in the K car on Detwiler at the point where the road curved right, out over the river, and a footpath angled to the left, forming a Y with the road. To our immediate left another road, Riverview, angled up a hill, away from Detwiler. It was isolated here — because of the trees and the angle of the roads, only one house had a direct view of this spot, and that house was back up Detwiler a little ways. Stu put the car into park and lit a cigarette.

We sat quietly after that for the five minutes it took him to finish his smoke. Several times he began to snap his fingers, which was a habit he'd developed for dealing with nerves. But each time he looked over at me after a few snaps and then stopped. Little moved in the neighborhood around us. Two kids played in the front yard of the one visible house until their mother leaned out the front door and called them over. She threw a glance toward the strange car sitting in the street. She said something to the kids and pointed up the road, toward Bank's house, which lay out of sight around a curve over a rise in the road. The kids nodded and walked inside. A minute later they reappeared in the fenced backyard.

We'd spoken to this woman several times yesterday. She and her kids had been away at the time of the disappearance, shopping.

A cruiser crept past. Stu nodded and the cop held up a hand.

I watched Jamie's ghost walk up the street from the direction of her house, toward the bridge. She had a gold-colored aluminum bat over her shoulder. She and Bank had bought it together at a Kmart clear over on the East Side. It hadn't been easy, I remember, for them to find one short and light enough for Jamie to swing. The team had some, but Jamie had wanted to practice at home. Then she insisted on taking the bat to practice because it was lucky. She carried her mitt over the end of the bat, in the manner that Bank had taught her. She looked good. I watched her walk along at precisely the same time she had the day before, but when she got to the split between the trail and the road, when she had to choose a direction, she disappeared.

"Could walk across to the other side," Stu said. "We don't know. Maybe it was here. Maybe over there." The trees in the ravine which held the river were old and dense and healthy. We'd been all through them a dozen times, men and dogs stomping and yelling and sniffing. Nothing on the other side could be seen from here, although it was only a couple of hundred feet across.

"I'll go," I said. "I'll walk the footbridge, wait five, then come back on the road."

He nodded, and lit another smoke.

This day would be as hot and still as the previous one, I could tell. I wore a clean shirt, but for some reason — I just was not thinking — I'd put on the same suit I'd had on the day before, and with all that activity and the morning's new sweat, it'd begun to stink slightly. I tossed the jacket into the backseat.

My shoes echoed on the wooden bridge. I moved slowly, peering down over the hand-rail into the dense foliage beneath. I caught glimpses of the water in there, ahead of me, flashing as it caught and reflected the morn-ing's light. Farther ahead, I could hear the traffic on Tecumseh Boulevard.

When I was directly over the river itself, I stopped and leaned over the wide wooden railing to look down. This was a particularly deep and narrow spot, a kind of chute where the water churned and frothed. Not much farther down it widened again, and slowed. The decision had been made to begin searching the water itself today, dragging it, maybe even putting in a diver. Although the water grew shallower past this rapid spot, it was still more than deep enough to swallow and hide a small girl.

Then, as my weight pressed against the railing, it shifted suddenly and I felt myself falling. I reacted, pushing myself backward and dropping to lower my center of gravity, all by instinct, but the railing had only given a few inches. One of the bolts was sheared off, I could see when I looked at its base. It wouldn't collapse because of this, but still needed to be fixed.

I shook it a few more times, testing its strength, then, without leaning against it, looked out over the creek again. But now, because of my change in perspective, I found myself looking more into the upper foliage of the trees that had grown up alongside the creek, which was at my eye level. And then, as if I had willed it somehow to be there, as if I had awakened suddenly into some slightly altered reality, I found myself looking at an incongruous glint within the leaves of the tree, a shine of yellow, and flat black next to that. Whatever it was, the leaves had all but hidden it, and to anyone searching below on the banks of the creek it would have been invisible.

Then Stu's horn sounded. He stood outside the car, waving me back.

Bank was in the garage with Captain Draves and Googie and a couple of other detectives when we got back.

"Something's up," Stu had informed me. "Over at City Med." City Medical Center was our city's third huge medical facility, besides St. Jerome's downtown and the Medical College hospital out in the South End. City Med was on the border, roughly, between the Old and New West Ends, on the edge of the huge old Heron Park that had been there for generations, in one of the prettier, if increasingly beleaguered, parts of our city.

"We were thumbing through the pink sheets off the hot-line transcripts," Captain Draves was saying. "One that come in last night sort of jumped out. Third-shift maintenance guy over at City Med. A runner. He was out yesterday morning, after his shift, running the trails in Heron Park there across the street. We sent a guy out to talk to him an hour ago."

Around nine-thirty, the jogger said, he'd been on one of the deep trails that at one point skirted the edge of a kind of rough circular open area inside the woods, large enough for a car to be able to pull into, but unpaved and accessible only by a pitted muddy lane leading off of Morton Parkway. The sort of spot kids would use for making out or drinking, not visible from the roads with all the foliage. As he came out into the section of trail alongside this clearing, near the end of his run, he heard a car door slam.

He saw a man standing in front of this car down in there. And he saw a kid in the front passenger seat. He'd been close enough to see clearly. He watched them for the few moments it took him to run past. The kid had on a baseball cap, so he figured it was a boy. The jogger had had no idea why that car would be there, at that time, in the morning, he said, and although he had no reason to suspect anything, it had just seemed odd to him. He'd gone home then, showered, slept through the afternoon, had dinner and so forth, and gone back to work that night. He did not turn on his TV or look at a paper. It wasn't until then, at work, around midnight, that he heard some people talking about this cop's kid who'd disappeared, and he heard a description, including the baseball hat. He remembered that car he'd seen in the park, but didn't know what to do about it. Finally, when the subject of this missing girl came up later in the break room, he said something to his supervisor, who called one of the hospital security guards down. No cops were hanging around the ER at that moment, so the guard had placed the call to the hot-line number, which was posted in the ER.

Bank listened as we asked Gene questions. Could he give a description of the driver? They had someone working an Identi-Kit with him right now, and an artist was going to sit down with him that afternoon, but it didn't sound like he'd noticed much.

What about the car?

Blue, he remembered. A light blue, and kind of a boxy car, older model. American, he thought.

And the child?

All the man could remember was the baseball cap. Dark, he'd said. With a red bill. That's what he remembered, anyway.

I watched Bank's face collapse when he heard this, watched his eyes fill and then watched him turn away and walk out through the rear of the garage into the backyard, where he stood with his hands on his hips, looking up into the old trees there. As I watched him, it dawned on me what I had seen before, at the river. I waited until he went back inside to tell Sarah about the car.

"Listen to me," I said, then. They all looked, Gene and Googie and Stu and the others. I pointed up the street, toward the creek in its ravine of trees. "Her bat," I said. They looked at me still, not comprehending. But I knew that that's what I had spotted there in the crook of a branch of a tall tree, caught where someone had thrown it — the taped handle of Jamie's golden aluminum bat.

10

Jeff Gramza lives three doors down from the Tamara Shipley house. He is bent and misshapen like he has cerebral palsy, his neck twisted so that his face aims upward, his thick lips separated in a permanent grimace framing his horse teeth, his head all skin and skull, too large for the wasted body, too large for the bird neck to hold up. If he suffers from CP, though, it isn't from that alone. He holds one arm permanently folded across his chest, its malformed hand, a pink lobster claw, tucked into his armpit. He has a problem with drool. In his good hand he holds a folded bandanna for this purpose. We sit in the living room of his mother's house, him strapped into an electric wheelchair, me on the couch. His mother — after protesting to me about bothering the boy (who is thirty-two years old) again after all that commotion yesterday, after complaining that the boy can't hardly talk anyway so how do we expect him to describe what he saw, and can he really have seen anything anyway? — agrees to leave us alone for at least a few minutes.

I perch on the edge of the couch, lean

toward him, and say: "So you win the prize for best answer as to the color of the car, Jeff. Purple. Those others, they were wrong with their browns and blacks. What do you think of that?"

He bucks, his head flopping forward and back, which I take to be an affirmative gesture, a nod.

"My colleague's notes," I tell him, "say you were sitting right out front here, in the yard. Just watching the cars go by?" Katherine's notes I'm referring to. The fact that she had questioned this man aided us immeasurably. I could see her kneeling down, patient, listening, learning the sounds, understanding that inside his head this man was whole. Underdeveloped, uneducated, treated like an idiot his whole life, but whole nonetheless. And so she got a brief statement. But then, according to the notes, Jeff's mother cut it off, saying enough was enough, and wheeling him across the Shipley/Salano front yard to the plywood ramp built onto the front of her own house.

"Eahh," he says.

"You like to do that? Watch the cars go by?"

"Eahh."

"Did you like Katherine? Detective Biasotti?"

"Eahh!" Jeff says and bucks again, the spit flying off his lips from the force of it.

"She's all right, isn't she."

"Eahh."

"So, Jeffrey. You been thinking about what you saw since yesterday?"

"Nah."

"No? You don't think you've remembered anything new about that car since then?"

His head waves like a heavy flower on its stalk.

"Katherine wrote that you think for some reason you couldn't see their faces very clearly. Why not?"

"On know."

"You can't remember."

He blinks, and rolls his head. A shrug.

"Three other people saw black men. You still think they were white?"

"Eahh."

"So what else, Jeff. Picture that car going past. Think back. You're sitting out there in the yard, in the sun, a quiet Sunday morning. People maybe going to church."

He bucks but does not speak. His loud breathing fills the small room. It rasps in and out and then stops hard, as if he's choking or has just died on me. Finally, after many seconds, it cuts loose and begins to flow again. A kind of moaning escapes him every so often, a deep involuntary swell that rises up when his muscles contract in a certain way.

Then, clearly, he says, "Mune-sic."

"Mune-sic?"

"*Mune*-sic."

"*Music.*"

"Eahh."

I check the notes again. No mention of this. I say, "They had on a stereo?"

"Eahh."

"You didn't remember that yesterday, either, did you, Jeff?"

"Nah." His head flops.

These little doors open. Sometimes you have to come back three, four, five times, knocking, before it happens. I look out through the window at the day, at the neighborhood. "Jeff," I say, "was the music so loud that you heard it through the glass? Or was the window open?"

He bucks and rolls his eyes to the ceiling and says, "O-ben."

"Sure?"

"Eahh," he says. He seems to laugh. His face twists and he begins to cough, a series of deep rasping barks that sound like death waiting. His mother pokes her nose in from the kitchen, but I meet her eyes until she backs away again. When he's calmed down, Jeff says, "Na guy's arm, anging out."

"What? His arm. The man had his arm out the window?"

"Eahh."

"This would have been the passenger."

"Eahh."

"So you saw his hand too. Maybe that's how you knew he was a white guy?"

"Un-oh." His head flops. "Nah. Gl-glove. Ad a glove on."

"He was wearing a glove."

"Eahh."

"Jeff!" I say, suddenly, sharply. I lean forward, closer to him, and press. "What'd you see? Think back. What is it about their faces? How'd you know they were white?"

He bucks again, his head lolled off to one side, the drool running down unhindered now, him not bothering to catch it in his bandanna.

"Like this," I say, pointing to the red cloth in his hand. "Maybe they had —"

"Eahh!" he says. "Mansk! Mansk!"

"Mansk?"

"Mansk!"

"Masks, *masks*. Right," I say. "What kind of masks? Like a bandanna?" I hold a hand up over my mouth.

"Nah," he said. "Win oles fer na face. Know?"

I do know. "Holes for the face," I say.

"Openings, you mean. Like ski masks?" I make a circle with my fingers and look at him through it.

"Eahh," he says, bucking excitedly.

"*Black* ski masks," I say.

"Eahh!"

"But underneath you saw white skin."

"Eahh."

"The others, they were too far away, weren't they?"

Jeff doesn't answer me then. He seems to have collapsed back into himself, to have folded up again, exhausted from these exertions.

I stand up and lean over him, my mouth next to his ear. He smells strange, antiseptic and yet faintly rotten. "This is very good, Jeffrey," I tell him. "I'll tell Katherine."

From my car on King's Court, across from the missing girl's house, I lift my radio to call Stu with my news. I'm parked behind a cruiser with a couple of uniforms sitting in it, keeping a watch. But as I look up at the sagging front porch, the peeling paint, I set the radio back on the seat.

This is not my case, I whisper to myself. I open the door and step out into the morning again, nod at the two patrol cops, then walk up across the front yard and onto the porch.

When the girl's mother, Rochelle, sees me standing there, she assumes I have bad news, and starts to weep.

I shake my head, say, "No, no," and tell her I'm just there to talk. She nods and composes herself and then opens the door.

She offers me coffee, which I accept. The house is quiet today, the big television on but playing silently. The other kids, Eddie and Geena, are at school. "And why not?" she says. "What'll they do here but sit around and watch me worry? Maybe school will keep their minds off it a little. Maybe they'll hear something, from one of the other kids, you know. . . ."

I nod at this possibility, and think for a moment of my own daughter and her mystery friend, Zelda, at their own school clear across the city.

"So why'd you come over?" Rochelle says then, her eyes boring into me again, her strength restored after the shock of my initial appearance, as if she knows I'm not really attached to this case, that I'm holding back whatever I can from it.

"We may have found the car," I tell her. I'm watching the floor, so I don't see her reaction, but I hear the sharp sucking in of her breath. "And I had a talk with Jeff Gramza."

"Him?"

"He's not stupid," I say.

"I know," she says. "I know that."

"Mrs. Shipley —"

"Rochelle," she says.

"I don't think it was black kids that took her."

She looks at me steadily again, but the eyes aren't so hard this time, the jaw not set so firmly.

"They were white or Hispanic."

"So —"

"I want to talk to Eddie again."

She shakes her head.

"I don't need your permission, but I'm asking anyway. I want to swing by his school, pick him up, take him downtown. Just to talk," I say. "Just friendly."

"Friendly," she says. "Well, I don't know what you want me to say, Detective. You think Eddie had something —"

"That's not it. I just want us to talk to him again, see what he knows. Who he knows. He's got to be scared."

She gives me the hardened gaze once more. She's tough, toughened by the life, the worthless men, the fucked-up neighborhoods, the constant grinding lack of money. She does not speak again, but turns away instead, to stare out the window.

I pick up her phone and dial. "Bill," I say,

"it's Mack." As if on cue a news brief comes on the silent oversized television, yet another update on the Tamara situation, this one a minicam report showing cops in the street rounding up black kids somewhere in the North End. A sea of blue uniforms armed with old warrants has spread out through the neighborhood, some stepping up onto porches, knocking on doors, some leading known or suspected gang members toward the wagons that wait with opened doors.

"Son of a *bitch*, Mack," Stu says, when I tell him what I believe. In his office, along with the snapping of his fingers, I can hear the sound of the same news report I'm watching.

"He knew the color, Stu," I say. "And the masks. He watched them coming. This is right. I feel it."

"*Son* of a bitch," he says again, then, "Get the kid in here," meaning Eddie. And then, out to Jeremiah, the day clerk, "Get me the commissioner. *Now*," his fingers snapping away.

11

If Bank was the agent of my eventual acceptance into the fourth-grade crowd, then football was the vehicle. We played it in rough backyards or the open fields of the playground behind the school with three-man teams, four-man, five when we could get the guys, every clear weekend and at least twice a week after school. And I was lousy at it to start.

In the beginning it was just Bank and me tossing a ball. He was amazed that I had made it to the fourth grade without learning how to catch, let alone throw, a football. I just said I was rotten at sports and so had never bothered to learn. But as we practiced, he told me I wasn't all that uncoordinated. I had a certain touch, he said, decent hands. And, we discovered, there was nothing at all wrong with my once asthmatic lungs. I could run, fast and long.

And so after a week or two of practicing, he decided that if I stayed at the position of receiver at all times, I'd be all right. On offense my job was to outrun the coverage, get open, and catch the ball. On defense, to stay with the receiver and keep my hands constantly in his face. But I was never to play on the line, where guys twice my weight would squash me, or quarterback, because, Bank said, I threw a ball worse than most girls he knew. And if I had to make a tackle, I was instructed to hit as low as possible. There was no way, weighing what little I did, I'd be able to body-tackle anyone. At the ankles, though, he said, any body could bring down any body.

And from him, then, emulating him, I learned to play, or at least aspire to play, with an abandon, a recklessness, I had never felt before. In the beginning when I got really racked, a foot in the head, an elbow in the gut, I let myself cry a little until once, as I lay on the ground curled into a ball, Bank got down next to me and said, "Come on, Mack. Hold it in. Just don't let yourself." So I bit down on my teeth and closed my eyes and waited until the pain ebbed.

"All *right*," he said, when I got up. He told me one time he didn't think he had cried about anything since he was six years old.

Bank's favorite position was fullback: he loved to get the ball and then launch himself as fast as he could run into the wall of opposing bodies. I watched him do this time after time, head up, face forward, teeth gritted, taking blow after punishing blow, once even chipping a tooth — and most every time he'd pull himself up from the ground with a grin. It was the violence as much as the game he relished.

Sometimes, though, he'd just go off. Someone would throw a particularly hard block at him or break one of his tackles with a stiff-arm to his face, and he'd come back to the huddle with flushed cheeks and a locked jaw, his nostrils flaring. He would not talk, not even to call a play. I knew then that he was gone, because Bank always liked to call the plays, or at least throw in comments if someone else was calling. But these times he'd just kneel there in the grass, fuming, and then when we'd run the play he'd focus only on getting back at whoever had angered him, ignoring what the rest of us were doing. No one else ever said anything, just letting him go until he exhausted the rage and came back. But I began to.

"Yeah, throw the game away," I'd say, without looking at him, and then commence calling the play myself. The group around us would go quiet, awaiting his reaction, but he did not ever get mad at me when I'd say things like this. I seemed to have a license with him that he did not allow others. Instead, after I'd start to call the play myself, he'd interrupt me, his anger replaced by disgust with my ignorance of the subtleties of the game.

And after all, he was a gamesman, and hated worst of all not scoring and winning. So when, after three downs of his pummeling the line, we had not covered enough ground, he called the Hail Mary, which, as I got better, involved me. We'd line up as if we were going to punt the ball. We did this on almost every series, so whoever we were playing against knew what was coming, but still they had trouble stopping it. Bank would switch to quarterback and get the ball as I hauled downfield. All I had to do was get a step on whoever was covering me. And then I'd look over my left shoulder and there, propelled by Bank's strong and coordinated arm, the ball appeared, spiraling downward, its trajectory and mine meeting, when the play worked, just as I crossed the goal line.

I suppose it didn't actually work as often as I remember it, but I know we completed a few nice passes in those autumn games. And I remember no feeling in my life quite like that exhilaration after catching such a pass and scoring — my lungs burning from the crispness of the fall air, hands stinging from the hard leather, Bank and the others cheering up the field.

★ ★ ★

My mother never fully made peace with my friendship with Bank. Her first experience of him, my explanation of how he took me on the bus when we both knew she was coming for me, colored their relationship, and after that she always expected him to get me into situations where I didn't belong. "He's the sort who knows how to find trouble," was how she said it. "And you're the sort who'll follow." This feeling was buttressed, then, whenever it happened, which it did often enough.

When she learned, though, that Bank's own mother had died of a brain tumor three years before our arrival, and his father of a heart attack in the year after that, and that Bank lived now with a foster family, that that was how he had come to live at all in this far-flung corner of the city, she couldn't help pushing on him some of her simple gifts — a piece of scratch-made Dutch apple pie, or a used item of clothing she thought might fit him, or a lecture. It was funny to watch because she always seemed a little resentful even as she poured him a glass of milk or held a sweatshirt up to his shoulders. She'd press her lips together, in the way she did when I had earned her disapproval, and watch him with her head turned, never quite looking at him directly. But she was as incapable of not giving him these things as he was of not taking them.

My father, on the other hand, accepted him immediately. They would remain friends for many years. My father was a natural mechanic, an instinctive engineer. There were few things he couldn't fix or mold with his hands. He built a wood and metal workshop in the third bay of our garage, and Bank would sometimes spend hours out there with him, watching mostly, or helping to hoist a heavy block or reset the lathe. I had not inherited my father's abilities, nor did I share Bank's interest in them, and so at times I felt a vague kind of jealousy, that in this arena Bank had usurped my place as my father's son. But the other side of this, of course, was that Bank and I had become, in essence, brothers.

12

Perhaps the single attribute of the new offices that has generated the most commentary is the pair of interrogation boxes, which are as different from the old box in Juvenile as the designers of this place could have made them. These rooms, located at the far east end of the suite, are bright and airy and even have windows, barred though they are. In short, they are not terribly unpleasant places. I've heard detectives swear this has cost them cases. The upside, I guess, is that these boxes are separated from each other by a third room with views into each through one-way glass, and equipped with video cams and built-in tape recorders.

Stu and I have not spoken again about whether I'm officially on the task force or not, but the question is fast becoming moot. I brought Eddie in; I help Googie interrogate him.

"So, you okay?" I ask the boy. "Comfortable? You need anything?" It took a little while for the administrators at his school to find him. He wasn't in the classroom where his schedule said he'd be. It turned out he

159

hadn't been there for weeks. The teacher, who said she figured he'd dropped out, had stopped sending down his attendance cards. This embarrassed the assistant principal escorting me, and he shot a withering look at the teacher as we left. It took a half an hour and some questions, but we found Eddie with a group of his friends smoking cigarettes under the bleachers of the football stadium. The AP's sudden appearance scattered the kids, but he whipped out a pad and pencil and started furiously writing down names. Eddie, who recognized me, didn't run anywhere. Like his mother, I think he thought I was bearing bad news. He was reluctant to come downtown with me, even after I told him his mother had okayed it.

"Thirsty," he says.

"Thirsty, yeah? We'll get you something in just a minute. You answer a few questions first, okay?"

He nods.

And so it begins. From the viewing room behind the glass Stu watches. The Q & A goes on for the better part of an hour, Eddie largely just rehashing what he told Bank about graffiti and black kids and gunshots and shoes.

"Man, I'm thirsty," he says.

"Yeah, we got that Coke comin', don't we

Mack?" says Googie.

"With ice," I say.

"Just tell us what we need," Googie tells him. "We'll set you up."

"Eddie," I say. I sit down across from him. "What do these other bangers have to do with you? Really, I mean. You tagging a little on their turf, you think that's enough for them to do this? Bottom line, you really think they did it?"

"Dunno."

"But why would they?" I ask.

"Dunno."

"Maybe it's something else, then," I say. "Anybody talk to you about your sister? Asking about her, you know, showing some kind of unusual interest? You know what I mean?"

Eddie nods, and then the door of the box opens and Bank, in a coat and tie, pokes his head in. "Morning," he says, though it's probably two in the afternoon.

I look at him and raise my eyebrows.

"Court," he says. "Thought I'd stop by since I'm down here."

"You remember Eddie, huh?"

"Eddie, Eddie," says Bank. "Name's familiar."

Eddie cracks a grin and shakes his head down at the tabletop.

"You don't want me comin' in here, do you?" Bank asks.

Eddie loses the grin and shakes his head harder.

"You talk to these men." Bank steps back out, and I hear the door to the observation room open.

"So, these bangers —" I say.

But Googie suddenly slaps his hand down on the tabletop, the sharp sound echoing in the small room. "They ain't got nothin' to do with it," he says to Eddie. "And you know it." Sweat rolls off his flushed face. Though Googie is an old pro at this, the give and take, the cat and mouse, the subterranean bullshit head-games of the Q & A, he's tired of it now, I can see, and is beginning his endgame.

"No?" I say, playing straight man. "You don't think?"

"Uh-uh," says Googie. "This boy's holdin' somethin' back. He thinks he's got an ace in the hole, so's he can make a deal. He just don't know it's about two minutes to too late. I walk out this room, we're done. Book him — accessory to felony kidnap. Hang his ass up. He can see his poor mother again when he's a full-grown man." Googie slams his notebook shut with another crack and lifts his jacket from the back of a chair. "I'm through."

"What d'you mean?" Eddie says.

"If you know anything and don't tell us, then you're an accessory," I explain to him. "Under the laws of Ohio you're guilty too."

"But I din' do nothin'," the kid says. "I din' help."

"Didn't help who?"

The kid doesn't answer for a long moment, then says, slowly, "No one."

Googie and I look at each other. Stu, watching from behind the glass, I imagine, has grown still, too, his breathing suspended. This is the delicate question: to press harder, or wait. Googie and I decide, without speaking, without signs, through some kind of gut-level telepathy, to wait. We move very little. I'm sweating, and I can see Googie and Eddie sweating too. The sounds of our collective breathing fill the room.

Then Eddie looks up at Googie and says, "What if I tol' someone and din' know, you know?"

Googie places his hands on the table and leans across toward the boy. He says, more quietly, "Din' know what?"

"Like if they ax me, you know, about her and I told 'em some shit, but I din' know why or nothin'."

"Then if you tell us, we let you go home. That's the end of it."

163

Eddie shakes his head. "It ain't nothin' anyway."

"Who talked to you 'bout this, son?" Googie says.

Eddie continues to shake his head.

"They threaten you?"

"You're safer if you tell us, Eddie," I say.

But he shakes his head more vehemently. "It wasn't nothing, really. Just . . . some questions. Like what you was saying before. How you said that." He looks at me.

"About somebody showing unusual interest in her?"

"Unusual interest."

I stop and straighten up and cross my arms. Googie pulls out a chair and sits his bulk down. Again, we do not press. Moments pass.

"She told me not to say nothing," says Eddie, finally.

"Who?"

"My ma."

"Your mother knows about this? Someone was asking about Tamara?"

He shakes his head. "It ain't nothin'," he says, and then before I can ask again, he adds, "Just this priest that was comin' around, you know."

"A priest from your parish."

Eddie shakes his head. A little bead of water runs down from that black point of hair, like a faucet dripping. I can't help but stare at it.

"You didn't know him?"

"Nah. I never seen the guy before. But he was a Latino."

"Yeah?"

"Father Morales, she called him."

"And this is who was asking you about Tamara?"

"Yeah."

"And your mother was there?"

"No. He come around and she was talking to him, you know, for a long time. I come in the room, and she went out to the bathroom or something, and that's when he started axin' me."

"Like what?"

"You know, like who she go with, where she stop, shit like that."

"Tamara?"

"Yeah. He told me call him Father Hector."

"And that's it."

He shakes his head again. "There was another time, I seen him hanging around the school. He was just wearing regular clothes, you know. I seen him talkin' to her. They din' know I seen 'em."

"Talking to who?"

"Tamara, man. Who you think?"

★ ★ ★

After five, when I pull out of the courthouse parking garage and begin to weave around Government Plaza, I roll down my window because it's grown warm out. The early springtime smell of mother earth hangs on the air even in the evening rush hour in the heart of the city. As I circle the plaza on the grid of one-way streets, I come across a demonstration, a gathering of thirty or forty people in Cook Park, across the street from the public library and next to the huge, ornate St. Ursula's Cathedral. The crowd appears calm enough. Most simply sit in concentric circles on the grass, praying, apparently. A few pass out flyers on the sidewalks. I can't figure at first what they're doing.

Then I make out one of their signs: WE LOVE YOU, TAMARA, it says.

13

Although they share the name of the river that links them, Heron Park lies a couple of miles to the east of Heron Hills, and was built decades earlier. It was designed by the architect who designed New York City's Central Park, and covers three hundred or so acres on what was, at that time, the western border. Now it forms the city's approximate geographic center. The WPA constructed a golf course in its midst in the thirties, but that still left many acres of trails and meadows and deep overgrown ravines that roughly outline the path the river carves through the park.

We met Googie in the parking lot next to the dozen tennis courts across Morton Parkway from the east side of the park. From the lot we had a view, down Morton a few hundred feet, of the saffron crime tape spanning the entrance to the spot where the runner had seen the car with the kid who might have been Jamie. Googie took Katherine and me over there to look around, but there was little to see. We'd had no rain for days, and so the car had not left any usable tread marks. The spot was in the midst of an arc of heavy growth covering much of the northern quarter of the park, its wildest section, and cutting across its western edge. The area is so dense in some parts, down close to the river, that it's virtually impenetrable by midsummer without machetes or sickles.

It only made sense to concentrate the search in this area of heaviest growth. We set up a command post in the tennis court parking lot, near where the Heron River exited the park and began its final course to the Ojibwa. The dogs were due to arrive shortly, and volunteers had already begun showing up. I'd guess that between the detectives and patrol cops, both on- and off-duty, and civilians, by noon we had three dozen searchers.

I was dressed poorly for a tropical-weather woodland search, in suit pants and a short-sleeved dress shirt, but there was nothing to do about it. Once the dogs were off and running and the other searchers had been distributed over a wide area, I set off on my own, to walk and look and question whoever I might run into as to whether they'd been here a day earlier, seen or heard anything relevant. I kept to the edges of the densest areas, since I wasn't equipped to get down into them and since I had no idea where to look anyway. But that left plenty of ground to cover.

When I was a rookie, before I was partnered with Bank, while I was training with a cop called Big Bird, we took a call one morning from a man who'd been walking his dog in this part of the park when the dog began to bark at something down in a dense growth of brush and trees. The man found several human-looking bones, including the components of a complete leg and foot. Big Bird and I had to hack a rough trail in to the spot. Then, twenty or thirty feet away from the leg, on my hands and knees with a flashlight, I lifted the edge of a bush where something had caught the light, and gasped at the human skull staring back at me. I yelled for Big Bird. We grew excited, figuring we had a serial-killer caper on our hands here, a psycho's graveyard, bodies and parts strewn throughout the deep woods. It turned out, though, to be just one skeleton, a man who'd been missing for a year or so. The remains had been scattered by animals throughout that part of the brush.

I kept in touch by radio with Googie and Stu, the search coordinators. Sometimes when the channel opened I could hear, far in the background, the baying of the hounds. I was well to their west at that point.

By one the temperature hit the low nineties

and the humidity eighty-some percent. I was in a rain forest. I do not remember much except for the suffocating air. I know I spoke to people and took some notes. I wandered down hardened dirt trails and narrower grassy pathways through the underbrush. I surveyed and tried to imagine.

By two, dehydrated, soaked through, sweat dripping from my nose and into my eyes, I felt relief at least from the exhaustion, which had burned off some of the nerves and anxiety and which quieted my stomach. Googie called me in over the radio to take a break, so I hiked back across the park to the lot by the tennis courts, where players, shirtless men and halter-topped women, batted balls back and forth and threw curious glances at the conglomeration of cop cars and utility trucks and volunteer searchers and suits and news types who had gathered so nearby.

A couple of long folding tables had been set up and electric and telephone wires run from nearby boxes. A computer and some radio rechargers sat on one of the tables, a selection of various-sized pitchers and thermoses and ice chests on the other.

As I crossed Morton, I spotted Katherine under a broad sycamore tree beyond the parking lot, talking to Googie. I didn't see Stu around, but Bank was there, standing alone at that moment, a cup in his hand, looking into the dense woods across the street.

Katherine waved me over.

"We just got word," she said. "Lab lifted a partial set off that ball bat. Adult thumb and two fingers, it looks like."

"Bank's, maybe?"

She shook her head. "They already ran it against his file set. And yours, too, Mack. No match."

"CSU's printin' the two coaches now," Googie said. "Stu's over talking to security at the college there. He wants 'em to round up these students a-sap." For elimination prints, he meant, to compare with the latents we had to see if they belonged to anyone who had some business touching that bat.

Three students from the college had helped out with Jamie's softball team at one time or another. Katherine and Googie had interviewed the coaches the previous afternoon, and two of the three of these students as well, and had pulled or ordered sheets and vehicle data on all of them.

"What about them?" I asked.

"The two I talked to," Katherine said, looking at her notebook, "Alan Norke and Jennifer Jonson, seemed all right. Jonson was with the team Monday morning, and by ten Norke was at a church in the south end,

171

where he works. It checked out. The third is on his way over here now. One of the coaches called him. He's been out of town, I guess, at his parents'."

Bank stuck with me after that. We spent the rest of the afternoon and evening as I had spent the morning, questioning park-goers, hiking deep trails, looking, pondering, breaking only for a quick bite in the tennis-court parking lot.

Near dusk, in the far northwest corner of the park, we came out at a spot I remembered from my own childhood but which I hadn't visited in years. The steep slope leading down into a natural amphitheater had been terraced with stone retaining walls. A set of broad stone steps bisected it. At its deepest point the city had long ago built a band shell with a concrete stage at its center. The sky-blue and orange paint was peeling and faded now. Off to one side a small cinder-block storage shed sat sealed with a rusty padlock. Graffiti covered the lower half of the inside of the band shell and the storage shed and even the surface of the stage. Some was just the usual profanity and renderings of enormous phalluses aimed at huge-breasted, spread-legged women, but most of it was gang, pentagrams and crosses and strange words composed of what looked like a cross between Greek and English letters. RUTHLESS ONEZ. DOGZ ASS 2 U. CRIP 4 LIFE FOOL.

A carpet of saplings and bushes and weeds and vines had grown in from the woods, enveloping the storage shed, and now approached the shell itself. They'd had concerts here once, years before, music in the park played by the city symphony. That was what I remembered. And some rock bands, too, in the seventies, but there'd been problems with the crowds and drugs and alcohol, so the city had stopped it.

Bank and I wandered down the hill on the overgrown stone steps, to the shell, and sat on the stage, which was only a few feet high, and rested in the quiet cool shadows.

"I remember this place," Bank said, looking up at the canopy of trees.

"Music," I said. "We used to come. My dad liked it."

"Maybe that's it," he said. He sat slumped over, looking around at the trees and the terraces rising up before us.

Mosquitoes buzzed past my ears, lighting occasionally on my cheeks or forehead. I brushed them away.

The radio clicked and Googie's voice came over. "Six ten, two two one." He was very close to the dogs. They sounded excited, their cries higher pitched and breaking into yelps.

"Two two one, go ahead," I answered.

"Might have a hit here." Googie's voice was oddly calm and professional, but beneath that I could hear the emotion and stress that suddenly racked me again too.

I looked at Bank, but he did not react other than to stand up.

"Roger," I said.

We ran then, up the steep steps of the amphitheater, through the dense oppressive air, east toward the tennis courts, into the deepening twilight. A patrol car was waiting to lead us around to where the dogs had made their find.

There. In the beam of a flashlight, in a tangle of black branches and small trees that had caught and gathered at the inside of a bend in the river, the color screamed out: the cardinal-red bill of a baseball cap that had washed downstream. If you looked long enough, you could make out the rest of the cap, navy blue and harder to see against the wet black bark.

The dogs, we'd been told, had gone into the water after it, but had been restrained before they'd reached it. A small area had been trampled by searchers and dogs in the brush along the river here, but the trees were heavy and close together so there wasn't much room to move. Someone had hacked a rough pathway in from the four-lane Andrew Jackson Avenue, which lay up an embankment maybe fifty feet away, so that the sound of the traffic penetrated but was muted too.

Bank parted some brush along the shoreline and squatted and looked out at the hat, which was too far out into the water to reach. Finally he nodded. He turned to us and said, "That looks like hers."

Googie said, "We need a diver. I want it tonight."

If the lab could make the hat, more divers would come in the morning and start working this stretch of the river, especially upstream, figuring a body wouldn't wash as far as a small cloth hat. The grid search in the area upstream would be intensified, the dogs brought back.

But now it was too late to do much else.

"Come on," I said to Bank. I led him to where I had parked my car that morning.

Late that evening, Stu Marek called me at home to say that the lab had run comparisons with prints from everyone who'd worked with Jamie's softball team, and from Sarah and Don and Carol as well. None had matched those from the bat. So we had now, in all likelihood, the situation we had all feared the most: a stranger abduction.

At 2:00 A.M. my phone rang again. "Max"
— it was Sarah — "Bank's gone. I woke up,
he wasn't here. The bed was empty. His car's
gone too."

"All right," I said.

My heart pounded. I dressed quickly, without waking Gloria or Naomi.

I had not been in the Arbaugh house but for
a minute or two since this all began. A deep
part of me had not wanted to step inside, into
the center of the universe of sorrow, where
fear lay so heavily on the air that it was pal-
pable. These people were more than my
friends. They were, in any real sense, family,
and yet the thought of sharing this directly
with them frightened me.

Now, however, with the house quiet and
cool, Don and Carol, who were staying here
until something broke, asleep, I felt less trepi-
dation. Sarah met me in a bathrobe at the side
door and showed me into the wide and open
kitchen with its cornflower-blue ceramic tile
counters. A large cooking island stood in the
center with a stainless steel stovetop, and the
outside wall had been expanded into a
glassed-in breakfast nook. We sat at the heavy
oak table in this nook. The only light was cast
by the small fluorescent fixture over the stove,

which kept it dark enough in the alcove that I could not make out the details of Sarah's face.

"Had he said anything?"

"No," she said.

And so we waited, Sarah reaching over occasionally to take my hand. To my relief, but not my surprise, she did not seem to want any sort of reassurances from me, or even to talk much about the situation. I noticed that her hands, which usually fussed when she was nervous, lay still on the table.

I suggested calling the watch commander downtown and having him put out a call with Bank's license number, so the patrols could keep an eye out for him. But she said, no, it would only upset him. She apologized, then, for calling me, but she'd been frightened and had wanted to sit with someone.

By three-fifteen Bank had not yet arrived.

"He's out driving, like last night," I said. "I can still call the watch commander and have him put out the license."

"No. I'm sure he's all right. Anyway, you need some sleep. You'll be up early again."

She walked me to the side door, through the mudroom off the kitchen, and stood with me there.

"Thank you," she said. "You're a good friend."

"I'm not," I said. "I should've come in

before, said something. I waited. I was . . ."

"We needed some solitude," she said. "And you were busy. I wouldn't expect you to be in here holding my hand."

I shook my head.

"You're always questioning your motives," she said. "But in the end you do what's right, what's needed. You're Max, and that's what we love about you. That's what Bank says. He always looks to you."

"God, no," I said. "It's not like that at all. You of all people know that's not true."

"Don't," she said.

"I'm so sorry," I said. And the grief I had not wanted to feel, that I had been able to hold inside, sealed off within some thick membrane that surged but held within my chest, even inside this house, even sitting at their table, was loosed now. It washed through me, the membrane ruptured as if by an invisible lance Sarah held in her slender hands, and I shook beside her. My face grew hot and wet, my mouth and throat tightening so that it became difficult to speak. "My God," I said, thinly, "if I could do anything. There's just nothing. *Nothing.*"

"Max," she said, "I believe it will turn out all right. Trust in that."

"I don't know," I said.

"Old dear Max," she said, and put her arms

around my neck. We're very nearly the same height, Sarah and I, so that we stood naturally cheek to cheek as she squeezed me tightly to her. I hesitated to touch her at first, my hands hovering over the small of her back, close enough to feel her heat, the texture of the cotton fabric of her blouse, but not touching her body. I rested one hand there, finally, in the concave curve of her spine, and felt the narrow tightness of the muscles, the dampness of her perspiration. I moved my other hand up to her hair, allowing it to skate down and stop at the nape of her neck. We stood thus for several minutes. I knew that it was I who was drawing strength from her, not the other way around, as it should have been. Again, I felt a wave of remorse over this, that I had so little to offer, that I had wanted to withhold even this, my own sadness, and that now, in sharing it, it was I who needed her more than she needed me.

But even this she sensed. She said, "Shhh," although I had not spoken a word.

I heard something then as we stood embracing, and looked out toward the kitchen. Bank stood in the dim illumination of the stove light, watching us. I couldn't tell how long he'd been there, but it did not look as if he'd just arrived. He stood slouched, with his arms crossed. He had made no noise coming in. I don't know why we didn't at least hear his car pull up.

"Bank," I said, letting go of Sarah and turning toward him. But he just shook his head, as if to hold me off, as if he were passing some kind of judgment, and then turned and disappeared into the house.

I looked at Sarah. She smiled sadly, wearily, and touched the side of my face.

"You call if anything happens," I told her. "Anything."

"Good night, Max," she said.

14

In the morning, by the time I've showered and shaved and dressed, the boys are up and having breakfast, Jack still in his PJs because it's spring break this week. The Tamara Shipley task force, to which I now officially belong, is meeting before roll call and I'm running late, so I quickly kiss each of them, Jack on the top of his head and Ben on his sweet-smelling cheek. They're watching some PBS show over their cereal and haven't paid me much attention, but Jack grants a "Bye, Dad," and Ben turns when I kiss him and gives me one back, wet with milk and right on my nose. Naomi is still asleep.

Peggy offers me her own cheek. She has a pretty face and brown hair that she wears cut just above the collar so it frames her features nicely. She smiles broadly when she smiles and her teeth are as strong and substantial as the rest of her.

What surprised me as much as anything about her, once we realized we were going to stay together, was that being involved with a cop pleased her. Not the anxiety, of course, the waiting up nights when I was out, the jumping anytime the phone rang. And never hearing the gritty details, the particulars. But she liked the sense of living with a protector, she said, an enforcer, a man who went out into the baddest parts of the world and touched it and dealt.

She is a good cop's wife. She came to me in the aftermath of Jamie's disappearance, at a time when my faith in my abilities to do my work, in my desire to do it, in the very possibility of it making any difference, were badly shaken. I thought seriously of resigning altogether, maybe finishing the law degree, or doing something else altogether. But when I mentioned the possibility, Peggy seemed disappointed. After we married, she became an integral part of the Job, until my being a cop and her husband were two halves of the same thing.

We talk now and then of my taking the sergeant's exam. It would bring in more money, but she does not push it with me.

"You guys find that little girl," Peggy says. "Call you?"

"Before eleven or after three." Mondays are grocery days. She not only finds coupons in her stuffed organizer to match nearly everything she buys, but hits three or even four stores to take advantage of all their specials. And now, with the break, she gets to drag the boys along as well. Peggy has her degree in elementary education and taught second grade until Ben was born, but we both agreed that the sacrifices of living on a detective's salary were worth the luxury of her staying home with him until he was in the first or second grade.

"We have to get eggs," she says. For Easter, she means. For coloring. Because, I suppose, of the religious neutrality of my parents, when I was a kid we acknowledged the big religious holidays in only the most cursory fashion. And Gloria and I, when Naomi was small, never got very excited about them. But for Peggy they're a big deal. She decorates and bakes and plays the music for weeks before, and she's taught the boys all the customs and rituals she learned as a girl.

"Right," I say, then check my watch and hustle toward the door. Jack has tuned in to my urgency and now he leaps up from the table, races into the living room and onto the front couch by the window. Ben hustles after him.

"Use the Kojak light, Dad!" Jack hollers as he bounces.

"Yeah!" echoes Ben.

I carry a twelve-volt flasher that sticks by a suction cup on the front dash and runs off the cigarette lighter. I almost never need to use it but it drives the boys nuts. So I plug it in before I back out of the garage and then make a point of laying down a little rubber as I tear off down our street. Wholly unnecessary, dangerous even, but more than worth it to see those looks of blind admiration beaming from our front window.

In the hallway I see that Bank has again had a busy night. A dozen young men, mostly Hispanic this time, recline on the bench and along the wall. Several of them, who eyeball me as I walk past, are old Juvenile clientele. I nod again at the same two patrol cops standing watch. They each force a half-smile for my benefit.

I actually catch a glimpse of Bank farther back in the suite when I come through the door. I'd like to talk to him, but don't have the time, and then I hear his voice rising, and Stu Marek's along with it. A moment later, as I pour myself a cup of coffee at the communal pots behind Jeremiah's workstation, the two of them stomp past me without a glance and into Stu's office. Then the yelling really begins. I cannot make out much of what they're saying, but I know Bank's getting chewed on for his nighttime rampages, and they're both very hot. I have a sudden urge to interrupt them, to tell them to cool down, then talk, but again I'm late, and besides, I think, they probably both need to blow a little off. I know Stu's feelings are mixed about what Bank's doing; a part of him would just as soon let Bank go, and see what develops. But Stu's undoubtedly getting pressure from on high to put a stop to anything that could lead to some bad press.

"*Fuck* that," I hear Bank yell as he drives his fist down into Stu's desk.

The other members of the task force are all already seated in the conference room and the lights are down when I walk in. On a small television at the end of the table one of our city's more famous black ministers rails as he points his finger at the camera, at the administration and the Command for this egregious violation of civil rights that has occurred. This is the inevitable backlash of our having too hastily ascribed the crime to two black men. I'm sure the Command and the politicians are up to their asses in it this morning. As the minister talks, the police hot-line number and other fax and phone numbers and e-mail addresses of concerned church groups and children's welfare organizations scroll across the bottom of the screen as the desperate search for new information continues.

Googie hits the lights and flips off the set. "Steaming loads of it," he says. "And all

flowin' downhill. Well, now it's our turn."
The task force, he means. Us.

The meeting focuses first on the car. CSU, once they got it in, combed and taped and vacuumed the interior, scraped the tires and undercarriage, and then began dusting and scanning for prints and body fluids. It was, in fact, a blood smear on the backseat.

"She was in it," Googie says as he passes around copies of the lab printouts. In addition to the blood CSU found several hairs stuck in a gummy substance, some kind of adhesive, lower on the backseat. The gum was still being analyzed. The hairs matched perfectly those taken from the brush in Tamara's bedroom.

All latent prints from the car matched eliminations from the car's owner and his family. So we knew at least that our abductors weren't stupid. At least not as stupid as your average car thief turned kidnapper.

"But," Googie says, then, "they lifted a strange one, a man's, off'a the inside of the bike's chain guard. Almost perfect, 'cause of the grease. Eighteen, twenty points."

"A neighbor helped her put on a new chain," Katherine says.

"Not a match," says Googie.

We contemplate this for a moment. The chances of it meaning anything are almost nil.

If there were no prints in the car, the print on the bike almost surely does not belong to the perps either. But who knew? Strange things happened at crime scenes, slip-ups, accidents, urgent moments. Easy to forget, take a glove off just for a second, touch something without realizing it.

Next, Googie tells us, several detectives will be assigned to continue canvassing at the Medical College for witnesses to the scene that played out at the loading docks behind the Food King. As far as Father Hector Morales is concerned, a couple of swing shift detectives drove out to the St. Thomas Aquinas Parish, in the Near South, to talk to him, but were told he was away.

Then Katherine says, "I know him."

"Yeah?"

She nods. "I see him now and then. I'll give him a call."

"Anyone talk to the mother about this yet?" asks Rick Simms. "Why she hushed the boy?"

"I was headed over there this morning," says Katherine.

Simms says, "You know we slapped a running tap on their line."

"The family's?" Katherine says. "What for?"

"Why not?" says Simms, acting a little surprised at her question. If it's not random, he means, then it's someone they know. Someone they may talk to. It's just another place worth looking. He also passes around royal-blue folders bearing the seal of the FBI and containing documents the Feds have generated — a couple standard background character statements, but also phone records for the past three months, up to and including the previous morning, and even a credit report.

Katherine shakes her head at this, too, as if it bothers her, but Googie just shrugs. This is maybe not standard OP, but it's hardly unusual for the Feds to look at these things in a case like this, and Katherine knows it. I'm a little surprised at her, too. She's usually the hard-ass of the group, refusing to give anyone any quarter regardless of how much pain they seem to be in. But this situation has gotten to her, I think, in the way it's gotten to Bank and me and Googie: echoes and bad memories.

Then, just as Googie begins to run through each of our current assignments, Jeremiah knocks on the door, looking for me. "Sorry, Detective," he says, "but I've got a guy on the phone for you. He called earlier. You didn't see the message?" I hadn't checked my box. "Some grocery-store manager," Jeremiah says.

"Oh, shit," I say, louder than I mean to.

The room stops and looks at me, but I'm already moving toward the phone.

When I step back into the conference room a minute later, they all stop and look at me again.

"Um," I say, debating with myself whether to admit that in the heat of new developments, I forgot to go back to the grocery store yesterday afternoon to follow up. I decide against this admission, and simply give a thumbnail of that conversation and what led to it. Then I say, "That adhesive they found the hairs in?"

"Yeah?" Googie says.

"A girl at that Food King," I say. "Early on Sunday, six-sixteen A.M., she sold someone two rolls of packing tape."

Googie's on his feet then. "Get 'er in here, now," he says.

There comes a moment in the afternoon when I find myself momentarily unengaged in any task, watching the buzz happen around me as if I am separate from it. While those of us on the task force are given over to Tamara full time, in fact most PC and Missing detectives on this day have spent some time on it.

The girl from the store turned out to be a break. She remembered selling the tape to a big guy, she'd said, but little more than that until a department psychologist and a sketch artist started working through it with her. They'd been at it for hours, now, and a rough likeness was beginning to emerge on the artist's computer screen. Though I was roundly congratulated for this turn, I do not feel good about having let it slip like I did.

At one point after lunch, when I got back after running down some hot-line leads to nowhere, Stu sat down with me to talk about Bank.

"You have to wonder," he said. "What's this do to a guy like him, his temperament, what he's been through."

I didn't say anything.

"I'll tell you, Mack, I'm worried. This is eating at him. I'm thinking hard on what I oughtta do about it."

"Like what?"

"Like cool him out. Stick him on a desk for a while."

"You want him off this?"

"No, but I don't want him suspended either. I want him there when I really need him. And I will really need him. He's the best we got. But he's raising hell out there. We got complaints, lawyers calling. And anyway, he works an f-car, not day-shift investigations. He comes across something, great. But this caper's got way too much heat on it. High command and politicians crawling all over. And the press. It ain't like he's exactly unknown to them."

After that I spent a little time going through the whole Tamara file again. Paperwork was being added at an incredible rate: FBI documents, supplemental lab reports, witness accounts.

So this is where I find myself in the late afternoon, with these papers sitting spread out on my desk but my head having gone numb from it, thinking about missing girls and Bank and where we've all been. I'm also thinking about heading home, so I begin to stack the paperwork, when I find on my desk, beneath all of it, tucked under the edge of the blotter, a slip of paper I hadn't noticed.

"Mack:" it says, in Bank's handwriting. "Baker Hawkes." A name I have not heard before. So I do what I would do with any strange name I come across. I punch it into the terminal on my desk. The system whirs and thinks about it for a few moments, then brings up a file: Hawkes, Baker, b. June 15, 1947, d. September 2, 1992. A dead man, I'm investigating. He had a short sheet, some first- and second-degree misdemeanors, a couple of felony arrests that led nowhere. Altogether uninteresting. I'm not sure what to do with it, and think of calling Bank at home, but then I type in just the last name, Hawkes.

This brings up a list of five or six files. And after a moment of scanning it I think I might understand. When I highlight one of these entries and call up the file, I know I do. And I am impressed once again with Bank's ability to get around like no one else I know.

After I read the file, I do not leap up and run screaming for the door. I calmly stand and lift my jacket from the back of my chair and walk. Stu sees me and opens his mouth to say something, but I hold up my hand to stop him.

"Where's Googie?" I say, without stopping.

"What — he's out somewhere."

"I'm going back to King's Court," I say, over my shoulder. "Tell him to reach me a-sap."

Stu watches out through the glass door after me. I do not run, but at the elevators I punch the button repeatedly, as if this will make some difference. When they do not come quickly enough, I duck into the stairwell because I cannot stand there any longer.

The boy and girl are at home with her this time, sitting in front of that goddamned television set. The mother, Rochelle, peers at me from the kitchen, but does not come out right away. I hear her talking on the phone. When she finally makes an appearance, she gives me that look again, of expecting bad news, and she sees in my face this time that something's wrong. She wipes her hands on her apron and grips the back of the new La-Z-Boy.

"I want to know who we missed," I say. "Who was it we had to talk to to tell us the truth? I mean, we've hit everyone — teachers, neighbors — and no one knew?"

"What are you talking about?" Rochelle says. "What's wrong with you?"

"Maybe this priest, huh, Father Hector?"

Eddie throws me a look from the floor. Rochelle shakes her head and presses a tissue to her mouth.

"Baker Hawkes," I say then. I put it to Geena, the nine-year-old, who's looking up at me now too. "He was your father?"

She nods.

"And Tamara's?"

"Yes."

"And when did you stop using his name?"

"Last year."

"Last year," I say. "A couple months after some policemen investigated the report of a missing eleven-year-old girl named Tamara Hawkes."

Rochelle's face has changed again, gotten that hard sealed look back to it of anger and obstinance. "But that's not it!" she says. "She

193

didn't run away. Not this time! That's why I didn't want to say nothin'. 'Cause you'll just think that's what happened. She's just another one of these druggies runnin' off. Like they told us before. You know, they didn't even look for her that time. She was gone two days, and they didn't even bother to look." She's spitting now, her face twisted by her rage and desperation. "But this time is different. There was a car, Detective. You know that. With two men in it, black or not, and they grabbed her. And I want you looking. All of you!"

I wait a moment for her to compose herself, then say, "You were never married to him."

"No. It was the girls' choice. They wanted to use my name. It was up to them."

"That's fine," I say. "But why change right after she ran away?"

It had been a routine call, handled by a younger detective, no longer in Missing. The girl showed up at home again within forty-eight hours. The family had moved since then, so the address didn't mesh either. So no one this time around picked up the fact that Tamara was a known runaway.

"Just happened that way," Rochelle says.

"This priest, Father Hector. Why didn't you say anything about him? What's going on here, Rochelle?"

There comes another knock on the front door then, and it opens and Katherine Biasotti pokes her head in.

"Hey, Mack," she says.

"Katherine," I say, "you're not going to believe this —"

"Yeah," she says, cutting me off. "You want to step on out here a minute?"

"Me?" I say.

"Come on, Mack," she says. So of course I do. Into the cooling spring evening, into the worn-out neighborhood.

"I know, Mack," she says.

"She was a —"

"Yeah. I found out. I've already talked to them about it."

"Katherine," I say, "what are you doing here?"

She looks at me for a moment, and then I say, "She called you when she saw me."

Katherine nods.

"You protecting them from something?" I think again of Katherine's uncharacteristic comments at the meeting that morning.

"No, Mack."

"Does Stu know this?"

She doesn't answer me.

"Googie?"

"No."

"Well, what the hell?"

"It's just not germane," she says. "This girl was snatched. That's the fact that matters. If the press or the investigators learn what she did, who knows how it would affect the way the case is pursued?"

"Yeah, but she changed her name," I say. "Doesn't that seem a little suspect to you?"

"Why?"

"That she'd run away, then after she shows up again, changes her name?"

"What's one necessarily got to do with the other, Mack? You're reading too much into it."

"I'm reading . . ." I begin, then laugh.

"This family's had its share of problems," she says. "We're in a dialogue with them about all of it, me and some people from Family Services. Believe me, if any of it has any impact on this case, you'll know. But most of it doesn't. Their problems and the fact that this girl was taken are two separate issues."

"Really," I say. "You're sure of that."

"Yes."

"Then what'd they say about the priest? Why'd we have to pull that from the kid?"

"He was counseling them," she says. "Working with Tamara. Trying to keep her off the street, which is where she ended up. Rochelle just didn't want to get him in

196

trouble. She didn't see the point of mentioning him."

"You talk to him?"

"No. He's not around. I don't know where he is."

I shake my head, unable to quite take it all in. Then my radio squawks and Googie's voice comes over saying, "Six ten, two two one, whachoo got goin'?"

Katherine looks up at me with her black eyes and her black hair. She's one of the best, most admirable detectives I know. I trust her implicitly. What am I going to say?

"Two two one, six ten. Negative on that. My mistake."

"Okey doke," Googie comes back. "Have a good one."

I'm staring at Katherine during this exchange, but I'm thinking not of her or Tamara or this family, but of an insight I've just had. Trying to keep Tamara off the street, Katherine said, about the priest. Two days ago Naomi told me that she had a friend who'd met Tamara on the street. I'd dismissed it out of hand. I told Naomi she was mistaken, that Tamara never lived like that. But I was wrong.

Naomi knew. More than I did, my own unreliable daughter knew the truth, and I had failed to listen to her.

15

The hat from the river turned out to be Jamie's. The director of the crime lab himself pulled a single fragment of hair from inside the band, which he matched to samples taken from Jamie's pillowcase.

Early Wednesday morning the divers were just getting themselves ready when I arrived, pulling on their blue wet-suits and checking the gauges and straps on their equipment. A blanket of mist clung to the river, hiding its surface from our view. The sun hadn't yet penetrated here, although we were upstream several hundred feet from the brush pile that had caught Jamie's hat, at a more open and accessible spot of hard-packed dirt and a few large trees near the river's edge. Googie was there. Stu had stopped by for a minute on his way downtown.

The riverbank here was steep and dropped off sharply at its edge. I sat up the embankment a little ways and watched as the divers waded the first few feet, then disappeared, sinking not, it appeared, into water, but into a smoky gorge.

We waited. I'd come more prepared today,

in jeans and a short-sleeved work shirt, and knew that grid-searches of various areas of the woods were being organized up- and down-stream, but I did not move to join them. I felt compelled to sit, or rather, disinclined to leave. It was a quiet and peaceful place, cool still in the morning.

Bank arrived half an hour later and sat near me on the embankment but did not speak or look at me or acknowledge me in any way. We sat thus for another half an hour, watching the divers come up a few times, empty handed, not speaking to each other, before I left to head back into the park.

At noon, when I got back to the tennis-court parking lot command center, I saw that Jamie's two coaches had also arrived, recently, I gathered, since they still looked dry and unbeaten. They had brought with them their sons, who were on Jamie's team, and a few of Jamie's other teammates as well, ten- and eleven-year-old boys and girls anxious to get out there and help look for their missing friend. The expressions on their faces, earnest and angry and frightened all at once, made me look away.

I had downed some cupfuls of Gatorade and was squatting in the crushed limestone of the parking lot, balancing myself with one hand between my legs, when one of the coaches, a man named Smythe, wandered over and stood nearby. He was in his thirties, almost white-blond, even his eyebrows, with a tanned country-club complexion. My pale skin looked sick by comparison. I waited for him to speak.

"So it was really a kidnapping," he said. "Wow." He looked dazed.

"Maybe," I said. "We're still not positive."

He knelt down beside me, forearms across his dark, bare thighs.

"But it's looking more and more that way," I said.

"God, the thought of it . . ." He went silent for a moment, then said, "It's strange. This is just what Alan said it would be. I thought sure if it was bad it would be the creek."

I reached down and picked up a stone and turned it in my hand. "Say that again," I said.

"Alan Norke?"

"One of the Libbey students."

"Right. He and Jamie were pals. He's in a doctoral program over there. Good guy. He called me."

"When?"

"Monday night, I guess. The day it happened."

"And he said he just figured it was a kidnapping. Just like that?"

Smythe shrugged. "He was just saying. We were talking about what could have happened, you know."

"What exactly did he say?"

"I don't know, you know. I said something like 'That river gets one or two kids every year,' you know, and Alan said something like 'It's not the river,' or 'I don't think it's the river,' something like that. And I said, 'Why would you say that?' and he said 'It sounds like someone grabbed her.' I said, 'A kidnapping?' and he said, 'Something like that,' and then just like changed his mind, like he didn't want to talk about it then, and said, 'I don't know.' "

The air was hot and still and dead and despite all the people gathered there the whole area had a kind of hush over it, so that I could hear a high ringing in my ears.

"Where is he today?"

"I don't know. Either at that church where he works, or classes, I suppose. He's taking summer courses, I know."

I looked over at Smythe, stared at him until he looked me in the eye. "Is this something you wanted to tell someone?" I said.

"What?"

"Are you just making light chat, or did you have it in your mind to tell a cop about this conversation you had, what, a day and a half ago?"

"I don't know. I guess I thought they'd find her by now."

"I mean, people have a sense about things, you know what I mean. We all do, not just cops. Sometimes somebody says something to you, or acts a certain way, it strikes you as odd. It eats at you without your really even realizing it. What I'm asking is, are we having this conversation just because you're here and I'm here, shooting the shit, or has this been on your mind? Did the way he talked about a kidnapping bother you?"

Smythe nodded. "I don't know," he said.

"Could be either?"

"Yeah. I guess it bugged me a little bit. Something in his voice. And he never called me before for anything. We never even really talked at practice, not about anything much, you know. Then he calls, wanting to talk about this. I don't know. I figured, you know, it was a big deal, this kid he works with disappears, he's upset, like all of us. But he just kept talking." He stood up. "I don't know," he said.

"That's all right," I said, standing too. "You did the right thing."

I pulled Katherine and Stu aside and gave

them the gist of my talk with Smythe.

"You talked to him," Stu said then, to Katherine. "How'd he seem?"

"Cooperative. Wanting to do whatever he could to help. He didn't even gripe about the mess when we printed him."

"His sheet's clean?" I said.

"We don't have it yet," she said.

"What?" said Stu.

"He's not in our system. He's from Evanston, Illinois. I faxed requests to the Evanston and Chicago PDs. Nothing's come in yet."

"What do you know about him?"

"His dad's some kind of engineer. Mom's a lawyer." She looked at her notes. "Drives a late model Camaro, dark brown, still bearing Illinois plates, clean driving record in Ohio. Lives alone off campus, in the Kestler Village. He's in the Ph.D. program in child psych. He wants to be a therapist."

"And what does he do at this church he works for?" Stu said.

Katherine regarded him for a moment before she said, "He runs the youth group there."

Stu just looked back at her.

"Goddammit," she said. For Katherine, a student of pedophiles, this all suddenly rang a rather piercing bell. Serial pedos often structure their lives to maximize their time around children. It's a standard part of the profile.

Around the Bureau Katherine tended to be as direct and edgy as any of us. But when she interviewed, her demeanor changed; she grew gentle, really. Her voice softened and lowered. She never yelled or swore. And this was not only with victims, but with the perps she dealt with as well, pedos and pornographers and rapists and flashers and phone freaks, which was an amazing talent. By not threatening, by appearing to empathize with their urges and demons, she led them to talk. In the end that was all that mattered. She hated them as much as the rest of us did, but had this ability to hide it and so to let them open up. In this way, over the years, she took great numbers of them off the street.

"So maybe you want to catch up with him again today," Stu said. "Have another chat."

"Oh, yeah," she said, and turned and left us standing there.

I fell asleep early that night, around ten, but slept poorly and awakened fully, finally, around two again, the house dark, Gloria breathing beside me. I lay waiting for something, it seems like now, in memory, knowing it would come. Then the phone rang.

"Max." It was Sarah. "He's gone again. I'm sorry; you don't have to come. I just . . ."

"It's all right," I said. I carried my clothing downstairs to dress there, and paused, wondering if this time I should call the watch commander. I worried about Bank only because he was so totally distracted from what he was doing. Also, although nothing had developed, Katherine had floated the name of the first potential target of inquiry, this college kid Norke, and I figured word of that could easily have gotten back to Bank one way or another. It would have been perfectly in character for Bank to try to carry out an interrogation on his own. I had actually lifted the phone to call downtown, to have them put a call out on his plates and have someone drive by Norke's apartment building, when I knew exactly where Bank had gone. I hung up the phone.

The ceiling of trees made it darker than the night. The moon sat up full and high as I walked across a meadow from City Med, where I'd parked. But here, where the earth fell into the encroaching forest of ancient trees, it was velvety black. I always carried a heavy Maglite in my trunk, and used it now to pick my way down the pathway between the terraces to the old band shell. Random bits of the colorful spray-painted graffiti leapt out in the circle of my light. Bank sat with his legs over the side of the stage, slumped in the same way he had been.

I did not speak to him, nor he to me, at first, continuing our silence of the day. I shut off the light and sat beside him and waited for my eyes to adjust to the darkness.

Eventually, Bank said, "I remembered the first time I came here. It was a long time ago. Before I met you, when my folks were still alive. I was sitting here figuring it out. We lived on Rymer. Central North. I woulda been like six. They brought me here. I don't remember doing much with them. But I know we came here. It was in the morning, sunny out, but kinda cool. I wore a jacket, I remember, a sport coat I mean, some ugly thing my ma'd bought.

"There was a man down here, on this stage, talking, waving his arms, yelling at us. He was preaching, see. It was a kind of religious thing. Some kind of revival meeting or something. I guess I just thought my ma was into it, although I don't remember any other time we did that. This guy was preaching loud, into a microphone, hollering and pointing. I was scared, I remember. But excited too.

"Then later, I remember her, my ma, going down, coming down here to where that man was. He touched her. He was touching other people, too, but I remember how he put his hands on her head and prayed. He pushed her forehead hard when he was finished. It knocked her backward. I thought my dad would get mad, but he didn't do anything. Just watched from up on the hill with me.

"This was in the spring. It was still chilly out. She died that summer.

"The thing is, Mack, I only just figured out, today, what it was. He was a faith healer. You know that? And she'd been told she was gonna die, she knew it and my dad knew it, and they couldn't do a thing for her. So she came here.

"It's weird how all those years go by and then one day it just comes back to you out of nowhere. You forgot about it, like it didn't happen, and then suddenly there it is, in your head, this whole event out of nowhere. Only now, when you remember it, you understand something. As a kid you had no idea."

We sat for a while after that, then finally both stood up simultaneously, finished with whatever had happened, and hiked up out of the amphitheater to our cars.

The following morning, Thursday, I drove downtown to check my mail, messages, and so forth. I hadn't been in to the Bureau in two days, I realized. Life was going on in the rest of the city regardless of what had happened to

Jamie Arbaugh. I'd dropped into Stu's office and was sitting there, across from him, sipping coffee.

"So Katherine finally caught up with this Norke at his apartment last night," he said. "Little different this time."

"How's that?"

"Said he'd told her everything he knew, and that was all he had to say."

"No shit."

We were sitting there, chewing on this and other matters, when Katherine rushed in, breathless and flushed.

"Listen," she said, her voice excited, urgent. "As of late yesterday nothing had come back yet from either PD over there. Big bureaucracy and all, I figure, who knows how long it'll take. But remember I did those sex crimes seminars over in Chicago a few years back. I met a guy there, from CPD Sex Crimes, named Pete Stamos. Nice guy, we hit it off, had a few drinks. So last night I gave him a call. I told him I was having a little trouble getting information, and wondered if he could help me out. I said I was looking for the sheet on Alan Norke, from Evanston. We pulled nothing locally, and there's nothing in the NCIC, but I just want to cover all the bases. He says he even heard the story on the news about this cop's daughter in Ohio, and

208

he'll get back to me. Then, right after I hang up, CPD faxes the kid's sheet from Cook County. Clean. No arrests, no convictions. So I figure that's that, right? I shouldn't have bothered Pete. And if they'd faxed that sheet an hour earlier, that would have been it.

"But today, Pete calls back. He said he remembered the name Norke from something, and was going back through some files, and doing some calling around. He just faxed this." She handed us each copies of a St. Joseph County, Indiana, criminal record report and an arrest warrant for Alan Norke from 1986.

I scanned them and saw first that the arrest led to no conviction. Only then, because I was not familiar with the style of this paperwork, did I notice the charge on the original warrant: aggravated kidnapping.

"Jesus," I said.

The charge, I read, had then been reduced to child stealing, and later dropped altogether for some reason. No indictment ever came down.

"The family's got money," Katherine said. "Mom's a lawyer herself. Who knows what strings they could pull?"

"But kidnapping?"

"I called Pete back. He doesn't know anything other than this. He remembered the name because of the kidnapping collar. The South Bend authorities had been in touch with CPD Sex Crimes to see if they'd ever dealt with Norke. Someone from Stamos's unit even interviewed the kid, I guess. So now Stamos is trying to track down the detectives involved, to see what the deal was."

My heart was pounding so hard, I could see it in my eyes. Still, what did we have?

"Not a thing," Stu said, as if I'd spoken my thought out loud. "Nothing that will get us a warrant, anyway. What about his alibi?"

"He got to the church at nine-thirty on Monday," said Katherine. "Jamie was grabbed about ten till nine. It's a stretch, but it's possible."

"And whoever owns the print on the bat," Stu said. "If this Norke was involved, there was someone else there with him. He had some help."

We looked at Stu.

"So go try to talk to him again," he said. "Just keep it clean."

One side of the Kestler Village Apartments, an extensive complex built in the fifties, backed up to the rear of an old abandoned factory called Kestler Coil, which had once made electrical components, coils, of course, and things like solenoids and alternators, for

210

Detroit cars. Someone, somehow, had climbed forty feet up the sheer brick walls to the blackened, many-paned windows and sprayed out a series of messages in gang code. I had wondered, at other times I'd been here, why they'd go to the trouble of climbing up there when the entire walls of blank brick were at their disposal. Then, I figured, the height would make it that much more visible. A billboard.

The Kestler Village complex — two dozen red-brick three-story buildings — were arranged three to a quad, forming a series of U's on either side of the heavily treed street. The center of each quad held an asphalt parking pad. Each building had four or five apartments. Kestler Coil had originally built it as cheap housing for its factory workers and their families. The company sold it off in the early seventies to raise cash, when times got lean, and it became a slum fairly quickly, a welfare ghetto, until it was bought by the college, which underwent some rapid growth in the eighties and needed as many buildings as it could get to house the hordes of new students. A college-owned shuttle bus now ran every quarter hour between the complex and the campus.

Because we didn't know what we might be walking into, because once in a while these things turned in ways we could not predict, because there was a chance that Jamie was inside this place with God knew who, we wore Kevlar. I also grabbed the short-barreled Remington twelve-gauge pump shotgun from our trunk. I stood behind Katherine on the third floor of one of the buildings backing up to the factory grounds when she knocked.

A young man in a business suit opened the door.

"I'm looking for Alan Norke," Katherine said.

"What for?" said the young man.

"I want to talk to him," she said.

"I'm Chad Walsh," he said. "I'm an attorney with the firm of Byelick and Wozniak. I'm here on behalf of Roman Byelick, who represents Alan Norke as of this morning." He pointed back into the apartment. My gaze followed his finger and there, peering out at us, stood Alan Norke.

"Alan, please," Katherine said. "I just want to talk."

"No talking," said Walsh.

"Alan —"

"Look," Walsh said. "If it makes you feel better, I'll tell you there's no child in this apartment, if that's what you were thinking. But from now on, Mr. Norke is not to talk to you without his attorney being present. And we'll be in court if you try to get a judge to issue any kind of warrant."

Neither Katherine nor I spoke. We just stared, not quite believing all this.

"Do you understand?" Walsh said. "He's not going with you. So you should leave now. If you want to talk to him, call Mr. Byelick." He handed Katherine a business card, and then closed the door.

A summer rain began late that afternoon and broke some of the heat. It fell hard while I grabbed some dinner, but then tapered off to a light drizzle by six, when I got back to the shoreline of the Heron River. Bank was there, too, and Googie. Waiting. The divers were working a new stretch, farther west, nearer where the river entered the park, closer to the amphitheater and City Med, but no less densely treed than where they'd searched the day before.

We had a view of the divers a hundred or so feet downstream from where we sat. So we saw very clearly the orange gas-inflated buoy that broke suddenly upward through the surface of the water. I remember hearing it, too, the startling shattering sound. This was, of course, a marker that a diver had inflated, which meant that he had found something.

"Oh!" Bank yelled, utterly involuntarily I

think, and without realizing at all he'd said it. It was just an instinct against the certainty he'd already accepted on some level but had still fought with his wildest, most vehement hopes. I went to him, to place my hand on his arm, but he broke away and ran, swatting trees and brush from his way as he crashed along the hundred feet to where the three divers had all now surfaced. Googie was listening to one of them and barking into his radio at the same time. It was just the three of us on the river's edge, Googie and Bank and me, and the divers surfacing to pull their mouthpieces and yell at Googie, then diving again along the line extending down from the fluorescent orange float that hung there, dragging against the current of the river.

The bank of the Heron along this stretch did not drop off so abruptly. In fact there was enough of a slope that the diver who finally pulled the bundle up was able to pretty much walk to the edge with it instead of having to roll it into a boat or float it along to an easier access. It was dark, black. He carried it in his arms as if it were a sleeping baby and laid it at our feet in the weeds and grass that grew there.

An old coat, I could see, made of black cotton fabric. Bank tore at it then, to open it, and the stench hit us all.

It was a dog. The corpse of a dead and rotten collie that someone had wrapped and buttoned with some bricks into this old coat and sunk into the river.

I heard a sound in Bank's throat then, as it swelled up from his chest and forced its way out, a garbled cry beyond pain and frustration, of a rage so white and profound, it fragmented sanity. Bank pitched sideways as his legs kicked out from beneath him, into me, knocking me over, knocking us both to the edge of the river. The diver moved quickly to hold us there, to help me hold Bank as Googie rushed to help as well. It took all the strength the three of us had to hold him down, to keep him from diving in his madness deeper into that water.

16

Bank has Tuesday nights off. I need to see him but I don't get to my own home until after six. Peggy and the boys have just sat down to dinner.

"Dad!" I hear when I step in from the garage.

Peggy says, "We waited. You just made it."

"Guess what, Dad," says Ben. "Naomi called Mom a bitch."

"Hey," I say.

"But *she* said it."

"And that means you should repeat it?"

Ben grins and nods.

"No," says Jack.

"No, no," says Ben then.

Peggy confirms Ben's story.

"I'll talk to her," I say, as I open the basement door.

"You know what, Mack?" Peggy says. "Just join us. We'd like to have dinner with you. Can we just do that?"

I look at her, the raised eyebrows, the hurt in her face, the confusion at this tempest that has been dropped into the midst of our fairly peaceful lives. It's not fair to her, what Naomi has done to us. It tears at me, because I can't stand seeing her hurt like this, but at the same time, I love it that Naomi's here. I missed her for all those years, more than I realized until I had her back. And now I do not want to let her go again.

"All right," I say. "Let's eat."

"Meat loaf!" Ben shouts. His favorite, not because of the meat but the thick layer of catsup Peggy bakes on it. Ben is a catsup freak. He eats it on everything he can, including even crackers and bananas.

I throw a loose headlock on him and say, "Catsup. Catsup! You're that bad guy we've been looking for. The catsup thief."

"Yeah!" Ben shouts. "Get the handcuffs!"

"Ah!" shouts Jack, as he leaps up from his chair and races from the dining area into the family room, then back again through the kitchen and into the living room.

I look over at Peggy. She shakes her head, but I can see the smile there, working its way out.

I stand again listening to the heavy beat from Naomi's headphones coming through the cheap door. I knock and do the trick with my arm. The volume drops and she opens the door.

"I can hear it out here," I say. "Do you

217

know how loud that is?"

She closes her eyes. She's enduring me, this look says, and this just barely.

"You'll go deaf," I tell her.

"I can't hear it if it's not up."

"See, it's started already."

Now she rolls her eyes. What eyes this kid has.

"Besides," I tell her, "that's not music, you know, rap."

"It is."

"Snoopy the dog."

"Doggy Dogg."

"Yeah. Music has notes, a melody."

"Oh, God, Dad."

"It does. Real music. Led Zeppelin. The Stones. Neil Young."

"Stop it!" she says, grabbing her belly.

"You even know who they are?"

"Yes."

"You listen to them?"

"No. Thank you."

"I heard."

"What?"

"What you called Peg."

"I did not call her that. I said it, like, under my breath. My God."

"She has good hearing. She didn't listen to rap music through headphones."

The eyes close again.

"I'm serious, Naomi. It's the same discussion over and over again. Why can't we just
. . ." I am set, primed to gripe again, again. But even I am sick of hearing it. And besides, a sudden inspiration has come to me. Not a solution, just a thing to do that feels right.

"I have to go out," I tell her. "And I wanted to talk to you anyway. You want to come with?"

"You working?"

"Kind of," I say.

"Is this about Tamara?"

"I guess so. Yes, it is."

"Cool," she says, looking at me, a little surprised, the tiniest hint of openness showing in those eyes of hers.

Music comes through the front door of Harvey's Bar too. It only took two calls to track Bank here. Harvey's, on Brentcroft near the university, is popular with cops, and especially with Bank. But I don't see him when we walk in.

Naomi holds on to my sleeve as we enter, as the sounds of the jukebox and the raucous barroom laughter and the smells of beer and liquor wash over us.

"He stepped out for a minute," says the nice-looking lady working the bar. She's in her early thirties, with rust-colored hair and a smirky kind of half-smile. She looks wise, like a good bartender should. Her fingernails are long and curved, and each has been painted with a different intricate little piece of artwork.

"Hey, Susie. This is my daughter, Naomi."

"Hiya, Naomi."

"Hey," Naomi says, with a little wave.

"Sue owns this joint," I say.

"Really?" Naomi says.

Sue nods.

"I love your nails," Naomi says.

"Yeah? Let me see." Sue takes Naomi's hands in her own and inspects them. "You bite?"

Naomi nods.

"Mm," Sue says, and sucks her tongue and shakes her head. "You got one here that's long enough. We can do it. Pull up a stool."

"Really?"

"Sure."

She pulls a beer for me and a Coke for Naomi. It's early, and a Tuesday, so the place isn't too busy, but still I count four off-duty cops. By the time I've gone around and said hey, Bank has come back in.

"This Father Hector?" I say. "You know him?"

"Nah."

"You hear anything?"

"I heard they still ain't talked to him."

We're in the farthest booth from the bar, next to the men's room and the pay phone. This passes for whatever privacy we're going to get.

"He's not around," I say. "Whatever that means. Where's a priest just up and go?"

Bank shakes his head. We drink on this for a little while.

I ask him, then, "How'd you snap to Baker Hawkes?" but it's the unanswerable question. Bank is loath to give up his sources, even to other cops. Even to me. He has always been this way, from the beginning. When we were on patrol together there were places he'd insist on going into alone, leaving me leaning against the side of the patrol car in the night, eyeballing the local wildlife, them eyeballing me, each of us holding the other in a kind of stasis until Bank came back and the balance of power rolled back into my court. But he'd never tell me who he'd talked to or even why sometimes. "I gotta see somebody" was all he'd say. Sometimes he'd be gone half an hour.

So now he just shrugs and sips his beer.

"Googie doesn't know about this," I tell him.

"You sure?"

"I think I'd know."

"So you talked to him about it."

I shake my head. "Katherine showed up at the house a few minutes after me. She's known about it. She kind of suggested that Stu might know something about it, too, but not Googie. What's this about, Bank?"

"She's protecting something."

"But this is hot, the investigation, the whole PR front they're throwing up."

"Maybe that's it, then. Maybe this information would change those things and she doesn't want them to change."

"That's not it," I say. "There's something else."

We listen to the music and the barroom conversations.

"I know this," he says finally. "The girl's out there, Mack, someplace she doesn't belong. What else do you really need to know?"

Which is almost verbatim what Katherine said to me a few hours ago.

"They're going to bench you, you know," I tell him.

"Bullshit."

I look around. Across the room Naomi and Sue lean across the bar toward one another, talking now, not working on Naomi's nail.

"Maybe you need to talk about it," I say.

"About what?"

"About what this might be doing to you. What's happening at night."

"Just the Job, Mack. You get on the street and you get yourself dirty and you find shit out. That's all."

"You're even hauling in your own snitches, and some don't look like they're in such great shape when you're finished. Your own people. That's not your MO."

"It takes what it takes."

"I don't think it's just doing the Job. I think this thing's into you, eating away, fucking with your head."

"I haven't done nothing wrong."

"Maybe not. But I have it on good authority you're going to find your ass riding a desk."

He doesn't say anything. Sue walks over with a couple fresh draws. She doesn't ask any stupid questions or try to make small talk. She knows how to run a bar. When she's gone I say, "I just think you ought to air it out a little if it's going to make you crazy. That's all I came here to say."

Bank leans toward me and places his huge hand over my smaller one on the table and says, "Shut up, Mack."

I look into his eyes, at the anger cooking in

there, and feel some of it myself.

He says, "You know, your problem was always that you were *too* goddamn smart. You think you know so much but you can't see what's right in front of your face."

"What does that mean?"

"Figure it out. You're the genius. But do me a favor, will you? Give me a little credit. I mean, I've got this far. Think about it." And with that he gets up and walks to the bar, throws down a bill, and leaves.

A couple of the off-duty guys at the bar look over in my direction. I meet their gaze, indicating nothing, but it pisses me off, him leading on like he knows something but not telling me. Me, who he dragged into this situation in the first place. I sit and finish my beer and cool off before I get up.

"Taken care of," Sue says, when I try to pay.

Naomi has actually two new nails. She holds them up for me to admire, stars and moons and glitter.

"Groovy," I say.

She does the eye roll and throws a look at Sue, who smiles.

"You all right?" Sue asks me.

"I'm fine," I say. "I'm not the problem."

"He'll be all right," she says.

"I don't know," I say. "How's he been around you?"

"Thinking a lot, I guess. Working on something."

"Aren't we all."

"I hear you."

"Take it easy, Susie," I tell her. "Anything comes up, you know, call me a-sap."

I glance out the front window and see Bank there still, on the sidewalk, talking to a couple. I watch as he waves at them and crosses the street to Heron Park. Then he just fades out of sight, like an apparition or a spirit, back into the night.

"You know it," she says.

In the car Naomi says, "She said she's been on her own since she was fifteen. She even lived on the street."

"What'd she say about it?"

"I don't know. Stuff. Not much."

Naomi goes quiet again then, thinking about that, and I wonder how much of the truth of it Sue really told her. I also wonder sometimes what Naomi herself knows about it. When she ran away from her grandparents' home in Columbus those several times, they never called me when it mattered. Mostly, I guess, she had just slept at friends' houses without letting anyone know. But at least once, I learned, she was gone for three or four days. Those two old farts didn't report it for over forty-eight hours, and neglected to ever call me. When I heard it from a Columbus PD cop a month or so later, I was furious. It was at that point, June of last year, that I knew Naomi had to leave that place.

"Naomi," I say, then, "I owe you an apology."

"For what?"

"Sunday, when you told me about Tamara Shipley being out there, I blew it off. I should have listened. It turns out she ran away about a year ago."

"You think she did this time too?"

"I'm afraid not."

She stays quiet.

"So listen, this friend of yours."

"Zelda."

"Yeah. Where'd she get a name like that?"

Naomi starts chewing on a nail and looking out the side window.

"Anyway," I say, "I wonder, how can I talk to her?"

"I don't know, Dad," she says. "She's really nervous about cops."

"Not to come down on her. I want to know about Tamara. Where she was, what she was into, who she stopped with, that kind of thing. It might be important."

"I don't think she saw her since then. It's a long time."

"Doesn't matter."

"I'll see," she says. "I'll talk to her."

"Soon?"

"Yeah."

"Tomorrow," I say.

"Dad —"

"I'm sorry, Naomi. I have to see her. It might make a difference."

She inhales and exhales and studies her nails as she thinks it over, and she looks very much like a grown woman suddenly sitting next to me there. I reach across and touch the raven-dyed hair, petting it for a moment in a way I used to do a long, long time ago.

"Daddy," she says, sounding sleepy. She leans her head against the window and closes her eyes. "I'll talk to her."

"Good girl," I say.

Midnight, I'm in the Tamara Shipley folder again, flipping through copies of the witness statements; of certain detectives' notes, including Katherine's and Googie's (noting that there are very few here from Bank); scene photographs, the alley and bicycle, the Chrysler interior and exterior; lab reports; the transcript of Eddie Munster's Q & A; and the Fed-generated documents — phone records up to and including the previous morning; the credit report showing, to my surprise, almost no card debt; the background statements regarding the family from people Simms had dug up. These last documents are the sorts of things that sometimes break a case like this. You find out about a deep debt, for instance, or a steady outflow of cash to a particular place, all kinds of things can lead from that. But it's all fishing.

Peggy went to bed at ten, and I've been reading since then, the same documents over and over. I know what they say. But when I put them down I feel this tug, as if something's talking to me from those pages. The lack of credit card debt is part of it. But there's something else. I wander out into the kitchen, pick at some of the leftover meat loaf, drink some water, then go back into the family room and look again.

The background interviews contain a few mentions of some tensions in the family, a statement from the family priest, for instance, of how he had suggested counseling, that sort of thing, but nothing remarkable. In the phone records an agent has marked a few numbers with question marks, including one, which appears twice, to a number in a Chicago area code. I wasn't sure earlier, when I saw this, why they had marked these at first, but I realized then that the second such call had been at 9:14 on Palm Sunday morning. The call to 911 had been recorded at 9:04. Why had someone in the house called Chicago ten minutes after Tamara had vanished? Next to the number, then, the agent penciled in "FF." Family Friend.

I close the file, shut up the downstairs, turn off the lights, and crawl up to bed.

17

On the Thursday night of July 13, 1989, Jamie's fourth night away, Sarah did not call me. I found out later she had taken a sedative. But I awoke anyway, at two again, and sat up in my bed. I lifted the phone, then replaced it, got up and dressed in jeans and a sweatshirt and running shoes. The rain had continued into the night.

I drove out to Brentcroft and east until I came to Heron Hills. I crept through the neighborhood, down the winding tree-lined streets, along the banks of the river, which trickled serenely on this night. Finally I turned onto Detwiler. The Arbaugh house was quiet and dark. No police cruisers or unmarked city cars blocked the street or the sidewalk anymore. Even the press vans had left, although they would be back soon enough, I knew, looking for the next chapter in the story, hungry for that up-close grief interview.

I passed the house slowly, then turned around at the end of the street and came back. I stopped there in front, in the street, watching, waiting for something. No one was up, or if they were they were sitting in the dark, at a window perhaps, watching me, wondering who might be sitting out there at this hour.

As I pulled into their driveway to turn around, my headlights washed over the side of the house, and then into the backyard and across the front of the garage. The old swinging-style doors stood open. The minivan was there, but the other bay was empty, where Bank's Jeep Cherokee should have been parked.

I spotted no Cherokee lurking about when I arrived at the Kestler Village Apartments that night. As I drove again through the neighborhood across from the complex, though, and into the lot in front of Norke's building, I saw a light. It was Norke's car, the brown Camaro. The driver's side door stood open, so the interior dome light was on. I grabbed my Maglite.

The front door into Norke's building was locked, accessible only by key at this hour. I rattled the door in its frame but it did not open and no one came down to open it. There were no buzzers or bells to ring, to rouse anyone. I went around to the back door, which was locked too.

A high street-type lamp at the rear of the

small yard behind the apartment building illuminated the fence separating it from the field across which lay the old Kestler factory. I walked back to this fence and looked out over the weedy lot there, and beyond it to the broken asphalt surrounding the building, and then to the building itself. There were a few maintenance lights on it, probably mandated by the city so that the place wasn't a total black hole. And then as I stood there watching, I heard a voice coming from that direction, floating on the air, barely audible. It sounded like a cry of some sort, an entreaty. I vaulted the fence and ran.

I see it in that dank July night of our history, this great deserted redbrick behemoth, symbol of exactly what had built this city, its downtown and its old neighborhoods and its museum, and of what had happened to it all. It stood there, impassive, monstrous, shadowed, its sheer walls rising into the night eight, nine, ten stories. Where I came upon it, as I ran across the broken, pitted asphalt, I saw no good entry, but saw no one outside either. A flat expanse, a single chained and padlocked doorway. I listened, then ran again, toward the west end.

This side held a series of old loading docks. Concrete ramps led up to some of them;

others opened at trailer height. I also saw, beneath a security light, Bank's red Cherokee.

I ran along past the docks, each closed with a locked steel gate. Until the last one. This gate was raised a few feet. After pulling myself up onto the lip of the opening, I rolled beneath the door, over fragments of glass and stone which cut my arms and shoulders. I lay still, then, in the blackened interior, listening.

Another shout, much clearer, though still distant, came from above me somewhere, impassioned but unintelligible. The sound echoed down through the old air shafts.

In the beam of my light the room filled with eerie hulking shapes: abandoned storage bins, piles of wooden pallets. With each step my shoes grated against the debris beneath them. I picked my way along through the old loading dock, through a high and open doorway into a much larger, more cavernous chamber. Thirty- or forty-foot ceilings, the twisting steel skeleton of conveyor lines still bolted to the floor in places. Voices again then, closer, but above me.

I had no idea where to find the stairs. But one part of the old line that still stood, including a four- or five-foot-wide rubber belt, ran up through an opening in the ceiling. Some of it had been deconstructed, but it looked solid enough. I shook it, then tucked the Maglite into my pants and climbed onto the flat black belt that had once moved tons of product.

I went on hands and knees, gingerly, the whole structure shaking beneath me as I crawled higher, the belt letting go and slipping now and then on the steel rollers beneath it. I stopped when this happened, grabbing frantically for any handle I could find. But I made it up to the next level, which was somewhat brighter because of the moon shining in through the dozens of holes broken in the high walls of blackened windows.

"Wait!" I heard, nearby. Bank's voice. Then running footsteps echoing, then the voices fainter again. I jumped off the line. As I did, the Maglite slipped from my waistband and clattered to the floor and rolled through the opening. A moment later I heard it hit the concrete below.

I ran, nearly blind now, toward the sound, which led me from this high assembly room and into a lower, narrower, darker hallway. A heavy door slammed ahead of me and then bounced open again. Inside it, in utter blackness, I felt a cold metal pipe railing running up along a set of steep iron steps.

I climbed one flight, then another, pausing after each to listen, to hear the footsteps still above me, then another, up into the black until I was sucking air, panting and dizzy with the exertion and the sheer adrenaline rush. So it was that when I opened the last door I found myself falling out of the musty, greasy stink and pitch of the old plant, into the coolness and rain of the night.

And the sounds of men. I heard running. I saw a light play out into the darkness. I chased it. The expanse of the tarred rooftop was divided into different sections, at different heights. As I followed the light, I heard Bank say, "Don't run!" My eyes adjusted slowly to the darkness. I tripped over a low wall and tumbled, and ran again.

And then the rooftop simply vanished from beneath my feet. I thought that I was dead, that I had come to the edge of the building or to an air shaft and had stepped off into space. I remember inhaling — there seemed no end to the depth of my lungs, no limit to my capacity to breathe in. I would have yelled but I could not stop swallowing air. Then I hit.

The drop had only been four or five feet, I think, an unevenness in the roofline where a new section of building had been added to the original. But with the impact, which I could not see and had not braced for, my knees had slammed up into my chest and head, and hot iron blood filled my mouth.

"Wait!" I heard, nearby.

Then, "Get away from me!"

Near the eastern edge of the building I came upon a set of huge gaping air intake tubes and exhaust stacks. As I crept around them I saw the scene in Bank's Maglite. Alan Norke cowered at the low foot-high wall at the very edge of the roof.

"What are you going to do?" Norke said.

"Just relax," Bank said, out of breath, but his voice soft and cajoling. "I want to talk. That's all."

"So you kidnap me?" Norke said. "You crazy bastard. I'll have *you* arrested."

"Just talk to me," Bank said. "Tell me what happened. I have to know. Who else was involved. Where is she?" Bank approached him.

"You fucking lunatic," Norke said, kicking himself away. "You leave me alone."

"I will," Bank said. As Norke rose to run again, Bank stepped closer, so that whichever way Norke went, Bank could stop him. "Just talk to me."

"Help!" Norke screamed. "Help me!"

"Shh," said Bank. "Quiet down."

And Norke did then, growing suddenly calmer, and cajoling himself. "I want my lawyer," he said. "I want you to take me in. We'll call him from there. We'll just go in together."

"Tell me," said Bank. "Who took her?"

Say something, I implored myself. *Stop this!* Tell him it wasn't Norke's print on the bat. But he would have known that. It didn't mean anything, anyway. And what's more, I wanted as badly as Bank did to hear what this kid had to say.

"I don't know," Norke said.

"Did you do it alone?"

"I didn't touch her. You're insane."

"You're not leaving here until you talk."

Norke released a kind of sob.

"I just want the truth," Bank said.

Then Norke laughed, a crazy tittering. And he said this: "No, Mr. Arbaugh. You don't. Believe me, what you do not want is the truth."

Bank and I drew a single collective breath. Even when you have a perp you know is culpable, it's an amazing moment when he finally says it. Yeah. I did it. It never fails, even now, after years of interrogating, to make my heart race when someone cops. Why do it? Why not fight it out in court? Why not make us prove our case? For there always, I tell you as someone who knows, regardless of evidence, regardless of what our guts tell us, there is always some tiny grain of doubt, the smallest possibility that we have missed some essential key.

The tough guys, the hard-asses and pros, they know this, that their best shot is always to not talk unless they have a clear deal on the table, a deal they need. Otherwise, no way. But so many of them, the ones who aren't careerists, have this huge guilt, this pit of disbelief, of hopelessness even, at the thought of what they've done. And what we offer them is the chance to confess. They swear and they run and they lie, but in the end they need us to listen. It's their absolution. We are a kind of priest to them, as self-righteous as that may sound, but it's the truth.

And for Norke, about whom we knew almost nothing, on whom we had no hard evidence at all, the priest was the father of the victim. The ultimate confessor, the ultimate absolution.

Norke knew the truth. He had as much as admitted it.

"Please," Bank said. "Please. I need to find her. I need to see her, wherever she is. However she is."

"No, you don't," Norke said. "And you won't." And with that he tried to bolt. But he was not a strong man, nor fast, and here he was trying to get around none other than Bank Arbaugh himself. As Norke darted forward, Bank's arm flashed out and caught him and flung him back toward the low wall at the edge of the roof. But it was dark and Bank was pumped up with emotion. Norke stumbled.

I imagine still, in retrospect, that I saw him pause there at the lip and actually lean slightly forward, away from the precipice. I imagine that I saw one of his feet come up and try to brace itself there. I have imagined the look on his face, which I believe I saw clearly, a look of amazement, and even perhaps of a kind of relief. But I do not know if I saw any of this.

Bank realized what he had done, that in his anger he had thrown Norke too hard. He leapt forward, extending his arms, grasping. But even Bank was not fast enough.

Alan Norke seemed to hang for just a moment, long enough for him to utter a single "No." He said it flatly, though. He did not scream or clutch at the air. And then he fell, backward, into the night, into the sky, into the arms of the rain.

I must have let loose a sound, of anguish, of regret, because I had so many questions to ask, because I saw already, in that flash, what might now forever go unanswered, and what hell that not knowing would bring with it. I do not know. But Bank heard me then and trained his light into my face.

"Mack," he said.

I stood, naked in that light, waiting for what would come.

"Mack," he said again. "Goddamn you."

I did not answer him, or say anything, and I never did know exactly why he cursed me. Because I had watched, perhaps, and failed to intervene when I had the chance. Or perhaps because I was a witness now to this horrid event, a coconspirator, a holder of the secret, and would remain so always.

After a moment of standing thus, facing each other, we turned, Bank and I, without another word and walked back across the roof, each of us helping the other climb back up to the higher level, to the iron staircase and down, then to a different set of steps I had not found, and so to the ground floor.

He never asked me what I planned on doing and I did not tell him anything.

The first thing we did was to check on Alan Norke. He lay in a small lake of blood. We knew enough not to get our shoes in it, to leave tracks, but we did not have to approach him too closely. I saw enough brain matter in the beam of Bank's Maglite to know that he had died instantly.

Around at the other side by Bank's Jeep I motioned for him to follow me back into the factory, to the great cavernous room near the loading dock. And there I searched until I found my smashed Maglite. When Bank saw it, he realized immediately not only the significance of its being there, but of my showing it to him. He got down on his hands and knees and tried to sweep together the bits of shattered glass. I knelt and joined him.

When we picked up what we could, we found our way back through to the dock and the opened bay door. Bank drove me around to my car. I drove home and got into bed. But I did not sleep much that night because I was afraid, I think, of what I would see if I did.

The apparent suicide of Alan Norke, which was taken as clear indication of his likely involvement in the disappearance, drove the press frenzy to a higher pitch but ultimately led to little more than that.

The CSU tore apart Norke's apartment and his car, the brown Camaro, although it bore no resemblance to the vehicle described by the runner in Heron Park, and although it was known that Jamie had ridden in it at least once before her disappearance. They vacuumed and taped clothing and carpeting and furniture, floor mats and trunk, and organized the trace evidence into an extensive catalog of fiber samples and other debris. They collected samples from the Arbaugh house as well, from furniture where Jamie had liked to sit, from her bedroom, in a bid to identify some thread that may have been transferred from that house to Norke's property. They generated reams of data, but no matches. None of Jamie's prints showed on any of Norke's property, either, nor did any print matching the one lifted from her bat.

Norke's friends and acquaintances were interviewed about any known pedophilic activity on his part or any associates of his who ought to be looked at, other cars Norke had access to. The vehicles of all of these people were checked out as well, both visually and by plate numbers.

In the end Katherine's friend, Stamos, from the Chicago PD, called back with the story about Norke's earlier kidnapping arrest.

"It was a custody thing," Katherine told me. "He was acting on behalf of a woman he knew, who he'd been counseling. He had his master's by then and had been working in a couple of clinics around the area. The father had partial custody in South Bend; the woman claimed the father was abusing the girl. Norke got involved. That's why the charge had been reduced to child stealing. Later, I guess, the parents reconciled and charges were dropped. That's all it was."

No suspicion of any child endangerment. The opposite, actually. Norke had been acting in the perceived interest of the child, which the laws of Ohio, and Indiana, too, I imagined, recognized and allowed for.

And yet, on the rooftop, he had all but admitted that he knew something. Whatever it was, it was lost to us now.

18

The mood in the conference room is less agitated, more somber, on Wednesday. Little new has come to light regarding Tamara Shipley. What's more, Father Hector Morales failed to show up again at his parish last night. Katherine talked to another priest there this morning who was concerned enough that he asked about filing an MP report. This makes us all nervous.

From the table, however, in front of each of our chairs, a face stares up at us — the computer-generated likeness of the man who bought packing tape in the Food King early Sunday morning. This man has a dusky complexion, heavy lips, a slightly bearded, slightly underslung jaw. He wears round mirrored sunglasses and a black stocking cap — the rolled-up face-mask Jeff Gramza remembered — but beneath that, the clerk said, she had the impression that he had very little hair. She couldn't say why, exactly, but she remembered this. All in all the girl did a fine job and we have our first solid lead, although it is a tenuous one at best.

"Every cop on the street's got one'a these," Googie says. "Press, Feds, county sheriff's deputies. Everybody."

"This is good work," says Simms, nodding at each of us around the table.

"Well, let's take it the next step," says Googie. "Let's find this son of a bitch."

We nod at this directive.

"Somethin' else's come to light," Googie continues. "I been thinking about it. Turns out this girl has a jacket here under another name. She took off once, early last year."

I wait for the reaction from those around the table who didn't know this, but there isn't one, and so I gather that this news is not really news at this point. And again I'm a little baffled at the clandestine nature of it, at why this wasn't just laid out and discussed when Katherine first found out.

"For now," says Googie, "I don't think it changes nothin', and I don't think it's gotta leave here." I catch Katherine's gaze, but she looks away from me.

Googie runs through the rest of the day's assignments and is about to adjourn when I hold up a copy of the phone records. "Quick question," I say to Simms. "This Chicago number. Any story here?"

Simms says, "The mother made those calls. Close family friend, she said."

"One was ten minutes after the disappearance."

"Happens all the time. People freak. They want to talk to someone they know. Someone who cares."

"Anyone check it out?"

Simms shrugs.

"I called over there," Katherine says.

"You did?"

She stares hard at me. "Yes," she says, "I did. I spoke with a woman who said she'd been friends with Rochelle for years. Almost family."

"Oh," I say. "I must have missed it in your notes."

"Sorry, Mack," she says. "I'll put something in the file."

"Great, Katherine," I say. We regard each other for another long moment, until Googie says, "All right." And we are finished.

Afterward, though, when I catch Simms hanging around the coffeepots at the front of the suite, shooting the shit before hiking back over to the Federal Building, I motion to him and step back into the conference room, and close the door behind us.

"What's up, Mack?" he says.

"Listen," I tell him, "can I ask you something? You keep this just between us?"

"Sure, buddy."

"That Chicago number."

"Bugging you, huh?"

I nod. What's bugging me really is Katherine, though I don't mention this to Simms.

He says, "You want me to have someone take a look?"

"Could you?"

"Course."

"I'm just being weird about it."

"No problem. I'll call the field office over there, have them pull the address, see who lives there, maybe talk to them."

"And on the QT."

"If that's how you want it."

"I do."

Rick nods and slaps my arm, and heads back to the coffeepots. I head on out, into the day.

I eat lunch alone at a diner called the Green Lantern, a classic grease hole in a double-wide trailer on a tiny gravel lot jammed between an office tower on one side and an old yellow-brick hotel on the other. Though I'm not heavy, Peggy's always after me about my diet, cop food being what it is, so instead of the house special — what we call around the Bureau the cardiac platter, a bacon-cheeseburger and cheese fries — I order the day's soup and a salad. I'm not that hungry anyway.

I sit on a high stool at a counter that runs along the front window, looking out onto Jefferson Street. I'm lost in my thoughts, I guess, because I don't notice right away that Katherine's up at the counter, paying for an order.

When she turns to leave, our eyes meet. I expect something vaguely hostile, I guess, because that's the way it's felt between us lately. I don't know what's up with her, or if it's just me. But when she winks at me and smiles, I am even more confused.

Stu intercepts me when I come back into the Bureau around four. He puts a hand on my shoulder and nods toward his office. Something in his face alerts me, and when he starts snapping his fingers, I feel a wash of sudden fear in my stomach. One of the kids, I think first, or Peggy. But in his office Googie's waiting too. So it's Tamara. I am certain now that she's been found dead. I know this is so. I know it in my bones.

"You want to sit?" says Stu.

"No. What is it? They found her."

"Mack," Stu says, "that print CSU lifted off the girl's bike? Well, you know, they ran it into the AFIS here this morning." AFIS is the Automated Fingerprint Identification

System, a computer database of all prints we and the county sheriff's department have on file and a scanner that can match, in seconds, a stray print to any one of these. Any moderately sophisticated police force has such a system these days.

"That's what this is about?" I say.

He nods. "We got a hit."

I look at him, not understanding why these guys look so beat up, why they needed to haul me in here to tell me this.

"Mack," Stu says, "they got a nine-point match off the latent from that damn ball bat."

I still do not understand what he's saying. I wait for more explanation but it does not come. And then I do understand. I feel as if someone has just hit me with a pole across the back of my knees. I fall into the chair in front of Stu's desk.

He's talking about Jamie Arbaugh's bat.

"Oh, Jesus" is all I can say at first. "How could we — how in the fuck —" I can't think. I can't even breathe. I find myself gasping, opening my mouth like a beached fish, loosening my tie, tugging at my collar until I rip the button off. Stu hands me a paper cup of water.

"Easy," he says.

I need to get outside, out of this office, out

of the Bureau, away. I need to think about this, how it fits, how it doesn't fit. I need time to understand that Jamie and Tamara are somehow, in some bizarre fashion, for some horribly wrong reason, connected. But something else occurs to me then.

"Bank," I say. "Does he know?"

Stu shakes his head. "Not yet. But I gotta pull him now, Mack. There's no choice. He'll go nuts out there."

"You think that's going to keep him off it? You think every minute he's not at work he won't be out there cracking skulls?"

"What else can I do? Lock him up?"

"No," I say, my thoughts racing forward, jumbling together, straining to sort themselves out. "Listen. You have to let him work it. Let him stay out there."

"Mack —"

"But reassign me."

"What?"

"Me," I say. "To nights."

"To Bank's f-car," Googie says. "Partner 'em up again."

Stu just looks at me, the fingers snapping away.

"It's the only way," I say. And it is. Stu and Googie look at each other. Stu gives a little nod finally, acknowledging the wisdom of what I've said.

THREE

19

Bank's foster parents, Ned and Frances Baxter, seemed alien to me in some way I couldn't name. They had no children of their own, but had, along with Bank, at various times, other charges, including a girl named Angela Watson, who was a year behind us in school, and several much younger children I remember. Angela only stayed with them through two school years, and the younger children seemed to come and go without design.

They lived in a smallish single-story house painted a pale robin's-egg blue one street over from us. The front door opened directly into the living room, which held the pieces of an ugly olive-green sectional couch oriented around a massive console color TV. Ned and Frances also had another, smaller color TV set in their bedroom. This was a remarkable thing to me. My family owned one television, a small black-and-white Zenith in a plastic putty-colored frame that sat on a bookshelf in the den in the front of our house. It was not until 1974 or -5, I think, that my parents finally bought their first color set, which my mother still considered to be a terrifically wasteful extravagance. But Ned and Frances loved that TV set. I don't remember ever coming in when it wasn't on, even if no one was around to watch it.

To the left, from the front door, was the open kitchen and dining area, a single long room that ran the width of the house. From the other end of the living room ran a dim, narrow hallway, off of which lay the three bedrooms.

Ned worked as a plumber. He was a big, jug-headed, heavy-thighed, barrel-chested man with a close crew cut, meaty lips, and enormous fleshy-lobed ears that stuck out from his head at a broad angle. Frances was no small thing either. Around the house she wore tight, stretchy pink or yellow pedal-pushers that came down to the middle of her calves, the effect of which was to accentuate not only her bulbous, protruding ass and heavy thighs, but also the alarming way in which they narrowed down to ankles and feet that were so tiny, I wondered sometimes how they supported her without breaking. She was heavy breasted, too, but wore loose T-shirts so these weren't as obvious. Frances's eyes were slanted and yellow like a cat's, and could have been rather attractive, I thought, if they hadn't been embedded in her face, separated by her pulpy nose and underlined by her wide mouth, which seemed always to be twisted into some nasty expression.

I was aware that Frances was quite a bit younger than Ned, though this didn't really impress me much at the time. I found out some years later the age difference was fifteen years, and that Frances, at the time I remember her, was only in her mid-twenties, which seems very young to me now. But then I thought of her as essentially my mother's age. I was also vaguely aware of the fact that there was some scandalous history behind Ned and Frances's union, but I did not know what and wasn't particularly curious.

Frances did not work out of the house, so she was almost always around somewhere when I'd ride over to play with Bank. But we had plenty of room there for football games or running, and places to disappear to when we needed. The house sat on a narrow but deep lot of a couple acres and ran back to a small copse of trees at its end. In these woods Bank had built himself a rough but serviceable wooden platform fifteen or twenty feet off the ground, and eventually he chided me to the point where I forced myself to climb up onto it. In the beginning I could only sit with my fingers dug in between the planks, tensing at every breeze that rocked us, blinded and deafened by the sense that the whole thing was on the verge of tumbling to earth.

Frances and Ned were rough, loud people, unlike my own parents. It was not at all out of the ordinary for either of them to swat one of the kids, including Bank, without even so much as a warning growl. Hit first, talk after, was their credo.

I'd seen it happen. One Saturday Bank and I were watching *Jonny Quest* on the color television — I remember this vividly — and little Angela, with her curled hair and her pale skin and her red lips and the haunted expression she always wore, had wandered in from the kitchen, where she had been eating a bowl of cereal. She stood behind us, watching over our shoulders. For some reason I happened to look back at her just as Ned was passing through the living room on his way back to the bathroom. I must have heard him come in the back door and through the kitchen. As he neared Angela, I saw him raise his opened hand, thick and yellow with calluses, and, without so much as slowing down, deliver her a full slap on the back of her head. Her mouth opened in pain and she bent forward as if it had been her gut where she'd been hit, but no sound escaped her. Her eyes filled and spilled over. She looked at him, but did not speak.

"Clean that shit up," he said back to her,

and pointed into the kitchen at the cereal and milk and her bowl which were still on the table.

Bank told her to sit down, and went in himself and put the cereal box and the milk away. After making sure Ned wasn't coming back yet, he pressed the spoon against the counter until he'd bent it in two, cracked the bowl in half against the side of the sink, then buried them both deep in the garbage pail.

I actively hated Ned for weeks after this, for I was nursing at that time a bad and secret crush on Angela and had been putting myself to sleep some nights imagining the time when we could run off together into a vague but perfect future. Now my fantasies included a duel first, wherein Ned tried to stop us from leaving. I won, of course, but only after Bank, at the point of my most desperate battle, stepped in to help by delivering a resounding closed-fisted blow that echoed off the top of Ned's wooden, crew-cut head.

Still, I had no impression that Ned and Frances were anything other than somewhat dim, callous people who for some unfathomable reason felt the need to take children into their house. (I did not know then that there was money involved in these matters.) Frances seemed always to be dragging at least one bawling, runny-nosed kid behind her as she cleaned and straightened and shined the house and their possessions — for the Baxters were, at least, clean people, and they prized their stuff.

Our school was more than half a mile from where we lived but we could get almost all the way there on back streets, that is without having to ride on the busy thoroughfares until we reached Liam Road, across from Our Lady of Lourdes church. The school was just down a little ways, at the corner of Pawtucket.

Behind both the church and the school, and continuing on to the east, across Pawtucket, lay a great swath of undeveloped land which was tied together by Lourdes Creek, named after the parish it bisected, and which ran from just beyond the rusted wire fence bordering the school playground through a high cement culvert beneath Pawtucket. Much of this land was covered in wild brown grass, some of which grew as tall as me by the late summer. Some was low-lying marsh. And some, at the back of the wildest, largest tract — that which lay to the east, across Pawtucket, what we called the Wilderness — was woods.

These woods were not much really, an old seven- or eight-acre stand of midwestern hardwoods, maples and oaks and sycamores and a few remaining elms. Grapevines as thick around as Bank's biceps hung down from the tops of some of them, and we would leap up and, grasping them, kick ourselves away from the trees as we gave Johnny Weissmuller's Tarzan yell. Dead branches littered the ground, perfect as weapons or nut bats or just for whacking against a tree trunk to watch the broken end sail off into the shadows.

It was on our second or third foray into these woods, late in the summer of 1968, on a day which by noon was already in the mid-nineties, that we made our way into them far enough to see first, and with some disappointment, that they gave onto nothing but a farmer's soybean field. The Wilderness was not endless after all. Beyond the folds of the field, tucked away behind a low rise, we saw the tops of a white house and a weathered-gray barn. So we turned east and skirted along the back edge of the woods, to make our second discovery — that the creek turned southward here, cutting along the eastern edge of the woods before winding down through the middle of the soybean field.

As we walked back along it, we came to a particularly dense section of bushes and trees and could not see exactly where it ran. Bank plunged in, swatting aside the low-hanging branches and pushing at the saplings and bushes. I followed, but at some distance to avoid getting smacked in the face by a rebounding branch.

And then Bank said, "Whoa!" We had come out into a kind of open clearing where the creek formed a natural pool maybe twenty feet across and at least that long. As we looked out across it we could just make out the sandy bottom. Boulders lay scattered along the edge nearest us, as if they had been tossed there. We leapt from one to the other. The far shoreline lay in perpetual shade, but the sun penetrated down through the opening overhead and fell on the center of the pool and the rocks where we stood.

"It's deep," Bank said. Then he raced back to the grassy embankment and peeled off his shirt.

"What are you doing?"

"Swimming," he said. He had his shoes off and then peeled down his cutoffs and ran back out onto the rocks. And before I could say anything or warn him, he dived. I waited, holding my breath with him, for a long, long second before he surfaced, spouting, and waved at me.

"Come on!"

"Is it cold?"

"Freezing. It's great."

I badly wanted to join him. But, though we were shielded from view by the woods on all sides, I could not bring myself to take off all my clothes.

"Keep your panties on, then," Bank called out to me.

"Shut up," I said, then added, "They'll get wet."

"They'll dry, dope," he said back. "It's a hundred degrees out."

So I did that, stripped down to my J. C. Penney briefs and with a yell followed Bank into the icy pool.

When we were finished, shivering and blue-lipped, I stood behind a bush and rung my shorts out before sliding them back on and my jeans over them. And by the time we'd ridden home I was, as Bank had predicted, pretty much dry. What I did after that was to sneak an old pair of swimming trunks along with me and then to leave them back by the pool, hanging on a bush where they'd be whenever we returned. My mother missed them at one point and asked me if I'd seen them anywhere. I just shook my head, as if not actually speaking somehow lessened the lie.

By the following summer, though, I had lost any trace of my inhibitions. Bank and I would strip and then run and leap side-by-

261

side into the cold water, screaming and slapping at it until our bodies acclimated.

Or he would say, urgently, "I just felt something on my feet. It's alive!"

"Oh, shit!" I'd yell, and cut for the rocks, whose sunbaked warmth I crawled up on only to fling myself a moment later back into the water.

Bank had invented a competition: who could hold their breath longer under the water. After a few rounds of this in which he outlasted me by as much as fifty percent, he began to compete with a worthier opponent: himself. I became the timekeeper, since I wore a waterproof Timex I'd received for my tenth birthday.

"Go," I'd yell, and he'd inhale to point of bursting, then plunge under. I started counting when he dived. By mid-August he'd made it to sixty-five seconds before he came shooting up through the surface, wet and shining and sucking in chestfuls of air.

The problem, though, the limiting factor, was the fact that he floated. To stay under he had to continually wave his arms upward. This, of course, took energy, and so cut into his time, which was holding fairly steady at just over a minute. That is, until he discovered a new way of staying under.

Near where it emptied into the pool, the

creek had deposited a collection of fairly large stones, ranging in weight, I'd say, from five to maybe twenty pounds. Bank figured that if he carried a few of these rocks to the center of the pool, then piled them on his lap, he'd stay under with no effort but that of holding his breath.

There was an aspect of reckless abandon to Bank's personality that others tended to see as one of his primary traits, though around me he tended to keep this part of himself in check. I didn't understand why — I just seemed to have a calming influence on him. But when he did have an idea that he saw shocked or scared me, it pleased him greatly, and he had to try it, if only for my benefit. Such was the case when he saw my reaction to this idea of piling rocks on himself underwater — disbelief that he'd do something so risky; the certain knowledge that he'd drown.

And I had to admit that he was right. The first time he did it, his time increased to seventy seconds.

"What if you pass out?" I asked him.

"You'll save me," he said.

"I won't be able to tell."

"I'm not gonna, Mack. Just relax."

"It's really dangerous."

But his time continued to increase, upward to nearly seventy-five seconds, and then once beyond that to seventy-eight.

Until one day in late August when the sun was scorching everything in a last-ditch effort to stay and the trees and undergrowth had gone from ripe into wild, Bank announced he was going to break the record, lifted a large rock, and held it to his belly as he sank under. I started to time. A vague sense of uneasiness seemed to me to overlay the creek on that day, as if something lay waiting for us out there in the trees. I stood in the pool watching the second hand on my waterproof Timex sweep past thirty seconds.

Then, suddenly, I did not want to be in that water anymore. Again I felt a dark sense of apprehension roll over its surface. I climbed onto the warm boulders and sat with my arms wrapped around my legs. The sun rode high and hot, spikes of it piercing the canopy of trees. It was just past noon.

Forty-five seconds passed, then a minute. Bank showed no signs of surfacing. Seventy seconds. Then eighty. The record. Bank had done it. I stood up and looked out across the water, but could see little except for the glare of the sun on its surface. Eighty-five seconds came and went. Ninety.

"Bank," I said. I hooded my eyes and scanned the water where he'd gone under, but I could not see anything.

I checked the watch again. It was now coming on two minutes.

"Hey!" I shouted. "Bank!" I splashed into the pool and over to the spot where he'd disappeared. I groped around beneath the surface but felt nothing. "Bank!" I screamed. I was openly frightened now and on the verge of crying. *"Bank!"*

A voice from far down the creek hollered, "Time."

He sat on a weedy knob alongside the creek fifty feet away, where he'd floated to under the surface and then slipped out while I waited. He'd been sitting there watching me. I crawled back out of the water and sprinted along the embankment toward him.

"You shithead!" I yelled.

He fell over in the grass, laughing. I dived on him, furious and relieved at once, and managed, because he was laughing so hard, to get him into the headlock he'd taught me to throw.

"Fucker!"

"You shoulda seen your face," he said into my armpit.

"Dick," I said. He laughed harder.

Bank managed somehow to get to his hands and knees and then to pull himself to his feet, lifting me on his shoulders with my arm still wrapped around his head. He ran back up along the creek toward the pool, carrying me. As we approached I saw what was coming. I began to yell. He yelled, too, a war cry, as he leapt from the grassy shoreline to the rocks, and then out into the air.

For a moment we hung there somehow, together, impossibly suspended in that dazzling light before continuing onward in our arc.

The summer of 1970, a year later, after sixth grade, was to be our last at the pool in the Wilderness. Bank had a girlfriend, so I didn't see as much of him as I would have liked. On our first day back at the pool in June, I saw that sometime in the preceding months he'd developed body hair. He didn't seem the least bit self-conscious about it but I was fairly shocked, not just at what it looked like on him but at the thought I'd have it soon enough myself.

Then it was September and we began walking the mile or so to the junior high. And here in this new building, with ten times the number of students we were used to and classes that changed every hour, a surprising thing happened: Bank and I fell apart so quickly, it seemed as if we had barely known each other. He made the football team and that defined his existence. I joined the band, having taken up the saxophone in the fifth grade, and there I found more friends than I could hold inside my head. Band weirdos, we were called.

After junior high Bank went off to a Catholic parochial school. Because he was a foster child the church paid for it. I stayed in the city system, at Warren Harding High School, which was just across a wide ten-acre field from the junior high. Also around this time Bank changed foster families and so moved away from the Baxters and from our neighborhood. He still lived in the far west corridor somewhere, but I remember seeing him only a few times in those four years, and always in passing: at a dance in our gym after a basketball game, hanging out at the mall, driving around the neighborhood. He had, by the time he was sixteen and a half, a jacked-up muscle car, a damaged orange Plymouth Road Runner he'd bought cheaply and begun to repair. Once or twice he brought it over for my father to see. They worked on it together out in the shop but I was too busy, I guess, to even go out and say hey.

I'd had at one time high plans of going off to college somewhere famous and far away, Johns Hopkins in Baltimore, I thought, or anywhere in the Ivy League, or clear out to Stanford. In the end, though, whether because of a crisis of confidence or a sudden diminishment of ambition, or — most likely, I think — that strange aimless contrariness that afflicts some seventeen-year-olds, I started classes that fall at Libbey University, about seven miles due east of my high school.

Bank, meanwhile, had joined the Marines. So there it was. I, the whiz kid who was supposed to go out and conquer the world, still lived in the bedroom where I'd grown up. Bank, meanwhile, who had always been headed for a blue-collar job, lived in either West Germany or somewhere in the Caribbean, depending on who was telling the story.

20

Midnight. We've just finished coffee and sandwiches at a cop hangout called Emilio's, on Riverside in the Far North End, and are pulling out of the lot onto the side street when a man steps up to the curb and waves us down.

"Renta," Bank says. A private security guard, working the lot at Emilio's. With all those cops inside, eating and drinking, it would be an embarrassment to have the cars in the lot getting broken into.

The man leans in the window toward Bank and says, "It's the Bankster. Hey, my man."

"How you doin, Frank?" says Bank.

"Awright, you know. What you up to?"

Bank shakes his head.

"Hey, listen, you know about this place here?" Frank points to the old house just beyond Emilio's fenced-in lot, a huge clapboard Victorian, sagging and badly in need of paint and shingles.

"Here?"

"They running outta there."

"Right here?" Bank says. "The fuck they are. Who is?"

"I seen a bunch of 'em I know, Bobby B., Bobby T., Elrod. You know them guys?"

"Yeah," Bank says.

"And that punk runner, Sleepy, been shuffling around out front. You know what that means."

Bank nods.

"Couple other ones I recognize."

"They got balls, anyway," says Bank. "Twenty cops sitting a hundred feet away."

"They jus' stupid."

"This is apartments?"

"Yeah, probably five, six families in there. And they running right out the front door."

"All right, my man," Bank says. "You take it easy."

"Awright." Frank slaps his hand on the door before Bank pulls away and says, "Hey, you know you my hero."

Stu had sent me home in the afternoon immediately after our conversation, since I was coming back for the night shift. He told me not to call Bank, that he'd let him know what was going on. So when I came on at eleven I felt nervous, not knowing what exactly Bank knew, not knowing how he'd react to my being forced on him. But when I walked past the night clerk and the sighing coffeemaker into the mostly darkened suite of cubicles, he saw me coming and just nodded and grinned a little and said, "Heya, Big Mack." Like it was just another shift.

He knew about the print, I could tell. He didn't say anything right away, but I knew. It hung there in the air between us, like a bad tragedy or great good fortune, unaddressed but all-permeating.

What has surprised me most is how calm he's acting. I imagined I'd find him all worked up, frothing at the mouth, itching worse than ever to get out and inspire some discourse, how I'd have to try to hold him back now that this link to his own Jamie had been revealed. But the effect is just the opposite. He drives and doesn't say much. He seems to want mostly to think. And when he talks to people, even on the street, there seems to be an almost gentle quality to his voice. In a way, this frightens me more than if he were yelling and swearing and beating on the dashboard.

We come out of the North End neighborhoods onto Lagrinka Avenue, the old heart of the district that bisects it into the Near North and Far North. A few of the old Polish meat shops still operate along here, selling their kielbasa and kapusta and czarnina, still making a go, but their windows carry heavy black grates now, the doors have been reinforced with steel plating and triple locks, and they all close by four o'clock. Lagrinka has become predominantly a strip of bars and carryouts.

We've gone five or six blocks when Bank suddenly gases the car up into the lot of a closed-up service station and whips out into the street again, headed back the way we came. He pulls up alongside the far curb and turns his headlights off.

We sit. Then someone taps on my window. I jump. He'd slipped up alongside the car from the rear without my seeing him. A good example of why I never liked it on patrol. I don't have those instincts. You let them sneak up like that, sooner or later you're going to get clocked.

But Bank does not react except to say, "Crack it." I roll down the window.

A greasy man with nappy, smelly hair that sticks straight up from his head pushes his face inside.

"Hey, yo, Bank, my man."

"Hey, Sleepy," Bank says. "How you doin'?"

"Awright, awright, you know."

Sleepy the runner. Sleepy hangs out on the street, nodding to passersby, signing to traffic, subtly advertising the product. A buyer pulls up, flashes a couple fingers, say, meaning a twenty-dollar rock, hands him the cash, Sleepy runs inside one of the buildings behind him, an apartment building or flophouse or a bar or a porn store, then comes back a minute later with the order. Nothing more than that.

Runners never carry clips of bottles or any other kind of volume beyond a few grams, a couple of rocks, so if they get picked up the most they have on them is the personal-use amount, well under the legal minimum bulk volume, so they cop only a fourth-degree felony. And usually, even if they do get collared, they turn up clean in a search, because they carry the bottle in their hand and when they see the Man coming, they drop it and crush it under their shoe.

Runners make a certain amount of cash, but they also take a kind of commission — between the room where they make the purchase and the sidewalk where they turn it over to the buyer, they'll stop somewhere and pinch a corner off each rock. Each pinch is enough to keep their ride going just a little longer, another fifteen minutes or so, and in this way, combined with the cash they make, they'll stay high the whole night.

Because they're the go-betweens, runners tend to know pretty much everybody both on the street and off, and who's up to what. Because they're stone pipeheads they're also always broke and desperate to turn any coin they can, in any way they can. This combination makes them A-level snitches. Sleepy is one of Bank's.

"Busy night," Sleepy says. "You gone watch awhile?"

"Nah," says Bank, "not tonight. Listen, where you been? I been looking for you around here."

"I been round."

"Bullshit you have," says Bank. "I know where you been. Up there by that house on Collins, behind Emilio's. You getting stupider or what?"

"What?"

"You know who goes there. Just 'cause you know me don't mean nobody else'll cut you any slack."

"Shit. I know."

"Well, the word's out. Somebody's gonna get pissed off, you guys flaunting the business under their noses, and they're gonna take you all down. You stay the fuck away, hear?"

"Awright, man. Awright."

"That's a favor, me telling you like this."

"I hear you. You the man. You my hero."

"Yeah. Now listen, I got something else on my mind. You heard anything about a priest called Father Hector Morales?"

"Priest?" Sleepy says.

"He's gone missing."

"Yeah?" Sleepy said. "I own know."

"Awright. How 'bout this girl that got grabbed over to the East Side? Tamara Shipley?"

Sleepy has some muscular disorder that has unsprung his eyelids. They hang down all the time, making him look more like a heroin junkie or a gone alkie than a pipehead. I've never been able to read anything from his face. And this time is no different, but his voice sounds a little excited.

"Oh, yeah."

"Yeah what?"

"I own know."

"What'd you hear?"

"Nuffin'. Jus' she got took."

"Her brother, Emilio Salano, was doing a little business. They call him Eddie Munster. He was maybe working for somebody trying to cut in over there. I don't know."

"Dey cut his ass. Them spics some *nasty* mu'fuckas. So you back into nar-cotics, now, huh?"

"What?" said Bank. "Nah."

"Din why you wanna know?"

"I'm just asking."

"Yeah? And you think some priest be sellin' shit?"

"No, fuck no. He just ain't showed up in a

few days. He knew the girl."

"Maybe dey done cut his ass too."

"Yeah, maybe, Sleepy."

"I own know."

"Well, listen, this is big time crime stopper. You give up info leading to that girl, it's like five long."

"Ho, shit." Sleepy's eyes opened a little wider. "And nese others in it too?"

"I don't know what the fuck's going on," Bank says. "Maybe."

"Maybe not," Sleepy said.

"Don't know."

"I can ask aroun'," Sleepy said.

"Yeah. That's the idea."

"Fi' long?"

"Only if it leads to the girl. But, you know, I'll slide you some you get anything."

"Shit, I be out looking, din," Sleepy said.

"Awright," Bank said. "Awright."

Two-thirty. We're downtown, just pulling into the ER at St. Jerome's, where Bank wants to visit a crack whore with a terrible gash across her forehead. This woman gave the hospital personnel and the cops who interviewed her a verbal ID that didn't scan anywhere. She had no license, nothing on file, zippo. They called in another detective and the woman gave him a different ID. Still zip.

But the girl did give up the first name of her boyfriend, who she said had clubbed her and that's how she got the cut. The name was Rodney, but she wouldn't say anything else. She just wasn't talking.

Bank and I were up in the suite by chance, running some paperwork, when the detective who got the call flashed a Polaroid of this girl with a big long hole in her head and her eye all swollen up. Bank glanced at it and said, "I know her."

"She's not giving up nothing," said this other detective, who was called Buster.

"I know her," Bank said. "Ah, shit, I can't tell you her name right off. But that boyfriend. I know who that is," he said. "Rodney something. *Rot*-ney. *Rot*-ney. Shit. I know. He goes by Knucklehead. Put that in."

And sure enough, Knucklehead brought up in the computer an immediate hit on Rodney Green, which led to a printout not only of his sheet of priors and his current stats, but a color laser copy of his ugly mug too.

"Old Knucklehead," Bank said. "Mack, let's go see this girl."

So in the ER, where this scared little whore will not say boo to anyone, it's really kind of a touching thing. Bank goes right in while some young pretty white lady resident sews up the cut, and he takes up this girl's hand and leans right over in her face, blocking the view of the doctor, and says, "Hey, hon. How you doin'?"

The girl looks at him a moment and says, "I know you."

"Sure you do," says Bank. "I'm Bank. Bank Vault. Detective Arbaugh. I was the one come over that time Rot-ney threw that dog off the roof and broke its leg. Remember that?"

"Oh, yeah," she says.

"So, old Knucklehead Rot-ney done cut you."

"Uh-huh."

"We gotta know your full name, hon, so's we can run the complaint and go arrest his old self."

"He hurt me agin."

"He won't hurt you. I'll kick his sorry ass myself, I have to."

"Yeah?"

"Yeah."

"Okay," she says, and gives it right up to him, her real name and address, which we phone in so Buster can run it down.

And then, here's the remarkable thing, just as we're getting ready to go, the girl says, "Hey, Bank. I tell you sumpin'?"

"Sure, baby."

"You know that little girl got took? Over the East Side? Tamara?"

"Oh, yeah. We looking all over for her."

"I own know her. I heard her name, though, aroun', you know. On the street."

"Yeah? What about her?"

"I own know. Kinda weird. Why people be talkin' 'bout her?"

He looks at her for a moment. "You mean they were talking about her before she got took?"

"Yeah."

"Saying what?"

"I own know."

"No idea."

"Nah. Jus' talkin' 'bout her." She looks away from him.

"You hear something, you call me?"

"Yeah."

Back in the car I say, "What was that about? What did she mean?"

Bank shrugs. "Who knows." But the way he says it, I think maybe he does know. Something at least. Or suspects something. Or is on the edge of figuring something out. But he's not talking yet.

I look over at him, at the waxy hands in the fingerless gloves on the wheel, the melted neck, the scars on his jaw, which tightens and relaxes as he drives.

For the second time tonight I feel the dynamic of Bank and the city circling each other over this girl. What's happened is that the jolt of the link to Jamie has shocked him into patience. Bank's working the case as surely as I am riding along with him. He just isn't chasing it anymore, trying to beat it into submission, into revealing itself. Instead, he's letting it come in to him. Which it will do. The nighttime city is his city. He knows its cadences and echoes better than anyone out here. And it's talking to him. If I listen, I can just begin to hear it too.

21

Bank began an indefinite leave of absence from the force so he could focus on the search for Jamie. His energies were given over to its various aspects: conferences with other cops and with the FBI; combing through the phone tips that were still trickling in, looking for the one lead that would prove worthwhile; helping distribute pictures of Jamie around the city, the state, the region, and to the organizations that would get them out nationally; using the press interest, while it lasted, to keep stories in the paper and on television. Bank even hired a private investigative firm to look in different ways. But he knew that the chance of finding her alive faded more with each passing day.

And so, in August, when Jamie had been gone a month, Bank and Sarah rented an old Deco-style apartment in toward the heart of the city, on the southern edge of the huge and beautiful Heron Park, opposite the river and its tenebrous ravines, on a redbrick street called Morris Hill, near the public golf course. This course, though not very well maintained, had been well laid out over steep hills and drops, with fairways that wound between dense stands of old-growth pine and oak and several ponds. The river ran through parts of it as well. Another worn brick-surfaced road cut through the center of this section of the park, but it had been closed to traffic and was now part of the bikers' and joggers' domain. Around the entire five-mile perimeter of the park the city had laid a six-foot-wide asphalt ribbon, a footpath.

One side of Morris Hill was open, nothing but park spreading out away from it. The apartment buildings lined the other side, none higher than four stories, none more than eight units, none newer than fifty years old, most in their seventies. This had once been a grand place to live, a single neighborhood away from the grand Old West End, where the original industrial magnates and engineers, the inventors and manufacturing geniuses and financiers and hustlers who built this city, all lived. Morris Hill, I imagine, was where they would have sent their children when they cried out for a place of their own. An elegant pied-à-terre on the park, not too many blocks away from Daddy's money. I envision the great motorcars that would have pulled up to some of these buildings of a fine evening.

Then in the forties the war came, and after

that the GIs looking for jobs and houses for their new families, and so the sprawl of squat bungalows began and spread west from the manufacturing plants at the edge of the downtown clear to this park, hives built for all the returning soldier-workers who were glad to get them, and who would live there for the thirty years of their factory careers, and then die there too. But by then the ambience of this place had already long since been lost.

I sat, sometimes, in those weeks of August and early September, at a picnic table in the park across Morris Hill, looking up at the third-floor south corner window of one of these buildings. I could occasionally make out Bank as he stood there, staring out, but I rarely spotted Sarah (although later it was she who told me most of the details I know of that time). I thought of going up and knocking, but then stopped myself, unwilling to interrupt the solitude they seemed to need.

From the scuffed maple-floored living room of the apartment they could see into an open corner of the park where rusted grills stood on single stork legs, surrounded by weathered picnic tables. The window here was wide and tall, forming nearly the entire outside corner of the room but composed of numerous small panes of glass, each encased in a thick lead border, so the effect was that of looking through many windows rather than one.

The interior wall of the living room was nicely curved rather than angular and led smoothly around into a dining area defined by a bay window jutting out over the side street. The bathroom, down a short hallway past the single bedroom, was still done in its original coral-and-black checkerboard of ceramic tiles.

I know Bank thought it would seem strange to people that they would rent such a place, since they lived only a few miles away. And truly they couldn't offer up a very good explanation, other than that it was a thing they needed then, a quiet place away from their lives, insulated by the city around it. And those few miles made quite a difference. The village of Heron Hills lay west of the low brick buildings lining the busy city thoroughfares and the old tract houses that spread between them, west still of the decay that had crept out from the central city, west of the university and the worn-out shopping strips of the fifties and sixties. But here these things surrounded them. The Hills was, of course, a quieter, more peaceful place in the common sense. But people knew them. The press knew them. Now they sought relief from a different sort of noise, Bank and his wife, Sarah. They did not install a phone.

The house where they'd lived for nearly six years had taken on an unexpected aura in Jamie's absence. It seemed new to Bank, and when he mentioned this to Sarah she said it did for her too. He said it was as if the whole place, the furniture and rugs they knew so well, the banister and kitchen appliances, had all just been installed. He found himself touching things, running a hand along the dining room table or the piano and marveling at their novelty. He remembered the way the sunlight fell on them and how that reminded him of his own childhood, when the light had had a more memorable quality to it.

The apartment, on the other hand, didn't seem that way at all. It had been lived in for decades, had grown comfortable with all sorts of people, and they could feel that about it. The floorboards had been worn white inside the front door and the windowsills all scarred with the burn marks of forgotten cigarettes. The place allowed them to relax, to feel unself-conscious in a way they found they could not in their own home or around their friends or family.

It had no air-conditioning. In the hot afternoons of the days they spent there, they would lie propped up on the narrow bed, half the size of the king they had at home, careful so that their bodies did not make contact at any point, and sip Tanqueray and tonics while listening to the sounds of the city outside. It was at this time, Bank later said, that he began to train himself to remain motionless, barely even breathing, while he listened.

In the beginning they spent two or three days a week at the apartment. Bank indulged Sarah, accompanying her to plays in the city, a symphonic concert. They saw every film that was released that season except for those aimed at children or that had to do with children in jeopardy. They had always gone to films, since they'd started dating. It was the one quasi-cultural event they could both enjoy. Now it became a way of filling many of the hours of those days they wanted so badly to pass.

For a couple years some distance had been opening between them. They had been failing together, gradually but inexorably. Nothing traumatic, no screaming fights or flung dishes. Just coolness where there had once been heat; silence where their language had once flowed. They made love, still, although it was rarer than it had ever been, driven by a chillier, more detached passion, the passion of necessity rather than desire.

Now, in the rawness of this new world, they

practiced touching each other in the old way. I could picture them standing in the apartment's tiny galley kitchen with the refrigerator door standing open to cool the space, him putting his hand on the side of her neck, her tipping her head and hugging his hand like that, between her shoulder and cheek. They seemed to be trying to capture something from a time when they were poorer and had been starting out, living in a place like this, with a kitchen no larger than the foyer in their present house, from a time when the world was confusing and hard but full of boundless possibility.

Bank liked to sit and look out at the park, which had begun to pass in late August from a pretty, cultivated city place into a kind of wildness, of growth gone too far. The trees seemed impossibly heavy with leaves. The grass looked untended the day after it was mowed. Weeds seemed to rocket up from nothing overnight. And down from the walking path in the valleys where the river ran, the undergrowth was so thick and snarled and dark that Bank could not have seen into it more than a few feet, let alone make out the surface of the water.

But he did not want to see the water anyway, or think too long about river ravines or the things that could be hidden in them, especially in the darkest, most overgrown spots. He would come to a point of almost forgetting, for one second, what had happened, and then he would do something like glance into a deep pocket of woods during an evening walk, or watch a child playing with her parents in a meadow, and the cold vacuum would grip him again. He would stop in his walk and breathe as his stomach seized, as he trembled and went momentarily blind from the intensity of his rage. He had felt plenty of anger in his life, and acted on much of it, but he had never felt anything remotely as powerful as this. And nothing as bewildering, as sickening, as the fact that he had nowhere to put it.

It would have been less painful, I thought, for them to find a place somewhere else, where at least they did not have to look at the park, at the trees and the river where Jamie had last been seen. But he wanted to stay here, near it, in it whenever he could be.

I imagined them, one late night in the apartment, after four or five gin and tonics, making quiet love in some passionless manner they had developed: lying on their sides, say, his front to her back, without kissing once or talking, except for his repeated apologies. Him knowing it was only the drinks that allowed this at all. Her holding on to herself, straining not to give in, but unable finally to resist the gin and the need. And so, as he began his climax, she approached her own. He squeezed her, one arm beneath her neck, the other over her chest, and kept on until she cried out and let it end. Afterward she wept, and he continued to hold her.

On another night he went out, leaving her alone in the apartment, which she insisted she did not mind. He caused some surprise by showing up at Harvey's Bar, the cop hangout across the southern end of the park from his apartment. I happened to be there. The other cops, especially the detectives, I think, felt awkward. None of them had spoken with him at all since the disappearance. And no one could think of much to say now.

But Bank didn't want to talk. He wanted to drink and so we drank with him, five or six of us lined up at the bar, watching a game on the TV. Sue set us up as we needed, every third round free, the standard deal for cops. Bank only nodded to me at first. After he'd had a few, though, he got a little friendlier, pounding my shoulder as he walked past to hit the head, or buying me a round now and then and raising a glass toward me, in a toast to nothing but getting drunk. But we did not talk much, and said nothing about anything meaningful.

I left early, not long after midnight, as Bank had said he'd meant to do, but I heard later that he'd outlasted everyone and closed the place. Instead of driving, he decided to walk home by cutting straight through the park, normally a dangerous journey at 2:00 A.M. But on this night, Bank said, he felt protected. Not just protected, but invincible. Of course that was the alcohol in him, he knew, but it was more than that. It was an aura he had. The aura of I'm drunker than you, of little left to lose, of come on with that knife, motherfucker.

"Think about it," Bank told Sarah the next day, after she found him sleeping slumped against the wall just inside the front door. "What's scary about a place like that? No lights, and no people except the bad guys you don't want to run into. No help nearby. You're in the wilderness of the bad city. Only, the thing is, last night, I was the guy you'd be afraid of. No banger or pipehead robber would come near me."

"I didn't know they asked you first for your resume," Sarah said.

"It's an attitude," Bank told her. "A smell. I know what it is."

Sarah did not seem angry over his staying out and getting drunk. He didn't know whether to take this as a sign of hope or of defeat. She stood in the little kitchen while he talked, frying eggs and perking coffee and not looking at him, and the good smells made Bank's stomach hurt with its emptiness.

With this apartment they sought newness, rebirth. Together. At least that's what Bank thought then. Eventually he would come to believe that Sarah knew already what they were really doing. She was, after all, in his opinion, magnitudes more perceptive and self-aware than he. But it took some time for him, during which she gradually pulled herself away from their days in the apartment and back to their home in Heron Hills. Sarah resumed her teaching. She came to the apartment less and less often. Entire weeks began to pass without her showing up there.

Bank, though, found that he was not able to do that, to pull himself away. In fact it was the opposite with him — by the time Sarah started teaching again, he was spending more nights alone in the apartment than he spent at their house. He needed to drink gin and watch from the windows. He needed to practice staying still, barely breathing, eyes closed, so that he could hear everything the city said.

It was a little later in the year when he finally came to understand that, although they had rented the apartment together, it had always been meant for him alone. It was to be his new home.

22

Three A.M. We spin through the East Side looking for Sleepy's equivalent, a Bank Arbaugh snitch, over in that part of town, but it's zipped up tight except for the string of bars on Woodlawn Avenue with their college kid patrons. No gangsters hanging anywhere. The East Side has been heavily hit since Tamara Shipley, patrols and detectives and Tac officers all beating on doors and watching corners, dragging in anybody they get their hands on. So of course word has gone around to stay off the street until the firestorm blows over. Bank grumbles at this hamhandedness. He says it just muddies the water so people who know what they're doing can't see what's what.

In the deepest night, around four, I doze while Bank drives. I worked nearly a full day shift and by the time I got home and ate and geared down, I only napped for about an hour before Peggy had to wake me to get ready to come back on. Naomi wasn't home for dinner. When I went downstairs, just before I had to leave, her light was out and she appeared to be asleep.

Bank keeps it quiet for me, so I manage to snooze for another jumpy hour or so.

In the dirty sunlight of earliest morning we circle north once more onto Lagrinka and immediately spot Sleepy gesturing wildly with his head for Bank to pull over. But when he does Sleepy backs off and pushes his hands toward us, waving Bank away again. Then he walks up the street. Bank pulls ahead, up into a Dumpster-lined alley on the next block. It's daylight now. If someone's around, watching, Sleepy doesn't want to be seen chatting with the Man.

He shuffles into the alley a minute later and hangs his head inside Bank's window this time.

"What's up?"

"I done heard somethin' 'bout that girl."

Bank tenses at this. His jaw tightens and his hand moves toward the wheel, ready to go if Sleepy names a locale. But it's nothing like this, nothing like what either of us would have guessed.

"Some ladies working round here, you know. We get to talkin'. One'a them name Atwinda say she know 'bout that girl."

"What's she know?"

"She wun't tell me. She say if you paying, she want some too."

"She around here?"

"Yeah."

"Let's go."

"I own know." Sleepy looks behind him. "I best bring her down here."

"Well, go," says Bank. "Hurry the fuck up."

Sleepy waits a moment at the window.

"Uh-uh," Bank tells him. "I gotta hear it first."

Sleepy shuffles a little faster back out toward the street, doing his version, I guess, of hurrying.

Five minutes pass. It's still pretty dark here in this narrow alley. Bank plays with the spotlight, aiming it out through the windshield and firing it up, seeing what retiring nocturnal creatures he can catch in the beam. No humans, but at one point he catches a monstrous rat crawling over the lip of a Dumpster. It freezes in the sudden light, its black-hole eyes glaring at us.

"Look at the size of that fucking thing," says Bank.

"I had a black Lab that big, once," I say.

"No shit," he says.

He kills the light again. We wait, watching the sky above the buildings in front of us lighten a little more.

Then we hear the shuffling again. Bank flips the light on and catches Sleepy, who holds his hands up over his face and says, "Turn that shit off."

A woman steps out from behind him. She has that old piped-up nobody-home look, the glassy-eyed, dull, affectless demeanor. Though it's chilly out, she wears only a thin, sleeveless cotton minidress, a pair of spandex shorts, and ratty old white canvas tennis shoes.

"Go on," Sleepy says, pushing her at the car. "This Bank. He awright. You tell him."

"How much?" she says.

"I gotta hear it first," says Bank.

"Shit."

"Jus' tell," Sleepy says to her. "I said he awright."

"I own know," the girl says. "I jus' know she a bad girl."

"Who?" Bank says.

"That girl they be lookin' for. Tamara."

"A bad girl?"

"Yeah."

"What does that mean?" says Bank. "She's twelve years old. What kind of a bad girl can she be?"

"Whatchoo think," says the girl. "Bad girl's a bad girl. You know what bad girls do."

"You this Atwinda?"

"Yeah."

"You a bad girl too?"

She laughs and touches the inside of her fingers to her lips. "I guess so," she says.

Bank looks over at me, then back out the window. We're all silent for a moment, contemplating this, rolling with it, but not really believing it.

Bank says, "You telling me Tamara Shipley turns tricks?"

The girl laughs. "Yeah, baby."

"She's out here working the streets?"

"I own know about that."

"Then what are you talking about?"

The girl looks at Sleepy.

Bank says, "Twenty bucks, but you gotta tell me."

"Fi'ty."

"Here." He sticks a twenty-dollar bill out through the window. She grabs it. "If it's good, you get another one when I hear it."

"We out on the street, you know," she says, "some mens looking for something . . . unusual. How dey gone find it? Ain't in no Yellow Pages. So dey stop a girl on the street who out sellin, and say, 'You know anybody who do such and such?' Whatever it is dey looking for, showers or pain or whatever. You know? Or some young. Some twelve-year-old. We out there, we know."

"So you tell."

"Some does."

"Not you?"

"Not 'bout no childrens. Tha' sick. I own agree with that."

"Well, good for you," says Bank. "Now, what about the girl?"

"When she got took, you know, everybody talking 'bout it. Some ladies I know said dey sent some mens round to her."

"Tamara?"

"Yeah."

"Where'd your friends send these men?"

"I own know."

"When was this?"

"Not long. Couple weeks. Maybe a month."

Bank looks over at me again, his mouth hanging open. Even he is thrown by this. Even he is at a loss for words.

"Tha's all I know 'bout it," Atwinda says. "I own know like who dey had to see or nothin'."

"Where're these friends now?"

The girl looks off. "Right now, I own know."

Bank pulls another bill from his wallet and hands it over. "I need to know where they sent these men. You can find out, or I'll talk to them myself. It's worth a lot more than forty bucks. You know what I'm saying?"

Sleepy and the girl both nod. Bank holds

out another twenty, which Sleepy accepts. I know this is out of Bank's own pocket. He won't be putting in for any departmental reimbursements. This is personal, now.

The girl leaves but Sleepy hangs in the alley next to our car, brushing his fingers against it every now and then.

"I ain't giving you no more cash," Bank says to him, finally. "What you want?"

"Sum else," he says.

"Yeah?"

"You know some half-brother, half-white mu'fucka name Abel Jackson?"

Bank has been sort of slouched over the wheel, but now he sits up straight and looks out at Sleepy. "Yeah. We go back."

Sleepy says, "You talkin' 'bout that girl's brother maybe movin' some shit."

"Eddie Munster."

"I hear Abel been spreadin' it around a little over there, on n'East Side. Maybe tryin' cut hisself out a little piece. Git it in wit' dem greasy spics."

A few years back Bank believed Abel had perped a series of nighttime B & E's in Central North — very clean jobs, no excess damage, always either houses in which no one was home or unattached garages. Which meant the thief had done some homework, stakeouts, phone calls, so he knew what he was going into. The thefts involved only clean goods, easily fenced — tools, gold, electronics — and, of course, cash and pills. In addition, Bank knew Abel was doing some small-time narcotics trafficking. Bank managed to bring him down once on an aggravated assault rap, when he split a girl's head open with a beer pitcher and took some of her change, but Abel walked when the only witness, the girl, failed to show. So after that Bank took any call he could that let him blow a little smoke up Abel's tailpipe. It had become a kind of mission with him.

Bank hands Sleepy another twenty and we leave.

It's time to go in, but Bank just drives us around aimlessly for a little while longer, while we both ponder what we've just heard, thinking about Tamara and Abel Jackson and Father Hector Morales. And poor Jamie.

Though I catch the end of the task force meeting this morning, I do not, at Bank's suggestion, speak of what we've learned. We don't know if it's true. Atwinda, if that was even her name, could have just been scamming some cash. So I'll wait.

After the meeting I find my way to my car, and westward on the e-way to the Alcore exit, and west again on Brentcroft. As I'm pulling onto my street, I notice two teenagers squatting against the low brick wall that announces the happy name of the subdivision. They are dressed in black, with black hair, and they're both smoking cigarettes. I'm past them, almost to my house, when it strikes me that one of the pair was Naomi. I pull the car into reverse, and back up hard to the sign.

When I jump out, they struggle to their feet to scramble away from this madman coming after them.

"Dad," Naomi says. Then she looks at the smoke in her hand, as if someone else had placed it there, and tosses it away. Her face flushes deeply. She thinks she's in trouble for it, that this is why I've come to a screeching stop and leapt from my car. Normally, she'd be right. But now isn't normally.

"Is this Zelda?" I ask, pointing at her friend.

"What?" Naomi says, then, "No." The girl gives her a funny, confused sort of look. "This is Janice, Dad."

"I have to talk to this girl, this Zelda. Today, Naomi. It's urgent now. It's . . . I just have to talk to her."

"Dad," Naomi says, "can we — can we talk about this later?"

"No," I say, "we cannot. It's important. What's her last name?"

"She . . . I promised her I wouldn't say. I told you, she's nervous."

"You think I can't find out in two seconds?"

"Dad," Naomi says.

"She into something?" I say. "I don't care. I'll protect her. She selling a little pot, something like that, I don't care. She shoplifts. I don't care."

Naomi's eyes are tearing up, now. Passersby on Brentcroft are slowing to stare at this grown man in a confrontation with two punk girls. A woman in the corner house has pulled her front drapes back to peer out at us.

"Okay," I say, holding up my hands. "Okay. I'm really tired. And confused. I didn't mean to upset you. All right?"

She nods as a big tear drips off her cheek.

"But, Naomi, I have to talk to this girl today, okay? I'm going to get some sleep, and then I'm coming over to the school. You have any classes together?"

"Mm, not really."

"Well, I'll find you. Then we'll find her. No threats. Just talk, okay?"

Naomi nods and wipes at her eyes.

"I'm sorry," I say again. I nod at Janice, then get back in my car and go home, where I can reflect on what an asshole I must seem to my daughter.

23

I saw very little of Bank in those first few months after Jamie went. In October, finally, I went up to the apartment after Sarah had told me she'd pulled out for good. I parked down at the lower end of Morris Hill and walked through the sharp fall day up to his building. The trees had not yet come into their color, but I remember being suddenly aware of all that foliage surrounding me, of the smell of the air, rich and pungent already with the change of seasonal death and its promise of renewal. It felt like years since I had been around autumn trees.

It struck me as odd, knowing this building as well as I did, that I had never been in it before. I walked up the three flights of creaking stairs and knocked at the corner door. I heard footsteps inside, then nothing. I knocked again. When the door opened, I knew then I had made a mistake in coming.

He looked as if he'd gained fifteen or twenty pounds, although I don't know now if it was really that much, or just the impression given by his bloated face. His pink eyes squinted out at me from their swollen beds.

The apartment was stifling, the temperature near eighty, I guessed, so he wore only gym shorts and a T-shirt. The flesh of his arms and his chest seemed to sag. He'd even begun to carry some weight around his belly.

I did not understand at first how this change could have happened so quickly, but the next sensation that struck me was the stale, sweet stink of alcohol permeating the room. It hung in the air, and on him. I noticed then that he was sweating and flushed, and realized that he was drunk.

He had made one end of the living room into his command center. A set of steel shelves stood against one wall, and stacked upon it were thick manila files and typed reports, phone books and directories. Next to this sat a computer and printer. I hadn't known he even knew how to use one. The wall was covered with tacked- or taped-up pieces of paper: phone numbers, photographs, notes to himself, pages from reports with single lines highlighted or circled.

Other than this the place was barely furnished — a single couch in the living room across from a small TV on a stand, a single floor lamp, the floor just bare wood. In the dimness farther inside — he had all the shades pulled — around the corner, I made out a little table and chair in the dining alcove.

"Any progress?" I asked, but he just shook his head.

We talked for a few minutes. I began to sweat. When he turned on the television, I sat with him for a little while longer, but we did not talk about much else, and I left shortly afterward.

I realized I should go and see him again, soon. That even though he needed to grieve in his own way and on his own time, and that he alone would know when it was finished, I had a duty to try to pull him out somehow. Or at least to sit with him. To listen or not. To be nearby.

But I did not go up again. As the weeks passed, a strange lassitude gripped me. I fell into a rut, a kind of reverse momentum in which work occupied every hour I wanted to give it, and though I felt badly for it, I did not go where I should have gone.

I spoke with Sarah, though, during this time. She'd call me from the house, or have me out for lunch. We talked of small concerns, mostly, or about her and Bank's lives after Jamie. Once or twice, in moments that touched tangentially upon the tragedy, we talked about the difficulties of simply moving on, of getting up each day and doing something.

One Saturday afternoon in the first week in

November, when I was just putzing around the house, the doorbell rang. Sarah stood on the stoop, huddled into her coat.

"I saw your car," she said.

In the kitchen, where I'd been cleaning, I poured her a cup of that morning's coffee. She sat quietly at the table while I worked. She wore a printed flannel dress over a turtleneck sweater and knit stockings, I remember.

She told me at one point that she had retained an attorney to draw up the paperwork to make the separation official, and to lead eventually to a divorce. It would be a simple matter, really. Bank could keep the Cherokee and whatever other personal items he wanted. He'd get some money from the house if she sold it. That was all. Bank's attitude toward all of this, the legal aspects, she said, was a vast indifference. He didn't care, he'd said, if she gave him anything.

When I was finished cleaning, I poured myself some of the thick, acidic coffee and sat down at the table with her.

"I like it here," she said, looking out the little window into the little fenced backyard. "It's nice."

"It's just a place to live."

"Families all trying to grow themselves up," she said.

She took a tissue from her purse and held it

against one eye, then the other. I waited, and finally she reached across the table and took my hand.

"Max," she said, "I have to leave here."

I nodded dumbly at her, the meaning not really getting through. I thought she meant my house.

"It just makes me tired, Max. All of it. Seeing people I know. Bank. The press. Looking in her room. I'm going to list the house."

"When will you go?"

She looked up at me and smiled sadly. "Very soon," she said. "I have to get away."

"I can understand that."

"I know you can. I know you. And I love you for that, Max. I do. I have."

"Come on," I said. I walked back into the family room and put in a tape I'd made of some old music we'd all grown up on. Sarah sat down on the couch next to me. She smiled at the music, and laid her head over against me, tucked in beneath my chin. I put my arm up around her shoulders. We did not talk after that. I could see the print of her dress sleeve against her wrist, and her pale hand resting in her lap, and her legs beyond that. If I turned slightly my face brushed her hair, which smelled clean and faintly of fruit. Her mouth was next to my chest, pressing on it so that I felt the heat and moisture of her breath.

Eventually her breathing deepened and slowed, its rhythm working beneath whatever song was playing. She grew heavier, her weight pressing into me. I shifted and slid her downward so that her head rested on my thigh.

The tape played itself over and over again on my machine, and finally the repetition of it, and of her breathing, put me to sleep as well.

A week later I got a note in the mail, written on fine expensive shell-colored stationery, the sort that's handmade, with rough edges and random particles scattered through the grain. It said:

Dear Max,

When you get this I will be gone. I'm staying with an old friend from college for a little while, in Indianapolis, just to clear my head. Then I'll decide what to do. I did not want to call and say good-bye. I thought of seeing you again, but it's easier not to. You've been a good friend to me, and I thank you for that. I'll miss you.

Love, S.

At the bottom she wrote "Temporary" and the phone number of whoever it was she was staying with.

I folded the note carefully and tucked it away in the top drawer of my dresser, so I would know where to find it, but I never called her at that number.

24

I swim upward toward a surface I cannot yet see. The water presses inward, dense and warm around me, but it is not silent. It hums, or buzzes, or rings. I cannot tell, exactly. I feel its pressure, its depth, but I do not feel it suffocating me. I listen to it. I breathe it in, tenuously at first, then deeply, and feel its heaviness inside me, pressing outward. Then the darkness begins to ebb slightly, revealing colors, greens and blues and far above them the golden yellow of daylight. The sound increases. I rise quickly now toward them both, the sound and the light.

Then I awaken, the phone ringing next to my head. The day shines brilliantly outside the bedroom window. I squint at its glare, and snatch the receiver from its cradle.

"Yeah."

Eleven fifty-six, the clock tells me. Noon. Peggy's out with the boys somewhere, I remember, which is why she didn't answer. Normally I turn the ringer off in the bedroom, but this morning I forgot.

"Dad."

"What?"

"Dad, it's me."

"Naomi? Where are you?"

"I'm at school, Dad."

"What's wrong?"

"Nothing. I'm at lunch."

"Lunch," I say, dumbly. "Naomi —"

"She's absent today."

"What?"

"She's not here."

"Who?"

"Zelda. Remember?"

"Zelda," I say. "Oh."

"You wanted to come over and talk to her. Remember? But she's absent today."

"Okay, Naomi."

"Okay. Bye, Dad."

"Naomi, wait."

"What."

"What's her last name?"

"I . . ."

"Or tell me where she lives."

"I don't . . . remember it, offhand. I'd have to look it up. I gotta go, Daddy. Bye."

"Naomi —"

I'm listening to the hiss of dead wires, then. I lie back on the pillow, listening still, holding the phone to my ear and watching the sunlight pour in. And I stay like this until the tone, raucous and irritating, cuts in.

★ ★ ★

Pat Grice is the dean of girls at Warren Harding High School, my alma mater, where Naomi goes now. I've known Pat for nearly fifteen years, since I first worked the western corridor as a patrol cop and she was a phys ed teacher who had a student one afternoon lay open the side of another girl's face with a razor blade. When I got my shield and moved to Juvenile, and Pat soon after moved into administration, we got to be good pals. Harding is not the school it was when I was a student here. The man himself, President Harding, grew up not too awfully far from here. I imagine what a shock it would be for him to watch, for a day or two, what goes on in this namesake of his. But it is no different than other urban public high schools. A secretary has asked me to wait in an outer office but it's not a minute before Pat opens her door, still talking on the phone, and waves to me. She holds a finger up as she finishes the conversation, then ushers me in.

The dean's office is the place students used to fear most. A thick oak paddle, with a series of symmetrical holes drilled through it, has been mounted on the wall behind where Pat sits, a warning to all who enter. But it's only a wall decoration now. Corporal punishment is all but gone from the public schools, as much

312

an anachronism as the kinds of petty pranks students once pulled to deserve it. Now the crimes are real — possession of drugs or weapons, assaults and rapes, grand theft, felony vandalism — and so we, the city police, do the real enforcing. This school has one full-time officer now all to itself. I stopped and spoke with him for a moment down in the lobby when I came in.

"Did we call you?" Pat says.

"No, no," I say, "this is my call. Um, a personal one."

"Naomi?"

"In a sense," I tell her. And then I explain the whole thing, Tamara Shipley, my conversation with Naomi, this Zelda character, and so on. She hears me out, then nods and folds her hands on her desk.

"There's no student here named Zelda," she says. "I can tell you that right now."

"I figured it wasn't a real name, anyway."

"So what you're saying is you want me to sleuth around a little, see who this girl is." Pat's always crisp and to the point. The chair across from her sits, by design, slightly lower than her own chair, so I find myself looking up at her.

I nod. "If it wasn't important —"

"No, I know," she says. "I can talk to some girls. Some of Naomi's friends, see what they say. But she'll find out, you know."

"I'll talk to her. She'll have to understand. I don't get this reluctance on her part, or how she thinks I won't find out anyway. I don't know what she thinks I'm going to do."

"She's fourteen, Mack," Pat says. "Only God and other fourteen-year-olds know how she thinks, and neither will ever tell us about it."

"Right," I say.

"I'll call you."

In the afternoon I run some errands I've been putting off, the hardware store, some library books to return. As soon as I pull into my garage and step from the car, I hear it. Seeping around the window frames, beneath the doors, through the very walls of the house: screaming. I wonder if the neighbors can hear it, too, because it's so loud this time. But they are probably not home from work yet, since it's only three-thirty in the afternoon.

I hurry to the back door, then stop before going in and close my eyes and breathe a moment. If it weren't for the boys in there, I feel like I might just get back in the car and leave again. But I do not. I turn the handle.

"You *bitch!*" Naomi screams. They're in the kitchen, the two of them.

"Don't you *ever* call me that again," Peg

hisses back through her teeth, her index finger directed at Naomi's face.

"You are! I don't care! You call *me* names."

"I do not."

"You just, *just* called me a thief. You're denying that now? Jesus Christ!"

"The money's gone, Naomi. I know I didn't use it. Mack never touches it. The boys didn't take it."

"And how do you know that?"

"I asked them."

"Well, you asked me too. You believe them but you don't believe me. So I'm a thief *and* a liar."

A moment of thick silence. "Well —" Peggy says.

"Oh, *fuck* this," says Naomi, and she stomps toward the basement door, the entry to her lair. But I am standing there, blocking it this time. She stops before me and crosses her arms over her chest, her lips pinched together in her fury, and she stares at the floor, waiting for me to move.

"What happened?" I ask.

Peg holds up an old pottery creamer we bought together at a flea market when we were still new to each other. She keeps it on the top shelf of one of the kitchen cupboards, and inside it she keeps the household petty cash, twenty or thirty dollars, usually. From it

315

now she pulls a single twenty.

"I deposited your check today," she says, "and took some cash out. Forty dollars. I put it all in here. Silly me."

Naomi shakes her head but says nothing.

"Where are the boys?" I ask.

Naomi makes a sound in her throat, and Peggy looks away from me as she points out through the window into the backyard. They're in their fort again, their tight little sanctuary from the violence. I feel as if I am falling, standing in my kitchen with the floor opening up beneath my feet, sucking me downward into the earth. I feel as if my life has done nothing but lead to this moment of grief and misery, of abject failure, of betrayed potential. I cannot even raise two boys without this for them to look at.

"I went to the hardware store," I say to Peg.

"What —"

I pull a ten and four ones from my pocket and hold them up.

"You never take this money," she says, sadly now, a little desperate as her eyes meet mine. "You never . . ."

I nod. She's not used to having me around during a weekday. I'm not part of the routine. "I just needed a few small things," I say. "I didn't want to write a check." I step aside so Naomi can go downstairs, but instead she bolts for the front door and runs outside.

At five Rick Simms calls from the Federal Building downtown. "You hear they're out looking for Rochelle Shipley?" he says.

"What happened?"

"You did," he says. He's a little out of breath, a little pumped. "Your call on that number in Chicago, the one you asked me to check out. I called them after we talked and gave them the deal, this girl, the number. Put in a request for someone to do a workup. They traced the number back to a house in the north city. A house, it turns out, but not a private residence. It belongs to an organization. So they put out a memo. Which this morning crosses the desk of certain agents who, it turns out, have been watching the place on and off for years. One of them just called me. This place is the headquarters," Simms says, "of an organization that helps relocate girls in trouble."

"Like pregnant?"

"Like abused," he says. "Like getting beat up or raped or whatever. In the home. On the street. They get these girls to some safe houses, where they can recover."

"Where?"

"That's the thing about it. The houses are all over, I guess. Like a network. Kind of

317

underground. Different people provide safe haven for these girls at different times. It all shifts. No one's really gotten a handle on it, except this house in Chi. But no girls stay there anymore, I guess. This place just coordinates. It's called the Sisters of Compassion."

"Catholic."

"No official connection to the church. The diocese there wants nothing to do with them. Couple of nuns started it in the late seventies. I guess they get some hefty private funding. Now it's different people running it all the time, all fragmented, so it's hard to trace out. Some of it's done on the Internet and like that. All kept very clandestine."

I say, "So why has the FBI been keeping tabs on them?"

"Figure it out. Where do these girls come from? They live with their parents, or if they're on the street, maybe they belong to somebody. People who might not be willing to let them go. These are cases where the system has failed. You know, if the authorities can intervene in an abuse situation, then they take the girl out. No problem. This group steps in when that doesn't happen, at least not as quickly as they think it should. It might involve a custody battle, that kind of thing, or overt danger. They've been known to go in and take these girls away."

"From their parents?"

"Usually, I'm told, in a situation like that, it's when one parent wants the girl made safe from the other. They arrange it. Someone with the group picks the girl up somewhere and off they go. Of course, that still raises all kinds of proprietary issues, the possibility of criminal charges, all that. Puts a new wrinkle in Tamara Shipley, doesn't it?"

"And Rochelle?" I ask.

"Googie went over there. Nobody home. I guess Katherine's out looking too."

By ten, when I'm ready to leave for work, Naomi has still not come home.

As I'm pulling out onto Brentcroft, I glance at the entrance to the subdivision, and in a weird replay of the morning I see her sitting there again, in her black-on-black, but alone this time. Not smoking. Just sitting, watching traffic. I wait at the stop sign and watch her. Eventually she looks over at me. For a moment we watch each other. Perhaps, I think, she is trying as much to understand me as I am to understand her. But that's not the case. We are both, I know, struggling mightily to understand Naomi.

I give her a little wave before I pull out into traffic, but she does not wave back. She looks at me stonily, angrily, as if I'm the one who's betrayed her somehow. And it occurs to me after I pull out that I have — at my behest Pat has been questioning Naomi's friends about Zelda. From the look on her face I can tell that Naomi knows.

25

Fall semester of my fourth but not quite senior year in college: I was in the library lounge smoking a cigarette, drinking a Coke for the caffeine, reading a political science text. A young woman I had not seen before walked in, looked around uneasily at the various Formica-topped desks along the outside walls, then chose a couch roughly across from the one into which I was deeply slouched. She had a nice face, distracting not so much for its attractiveness as for the pain it reflected. Her eyes looked a little swollen and red, but they were pretty eyes, dark and wide-set. She had dark hair, too, a sharp nose, and a pouty full-lipped mouth. I couldn't help but steal glances. Then a man came in and sat next to her, a big man with short hair and thick arms. He did not speak to her, simply stared across the room, as if she weren't there at all. I barely glanced at him. And then I felt him watching me, because he'd noticed me looking at his woman and he was going to kill me, I figured.

"Hey, shithead," he said.

Then he laughed, a big laugh coupled with

a big grin. The shock of seeing the adultness of his face, its squareness and manliness, the size and angle of the jaw, the heaviness of the brows, the fleshiness of the nose, struck me before anything, this face that to me still belonged to a little boy. But then that grin, I saw, was just the grin it had always been, cocky and broad and sincere.

"Hey, you dumb jock," I said back.

"You smoking that shit," Bank said. I looked at the butt between my fingers, shrugged, dragged on it one last time, and ground it out.

"Shit'll kill you," he said. He came over and yanked me up out of my couch. He stood what looked to be a full head taller than me. One huge hand enveloped mine and squeezed, while the other locked on my shoulder. Just like that, it was as it had always been between us, as if only a month had passed instead of nine years. And yet I saw in his face how much I had changed, and I wondered if he saw the same in mine. I had missed him, I realized. He was a part of me, a part of my history, of my family, and I knew I had been wrong to let him go.

"I heard you were going here," he said. "What're you doing?"

"Working for some lawyers," I said. "Going to law school in a year or two."

"Sounds about right," he said.

"You?"

"I was in the Marines, you know," he said.

"Semper Fi."

"Right on, Mack. I was an MP. You know that?"

"No."

"I really liked it."

"Yeah?"

"So I'm gonna be a cop."

"Hey," I said, and I smiled because it fit him so perfectly. Officer Bank.

"I'm waiting to get into the academy. Taking a few courses out here while I wait, on Uncle Sam's nickel."

"All right," I told him.

"Hey," he said. "This is Sarah Garrison. Sarah, this is my old buddy, Mack Steiner. We go way the hell back together."

I sat down on the low table in front of her and nodded and glanced again at her face. The nose was a little too angular, I decided, the mouth a little too pouty, but the eyes were knockout. I pulled out my pack of smokes, removed one, and noticed her watching me, so I shook another one free and held the pack toward her. She accepted the cigarette. I held a light out for her, and she cupped my warm, moist hand in hers, which was cool, and sucked on the flame and the whole time her eyes did not leave mine.

"Jesus," Bank said, somewhere off in the distance. "That shit'll kill you both."

He'd gotten back in June and met her in a club. She was twenty-four, two years older than Bank, nearly three years older than me. She lived with her parents in Heron Hills.

Her maiden name was Lyell, but when she was a senior at Kenyon College, in Gambier, Ohio, she'd fallen in love with a forty-nine-year-old divorced anthropology professor and married him, much to her father's chagrin. The prof suffered a massive cerebral embolism six months after their wedding. Though he did not die for another three months, he never regained consciousness and did not know at the end that Sarah was pregnant. She had, now, an eighteen-month-old daughter named Jamie.

It was not at all a mystery why Bank had been drawn to her, for not only was Sarah beautiful and well off and well educated, she was sensitive and careful and attentive. What was harder to fathom was her attraction to him, this beefy Marine with his nearly shaved head and his new tattoo and his muscles. I decided that it was probably that fact, that Bank was so unlike any boy-man she had ever dated at her private schools, and certainly as different from her dead professor as he could have been.

But beyond any of this they were clearly very much in love with each other. I kept coming back to the two raw emotions Bank inspired in people, even as a kid — love and fear — and added to that formula a third element: a fierce and violent loyalty to those he loved in return. Sarah seemed to rely on that loyalty, to need it, to seek it out. And Bank, in turn, seemed to want nothing so much as to give it, and to get it back.

Still, sometimes when I saw them around campus or on the occasions when we went out together, I gathered that they had just finished fighting. They seemed to exist at one extreme or the other — either they were locked together, whispering, laughing, touching; or they sat apart and barely spoke, and if they did, it was more at each other than to. Perhaps, I thought, this was just a natural consequence of the fact that their relationship was so intense, and so new.

I studied in the lounge most of the time because I could smoke there and drink coffee. Bank and Sarah tended increasingly to show up there, too, and would sit with me at whichever table or couch I was using. I noticed, though, that Bank had taken to leaving Sarah and me alone together for fairly long periods of time. She would read — good books: Charlotte Brontë and Pearl S. Buck and Doris Lessing — or write for a time in a notebook she carried, but inevitably she started talking to me until I stopped working and listened. Though this cut into my study time, I did not begrudge her the attention. I liked talking to her. Aside from all her attributes, she could also be dark mooded in the way I imagined all mysterious women were.

She eventually allowed me to see some of the flowing prose-poetry she wrote, full of images of loss and angst. It seemed to me at the time remarkably polished and perceptive. I grew more impressed with her. What I did not understand was why she was spending so much time with me, while Bank was in class.

The lounge had a kind of anteroom with soda, coffee, and cigarette machines. One afternoon I was walking out there for coffee, but stopped at the doorway to finish my cigarette. I heard Sarah's voice. She said, "I don't want to stay in here today. It's nice out."

"You can't wait an hour in here for me?" Bank said.

"Just meet me out there."

Silence. Then Bank said, "Stay with Mack."

"Bank —"

"Sarah." He paused, then said, "Please."

And then I got it. I was a baby-sitter. That's what it amounted to. Bank had me watching his woman so other guys wouldn't. For the first time I saw him as a purely muscleheaded asshole.

Why do you let him? I wanted to ask her, as we sat there together in the smoke. *Why would someone like you let anyone do that?* But I did not ask. Instead, I said, "Come on," and grabbed my cigs and left. She followed.

We walked through the library and out into a paved quad, and across that to a small café in the union where you could get, in those years, a large slice of cheese pizza and a good-sized beer for a dollar. We ate and then had another few beers, at the end of which she had revealed to me nothing at all about her and Bank, though I kept trying to steer the conversation around to him. She would have none of it, none of the comforting I imagined myself giving her. Instead, she talked about the graduate program in art history here at Libbey she was thinking of enrolling in, and how she loved art and wished she were more talented as a painter but that she knew she wasn't, and about writing and then about books, and finally language itself. We quoted to each other lines of prose and verses of poetry we loved. We were drunk, of course. But what struck me was how much she simply needed someone to talk to in this way. Because Bank, I knew, had no use for books or art or most discussion. It all struck him as a waste of time. Because it wasn't *doing* something.

I wondered again at the strange nature of the relationship between these two people.

At the end, when it was time to get back to the library to meet Bank, we picked up our things and walked out of the dim café and into the sun-pierced atrium of the union. I held doors for her and she brushed against me as she passed through them, so that I smelled her perfume and, beneath that, the native scent of her skin itself.

For the remainder of my last year of college we formed what to my mind was a rather strange triad, Bank, Sarah, and I — going out to dinner together for Lebanese or Greek or Hungarian, drinking late into the night at the Blind Pig near campus or at a better, darker, more dangerous bar called the Westgate Lounge farther into the city. Sarah and I would smoke and talk while Bank looked on, smiling, the beer working its way into our heads.

I didn't know why they wanted me along — it was they who asked me, most of the time — but I had an idea. One or two nights a week, while he was in the academy that winter,

Bank rode along with the detectives or patrol cops from downtown, and he left it to me to be with Sarah on those nights, going so far as to even suggest things for us to do. More baby-sitting. It amazed me that she'd allow it, and that he would just expect us to go along with it. But I loved going out with her, whether Bank was there or not, and so I didn't care what motives were behind it.

Bank was also still in the Marine Reserves, which meant that once a month, for a weekend, he had to go off to the Wright-Patterson Air Force base, near Dayton, and play MP.

One afternoon in March of that year, 1980, he found me in a study carrel up on the sixth floor of the library. He hung over the privacy wall of the carrel, his thick arms dangling down toward my books and papers, and said that he'd just realized something about the date of his reserve duty coming up that weekend. Sarah's twenty-fifth birthday fell on Saturday.

"Change it," I said.

"This is the Marines, Mack."

"Then you have to tell her. Get her something nice. Take her out. Celebrate early." He shook his head and hung there like some chastised dog. Then he said, "Whyn't you take her out?"

"Bank," I said, "I'm not going on a date with your girlfriend."

"Not a date, moron. Just out. For her birthday. So she's happy."

I felt myself growing angry.

"I can't."

"Mack, come on. Do me a favor. I'll cover it."

"You don't have to cover it. I can afford to take her out."

"All right," he said. "I owe you big." And he was already walking away.

Sarah called me that night.

"I was just looking forward to his being there," she said. At the party her parents were throwing at their condo in Heron Hills, she meant. Bank was to have met her relatives for the first time.

And then I heard myself speaking, but didn't believe it was me. "If you're looking for some company," I said, "we could grab dinner later on or something."

"That's so sweet, Max," she said. She had always called me that, my given name, Max. "But just come to the party."

Sarah did not come across as a spoiled child of the affluent, although she easily could have. She never seemed to me like other privileged children I've known. She had a hard and unbending edge to her attitude regarding work and money, a kind of discipline that one generally sees in those who have had to struggle for what they've earned. The kind of edge, for instance, that my father had. A self-driving, judgmental, parsimonious attitude. On the other hand, her family had been well enough off from the time she was a child so that she had come naturally to assume the world would work more or less the way she expected it to.

I went late, thinking that with dinner over things would be dying down. But the party appeared to have just hit its stride. Sarah's father, Don Lyell, threw an arm around my shoulders and said, "We've got all the hooch you can drink here, son. Good stuff too." He was a red-faced man who always seemed slightly boozy to me, but powerful, too, and capable of being damned mean if he had to. I never saw him that way, but I believed it was there when he needed it to be. The steel business, I imagined, would call for that now and then.

"Eat," Sarah's mother, Carol, instructed me, and shoved a plate into my hands. She struck me as a simple woman who'd been thrust into a life she had not anticipated. She seemed to enjoy the life but not to trust it, somehow, so that she needed always to remain just a bit wary.

I was introduced around as a friend of Sarah's. Some mistook me for this new boy they'd been waiting to meet, but when I told them, no, that wasn't me, they didn't seem to care one way or the other. It was a fine party. I ate a little of the good food and drank a lot of the good liquor and stayed until nearly midnight. Jamie, who was turning into a beautiful bright-eyed girl, ran excitedly among us until she fell asleep on a couch.

Afterward, Sarah rode down in the elevator with me and walked me outside, slipping her hand through my arm.

"Thank you, Max," she said. "It means a lot."

"Bank wanted to be here."

The parking area was bordered at the rear by tennis courts surrounded by a high linked fence. We walked along its edge, past the asphalt and the expensive argon lamps, to the far corner of the courts, where Sarah produced a pack of Benson & Hedges and a Bic. I lit both cigarettes while she held the flame in one hand and shielded with her other. We smoked, shivering against the last of the winter winds. She moved closer to me, for warmth, so that I had to turn my head to keep from blowing smoke in her face.

When we had finished and ground the butts

under our shoes, we stood still for a few more moments in the chilly breeze and the darkness. I felt her hand on the lapel of my coat.

"Happy Birthday," I said.

She smiled and leaned up for a birthday kiss, which I gave her. And then I kissed her again, a little harder, more earnestly, and after a moment or two she responded, putting one of her arms up around my neck. We stood like this for some minutes, embracing here in the shadow of her parents' building, our tongues twisting together, while Bank enforced the rules of the military far away from us.

When I left, she walked me back up to my car and waited while I unlocked it, but we did not say anything to each other.

I woke up crusty eyed and brick headed when Sarah called me the next morning to ask if she could take me to lunch. She picked me up at noon in her Cutlass Supreme. We drove in to the Westgate, which, in the light of day, seemed not so much dangerous as simply seedy and run down. They served food in colorful plastic baskets, all of it fried, battered shrimp or cheeseburgers or chicken. One of these baskets with a single pony beer and three aspirin was guaranteed to cure any hangover.

We spoke little during the drive or through

lunch, although she did not seem upset. After the grease and beer, when I could look up without the light pounding into my head, I felt ready.

Listen, I would say. *I'm sorry about last night. But, I'm not sorry, Sarah. We'll tell Bank together, and if he wants to, he can take it out on me.*

Sometimes in life, at certain moments, we realize that our failings, our inadequacies, work probably as much to our benefit as to our detriment. My trouble with emotional discussions, my lack of verbal facility, held me silent while I ran these words through again and again, deciding how I wanted to phrase them.

Sarah said, while I was still thinking, "I talked to Bank last night."

I felt cold, suddenly.

"He's so sweet," she said. "He sent me roses yesterday. And when I woke up today, a bouquet of wildflowers was waiting."

"Old Bank."

"He cares about people."

I nodded.

"He cares about you, Max."

I looked up at her, utterly at a loss now as to where this was going.

"I know what you think about him, some-times. Some of the things you say or the way you look. I think you have the wrong impression." She leaned forward, pushing her pretty face closer to mine. Her voice changed. She was serious, now. She said, "He thinks you're lonely, Max. He thinks you don't have any friends."

"I don't, really," I said.

"I understand that," she said. "You're solitary and you're working hard at school. But, Bank, he doesn't. So he wants us to keep you company. 'Let's call Mack and see if he wants to go out.' 'He just sits in the library and smokes. Sit with him.' And I know he asked you to take me out."

"But I wanted to," I said.

"I know. We're great, you and me, but that's not the point. The point is, Max, why he does this stuff, why he sets it up for us, is because he's afraid we'll be lonely when he's not around."

I had not considered this. But then I had not considered many things. I'd wanted to see them, Bank and Sarah, in a certain light because of how I felt, how I wanted things to be. I took out a cigarette and played with it.

"He's *good*, Max," she said. "He's good to me."

I knew she was right. But still, a part of me believed in the possibility that something else motivated Bank to push Sarah and me

335

together besides just his concern about my loneliness, that he wanted to see what would happen between us. As if he were testing us. If so, then we had failed.

"I should apologize, I guess."

"Listen," she said, "I wasn't trying to lay down some guilt trip. I'm just saying."

"What about last night?"

She shrugged. "How many drinks did you have?"

"I don't know," I said. "I was hammered."

"Me too," she said. "A girl gets drunk on her birthday and kisses the only kissable guy for miles around, what can you say about that?"

I felt stupid, then. My headache had come back and my stomach turned with the grease. I needed to lie down. But I also felt relieved, and vaguely happy, in a painful, longing sort of way. You have this woman as a friend, I thought, and you have Bank. Whatever the truth is, you are lucky for that, and you do not deserve them. You do not.

"What we have, Max," she said, "is a secret, you and me."

I picked up her hand, which was cool and dry, as it was on the day I met her, and tried to read her eyes. But they were enigmas. We sat, her hand resting in mine on the table.

"A secret." *I have a secret,* I wanted to say. *I*

could tell you *something, Sarah Garrison.* And as if I had spoken this aloud, she waited. She seemed to hold her breath. Because in spite of what she'd said, I wanted to tell her how I really felt about her, what I thought about the night before, what I wanted now. What could happen. With us. What possibilities existed. And I believe that she wanted to hear it.

But of course, I could not speak. Bank precluded it.

I have thought of that moment more times than I can say.

Bank graduated from the academy in May and was soon in another uniform, in a cruiser, watching over us all. He worked nights to begin, partnered with a guy I knew only as Dirty Red. I should have graduated in June, but I was a few hours short and so had to take a couple summer courses. Sarah had started back, too, working toward her master's degree. We often met for lunch in the union or shared a study room in the library.

Bank would come by after he'd slept and find us. Sometimes he'd just stick his head in the door and nod. And Sarah would get up without a word and leave with him. This meant they'd been fighting. Other days, though, Bank would greet us by pressing his face up against the glass panel in the door, flattening his nose and lips. This was a good sign.

"How can you sit in here on a summer afternoon?" he'd ask.

"Well, here you are," Sarah would reply. These were lost hours, for Bank could never sit still enough for us to get any work done. He'd tell stories about his nights. I liked to watch him then, his eyes lit up as he relived the excitement off which he fed. I envied him terribly.

Sometimes Bank baby-sat at the condo, when the regular sitter was off and Carol had to run out. In this way Jamie came to know him. She called him "Ba," short, of course, for Bank. "Ba, ba," she'd say. He in turn called her Little Lamb. It was her street name, he said, in case she ever had to go out among the junkies and crack runners and thieves.

He and Dirty Red would swing by sometimes in the early mornings in their blue-and-white and let Jamie turn the lights on and off. "Dirty Red," Bank would say, "this is Little Lamb."

I graduated in August and started law school immediately. In December, a year and a half after they'd met, Bank and Sarah were married. The best man was a Marine buddy of Bank's from Kansas City, to whom he'd promised that role while they were serving together, before he even knew Sarah. He apologized to me. It was fine, I said. I stood up there, too, though, in a powder-blue tuxedo that was too big in the chest and too tight in the waist, feeling silly and insipid next to Bank and his best man, who wore their dress uniforms. They looked so sharp and powerful that I did not see how any woman could have refused marriage to either one of them.

A couple of weeks after the wedding, at a Christmas party thrown by some law students, I met a woman named Gloria Harris and took her home to my apartment. By February she was practically living there. In April she told me that she was pregnant and that she was having the baby regardless of what I thought.

Bank found me in a bar one afternoon. I was nearly in tears, my nails bitten bloody, my breath stinking from the cigarettes, my head hurting because I was drinking way too much at that time. He said I should be disgusted. He certainly sounded disgusted. First thing, he said, was to get myself together and stop feeling sorry. What happens, happens. Grow up, he told me.

At his urging that month I took some civil service type exams on which I scored in the ninety-ninth percentile and which gained me admittance to the summer police class of 1981. In May, when my semester was over, I informed the law school that I would not be back. And by the late fall of that year, in what seemed like a running dream, I found myself in a uniform, in a cruiser, and going home at night to my very pregnant partner.

My daughter, Naomi, was born on January 2, 1982. She weighed nearly eight pounds, and looked even then as if she would grow up to be healthy and solid.

"It's a good thing, however it happened," my father told me in the hospital. "Appreciate it."

"This living-together business, it's too modern for me," my mother said. "You should get married. Give the baby a name." We were standing at the window of the City Med nursery, looking through the glass. "Whose name is she going to have, by the way?"

"Both, Mom," I told her. "Naomi Harris-Steiner."

"Both," my mother said. She looked a moment longer. "Your mouth," she said, then. "Poor girl. She has your unhappy mouth."

26

I fall like a tossed brick back into the night rhythm. I've worked nights before, at odd times, but first and longest when I was a young cop, a patrolman working my way up that ladder which only seniority, not talent or brains or luck, orders. So before I got the good day-shifts, the western or southern suburban neighborhoods where nothing ever happened but some car wrecks and drunk parties and the occasional domestic dispute, I had to work the shit. And the shit was nights, in the ghettos, in cracktown, on the East Side. Bankland.

After a while on nights — it takes a few months the first time you do it — you catch the rhythm of it, of waking after noon and eating a breakfast of cold cuts, of late dinners, of having your lunch, as everyone calls it, at 1:00 or 2:00 A.M. in some cop trough or fast-food joint. And then of doing your drinking, if you're a drinker, in the morning, of knowing the bars and lounges and bowling alleys and strip joints that start serving as soon as it's legal under state law, at seven. Not many do. But enough.

Once you catch it, though, you have it for life. Like alcoholism or an affinity for a certain sport or the ability to play an instrument, you can let it go for years, but when you touch it again, you're there. Not like when you were in it, when you were good, when it was your life, but you can feel the grooves still there inside you and you can feel yourself fitting back into them.

Abel Jackson's girlfriend, Bank informs me, lives on Hudak Street in Central North. I do not ask how he knows this.

Bank raps on the metal storm door with his Maglite. It's after midnight.

"Who is it?"

"*Po*-lice," he says. "Open the door."

The inside door cracks open an inch. "What d'you want?" says a woman.

"Looking for Abel Jackson. I heard he stops here now."

"He ain't here."

"He stop here, though?"

No answer, then, "Who's Abel? Abel who?"

Bank says, "Fuck," under his breath and shakes his head and looks around at me. I'm standing down the steps from him.

He says, "What's your name?"

"Kendra."

"Kendra. You don't know no one named Abel?"

Silence, then, "Yeah. Well, Abel who?"

"Abel *Jackson.* How many damn cocaine dealers named Abel do you know?"

"I don't got nothin' to do with no coke."

"Yeah?" says Bank. "Well, you better tell me about Abel or you're gonna have something to do with it. This your house?"

"Yeah."

"We make a bust here and find some blow or some rocks, you know what's gonna happen, don't you. Nobody cares whose shit it is, you know that. How the system works, we'll just take this house. You can kiss it right good-bye. That's straight up."

She looks out at him, a fat homely white girl in a worn-out pink bathrobe.

"You should talk to me about Abel, Kendra," Bank tells her. "You don't deserve the shit he's bringing down."

"Abel ain't here."

"You're gonna make me come back, ain't you," says Bank. "Every hour tonight, I'm coming back here and waking you up till I see Abel. Okay?"

"He ain't here!" she says, and slams the door.

"Fuck," says Bank. We ride. It is now just a quarter past midnight.

343

In spite of the fact that I feel adjusted to nights already, I'm still a little tired, so after Abel's house we head for Emilio's, up in the Far North, where I can grab a cup of joe and listen to Mamie the barmaid, the foulest-mouthed woman I have ever met.

Bank and I sit at the far end of the bar, out of earshot of the other cops and lay drinkers in here tonight. I need to talk.

"You knew before anyone that Tamara was a runaway," I say, after Mamie serves us our sandwiches and coffee. "Not just Baker Hawkes and the call last year, but that she's a chronic runaway. She hangs on the street sometimes for days, doesn't she?"

He nods.

"And her mother just stopped reporting it after that first time. She figured the cops wouldn't do anything anyway."

"That's right."

"I think you knew all that before any of us came to work on Monday morning. You just chose not to share it."

"I shared it," he says. He purses his lips and watches his cup as he stirs. "I clued you in."

"The tip of it, maybe. But I think Katherine knew too."

"I don't know," he says. "We don't talk much."

"Well," I say, "this afternoon, I heard something new. The mother, Rochelle, was in touch with a group out of Chicago. The Sisters of Compassion." He does not respond or look at me. "They relocate girls," I say, "who're in trouble. Sometimes maybe a little illegally. They've been known to make grabs themselves."

He looks at me, finally.

"You knew about this too?" I said.

"A little," he said. "Not much. Just some things Rochelle said. I kind of put it together. No facts, no names, nothing like that. Nothing about Chicago. She told me how the girl was running off all the time, doing God knows what, but Rochelle thought she was taking some abuse. Well, it turns out she was right, wasn't she? Anyway, they'd found this place where Tamara could maybe go away for a little while, get away from all the shit. That's all."

"You know where it is?"

"The place? No."

"What I mean," I say, "is could it be these people who grabbed her? Could her mother be in on it?"

"No," he says, looking around us at the other people in the bar, "she ain't in on it."

"How about the fact that she's got no debt on her credit cards?" I ask. "That new TV, new chair in there. You thought about that at all?"

He nods, but says nothing.

"Let me ask you something else. Everyone on the task force acted like they already knew about Tamara's file when Googie finally said something about it. I wasn't the only one you tipped off, was I?"

"No."

"You've been running on this for days now, letting the rest of us catch up, feeding out little bits of insight, keeping it all clandestine. Why?"

"I don't know what it is, yet, Mack," Bank said. "Is that what you're asking? If I did, you think I wouldn't turn it all over? I don't know where she is or who has her. But I think we're getting closer. And I like the water clear."

"Bank," I say, "I've got a . . . problem of my own with all this, now. With Naomi."

"Naomi?" He looks directly at me again. I tell it to him.

"I didn't think it was anything," I say. "Even after I found out about Tamara's file, I figured it was just a chance thing. Now it's gotten to be this emotional issue, this big secret."

"You're just Dad talking now."

"Maybe."

346

"I'll talk to her. Let me take care of it."

"Yeah?"

"Yeah. Problem is," he says, "you guys from Juvenile are only good up to about twelve-year-olds. After that it takes a real detective to muscle these hard-asses. Especially the girls."

"Right," I say.

"Right," says Bank. "You should'a said something sooner."

"Bank," I say, "you think there's a possibility it's this group, that Tamara is somewhere safe right now?"

He looks at me for a long moment with heavy eyes, his face sagging around those tight rubber scars on his throat and ears and cheeks. He looks older to me at this moment, in this light, than I have ever seen him. It's as if all the trauma of the past seven years has finally just caught him.

"Maybe," he says. But his eyes tell me that he does not believe it.

Around three Bank pounds again on the door of Abel Jackson's girlfriend's house on Hudak Street. Lights come on, the door cracks open again.

"What!" she shrieks. "Why're you doing this to me?"

"I want to talk to your boyfriend," Bank

tells her. "I want Abel Jackson."

"I *told* you," she says.

"And I told *you*," he says. "Vice comes down on this place, the city's taking it. Bye-bye house. Bye-bye yard. Bye-bye tree in the backyard. Bye-bye garage. Bye-bye driveway. Bye-bye nice neighborhood. Bye-bye down payment. Bye-bye tax break."

"I'm calling the cops!" she screams at him.

Bank laughs at that. He laughs and laughs, even as we're driving away.

Hudak Street again. Five twenty-five A.M. Bank parks three houses down from Abel's girlfriend's. I watch with him for a little while, with a cold cup of coffee stuck between my legs, but soon I nod and fall into a shallow, uncomfortable sleep. I wake up the first time Bank starts the car to heat it up, but then settle in against the door and let myself fall.

At six-forty Bank slaps my arm. I come to, wide eyed and confused, trying to see what he's pointing at. It's the woman, Kendra, coming out of her house, dressed now, wearing a long winter coat because it has gone back to cold this morning. An expensive coat too. Leather and fur. She looks much better than she did in the middle of the night. Bank waits for her to get clear of the house, then opens his door.

"Come on," he says.

We run up along the sidewalk, across the front yard, to the driveway.

"Hey, hon," he calls out to her just as she pulls open the garage door, startling her so badly, I see her jump.

"What!" she yells. "What do you want from me?"

"Abe. Ul," says Bank. "Jack. Son."

"Jesus *fucking* Christ," she says. "He ain't *here!* I *told* you that fifty *fucking* times already!"

"Yeah?" Bank says. "So, uh, where is he? Where's he been stopping? Where's he hanging? What's he been up to? I just want a little bit, hon, something to chew on, then I leave you alone."

"I don't know nothin'," she says. "He just ain't even been around. Been out doing somethin', some shit he's been working on. Some big important thing, so the asshole can't stay around here no more with me." To my amazement she starts to cry then, big, ugly sobs coming out of her twisted mouth, her fresh makeup running at the first tears.

"Yeah?" says Bank, softly. He touches her hair.

"Like I'm not even here no more," she says. "The bastard. I ain't seen him. He just goes around with these other shitheads."

"Who?"

"I don't know who they are." She takes Bank's handkerchief and holds it against one eye, then the other. "Stupid spigs."

We are all three of us quiet. A beat passes. Bank says, "What?"

The lady sniffles and wipes at her nose with the back of the hand in which she holds the handkerchief. She looks at us, her mouth half open, pain and confusion and anger smeared all across her face, not because of Bank, but because of her own lousy life. "Spigs," she says. "Wetbacks."

She looks for a moment as if she's on the verge of saying something else. Then she spins and jumps into her car. I expect Bank to go after her, to pull her back, but he doesn't move as she backs hard down the driveway. In the street her tires squeal when she brakes, and again when she accelerates away.

It is just like Benny Escobar last Sunday on Moon Street. Bank hounds these people, badgering them to the point of harassment, for what seem to me the most tentative reasons, the flimsiest inklings. And then, to my wonder, they produce. They validate his hunches. I can only shake my head. My approach to the Job has never been, and will never be, this intuitive. I'm a plodder, a thinker. I get there, but never as quickly or elegantly as Bank.

Sleepy's tip was right: Abel Jackson's been consorting with the Hispanic gangs. Abel Jackson's attempting to cut in, to set up a little narco-pipeline into the East Side. What this has to do directly with Tamara Shipley, I don't know, and I don't think Bank does. But it's a direct strike into her neighborhood, into the dim world where her brother, Eddie Munster, tries to cull favor and sell rock, where Benny and Mario Escobar and their brethren run their own little cartel.

27

On the last Friday night in November of 1989, after an on-call swing-shift that had me running most of the night, I drove out toward Heron Park, to Morris Hill, and parked down the street from Bank's place. I knew he'd be up. I thought I'd surprise him, maybe draw him out a little. He had still not decided to come back to work, though he had always loved the Job, loved being out there mixing it up, and I thought it was past time for him to return. I worried, too, about the drinking, although he'd told me that it was not a regular thing. He had bad days, that was all.

I sat for a few moments after parking, before going up, watching the park, the night. And as I sat, a figure passed from Bank's building, a large figure shrouded in black. It crossed in front of my car and disappeared into the park.

My head spun. I knew, somehow, immediately and with certainty, what he was doing. On that night I just sat, contemplating what I'd seen. But then I began to prepare myself to find out what I already knew.

★ ★ ★

Heron Park, where Bank lived, where Jamie was last seen, is a great park, as I have said, in size, in design, in the amenities it offers the people of the city. But it is also, of course, in the manner of all great city parks, a crime incubator. A black hole in the city's midst. One long side of its golf course lies just across from a particularly garish and seedy section of Brentcroft that is lined with bars and strip joints and Triple-X video stores and carryouts that turn their coin selling malt liquor quarts and condoms and plastic food for the 2:00 A.M. drunks. The park is known for the muggings and beatings and rapes that take place within its borders. When we were young patrol cops, in our mid-twenties, Bank and I would come to this park to breathe. It wasn't so far from the stench of the burned-out old city. We would come here in our blue uniforms and park the car, and walk into the blackness, nightsticks bouncing on our legs, Smith & Wesson .38 Specials at our sides, the leather of our gear belts creaking in the night, looking for any trouble we could find.

We found it always, always. I do not remember a night when we did not come upon some offense, moral or legal or spiritual. A man beating another man in the face, blood and wet flying, the beaten man semiconscious

353

and barely breathing. A stolen car being stripped for parts right in the middle of the third fairway, the most accessible from Brentcroft. A man bent over forward, his hands gripping a low branch of a tree, his pants around his ankles, another man behind him, inserted, teeth gritted and eyes squeezed shut to hold in the bliss, humping and pumping away. Drunks drinking, pipeheads smoking, whores whoring. Once, we found a man lying in the middle of the old road, shot in the stomach, the aftermath of a bad narcotics transaction. A college girl once who had been raped and beaten and was wandering, naked and dazed, her face streaked with mud and mascara and blood, her hair torn and wild, prey for the next lowlife who found her. We'd freeze this all in the beam of our sudden lights, but not before we watched. This was a part of our school, Bank's and mine, because we learned that, once our eyes had adjusted to the darkness, we could see fine. And so we'd watch. And listen. We'd come silently upon these scenes and stand in the deepest shadows watching, unless a life or someone's well-being was immediately at stake, learning what it was that bad guys did, what they talked about, how they moved and treated each other, what moved them.

Another night that week, dry but cold. Little snow had fallen so far that year, so the ground was barren and hard. The days had grown short, the sky close and dark by late afternoon and controlling the mood of the city, which was pensive, now, waiting for winter. Late nights such as this you could park the car, get out and walk off into the blackness, and feel it then, in that night air, a hint of the frigidness of the Arctic borne in its currents, waiting to come down on us.

I felt it. I had parked at the very south-eastern corner of the park, just off Brentcroft, at the end of that old brick-paved street called Morris Hill.

The rubber soles of my duty shoes slipped on the red bricks, which seemed always to be damp or iced over, as I walked up the hill, into the night. The street was not well lighted. I found the picnic table in the park where I could sit and watch the old blond brick building with its white steel awnings and leaded glass windows. It was 11 P.M. Just the time. I had been coming here like this for several nights running. I, too, had just lost my family. Gloria and Naomi had moved to Columbus a month earlier. I, too, now lived alone, and had come to dread going back to that dead, empty house. I preferred, actually, spending my time sitting in the cold night. Waiting.

Now, on this night, I had only been sitting huddled into myself for half an hour, my feet and hands just starting to go numb, when the living-room light in the third-story apartment went out. A moment later I watched the dark figure pass again beneath the safety light over the front door of the building.

We crossed over to the golf course — me hanging fifty yards back from him, walking soundlessly on the frozen earth, between the barren trees — past the crusted-over frog pond near the clubhouse. Here, because of the lights on the clubhouse, I walked out into the darkness of the first fairway, to stay concealed. I thought I had lost him at one point, but then I heard him crossing the tenth fairway and climbing the steep hill leading up to the eleventh green. We crossed a split rail fence and passed an old boarded-up brick shelter house. The bright antiseptic halogen lights of City Med illuminated the northern horizon, but soon these disappeared, too, as Bank led me deeper into the park, where no lights from the city penetrated.

We walked like this for an hour, seeing little, hearing little. An uneventful, pleasant, if surreal, nighttime stroll, enough activity to keep me warm. At one point he sat down on a steep, grassy slope. I waited above him. He rested for five or ten minutes, sipped from a water bottle he carried in the day pack on his back, then continued on.

I hung back, rarely closer than fifty yards. Like Bank I had dressed for this, darkly, in layers of thermal and wool shirts covered by a hooded navy sweatshirt and black jeans, a knit cap, and gloves. He never once paused to look back in my direction.

Then, at the edge of some deep woods, he stopped suddenly and crouched, pulling his Maglite from the metal loop on his belt next to his gun. We were in the region of the amphitheater now. He waited, then crept forward on his hands and knees, into the dead brush. I crouched behind him, waiting. I could not penetrate far into the woods here without rattling too many branches and dead leaves. I really could not see him at all now, as he wormed more deeply into the trees. I heard him, though, creeping. One step, wait fifteen seconds, then another. Like any good still-hunter. I decided to take the chance, so I crept slowly forward, on hands and knees, along his path.

And then I heard what he had come in here for. A party. I saw, a little ways ahead through the undergrowth, the light of an occasional conical blue flame, and heard the faint sound of the rush of escaping gas: a butane torch. I heard the exaggerated inhalings of freebasers. This was unusual, I thought, freebasing expensive cocaine powder out in the park like this instead of just smoking crack rocks with a cheap lighter and stem. These partyers had a little money. So why come out here into the cold dark?

I crept closer. Now I saw Bank again. He had crawled to within ten feet of one of the smokers. They were four kids, two boys and two girls, sixteen, seventeen, which explained things. They might well have been from Heron Hills. I had no idea how he had found them, because I'd heard nothing as we walked. But these kids were in danger here, especially all smoked up, with money in their pockets. They were the sort who'd end up dead, one morning's lead news, and then good-bye forever.

Bank cleared his throat. The butane flickered out. One of the kids said, "What was that?"

Bank waited, thirty seconds, until the torch came back on. Then he cleared his throat again, more loudly this time. Two of the kids, the boys, pushed themselves frantically back and scrambled to their feet, then stopped again to listen.

"Shit," one of them said.

No sound. I was close enough that I could

hear their breathing, fast and loud from their free-based high and apprehension.

"Hey," Bank said, in his best ghetto voice, in a loud, haunting whisper. "You be dead, children." The four of them scrammed then, running hard through the trees, northward toward their car. They left behind their torch and their pipes.

I heard the butane hiss again, then saw it leap to life, longer now, blue tipped orange, the valve turned wide open. Bank sat holding it, watching it heat the wintry air around him. He turned it upward, pointing the flame at the sky, then down toward his feet, then out-ward at the trees, burning it all off. For ten minutes he sat there, his face and torso eerily lighted.

I watched him watching until the flame had died. He laid the torch in the beam from his Maglite and pounded the nozzle out of shape with a rock, so it couldn't be used again, then tossed it into the leaves. He got to his feet and walked directly toward me. I tucked and froze, my heart thumping wildly. He passed within feet of me, his boots shuffling loudly now through the undergrowth, and back into the open park.

I did not follow him anymore on that night. I had to work in the morning. But I'd learned something: why he had not felt compelled to come back on the job. Because he was working anyway. His own job. Bank the night cop, patrolling Heron Park.

I knew that he would be out here for hours that night, and the nights that followed, for a full shift, until five or six in the morning, until dawn, when the bad guys and freaks and dopers went home. Watching, chasing, breaking up, protecting. Forcing his presence, his will, his law, on anyone he found who dared to come here, into the park, into his night.

A couple of weeks before Christmas, not long after the first deep snowfall of the season had finally fallen, two patrolmen responded to a 1:00 A.M. burglary involving a car in the lot of a carryout at the corner of Morton Parkway and Andrew Jackson Avenue, only a quarter mile or so down from those tennis courts where we'd set up the command post for Jamie the summer before. No eyewitnesses. The cops got a call first from dispatch. Someone in the store heard a crash and called it in. Outside, the patrolmen found the car with a brick in its front seat and its stereo ripped out.

But they got another call at the scene, only minutes later, this from their watch commander, saying he had a report of a collar in the park.

A collar?

Could they see anything?

Like what? The patrol cops peered across Andrew Jackson toward the darkness of the northeast corner of the park.

Go on over there, the WC told them.

Go where?

Just across Jackson, he said. So one of the cops cut over in the squad car and pulled up onto the icy asphalt walking path between the road and the woods. He shone his door-mounted spot up and down along the line of trees. Then he heard a voice. "Help me!" a man shouted. "Help!"

The cop swiveled his light around toward the source of the cry, and found a skinny white guy standing there all hangdog, hands behind his back. Like he was just waiting for something, the cop said later, in telling the story. The stereo from the car lay on the ground at his feet.

The cop pulled his piece because it was just too weird and dark in there and he had no idea what was going on. But this perp turned out to be tied to a small tree, his wrists so tightly bound with plastic clothesline, it took the cop several minutes to cut him loose.

The man said he didn't know what happened. Something knocked him down. Next he knew, he was tied up.

Stories began to circulate around the force and out into the city itself. Reporters called down, asking about a possible vigilante in Heron Park. Bank's name was tossed around because it was known now that he lived there, but no one had any kind of proof or indication that he was behind any of it. Googie, though, I think, voiced the sentiments of most rank-and-file patrolmen and detectives when he said, "Bank wants to run around on his own time and try to clean up Heron Park, Christ, I say let him."

When the Command started talking about questioning Bank about this, Stu Marek came up with a different solution. He called Bank one day and told him it was about time he got his ass back down to work. Bank said he'd think about it, then called Stu back the next day to say he wouldn't mind coming back, but not to the Gang Squad or any organized unit. He wanted only, he said, to work the graveyard in a felony car. Alone. Nothing more than that. No open cases. No team-work. No operations.

He was a good cop. The Command was glad to have him back, and gladder still to have a solution to this budding problem of Bank Arbaugh as possible vigilante, to the problem of the rumors coming out of events in Heron Park, to the increasing press interest in these phenomena. Having Bank back to work, they figured, would end it.

But it did not end. The stories still floated around, reports still came out of the park from junkies who were rousted by some invisible figure in the night or passers-through who felt themselves being escorted by a force they could not see or hear.

And I continued, sometimes, to follow. Not often, but when a shift left me antsy instead of tired, an empty evening had me feeling sorry for myself, and I knew Bank wasn't working that night, I'd go out there and sit. And as often as not, Bank, alone now in his apartment on the park, still stewing in his rage and despair, would come out to roam again through the night.

Through all of this, from the time of Jamie's disappearance, the press never stopped trying to gain access to Bank. Even after the locals gave it up, having been rebuffed so many times, the occasional outside reporter would come in to seek an interview. None ever succeeded.

In the new year of 1990, though, this was all to change. But the agent of that change — no, the catalyst — was, in the end, I believe, not Bank himself, but me.

28

Bank and I have breakfast after our talk with Kendra, though neither of us says much during the meal. Afterward we hustle back downtown and up to the suite. Bank has paperwork to finish and I want to catch the task-force meeting at eight. When we step through the glass door, though, the place has the feel of a buzz on and the conference room is empty. Stu comes out of his office when he sees us, and says, "We found Rochelle Shipley. Katherine's got her in the back."

"Who's doing her?"

"Katherine. Why?"

Bank and I look at each other. "Stu," says Bank, "the girl was whoring."

"What?"

"Tamara. Might be she was out selling it."

"Who —"

"We don't know yet, Stu," says Bank. "We don't know nothin' for sure."

Stu stands a moment, digesting this, then hurries back toward the boxes. Over his shoulder he barks, "Well, come on."

★ ★ ★

Stu pulls Katherine out of the box, and nods toward us. "Get this," he tells her. Bank delivers a brief recap. Katherine's lips tighten, but that's her only reaction. Again, I get the impression that she's more concerned with the fact that we know what we know than with the knowledge itself — it doesn't surprise her in the way it should.

She nods and steps back into the box.

"Can I go in too?" I ask Stu.

"No," he says. "Leave 'em alone." Bank and I follow him into the viewing room. Googie and Rick Simms are in there already, so it's pretty crowded now with five men. We all go silent as Katherine starts up again.

Rochelle Shipley weeps. The circles under her eyes are the darkest I've seen them. Her skin looks even pastier.

"I don't know!" she says, when Katherine tells her what she's just learned. She pounds the tabletop. "I don't know! It might be true. It might be. But she's into some badness, whatever it is. I know that now. I been trying to put a stop to it. You think I haven't? But I can't control her anymore. I lost her."

"We've heard about this place," Katherine says, "called the Sisters of Compassion."

Rochelle nods. "They were gonna get her

out. Someplace she could grow up a little, have some safety."

"How did you hear about it, Rochelle?"

She shakes her head.

"You don't want to say?"

"A friend," she says. "Does it matter who it was?"

"No," says Katherine.

"Yes, it does," I say, under my breath, from behind the glass. I catch Stu's eye and shake my head, and feel myself growing a little hot. *Push her,* I want to say. But Stu just looks back into the box.

"How about Father Hector?" asks Katherine.

"He knew she had problems. He was helping out."

"How'd he know?"

"What?" says Rochelle. "I — I called him, I guess. Somebody at the church gave me his name, I think. I don't remember."

"Okay," says Katherine.

"Okay, what?" I say out loud. "Stu . . ." The others in the viewing room look at me. "She's holding her hand," I say. "How about Chicago? Katherine's the one that followed up on that. She said it was nothing. What if I hadn't raised it again?"

"What's your point?" Stu says.

"Katherine's walking her through this."

"Mack," says Googie, "take it easy. We got all day. She don't gotta pull her guts out first thing."

"Fine," I say, and vow to shut up. Fuck the whole case.

"Who'd you talk to in Chicago?" says Katherine.

"Some lady named Keira. I don't know the last name."

"Do you know anyone else's name there?"

"No."

"So you were going to let complete strangers take your daughter away. Just like that."

"You think that's worse than what she's going through now?" she asks. "The only thing they could do worse is kill her, and I don't think they would. Maybe it's too late, now, anyway."

"Where was the girl supposed to go?"

"Someplace in Ohio. That's all I knew. They didn't say just where. Not yet."

"Rochelle," Katherine says then, "listen to me. This is what we have to know. Do these people have Tamara now? Is that who picked her up on Sunday?"

"No!" she says, and slaps the table again. "God, I wish they did. They were s'posed to come around soon, but then it was too late. It was too late. Too late."

It goes on. I listen with half an ear, still feeling in some way that Katherine is coddling this woman. But I don't care anymore. Something else is trying to occur to me. I'm standing here in this hot little room, watching through the glass as this woman talks about her daughter and some organization in Chicago and kidnappings. It occurs to me quite abruptly how blind we've been. Chicago. I turn suddenly enough to startle the others in the room.

"Sorry," I say. "Excuse me." I squeeze through to the doorway, and open it and bolt out into the suite.

"Jesus," I hear one of them say behind me, "what's up his ass?"

A civilian clerk named Jan Lupino works the front desk in Records, in the cool basement of the PS Building.

"Detective," she says, in her smoky voice. Jan's been here for a long time, in the job she got as a political favor to her uncle or someone back in the seventies.

"Jan. What's doing?"

She pushes air between her lips. "Oh, today's been just exciting."

"Yeah?"

"You wouldn't believe the action."

"Couple's shootouts?"

"Couple?" she says. "Lucky we ain't all dead."

"And they still haven't given you a gun?"

She cackles and winks at me. She's only fifty, but all the cigarettes she's sucked down over the years have crevassed her face. She used to keep one burning perpetually on her desk until they banned it in city buildings. Now she hustles out front for a quick drag whenever she gets a minute.

"You pull an old jacket for an old cop?"

"Sure thing, sugar. We let you guys see a file once in a while, special occasions and the like."

I write the name down on a piece of paper. She glances at it and then up at me again, a question in her eyes.

I nod.

"How's he doing, anyway?" Bank, she means.

"Same old. He's a busy guy."

"Tell me about it. Takes me half a morning sometimes to get through his paperwork." She leaves, and is back inside a minute with my request. I carry it out to a wooden bench in the hallway.

Jan pokes her head out the door. "You can check that out if you want, bring it back later."

"That's all right," I say. "Thanks."

I've seen it before, this file. My name's all through it, in fact. On the front, imprinted in black letters on clear tape, is the name of its subject: Alan Norke. The boy from Chicago who was once arrested while transporting a girl out of a possible abusive situation.

It doesn't take me long to find the notes that the CPD detective Stamos faxed to Katherine in the aftermath of Norke's death. And there, in those notes, I find it: an address and phone number in north Chicago. The same address Simms's fellow agents in Chicago just told him about. And the very same phone number that showed up on Rochelle Shipley's records — the Sisters of Compassion. Norke had at one time worked with the same group that was now trying to save Tamara Shipley.

I knew it, I guess, before I came down here, but it rocks me anyway. Another direct link between Jamie and Tamara. But what does it mean? I still cannot put it together.

I sit for a little while, trembling and breathing and trying to understand. Perhaps, I pray, it is just a grotesque coincidence. But like any cop I do not believe in such things.

I read on.

Norke was arrested in Indiana. He was transporting the girl to a safe house in that state, not in Illinois. He was arraigned in a district court in South Bend, where he'd picked up the girl, though he was arrested some fifty miles from there. His attorney drove over from Chicago. This attorney's firm, I see now, handled many cases for the Sisters of Compassion, all pro bono. The same firm, it turns out, that Norke's mother worked for.

I begin marking the pages I want Jan to copy.

Upstairs, the interrogation of Rochelle Shipley is over, or at least on a break. I hear Rick, Googie, and Stu in the conference room. I wander back into the suite, though, looking for Bank. And then I spot him. He's sitting in Katherine's cubicle. She's at her desk. She smiles at something he's said. I feel betrayed somehow, without understanding exactly why.

Then she spots me.

"Mack," she says. Bank leans around and looks at me too.

"Your wife called," he says. "We been looking all over for you. Where the hell'd you go?"

I hold up the copies I've just received, to show him, but of course he has no idea what they contain.

"Call her," he says. "She said it's important."

So, from my own desk, I do.

"Mack," Peggy says, her voice subdued and frightened.

"What is it?"

"Naomi," Peggy says. "She left, Mack."

"What do you mean?"

"She came in last night, not long after you left."

"Yeah," I say, "I saw her."

"Well, she came in and went straight down to her room. I tried to apologize to her. She wouldn't talk to me. So I just left her alone.

"This morning the boys and I were up, you know, having breakfast, and it was getting late. She was going to be late for school. So I went down there. Her door was open. And she was gone, Mack."

"She left early."

"She hadn't slept in her bed."

"Maybe she made it," I say.

"She never makes it," says Peggy. "But I know she didn't, because I changed the sheets yesterday. And I made it then. And it's still that way. So I checked, and the dead bolt on the front door was open. Mack, I locked it before I went to bed. I think she left last night."

★ ★ ★

Though it's not protocol, because it hasn't been twenty-four hours, Googie takes a Missing report, mostly, I think, to make me feel better.

"She got pissed and took off, Mack," he says. "She's at a friend's."

"I'll go out there," Bank tells me. "We'll take care of it."

Stu's pounding my back, telling me not to worry. Katherine and Simms are hovering about too. It's all a little silly, really. But it does make me feel better.

"She might've just gone in to school, you know," Katherine says. "The routine. She'll need that."

I pick up a phone and dial Harding High School. "Pat Grice," I say, when the student aide answers. A moment later Pat says, "Yes."

"Pat, Mack Steiner," I say. "Naomi —"

"Mack," she says, "I was just going to call you."

"Is Naomi there?"

"In school? I don't know. Why — let me check the cards." She puts down the phone. "No," she says, when she comes back. "She wasn't in homeroom. Mack, I didn't get any-where yesterday. Her friends, the ones I talked to, they all denied knowing anyone

373

who goes by Zelda, or who Naomi might call that name. They were covering, of course. But this morning I got hold of a couple of other girls who know Naomi and got them in here and scared them a little. Mack," she says, "they both told me, separately, that Naomi calls herself Zelda."

"What?" I say.

"Naomi," says Pat. "She *is* Zelda. She's the one who met this girl Tamara Shipley."

29

One February night in 1990, seven months after Jamie had gone, while sitting alone in the family room of my empty house, sipping my third beer, staring at the television, I heard a car pull into the driveway. It was just after midnight.

I peeked through the window and made out the figure of a woman. It was Sarah. I hadn't seen her in the three months since she'd left. She looked nice in a knit navy dress and a long wool coat, but disheveled, worked over a little, at the same time. Her hair was mussed, her lipstick smeared in a couple spots, and her eye shadow had smudged into dark bruises beneath her eyes.

"Max," she said.

"When did you get back?"

"Just today. I should have called. I'm sorry." She stepped inside and kissed me carefully on the cheek. She smelled of perfume and cigarette smoke and liquor. I turned to walk back into the house but she paused in the little foyer, as if to compose herself, and then felt her way into the darkened living room and fell into the first chair she came to.

I sat down on the couch across from her.

"Did I wake you?" she said, her words a little slurred and lazy sounding.

"No. I worked late, actually."

"I'm sorry about this," she said again.

"Stop it," I told her. "You know I'm glad to see you."

She sat for a moment before speaking. "I had this dinner party I'd promised to come back for. Old friends, you know. It was horrible. They don't tell you they're inviting another man, divorced, to seat next to you. Not to try to fix you up, mind. Just so everything balances. God. So you know what I did, Max? I left after a little while, and went out and had a drink all by myself. I don't think I've ever done that. Well, I had a few drinks. And it was just one man after another, coming up, wanting to buy me the next one. My God. The slobs all think you came in for one reason, and they're it."

I felt a flare ignite in my chest at the thought of her sitting alone at a bar as men in bad suits and open collars send drinks and napkin notes, or lean in next to her, their boozy breath blowing in her face.

She said, "It was just as well, though, my coming back. I had to sign papers. The divorce is final, or nearly so. That was quick, wasn't it?"

"Are you all right?"

"Sure," she said. The streetlights painted her silhouette in the window. She breathed heavily through her nose. "I meant to call you, Max. I wanted to see you. So while I was driving back to my hotel, I thought I'd stop by, see if you were up. I thought maybe you'd want to go out and have a drink or something."

"No," I said, "not really."

"Okay."

She stood. I thought she might leave then, but she slipped her coat off and dropped it, then came over and sat next to me. She leaned her head on my shoulder. Her breath was hot and sweet with the liquor. I breathed it in, getting drunker on it, going a little light in the head myself.

"I've missed you," she said.

"How drunk are you?" I asked.

"I had a few," she said. "I'm not that bad."

"I'd hate you to be," I said. "I'd hate that to be why."

"It wouldn't be, Max, even if I were."

She pulled my face around toward her and kissed me first on the cheek, then the mouth. She stood up and in a single fluid motion pulled her dress up and over her head. She stepped out of her shoes, then peeled her hose down so that all she had on were panties and her bra. The air felt heavy around me, the beers I'd had and the smell of her making me dizzier. She reached back and unsnapped her bra, but held the cups against her breasts. I held my hands out toward her but she stepped backward.

"No," she said. "You too. Stand up. Let's see you."

And when I was naked before her, she dropped the bra to the floor, and bent and slipped off the panties. I could make out her neck and her belly, her small pointed breasts with areolas so dark, their pigmentation so heavy, that they looked almost purple in the faint light.

I sat back down on the couch. She stepped toward me until her breasts brushed my face. She pressed herself into me, her pubic hair brushing against my belly. I took the nipple, the entire areola, of one breast into my mouth. She pushed it more deeply into me.

I moved her back so that I could run my hand up between her legs. I touched her, then slipped my fingers in. She moved against my hand, rocking herself as she gripped my face until her legs gave and she sagged against me.

I lay back on the couch and pulled her toward me. It was purely sex that first time, hard, slapping sex with her knees pressed up along my sides, as if this single act held within it the potential to purge us both of missing years, of unfulfillment, of horrid loss itself. We both came quickly and hard, then lay together afterward until our sweat evaporated and we grew chilled except for the places where we touched.

Upstairs, after lying tucked into each other for a while longer, warming up, talking a little, Sarah began to touch me again, in ways I had not quite been touched before. When I was ready she crawled on top of me and reached between us. I felt her hand on me again, gripping me this time, rubbing me against her, and then positioning me until I felt her there, her heat and openness, just barely touching me, but ready. Before pressing herself down upon me, though, she paused for a moment to look into my face, and to kiss me, once, softly.

We moved quickly and then we moved slowly, and for some time, neither of us in any hurry to finish or even to get there at all. We might have fallen asleep like that, with me inside her still, and been fulfilled, so slowly did we move at times, but in the end we did not fall asleep until we had exhausted ourselves.

I awoke shortly after sunrise, my head full, and saw that she was awake already. She moved over to me, slipped an arm beneath my neck, and rested her face on my chest. She draped her other arm across my belly.

"Old Max," she said.

"You're the only one besides my parents who calls me that."

"I'm not one for street names, I guess."

I touched her hair, running my fingers along it, tracing its edges against the skin of her back.

"I don't think I'll be coming back here anymore," she said. "We're moving home, near where I grew up."

"We?"

She kissed my chest. "My family, Max. My parents have sold their place. They don't want to be around here either. We're all going home."

"That sounds nice."

We lay still together.

"Sarah," I said, "have you ever wondered?"

"About us?"

"Mm-hm."

"Oh, Max, you don't know. I don't think you'll ever know."

"Will you call me?"

"Sure I will, Max."

She let me hold her like that for a few more minutes, and then we got up and showered. I cooked her breakfast, scrambled eggs and toast and coffee. We ate at the table in the dining alcove next to my kitchen, looking out at the backyard she had said she liked so much.

"Let me know when you get there," I said. "Wherever it is."

She nodded.

I walked her out to her car and leaned in the window toward her. She kissed me on the cheek and said, "Good-bye, Max," into my ear before she drove off.

As I turned to go inside, I noticed a red Jeep Cherokee parked six or seven houses down the street, its engine running, the driver sitting inside it, watching. It was Bank. He must have known about her coming back to sign the papers. Maybe even the party. Why would he come here, though? I did not know. Perhaps he knew I'd been following him in the park, and was just returning the favor. I wondered if I should go and speak to him, explain things, try to justify. But I didn't think he'd want me to.

I simply looked at him for a moment, and then went inside to get ready for the day.

I did not talk to or see Bank in that week. I did not try to call him, to comfort him in his new loss, the final unequivocal departure of his wife, nor to comfort him in the face of the fact that I had finally consummated my own relationship with her, a relationship that went back very nearly as far as did his own.

I did not do any of these things.

One night the following week Bank was cruising alone in his f-car when a call came over. Some kids had taken a ball bat to a mail drop-box off Riverside Drive in the Far North, just a block up from a newly opened bar and sandwich joint called Emilio's. The place had quickly become popular with cops, so Bank knew there were plenty of units in the immediate vicinity to cover the offense. He didn't have to respond unless there was an arrest. But the night had been stiflingly quiet, so Bank headed up that way. He laughed when he got there. Because of the proximity of Emilio's, five or six squads had responded. The presence of all the flashing and spinning Visibars made the scene look like some major bust. But the only signs of a crime were some fragments of a wooden bat and a concave mailbox.

Riverside Drive just north of this spot opened to four lanes, then followed a broad curve as it fed directly into one of the expressways belting the city. It hummed during the day, but now, after 1 A.M., was largely empty.

What happened was that two kids in some old heated-up muscle cars were tooling south around that curve, one in each lane, seeing who would be first to where the road narrowed to two lanes. It was a natural drag-racing spot. Wide-open blacktop, a dry, clear night. Estimates had them doing close to a hundred miles an hour as they came off that curve.

But what these kids saw, instead of empty road, was a phalanx of lit-up squad cars. One knew enough even in his surprise to go soft on the brakes, figuring he was busted whatever happened. The other, though, an eighteen-year-old in a '69 Camaro, panicked and locked it up, which cost him his steering. He skidded across the concrete turtles into the northbound lanes of traffic, where he almost missed the single pickup truck there. His left front bumper tore the rear bumper off the truck and spun both vehicles. The Camaro continued southward through three revolutions, tires screaming until they gripped the road and flipped the car into the air. It rolled at least four times before coming to rest on its roof.

Some of the cops jumped into their squads. Others, including a couple of off-duty drunks, raced northward on foot toward the vehicle, but stopped when they got close. Flames leapt upward from the rear end. Several said later they could hear the kid inside screaming.

Two cops got to the car and tried the door, but it had jammed. The flames grew, forcing them back.

Bank, in no apparent hurry, drove northward in his unmarked Plymouth to within a few yards of the burning car. He got out, pulled a folding Buck knife from his pants pocket, and opened the blade. He lifted his trunk lid and removed a blanket he kept there. Then he approached the driver's side of the inverted car, took a step forward, and drove his booted foot through the glass. All this new fresh night air fed the flames licking into the rear of the passenger compartment. They engulfed the backseat.

Now even the cops still at the original scene could hear the screams. Smoke poured from the driver's window. The plastic seat covers had begun to melt around the boy. His hair had ignited. Fire engines and rescue squads raced northward in the distance.

Bank kicked the remaining glass from the window, wrapped the blanket around his own head, then lay down on his back so that his head was next to the broken-out window. He scooched himself backward, into the car, into the fire.

He sawed with his knife at the seat belt (which had saved the driver's life, actually) until the boy fell onto his chest. Some of the other cops grasped Bank's feet and pulled him and the burned boy over the glass and asphalt and away from the burning wreckage. They lifted the boy off and laid him on the street. And then, upon turning to congratulate Bank, or chastise him, they saw that his shirt was smoldering, that his hands were blackened, that the blanket, which was not cotton but some synthetic blend, had melted around his face. Bank grunted and sucked at the air, which he could not get in because of the smoke that filled his lungs.

By then the first rescue squad had arrived.

A St. Jerome's ER nurse I knew let me back into the trauma section. Bank lay on his back, oxygen mask on his face, elbows pressed to the sides of his chest with his scorched hands held up in the air, pieces of the blanket still attached to his neck and the sides of his face.

"Hey," I said, leaning toward him.

He looked up at me, then shook his head and turned his face away. His life was gone, every shred of it, including me, his best friend who had slept with his wife. And so he had tried to end it. Not consciously, maybe, but he had crawled into that car not caring if he survived. Even, perhaps, hoping he would not survive. He wanted to die. And I was in part to blame.

"I'm staying." I leaned down toward his burned face. "You stubborn bastard," I said to him, "I don't give a shit if you hate me. I'm staying here, and so are you."

30

Janice Ewell, the girl I frightened with Naomi yesterday morning, huddles down into the chair across from Pat Grice's desk and looks up at the three of us: Pat, Bank, and myself.

"Janice," I say, as gently as I can with the dread I feel inside me welling up and filling my throat. "Janice," I say. "This is terribly important."

She nods.

"We have to know what you know. I know it sucks to rat, but, Janice, Naomi could be in a lot of danger. You understand that?"

Her eyes widen.

"Do you know where she is?"

"No."

"No idea."

A pause.

"Janice?"

"I mean, no, I don't know. I have an idea, but I don't know where it is or if she's there."

"Where?"

"I don't know."

"Janice," Pat says, a hint of steel in her voice.

"I *don't* know," Janice says. "There was this

place she wanted to go. This retreat thing she heard about. A safe place. For girls."

Bank raises his eyebrows.

"How did Naomi know Tamara?" says Bank.

"When she was still living in Columbus," Janice says. "She ran away."

"She ran away a few times," I say. "But I don't see how they could have met. Tamara was here —"

"Naomi came over here looking for you," Janice says, to me. "She just got on a bus."

The time she was gone for several days. I am furious all over again at Gloria's folks for not calling, not making a report, not ever telling me about it.

"I mean, I don't know everything," Janice says. "I know when she got here it was already night. She was gonna call you, but then she said on the way over she thought about it and got afraid you'd get mad at her. So she decided not to call. She said she didn't have anywhere to go, really, and not that much money, and she was about to call you anyway, then these girls hanging around the bus station saw her sitting there, crying. And one of them came over and sat down with her. That was Tamara. She talked to her, I guess, for a long time."

"She told you all about this."

"Sure. A lot of times. Like Tamara was some kind of guardian angel or something. She said she sat with her there way into the night, just keeping her company. Tamara told her she had a place Naomi could stay if she wanted, but she might not like it. Naomi didn't go. Later, Tamara left with some of her friends."

"What'd Naomi do?"

"She got on another bus, like at two in the morning or something, and went back to Columbus. In the morning she went to some-one's house she knew. But after that they talked on the phone."

"Who?"

"Tamara and Zeld— Naomi."

"They talked?"

"Yeah. At least once, I know."

"Janice," says Bank, "did Naomi ever say anything about Tamara doing a little prostitu-tion? Selling herself?"

"What?" says Janice, her face flushing pink. "No. Uh-uh."

"What's with the Zelda thing?"

"Zelda Fitzgerald," says Janice. "We read *The Great Gatsby* last fall and Naomi loved it. All those big old houses and waiters and stuff, and the ocean. And we had to do reports, you know, on something from the book, the time period or whatever, so Naomi did it on Zelda

Fitzgerald. She says she was a tragic figure. And after that she started calling herself Zelda, and she wanted me to call her that, too, and a few other girls. We each picked different names. . . . She thinks that's where Tamara is, you know."

"Where?"

"At that place. That house. She doesn't think she was really kidnapped. She thinks these people took her away to someplace better. And that's where Naomi wanted to go too."

"How does she know where?"

"That was the problem. She said she'd have gone right away, but she didn't know where. So, finally, when things got really bad for her, that thing with Peggy and all that —"

"And me," I say.

Janice looks at me, nods, and then continues. "— she said she was going to find out where it was."

"How would she do that?"

"Naomi thought some of Tamara's friends would know about it too. She said she thought she could find some of them."

"Tamara's friends?"

"Yes."

The panic comes back, now, clawing at my throat, swelling it. I look at Bank, begging him, imploring him to do something, to find her. Because he knows as well as I do what might happen to Naomi if she should happen to hook up with the people Tamara runs around with.

Outside, as we're walking to our car, Bank says, "No way she'll find them."

"No?" I say. "Maybe they'll find her."

"Or maybe she really will find this place, and go there."

"Like Tamara?" I say.

Bank shakes his head. "No," he says. "Not like that."

In the daylight Bank is diminished. The city looks alien through his eyes, strange and distant and uncommunicative. People are not where they belong. The traffic distracts him. Places that are open should be closed, and vice versa. This is my world, not his, but my being with him makes it feel unnatural to me too.

I ride numbly, unable to do much but mumble a few words, a suggestion, a thought.

After the school we drive to my house, where Peggy frets and the boys know something's wrong but have been warned, I gather, not to ask. I take Bank down to Naomi's room, which he rifles. Another betrayal, but the diary is gone from her drawer, anyway, and with it the two hundred dollars she showed me. Bank finds nothing else here to help us.

We hit the bus station and pass around Naomi's last school picture. No one remembers seeing her. We sit in the lot for an hour, watching, then head back to the PS Building. Googie tells us he has good people on it, and that we should both go home and sleep a little, since we've been up all night. We're due, actually, to come back on at eleven, but Stu shakes his head and tells me I'm on a leave until my daughter turns up. I protest. He ignores me.

So Bank drives me home again, to the western corridor, to the subdivision, past the brick wall where Naomi liked to sit. There — the past tense. I'm doing it too.

At dinner the boys, especially Ben, cannot help asking about their sister, pretending not to notice the looks their mother throws them when they do. I do not know what to tell them, not wanting to lie, but not wanting, either, to upset them too much. We're just not sure, I say. But we think she's with her friends. Why don't you just call them? Ben asks, but Peggy brings her palm down onto the table, and that puts an end to the questions.

I manage to doze for a couple hours after dinner, a shallow, irritating sleep that leaves me feeling more tired than before I lay down.

In spite of Stu's admonition I show up downtown at a quarter to eleven, wanting to see Bank, wanting to ride along even if I'm not on duty. But he's not here. I sit in my cubicle, pondering.

"Heya, Mack," says Stu.

"What're you doing here?"

"That's what I'm supposed to ask you."

"What am I supposed to do?" I say. "Sit around?"

"I don't know, Mack," he says. He leans up against a divider and crosses his arms.

"So where's Bank?" I ask.

"Out already," he says. "I guess he's been out for hours. He's not even on the clock till eleven."

"Something come up?"

"Yeah, Mack," he says, "something did. Father Hector."

"They found him?"

"No," he says. He swings a chair around and lowers himself into it. "We sent a CSU team out to run his room at the church, start a workup. They lifted some latents and scanned 'em in. Turns out he's the one who fingered Jamie Arbaugh's ball bat and Tamara Shipley's bike."

"They were his prints?"

"Yeah."

"Father Hector Morales?"

He nods. So this is why he really came in — to tell me this news himself. I thank him for it. He nods, says to take it easy, and leaves. I sit. I'm still sitting a few minutes later when Katherine wanders past. She stops and looks down at me.

"You come in to talk to me too?" I say.

"I thought you could use the company."

"No, thanks," I tell her.

"Go on home, Mack. We'll find her."

"Bullshit."

"Excuse me?"

"You heard about this print business with the priest?"

"Yes."

"Your old buddy, Father Hector."

"What's wrong, Mack?"

"Besides the fact that my daughter's out roaming the city, looking for some people who would love nothing more than to put her out on the street or stuff a crack pipe in her mouth? Besides that, you mean?"

"Mack —"

"Or, say, the fact that you, of all people, are running around behind all of our backs?"

She just crosses her arms and waits, now.

"Tamara's a runaway. Tamara's a whore.

Tamara's mother knew all about it. Tamara's mother was arranging to have her own daughter taken away by some strangers, the same group, just coincidentally, that Alan Norke was working with. Alan *fucking* Norke, Katherine, the guy you chased down seven years ago. And now this goddamn priest —"

She shakes her head.

"You deny knowing any of this?" I ask her.

"No."

"But you won't talk. You're acting very strangely. And it scares me, Katherine. Because it's you. You, who I trust."

"We're all trying to find this girl," she says. "These girls. That's all."

"That's not all. Something's going on. It's your business, I figure. But I'll tell you something — if it turns out you knew anything and kept it in, and Naomi gets hurt —"

Now, finally, she reacts. "You think if I knew anything, *anything*, about Naomi I wouldn't say so?"

"I hope you would."

"Hope? You son of a bitch. If you think that —"

"I don't know what to think, Katherine," I say. "About anything. I don't even remember how to think anymore."

I find myself on Andrew Jackson, angling

northwest out of the downtown, through the ring of burned-out houses that surround it, past the City Shelter, where the indigents line up every day for free meals, past the girls who regularly work that strip, past the city's museum of art, onward until I come to the edge of Heron Park. I pass it, then turn off near City Med and slow down. I like it back in here, the heavy foliage, the quiet, twisting streets. I follow them a little ways, until they bring me out to Brentcroft, then cut back east, and turn finally onto Morris Hill. I don't know why, but I feel drawn here.

I park, and walk up into the darkness and find my old spot on the picnic table across from Bank's building. I sit as I used to do, watching, listening, waiting for nothing, and everything. And then, while I'm looking up at Bank's place, a light snaps on and someone's shadow passes before the wide corner window.

Sue, who owns Harvey's Bar, answers when I knock. She stays here with Bank, sometimes. I have never asked for any details about the nature of their relationship, and I don't think either one would care to tell me much. Now, she does not ask me any questions. Just opens the door, motions me in with a flick of her head, and hands me her beer, which I gratefully accept.

She picks up the phone, dials a number, and hangs up. A moment later the phone rings. When she picks it up again, she does not wait to hear who's called. "He's here," she says, simply. Then, "Yeah," and hangs up again.

She'd called Bank's pager. She gets another beer from the fridge and sits down next to me.

"I'm sure Bank asked you," I say, "but did Naomi say anything to you at all? About this place she wanted to go? About who she might ask to find out?"

Sue cocks her arm and rests it on the back of the couch, watching me.

"Did she?"

"Drink the beer, Big Mack," she says.

"Right," I say.

"Right," she says. "You know Bank'll take care of it."

I drink with her. When I finish the beer, she hands me another, and I drink that too.

Then the door opens and Bank walks in.

"Come on," he says.

We cross into the park, past my old picnic table, on toward the lights around the golf course clubhouse.

"What do you know?" he says, finally.

"This group, the Sisters of Compassion. Norke was working with them when he took that girl in Indiana."

He stops and kneels down in the grass.

"You figured this out?"

"It's in the file," I say. "Katherine knew it too. What's going on?"

He stands again and walks.

"Katherine," I say. "I cannot figure her deal in all of this."

"Listen to me," he says then. "Just be quiet and listen. And, Mack, this is between us, and no one else. I mean it."

"Sure," I say.

"Listen to me," he says again. "I came across an address."

"Where she is? Oh, Jesus, Bank," I say, fear shooting cold throughout me. "Why aren't we there, now? It must be bad. . . ."

"Shhh," he says. "It's not like that. What I'm gonna tell you, this never goes anywhere."

I nod.

"Forever. No matter what happens, no matter how it turns, you don't ever give this up, not to no one. Okay?"

"Yeah. What is it?"

"Come on." We turn back toward Morris Hill and his apartment.

"This address, I need to run it down, but I

can't right now. It means a drive."

"How far?"

"I'm not sure."

We cross the street again and walk in silence up to his place. Sue's gone. Inside, Bank goes to the workstation in the corner, which he used once to track all the information on Jamie, information he had gradually taken down from the walls and the bulletin board and filed away. The computer still sits there, but I don't think he uses it much anymore. He opens a drawer, removes a single sheet of paper, and hands it to me. It contains nothing but a rural route number outside the town of Phillip's Landing, Ohio.

"Where's Phillip's Landing?"

"South, I think," he says. "South central. Get a map."

I'm about to ask him what it is, when I know. "It's a Sisters of Compassion house."

He just looks at me.

"Do you think she's there?"

He does not answer.

"And Tamara?" I say. "Rochelle said they didn't have her."

"What else was she gonna say? She's gotta cover for them, too, especially if they got the girl."

"And Katherine," I say.

He shrugs. "I'll tell you this," he says.

"Whatever you find out, you had better not breathe a word of it."

He's right. If Tamara's safe, if these people managed to get to her, then that's the way it should remain, and no one needs to be any wiser. If I get Naomi back, I don't care if anyone knows how it happened.

"Wait till the morning, Mack," Bank tells me. "You're tired and emotional right now. Nothing's going to change tonight. Promise me that? You'll wait?"

I nod.

"Okay," he says. He walks to the wide corner window and stands, hands clasped behind his back, looking out at the night. As I'm leaving, he turns and says, "Wait a minute." He goes to the desk again and unplugs his cell phone from its charger and tosses it to me.

"Take that with," he says.

"You might need it."

"I'll be fine," he says. Then he resumes his position at the window. He does not turn again, even when I leave.

31

I learned the ways of the burn unit, how to tie on the sterile gown and mask and bonnet and shoe covers in the transition room, how to pull on the latex gloves before helping one of the nurses with Bank's dressings. I learned the smells of that place, the sounds of its agonies and the incongruent cynicism and concern of its nurses. I learned to watch the debridement process, which is the picking off of destroyed skin, and the bathing, when they lift the burned patients in a cloth sling and lower them into a whirlpool. I learned what a face can come to look like.

Bank himself was not critical, at least not after the first week or two. The risk with him had been his lungs, the smoke inhalation, the questions of what permanent damage had been done. Some had, but not so much that he couldn't recover. His face was burned, too, but again not horribly. His neck, where the blanket had melted, was worse, the skin there healing eventually into a waxy-looking mass. The worst burns were on his hands, which in the beginning were wrapped thickly in white gauze, as were his head and neck, but in such a way that the elements of his face still showed.

Much worse off than Bank was the eighteen-year-old driver of the car, whose name was Denny Merkin. He had third-degree burns on forty percent of his body, including his face and hands. His lungs were also damaged, and on top of that he'd broken his left leg and arm in the crash. I sat with him, too, or with his parents sometimes. The burn unit is a place where you learn patience.

Sarah called me a day or two after the accident, when she heard what had happened. She did not say how she had heard about it or where she was calling from. I had thought she would come back, at least to see him, but she did not ever. She called once more, a few days later, when it had begun to become clear that Bank would not only survive but stood a chance of recovering more or less fully.

That was, by the way, the last time Sarah ever called or wrote to me. Somehow, I had known it would be.

Bank and I spoke about passing events, things he'd heard about the Job or the street from other cops who came up. He did not ever mention to me the night I had spent with his wife. In time we came to talk again as old friends do.

And strangely, my own life flowered during this time of the aftermath of these awful events. That summer I met a woman named Peggy Cook and her two-year-old son, Jack, and fell in love with them both.

In time, after numerous surgeries and grafts and hours and months of agonizing physical therapy, to which he brought every scrap of his strength and will and stubbornness, Bank would regain most of the use of his hands. Though he spent many painful hours at the city firing range, squeezing off clip after clip of ammunition, it would be nearly two years before he could fire a gun well enough for the Command to allow him to go out alone again, into the nights. But he rejoined the force in a desk job in the fall of '90, only nine months after the accident. And in the spring of 1991 he stood up next to me at my wedding. I convinced him to wear his dress blues even though his reserve duty had ended years before.

One of the images I remember most vividly from these months happened not too long after the accident itself. The news of Bank's actions, of his having risked his own life to save this eighteen-year-old boy, coupled with the pressure that had built from the rumors of Bank in the park and the still intense interest in Jamie's disappearance, drove the collective press into a new frenzy. Groups of reporters hovered on the sidewalk outside the front doors of St. Jerome's, as if some famous politician or actor were inside recuperating instead of a beat-up old detective. Again, this was not just local press. I spotted crews from stations and papers around the region. I myself was one of their targets. Some of the locals knew of my relationship with Bank and this knowledge spread quickly, so that I had trouble for a time entering or leaving through that door.

After Bank had recovered to the point that he could converse, but while he was still a full-time patient, still a badly injured man, I came to see him after my shift one afternoon. As I walked up the hallway, I knew that something was different. The light from his room, with its wide glass panels set into the walls, was too bright. A chill ran through me. I had seen the crash crews run stat emergencies when someone's heart or breathing had stopped, the room filling with people and portable equipment. I quickened my pace. There, inside, Bank sat up on his bed, fresh dressings around his face and hands. Next to him, in a pretty green suit and TV makeup, stood a local scene reporter named Holly Sawyer, and across from her a cameraman and his video setup. These were the lights I had seen. Bank waved at me. The piece, Bank's own account of his heroics, ran that night.

And after that it became common to find a camera crew and an interviewer set up in his room, or a print reporter sitting with him, notebook opened on her lap, a tape recorder running on the bed between them.

Later, the FBI's *Law Enforcement Bulletin* included a piece about Bank's rescue on its "Notes" page, and one of the national tabloid cop shows reenacted that night, with Bank appearing on camera afterward, one of his arms still in a sling from a surgery, a turtle-neck not entirely covering the scarred neck, the fingerless gloves he would always wear on his hands, to comment on the experience.

When he finally got back his nighttime f-car, he began taking local reporters with him for ride-alongs, giving them tours of the nastiest neighborhoods, never failing to find a situation of some kind they could record: Bank making a bust, squad cars converging suddenly in the dark night around him in support; a buy going down after Sleepy or one of his other crack snitches set up a deal so the cameras could record it.

I did not ever ask Bank what had caused him to decide to embrace the press in this way. But embrace them he did. And they in turn made him into nothing less than a true-life hero.

There is little else to tell of the years before Tamara Shipley. After his recovery I know that Bank continued to go out into the park, in the night, on his own, but I do not know how often or what he did there. I had a new family and could not run after him anymore.

I stayed on the day-shift, in Juvenile, until the changes hit our force and I was moved into Personal Crimes. Bank and I kept in close contact, though. I took to riding with him on my on-call nights. He enjoyed my kids I think sometimes as much as I did. They called him Uncle Bank.

With this new family my house needed work, and Bank and my father pitched in to help me do it. We built new shelves and closets, remodeled the kitchen, ran new electrical lines and outlets, repaired pipes and flooring. And when it was time for my daughter to come back into our lives, we built her a room.

I say "we," but they did most of it, my father and Bank, as solidly and carefully as they knew how. I felt happy seeing them working together again, and at the memories it brought up. I'd sit sometimes upstairs with my mother while they worked in the basement. It reminded us both of the way things had once been.

32

Perhaps because I had a direction, a lead, perhaps because Bank had led me to it, or perhaps just because I was exhausted, I slept almost instantly, and deeply, dreamlessly. But then at 6 A.M. I awoke just as suddenly and completely, finding myself abruptly open eyed and lucid.

When I step out of the shower, I see that I woke Peggy too. She leans against the sink, sipping coffee from a mug. Another mug, mine, steams on the sink.

"Thanks," I say.

"Feeling any better?"

"Fresher, at least. You?"

"No."

"Don't beat yourself up about this, Peg."

She nods but looks sad still, disappointed in herself. I rest my hand on the side of her face for a moment, until she smiles, then bump her aside with my hip and wipe the mirror with a towel so I can shave.

"We're coloring eggs today," she says.

"That's right," I say, then tell her — "I'm headed out of town."

"Where?"

"I don't know, exactly. I'll be back by this evening at the latest. Maybe sooner."

"This is about Naomi?"

"Of course. But, Peg, don't say anything, okay?"

"What do you mean?"

"I mean, someone calls from downtown, you don't know where I am."

"You're scaring me."

"No, don't be scared. This is just a thing. No danger in it, nothing like that."

"What if something happens here?"

"I've got Bank's cell phone. You call me."

"Bank knows about this? Now I am scared."

"Just hush, okay?" I lean over and kiss her. "When we get her back, we have to do something. Counseling, I suppose."

She nods in agreement.

"I know some good people."

It feels strange, exotic, to drive west instead of east, to head away from the city on the four-lane spur that ties us to I-75, and then to head south on that superhighway with the truckers and salesmen and old people on vacation.

Phillip's Landing, I see when I dig out the map, is actually quite a distance, tucked away into the hills of south-central Ohio, east of the

Wayne National Forest. Ohio is a state of cities, with seven metropolitan areas of at least a half a million people, all connected by major highways. But Phillip's Landing, equidistant from several of them, is accessible in the end only by remote secondary roads.

It is a perfect spring day in any case, the sun strong and high and clear, the air cool, the trees greening on the day before Easter. The concrete of the highway itself looks especially clean and white, perhaps in preparation.

The land is steep near Phillip's Landing, Ohio. The hills, though not high, rise almost from the center of the town itself, from the banks of the narrow brown river winding through it. The single main road, two-lane, pitted asphalt, follows the narrow valley, the route of the river. From it side streets shoot off along shallow draws or up the hillsides themselves, and are lined with old tall houses that all seem to lean slightly toward one another. Whatever industry or circumstance had built this place had also long since abandoned it.

In the downtown, which is all of three blocks long, I stop at a gas station across the street from a Sears catalog outlet with CLOSED written in irregular, chalky-white letters

410

across the window front. I top off the tank, though it comes to only three dollars and change, and then ask for directions to Rural Route 68 when I pay.

"Sixty-eight?" the man at the counter says, the underpinnings of a drawl in his words. This is Ohio, not the South, but these hills are where the South begins, though people from other places don't realize that. The man is small with a high, leathery forehead and deep encrustations of grease in the creases of his hands. "You on it, bud."

"This?" I say, pointing out at the road. My map was not clear on this.

"Yep. Main here. Sixty-eight ever where else."

The land opens out some east of the town, still rolling but lower, broader, less constricted. Farmhouses dot the hillsides, and fences cut them, some holding in livestock. The residents do not seem to place a priority on maintaining the numbers of their houses. I pass a RR number below the one I want, then later one well above it. I counted at least three unmarked houses between them, so I choose one of the three and pull up the long dirt drive to ask. Beyond it lies an open field that has already been worked some, bounded by a pine woods on one side and a steep, rocky incline on another.

It is a large place, an old redbrick farm-house that has had added on to its rear a two-story addition that's nearly as large as the original house. It makes a rather impressive building, though the bricks of this addition still look new and so do not quite match the original ones. Behind it, at the edge of the field, sits an old barn that does not look like it's used for much anymore. When I stop in the driveway a slow dog walks out to investigate, but he does not bark or threaten me. I let him sniff, then accompany him to the wide front porch.

A girl of about fifteen opens the door and looks at me with furrowed eyebrows and a frown. She does not speak.

"I'm looking for this address," I say, and hand her the sheet Bank gave me. I wait there for some time in the cool shade of the porch. The sunlight looks especially bright out beyond where I stand. At one point someone else opens the door a crack and peeks out.

Finally the door opens fully and a woman smiles out at me. She holds my paper with the address on it.

"Can I help you?" she says.

I cannot answer her. It is all I can manage to just stand there, looking. Her hair is tied back, her sleeves rolled up as if she's been working at something. She looks nice, still, with her pretty dark eyes. As nice as I remember her ever looking.

The smile passes from her face. Her eyebrows frown in confusion at first, and then rise in wonder.

"Max?" she says.

"Hello, Sarah," I say to her. She steps out, and I put my arms around her.

From the high foyer I can see into one of the front rooms, which holds a spinet piano and a couple of mismatched couches. Two teenaged girls, neither the one who answered the door, sit with their heads nearly touching as they talk.

"You're running this place," I say, "for the Sisters of Compassion."

She nods. I follow her back through the massive house to the huge open kitchen in the rear addition. A counter lined with half a dozen oak stools separates it from a dining area with a long oak table and chairs. I sit on one of the stools. Sarah sets a mug of coffee in front of me, cream, no sugar, the way I have always taken it.

"How long —" I begin, but stop because there is simply so much to ask, so much to talk about, that it overwhelms me.

"These girls —" I say.

"They're from all different places," she says. She stands across the counter from me, leaning forward on her arms, watching me with as much curiosity and fascination as I am watching her.

"How did you —" but again I stop. Another girl is coming down the hallway from the front of the house, looking me over. She seems unsure, somehow, uneasy. She is, I notice then, when she emerges into the light of the kitchen, older than the other girls I've seen, a young woman of eighteen or twenty. I look from her to Sarah, and see that Sarah has grown uneasy now too. She looks as if she wants to say something but cannot.

The girl comes toward me, her head tilted to one side as she inspects me. She's very pretty, with pale eyes and dark hair.

"Uncle Mack?" she says.

I look from her to Sarah again, confused, then frightened suddenly at the chasm I feel opening within me. I stand up.

"Do you know who I am?" she asks me.

And I do. I nod, but she tells me anyway.

"Jamie," she says.

She steps toward me, as her mother did, and I hug her too.

"I'm okay," she says. "I'm okay."

I begin to cry, then, as I hold her, not just

because of the shock at the knowledge that she is alive, but because at this moment I have begun to suspect the horrible truth.

FOUR

33

After Jamie excuses herself, Sarah freshens our coffee. I ask her first about Naomi, who, it turns out, is not here. Sarah's confused as to why I would think she might be, but leaves it for now. We have other things to talk about.

I follow her out back into the sun and air, into a wide yard with Adirondack chairs scattered about, to a white gazebo on the side opposite the barn, near a wooded ravine. We sit, but do not begin right away. We wait with each other, watching out over the distant fields, gathering ourselves because there is so very much to make up for.

Finally Sarah takes a deep breath. "The sad thing, Max," she says, "is that this case was really about love. A terribly inappropriate, misguided, ultimately destructive love, but love nonetheless. Which is why, maybe, it was so hard for me to see it. I needed help. Someone to say, 'Hey, you look at this.' "

"Alan Norke."

Sarah nods. "I met him that spring, when he was working in the school. We just shared a few words; he had some nice things to say

419

about Jamie. But he also caught me off guard. He said a couple of issues had come up when he'd talked with her that he'd be interested in exploring a little more fully. What issues? I asked him. He wouldn't really say, and didn't push it.

"Then in May he started helping with the softball team. Jamie sort of befriended him and they talked some more. One day he brought her home. I invited him in and made us some iced tea. Well, eventually he got around to asking some rather pointed questions about life in our house, about Jamie and what was going on with her. I think that not long before that I had actually begun to suspect something, or just to wonder a little. Something didn't feel quite right. But I hadn't faced it yet. So when he asked me this, it frightened me. I told him, actually, that I thought he should leave. Which he did, without any protest. But of course, the door was open then.

"In my gut, Max, I knew. So I called him one day a week later. He came over while Jamie was at school and Bank was at work. I confided my worst fears in him. And he told me that from the little Jamie had told him, he believed I might be right. But what to do, then? Before anything I had to know for sure.

"So Jamie and I took a trip one weekend. I

told Bank we were going to see an old friend of mine in Columbus who had a daughter Jamie's age. Which we did, actually. No big deal. But while we were there, we saw a psychiatrist at OSU who Alan referred us to. The man spent several hours on each of two days with Jamie, trying to draw her out. She said very little about what had happened. I think she learned the art of stubbornness from Bank. But this doctor was convinced at the end that she needed to be removed from the situation very quickly."

"And Norke had told you about the Sisters of Compassion."

"We'd talked about them, yes. But that wasn't what gave me the idea. One day Bank was talking about an old case he'd come across of some guy who'd disappeared one day. Just never showed up at home. And suddenly, there it was. I knew what I was going to do. I went to my father."

"It wasn't Norke's idea?"

"God, no. He was horrified when I told him. We argued about it for two weeks. But when he saw that I was serious, that this was what I wanted to do, that my father was already making arrangements, he put me in touch with the Sisters."

"And they condoned this, a staged abduction?"

"They said nothing about it. It was my decision. All they did was arrange to have someone pick her up at the time and location I specified."

"Father Hector Morales."

"That's right. I met him once beforehand. A very sincere man."

"And the safe house where they kept Jamie, that was in Indianapolis," I say. "That's where you went yourself, when you finally left."

She nods.

Then it is my turn to take the deep breath. I sip at the good coffee and look again out over the moist turned fields. "I guess," I say, "what I want to know is why you did it like that. And then how you could stay around for months after that with Bank, sleeping with him still. Lying to us all. There had to be other ways of dealing with this. And you, of all people, had access to them. You could have asked any of us for help, and we'd have been there."

"Would you, Max?" she says. "I mean, yes, I could have asked. I could have had help. Lawyers, cops, judges. You, maybe. Maybe not."

"God," I say. "What you had to engineer to carry it off. What you had to act your way through."

"It wasn't really acting. I was so torn up inside that if she'd actually been snatched by some stranger I'm not sure I'd have felt much more frightened. My tears were all real. And made worse by the fact that I couldn't talk about it. You think I didn't want to tell you? You think I didn't rehearse that speech? Didn't begin it with you a hundred times?"

"Then why didn't you?"

She shakes her head.

"You thought I'd say something to him."

"I don't know, Max. And I don't think you know what you'd have done then either."

"But, Sarah," I say, "I thought she was dead. I ran around with a hole in my chest looking for this girl I loved who I thought had been strangled or drowned or shot some-where. What kind of torture is that?"

"You want me to say I'm sorry?"

I don't answer.

She says, "Well, I am. I'm so terribly sorry, Max, and have been for seven years. I will go to my grave sorry for what I did. But you have children, you have a daughter. What lengths wouldn't you go to protect her? To save her from a thing that would damage her for the rest of her life? What lengths, Max? I know you, and I know there are none. You'd kill. You'd lie. You'd hurt everyone you know to save that girl, or one of your boys."

In the distance, beyond a rise, puffs of diesel smoke rise from the stack of a working tractor. But this hilly land does not look very productive with its light rocky dirt, so unlike the rich black topsoil of our Ulysses County.

"But you didn't even give him the chance to say anything."

She shakes her head and says, "I don't think you understand yet quite what happened. I don't think I've been clear.

"It was never obvious. It didn't just happen one time. I mean, he didn't throw her down and rape her. You hear about these families where the mother knew and didn't do anything. Maybe she was so desperate to keep a husband that she'd sacrifice her daughter's sanity for it. You think how sick that is, how this mother should be punished. But then, like anything else, when you find yourself in it, you realize it's not like that. It creeps up so gradually, like cancer, like getting older, that you just do not see it. One tiny little event at a time. And each of these small events is nothing in itself. You laugh it off, or ignore it. You push it away. A tickling session on the floor that seems just a little too aggressive, a little too touchy. But they've done it since she was a small girl, so it doesn't mean anything. She gets scared one night, though she's a little too old for that, she's nine years old, say, but he goes in as he's done since she was small and lies in the bed with her. He stays in there most of the night, but you assume he fell asleep with her, and don't think anything about it. On subsequent nights sometimes you wake up and find that he's not in your bed, that he's in hers, but you assume it's the same thing. They've always had a bond so when she gets frightened she comes to him, and he goes with her. That's what you assume, though you were never awakened by her coming in, and usually you wake immediately. Still, you would never guess, never allow yourself to guess, that he initiated it this time, that he's the one who went in and woke her up.

"But when you finally start to realize, when it begins to dawn on you, you ask yourself how it started. I spent days doing nothing but wondering about this. I think it was a long and nearly imperceptible seduction, not just of the child, but of the man. The man — let's assume he'd never done this before, he wasn't a pedophile in the common sense, could never imagine himself being a monster like that; in fact he's the sort of man who busts pedophiles, who prefers to beat on them a little before taking them down to where they are kept — he himself falls so gradually into the act, he approaches the line so slowly, that when he finally reaches it, he's barely aware anymore that it exists. We're talking here of maybe years.

"And what of the girl? What must it be like for her, this gradual seduction? The touching in itself, Max, which must be gentle, teasing, barely even there at first, is not unpleasant. She, like any child, is as physically sensitive as an adult. It feels good to her to be touched in certain ways, in certain places.

"But the thing is, Max, she has no context for it. Does it seem wrong to her? How could it? She has no way of judging, of evaluating, such a thing. It happens in such a profound vacuum that she cannot know. Or perhaps it does not seem right to her at first, especially if she's a little older. But this man who's touching her, this is the person to whom she's entrusted her life, the person she looks to for everything she has, the strongest, safest, best person she knows, who protects her from the world. And if he says it's right, then it must be. If he tells her she must not talk about it to anyone, not even her mother, then who is she to question that? If it ever hurts, if it's ever uncomfortable or frightening, he backs off, he stops and cradles her and caresses her, and he doesn't begin again until some time has passed, until she has healed. The next time he can push it a little farther.

"Until at some point he's committing the

ultimate violation. But, you see, Max, it never quite got to that point with us. *That's* why I did what I did, why I had to rip her out of there in any way I could, as quickly as I could, without having to fight Bank about it, because, Max, I stopped it. I *prevented* it."

"Prevented what?" I say, stupidly.

"The act itself. The rape. He did things to her over a long period of time. Sexual acts, I mean, fondling, kissing, stimulating. I think she did things to him. He and I hadn't had much in the way of relations toward the end. But he didn't do that. If she'd stayed, though, how much longer would it have taken? A week? A year? I didn't know, but I knew that eventually it would have happened."

"Sarah," I say, confused now, my head spinning, "how did you know all this? How do you know *what* the truth is?"

"I knew it hadn't happened yet because I had her examined. I knew he'd done other things because of what the psychiatrist discovered."

"Psycho-bullshit," I say. "You can find a shrink or a psychologist to say any damn thing you want. Ask the lawyers. And do you know how easy it is to plant a memory in a kid's head?"

"I knew," she says, "because of what I saw.

I knew because of how she acted when I asked her about it."

"Did she tell you it happened?"

"Eventually, yes."

"No, I mean in the beginning, before whatever therapy you must have put her into. Did she tell you then?"

"I knew her, Max. And I knew him, maybe better than you even. I *knew*. For a dozen different reasons, once I realized, I knew. No, she didn't tell me in so many words. She wouldn't talk about it. That's not unusual. But I knew. And later she did remember. She came to understand it herself, and to talk about it. When she was healed."

"When she was brainwashed."

"*Max* —" she says, her voice rising. Then she stops.

Some of the girls have come outside and are walking toward the old barn. They wave toward us. I wave back. When they've gone in, I say, "I just can't believe it of him, Sarah. I don't believe it. You should have talked to him. You should have —"

She says, "What really would have happened if I'd done that? Think about it. You think he'd have gone gently? You think I could just have said something and he'd have slunk off to some therapist's office? We'd have separated and that would have

428

been it? I don't think so.

"He'd have fought me with all his strength and bravado and cunning. And I had no hard proof of anything. I admit that. But I knew what would happen, sooner or later, if I didn't act. What the next logical step was between them. I had to stop that at any cost. And if I had stayed and fought, and it got out, can you imagine the spectacle? What it would have done to Jamie?

"Or to him. That's the other point. The allegation alone would have destroyed him — his reputation, his career, his almighty presence in the street, his friendships, what you thought of him, what your parents thought, his status in the eyes of all the cops who look up to him. He'd have gone from being a hero to being the worst scum of the earth."

I shake my head.

She says, "I don't think you've ever understood the mentality that led to this bizarre attachment he had to Jamie. He was *so* protective. He loved her so, so much. In the way he loves people, Max. In the way he loved me. In the way he loves you, how he's always loved you. He *possesses*. You know he'd die for you if you needed him to, or move the earth. And sometimes you believe he *could* move the earth. In the end, though, at least with Jamie, it was too much, it went too far.

"But the strangest thing of all is that I don't hate him. I feel sorry, more than anything. People are only what they're taught, right? And after what happened to him, growing up — I think later he simply willed himself to become powerful, so he would never be helpless like that again. So he could protect what was his, what he loved, protect the whole world, even. Or at least his city.

"But it's all mixed up in there. Where that line is, you know. That's the really tragic part of it." She looks at me and says, "What?"

"Are you talking about his parents dying?"

"Well, that's part of it," she says. "But I meant after that. The people he lived with . . . You know?"

I just watch her.

"Early on," she says, "when we were dating, he told me something once, almost in passing. It was the only time he ever mentioned it. I tried to pursue it with him but he made it very clear that it was a place I was never to go."

"Something about what?"

"What they did to him, Max. You really don't know?"

I can see the horror of my expression reflected in her face.

"Max —" she says, but I say, "No," and I hold my hand up to stop her talking. I don't want to hear her say it. Because I do know what she means.

I know.

It is not that I remember. It's not that simple. I've always remembered. These images have been with me for twenty-seven years, waiting not for me to see them, but to name them.

34

My knowledge of the rot that existed in that household began in 1968. June, I guess it was, because we had just watched, only a week or two earlier, the televised funeral of Bobby Kennedy. The summer was colored by that death, and the death just months before of Dr. Martin Luther King, Jr., and by the college protests that I was dimly aware were beginning to rage in earnest at the universities around us, in Columbus and Madison and Kent and Ann Arbor and far-distant places called Berkeley and Columbia, and by the body counts from Vietnam that Walter Cronkite dutifully reported every single night, it seemed, as we were getting up from dinner, and by some exotic holiday we'd recently learned of called Tet. It feels strange to look back at that remarkable, horrible year now and to see its place in history, when then it was nothing more than every day, than news reports and a few young men in the neighborhood who were plucked up by some invisible force called the Draft and made to vanish from that place, as if they had been stolen.

One hot, broadly sunny afternoon, I rode my bike over to Bank's, dumped it in the front yard, and knocked on the screen door. Angela let me in. The TV was on, of course, so I sat down with her. She was watching a soap opera called *The Edge of Night*. Several minutes passed and Bank did not appear.

"He know I'm here?" I asked Angela.

"Bank!" she hollered, without ever looking away from the screen. "Mack's here!"

It was still a while before I heard a door open and close, and Bank finally emerged from the hallway. I had not seen Frances around.

"Hey," he said.

I jumped up from the floor. "I brought my mitt," I said.

He seemed nervous, though, and uncharacteristically unfocused. I followed him out to the garage where he took out one of Ned's golf clubs, which he was expressly forbidden to touch, and began swinging it hard in the grass.

"Ever golf?" he asked.

"No. You?"

"Nope. I'm gonna, though. You want to see something?"

"What?"

"You can't tell no one."

"What is it?"

"I'll show you, but you gotta promise. You promise?"

"I have to do anything?"

"Jesus," he said. "No. It's just something to watch. You'll like it. But you can't tell no one. Swear."

"Okay."

"Say it."

"I swear."

He led me back into the house, through the kitchen and then the living room, where *The Edge of Night* had ended and *Dark Shadows* had just begun. Angela was still sitting there on the floor, staring at the screen. I do not think she had moved since I left. *Dark Shadows*, by the way, was a show I was forbidden to watch, but did anyway, sometimes, at Bank's. The vampires Barnabas and Quentin showed up regularly in my nightmares, and when I told my mother about it her sympathies were tempered by the fact of my disobedience.

On this day Bank stopped to watch for a moment but I got the impression this was only to cover what we were up to, so that Angela wouldn't get curious. After a minute Bank nodded at me and I followed him into the hallway. The doors at the end were closed: one of these led into Ned and Frances's bedroom, the other into the room that

Bank shared at times with some of the smaller children, but which at that moment he had to himself. I assumed this was where we were going. We spent a fair amount of time back there. I was always impressed at how neatly Bank kept his stuff, although neither this fact nor my mother's unceasing efforts succeeded in changing me over.

Bank stopped me, though, with a hand on my arm and pulled me into the bathroom. He glanced out through the door before closing it softly and turning the lock. He held a finger up over his lips. Then he stood in front of the sink and pulled open the medicine cabinet, holding his hand against the mirror to dampen the sound. I had no idea what he was up to. One of the few remarkable features of Ned and Frances's house, though, was this medicine cabinet. It had no inner wall, and was shared by both the hallway bathroom and the bathroom in the master bedroom. So if someone in each bathroom opened the cabinets at the same time, they'd be looking each other in the face. I remember, in fact, some television commercials at that time being designed around this gimmick.

"Morning, Sam."

"Morning, Bill."

Bank looked at me again, removed some bottles and a brush from the cabinet, so one shelf was clear, then reached through and pushed against the inside of the opposite cabinet door until it popped and swung open. I froze at the noise, though I couldn't imagine what we were looking for. Now he waved me closer. I stood next to him at the sink, our arms and shoulders and hips touching, and peered into the cabinet, into the darkened bathroom on the other side. And beyond that. The bathroom door was open, so that we could see clear into the master bedroom, could see, in fact, the bed with its head up against the far wall, its foot toward us. It took me a moment longer to notice that Frances was lying in it, and a moment longer than that to see that she was writhing somehow, as if she were in pain.

I looked at Bank but he kept watching. Frances rolled her head back and forth on the pillow. Her knees were spread apart and jutted up beneath the bedspread. Her whole body seemed to be moving and I thought at first that something was wrong with her, but Bank did not appear concerned. At one point she lifted her head and looked directly at us. We must have made some noise. I ducked, but she could not apparently see us through the darkness of the bathroom. A moment later, Frances flung off the bedspread, revealing to us the mound of her young, abundant and utterly naked body.

Bank kept, in the tree house he'd built, some greasy copies of *Playboy* he'd found in a Dumpster somewhere. But in 1968, or whenever these issues were dated, they had not yet begun to show total frontal nudity, so I had never seen pubic hair on a woman. I knew they had it. But seeing it then on Frances's otherwise smooth body shocked me in some deep way, more, at first, than the fact of her spread-legged writhing.

We were far enough away that we could not make out minute detail, but our vantage was virtually straight up between her legs, so we could see whatever she did there. Beyond that her great breasts flopped off to either side of her chest.

As we watched, Frances moved one hand so that it covered her pubic hair. Her fingers began working there, rubbing, slipping in a little. Then she stopped and placed the tip of one finger at a certain point and moved the finger rapidly back and forth. She lifted her hips from the mattress as she did this, higher and higher, and then plunged the finger into herself and fell back. Little muted noises escaped her, but something in her manner told me that she wanted to be louder, to cry out. She did this thing again and again with the finger, until she had worked herself into a sweating frenzy. And then, abruptly, she stopped. She lifted her head again and looked around, her eyes sweeping across the open bathroom door, but again apparently not registering us. She rolled to one side, revealing the crack running up the middle of her monstrous ass, opened the drawer in the bedside stand, and removed a long, off-white, banana-shaped object. She placed one hand between her legs again as she licked this object as one would a Popsicle. Soon, though, I saw what it was for, when she began rubbing it between her legs, where the fingers had been, and then it disappeared into her.

In the midst of this remarkable event my little hyperrational brain was still whirring away. For as I watched Frances pump this fake bone-colored dick into herself again and again, as her motions grew quicker and quicker, I realized that this answered a profound question I had been carrying around. I had just learned earlier that year what we called the Facts of Life. The existence of these Facts had been whispered around school long before I ever knew what they meant. The girls, of course, all seemed to have grown up knowing, and they acted disgusted at the mere mention of it by us boys, or rather disgusted at our ignorance of the whole subject.

But as the fourth grade wound on, certain boys were told by their parents, and warned not to tell others, so their own parents could tell them. Still, the gist of it got out. And I, quite simply, did not believe it.

But I began subtly pestering my parents to tell me, so I'd know for sure. The Birds and the Bees was another euphemism for it. This is what I asked about. What does it mean? I'd say, feigning complete ignorance. I tried asking Judy a couple times, too, but she just rolled her eyes and stalked away. And finally my mother told me one afternoon, but only in the sparsest detail, the minimum necessary to clue me in.

I remember sitting or lying around the house for long stretches of time after that while I contemplated this bizarreness, trying to picture it, to picture my parents (!), and to understand the mechanics of it, which I could not. The fault with my mental model, I now realized on watching Frances, was that it had no motion. I had the man inserting his penis, which stuck at a perfect ninety-degree angle from his body, into some mysterious gash, and simply holding it there for the requisite time. Now, I could see, what it was about was friction. And apparently, judging from Frances's movements, lots of it.

She grew louder, unable to hold her sounds in any longer. Still, she did not shriek. She cried out, saying "Oh," or "Mm," and grunting as she did, as if she were trying to make herself shit. The fake dick had become a blur, so fast was she whanging it in and out. She had now lifted her ass and her back completely off the bed. In fact, the only parts of her that seemed to be touching were her shoulders and her tiny feet.

And then she arrived at some moment, some peak, for after giving three or four particularly violent thrusts with her pelvis, Frances jammed the dick deeply into herself and held it there, her entire body locked in a kind of spasm or contraction. I held my breath, too, until she released a long, seamless groan, fell back to the bed, and commenced moving the phallus again, but more slowly, her real energy obviously dissipated. I was suddenly aware of my stiff erection, of the painful rubbing of my own little penis against my shorts.

And then a knock came on the door of the bathroom. Bank calmly closed the medicine cabinet and said, "What."

"I gotta pee," Angela said.

Bank unlocked the door.

"What are you guys doing in here?" she said, brushing past us.

"Talking," said Bank.

"Weirdos."

"Shut up," he told her.

She unsnapped her jeans and waited for us to leave so she could pull them down. Normally the prospect of catching a glimpse of this would have interested me, but I had seen far too much already. I quickly pulled the door closed.

I remember grappling with myself over whether to tell my parents, that I thought often of mentioning the incident to them, that I wanted to, and nearly did on a couple of occasions. I suppose I was afraid they would be angry at me, and at Bank. We had, after all, watched. I knew without doubt that my mother would stop me from going over there, and maybe even from seeing Bank again.

I remember that Frances seemed especially nice to me in the weeks following that afternoon. I never thought she'd even noticed me around before that; now she smiled at me when I came over. I remember feeling enormously self-conscious and uncomfortable in her presence, though, and thinking, at first, that because of this I was just noticing what I had missed before.

But then, later that summer, something else began to dawn on me. One morning when Frances was out, Bank went into their room to get something. I went in with him, and stood by the bed and looked into the bathroom. I could make out the medicine cabinet quite clearly, even with the lights out. I knew then what I had begun to suspect — that Frances would have had no trouble at all seeing the faces of two peeping boys as she lay there in her ecstasy. She had to have known we were there.

What I did not understand then, at the age of nine, was why. Or what this hinted at about other things that were going on in that house.

It wasn't until a year later, the following summer, that I knew really that something was wrong. In my mind, in memory, I have all of this taking place on that same afternoon I've described, when Bank sank beneath the surface of the pond in the woods in the Wilderness and did not surface, leading me to think he had drowned. In truth, though, I don't know if it all happened on the same day or not. What I know for sure is nothing more than a series of images, really. I have stitched them together into a kind of narrative line, but I would not be surprised to learn they did not happen in this way.

They begin with Bank and me lazily riding,

one morning, through the neighborhoods behind and south of our street. Some of these were so heavily treed that, even at its zenith, the sun could only reach the very center, painting a bright, blotchy line there that we rode back and forth across, weaving our way until we came out at the berm of Liam, into the cooling artificial breeze created by the cars ripping past. We crossed over to the church when traffic abated, then rode east, toward the school, past the spot where the buses lined up, then to the intersection at Pawtucket, and across to the Wilderness.

Normally, we'd creep along the steep, hard-packed dirt banks of the creek, watching for game. Bank had that combination of stealth and quickness that allowed him to catch frogs bare handed. After spotting one sunning itself at the water's edge, I'd watch from the grass as he crept on his belly over the crest of the bank and slithered down the slope, serpentlike, slowly, slowly, to within a couple feet of the frog. Then his hand would come up even more slowly, the movement barely perceptible, his arm not trembling or moving in any extraneous way, until he struck. His hand flashed forward, too quick to see, and then shot up over his head. He wasn't always successful. Sometimes I'd hear a splash out in the water where the frog had launched itself to. But often enough I'd see that little yellow-green snout with its bulbous black eyes peeking out from between his fingers.

On this day, though, we saw no frogs and I realized that we had not heard their usual croaking as we approached. Then, as we squatted on the bank, scanning the creek's reedy edges, a movement out on the water caught our eyes. A snake, three feet long and as thick around as my wrist, swam past us, its brownish body a darker shade of the color of the water, its sinuations sending out an endless series of S-shaped ripples as it fought the current. I felt the hairs on my neck stand up and scooched myself back up the embankment, but Bank stood at the edge and watched it. I know he was figuring a way to catch it, but in the end he did not come up with one.

"I bet it was a water moccasin," he said afterward, as we sat on the dirt, contemplating the moment.

"They're not around here."

"Yeah, they are. I heard about it. Some guy got killed in the Ojibwa." The huge Ojibwa, which bisected our city as it ran northward toward the Great Lakes, and into which this creek eventually drained, lay many miles to our east. I had only ever seen it then from one of the high bridges crossing it.

"Uh-uh."

"Yessir, smart-ass."

"I bet it was just a big garter or something," I said.

"They can't swim," he said. "I bet it was a water moccasin."

I'd read plenty about snakes and knew perfectly well that there were no water moccasins within three hundred miles of us, and that most any species of snake could swim, but I was not sure garter snakes got as big as the snake we'd seen, or came in that color. In any case, I didn't feel like arguing about it. The sight of the snake, though, seemed to spur us onward.

At the pool back in the woods we swam for a little while, but I kept seeing that snake winding its way upstream, its undulating body cutting through the water, its head held up slightly above the surface. I soon crawled onto the rocks to get warm. Was this the source of the sense of foreboding I remember feeling when Bank faked his drowning? Was this, then, the same day?

Perhaps. In this image, though, I do not sit on the rocks, but crawl farther back, onto the grassy bank, and huddle next to the pile of our clothing.

Bank announced he was going to break the

445

record in his ongoing breath-holding competition, as he did on any number of different days, and dived under. I started to time.

As the silent seconds rolled past, I happened to glance to my side, toward our carelessly discarded clothing. Bank's underwear lay on top of the pile and something in them caught my attention — a half-dollar-sized stain. I smiled at first and told myself to remember to tease him about this.

I looked out over the water. Bank showed no signs of surfacing. When I looked again at the clothing, the stain seemed odd to me, coppery and shiny in a way it should not have been. Like blood. Did I realize this then? I must have. I remember thinking that perhaps Bank was sick, and wondering if I should ask him about it. I knew he'd get mad if I did. But I sensed that this was a thing someone should look into, whatever had caused it.

My parents, I thought. I should at least mention it to them. Then my father could ask Bank about it in private, out in the shop. Or maybe not.

At this point either Bank did not surface and I began to panic, or he did and I called out his time. In either case I have a terribly specific, vivid physical memory of glancing once more at the blotchy reddish stain, then standing up. Of the heat and brilliance of the sunlight enshrouding my head. Of the certain knowledge that Bank was in trouble.

But I did not tell him what I had seen. Nor did I mention it to my parents, nor to anyone else. And the question, of course, was why? I didn't know. But something stopped me, some fear, some selfish instinct, indissolubly fused, I think now, to the incident with Frances, the guilt and confusion I felt about it.

In any event I failed again. My own weakness kept me quiet, and eventually shoved the whole issue out to the edges of my consciousness. What loss that would engender years later, I am only now, in the nakedness of the present tense, beginning to see.

35

"In the end," Sarah says, "knowing that helped form my decision."

"Because it was done to him, he'd do it too?"

"I think it allowed him to do what he did."

"You said yourself how much he loved her, how much it meant to him to protect her. Don't you think that's the last thing he'd do to her?"

"I don't think it's that simple, Max."

"No, what's simple is to say victims become molesters. It's an easy formula. An easy way of justifying."

"I don't know," she says, sharply. "That was just one part of it. All I knew at the time, at that moment, was that I was very frightened and confused, but very certain of what was going on, certain he would have fought me, that he would not have let her go. And certain of what I had to stop from happening. Whatever it cost."

I open my mouth to argue some more, then shut it again. It was, after all, seven years ago, and nothing I say now will change any of it.

★ ★ ★

Later, I ask, "How was it on her?"

"In the beginning, awful. She didn't want to go. I don't think she understood what was happening, or why. She just knew she'd been taken away from her mom and dad and that she was being kept in this place. But I called her whenever I could. So she knew she hadn't been abandoned. I told her there was an emergency, a very dangerous situation, and she had to just not ask too many questions and trust me. The women who ran the house lightened her hair, and whenever they went out, which wasn't often, they made her wear glasses and a hat. That made her mad, too, but they said someone might try to hurt her. She had to stay hidden. I think she told herself it was an outcropping of Bank's work, some police issue, and that she was a target or something. After a while she just went along with it. There was a time when she was convinced Bank had been killed at work and that that's why she was being kept in the dark. But I told her that was not so. Once she settled into her counseling, once she started to realize what had been done to her, I think she put it together. At some point not long after that she stopped asking about him.

"We were in Indianapolis together about six months. We took an apartment. I had her

449

home-schooled by people connected with the Sisters so she wouldn't be recognized. And then that summer we moved back to this area, farther east of here, actually, where my parents are from. A few of the family, the ones closest to us, and a few very close friends, knew. And they all, every last one of those good people, just accepted it as a matter of course and took that girl into their lives. She stayed at different houses, played with different kids, just for variety. I didn't send her back to school right away even then. So it was some time before she understood what a furor her so-called kidnapping had raised, not before she was fifteen or so. She found a clipping in the library. Then I told her everything. She seemed to accept it without much question. We talked it over now and then for a few days, and that was it."

"She doesn't ask about him?"

"No," Sarah says, "but she found clippings of some of the articles about him. She still has copies of them."

A little later she says, "Are you hungry?"

"Starved."

"Come on, then. We'll eat with the girls."

During lunch I speak with some of them about where they're from and how long they've been here. Tamara Shipley is not among them. I feel a stinging disappointment upon learning this, but my shock at what else I have learned is still so disorientingly great that this disappointment, and even my fears for Naomi, seem distant from me, attached to another life.

The girls and I talk about what they want to do one day. Some of them are particularly interested to learn that I'm a detective. They've had plenty of experience already with my type and find it a novelty to sit with one over lunch and chat as acquaintances rather than adversaries.

Jamie sits beside me the whole time. She seems to need to make sure that I am real. I notice her touching my sleeve or leaning in close to listen when I speak. I do not ask her or any of the girls any direct questions about their situations. Once, though, when I said her name, she said, "I'm Jane Lyell now, you know. We changed it when I went back to school. I took Mom's maiden name, and made my first name Jane. Janie. Almost the same."

Afterward, Sarah gives me a tour of the house with its six huge bedrooms, the old original parlors, the cavernous basement that has been finished off into a series of new rooms.

"We've had as many as fifteen girls here at

one time, though not for long. We're best at around eight, I think."

"So when did you decide to do this?"

"I started thinking about it when we were still in Indianapolis. They didn't have a house in this area, so I broached the subject actually with Diane Norke, Alan's mother. We spoke on the phone often, then. She had tremendous difficulty with his suicide, and it helped her to talk to me."

We're in the kitchen again. I sit down at the counter and rub my eyes.

"Sarah," I say, "there's something you should know." She sits on the stool next to me. The room is empty but for us. "Alan Norke," I say, "didn't commit suicide."

She does not say anything. She just stares at me, waiting.

"I was there when he fell."

"Oh, Max."

"And so was Bank."

"Oh, God," she says, a sad, sickened sound. "I killed him."

"Listen," I say. "It was an accident, not a murder. I don't know what I'd have done otherwise. Bank waited that night outside his building. When Alan came out, Bank showed him his badge and told him to get into the car. I think Alan didn't recognize him at first. Bank drove him around to that old factory and said they weren't leaving until he knew the truth."

Sarah watches me, her hand across her mouth.

"Alan got away from him and ran into the building. Bank chased him. I caught up with them on the roof. Alan tried to run. It was an accident. I swear to you it was. Bank wanted to know, not get revenge. At least not then. When Alan died, we both knew it was over."

She sits very still, staring off across the room. She does not speak for some time. When she does, she says, "His mother should know."

"We've always had secrets, you and me," I say. "And now we do again. Darker ones. More dangerous. You need me to keep yours. And I need you to keep this one. Please."

She looks at me. After a moment she appears to nod.

"Tamara Shipley," I say, a little later.

"Tamara —" says Sarah. "The girl who was kidnapped."

"I hoped she was here. And Naomi."

"Why would she — why would you think they'd be here?"

"We know about it, Sarah. Tamara's mother was calling the Sisters of Compassion in Chicago. She was arranging to have the girl

taken away. You knew she'd been a prosti-
tute?"

"Knew —" she says. "Max, I'm not sure
I'm following this. Did you think someone
from the group took her?"

"I didn't know —" I say. "We thought that
was a possibility, that she was at one of these
houses. Then I found this address."

"Why would you come then, anyway?"

"Naomi knew about it too. She wanted to
come. I hoped —"

"How — how could anyone say either of
them might be here? That doesn't make
sense. There are lots of these houses."

"Tamara was supposed to come here,
wasn't she?"

"I don't know. No one knows until the last
moment. I don't know I'm getting someone
practically until she's here. It has to be that
way. So who could have . . . where did you get
this address?"

I do not answer.

"Max — almost no one knows where the
houses are. Even people in the group, people
who help us, don't know. They don't want to
know."

"Bank knew," I say.

She makes a sound, a sort of gasping, and
her eyes widen with fear. "No one knows,
Max. Just a couple people in Chicago and the

few drivers we use." She stands and feels in her pockets, then pulls out the paper Bank gave me with the address on it. She lays it on the counter. I see then what I did not notice before, what perhaps I did not care to notice — that it's an old sheet of paper, yellowed around its edges. And the ink with which he wrote the address has faded. I remember then that we had to go back to his apartment to get it, that he took it from a file. Why, if he'd just come across this information, would he have filed it already? Why wouldn't it have been in his notebook still?

"He knows," Sarah says.

I correct her. "He's known. For years. But he's left you alone."

"How —" she begins.

"When he crawled into the car after that boy, when he was burned, I knew that night that he didn't care if he died. That maybe he wanted to. And I thought I knew why — because of losing Jamie, and then because I'd betrayed him, with you. That morning when you left my house, he was there, watching. But that wasn't all of it. He'd found you and Jamie. He knew the truth."

"I still don't see how."

"Those PI's he hired, to keep looking for Jamie. He had this whole center set up in that apartment. He worked with those guys for months looking for her, paying them a lot of money. And then, after the burn, it all stopped. He cut them loose. Why? Why stop looking?"

"Because he'd found her," Sarah says. "He must have had them follow me to Indianapolis. And they saw us together."

"But the burn stopped him from coming after you. After he started to heal, he was changed. He acted differently. That's when he started going to the press. Another way of making the world the way he wanted it to be. A way of reinventing himself, to keep from crumbling."

"But we left Indianapolis," she says.

"Once he knew where you were, it would have been easy to have someone keep tabs. Maybe the same PI's."

But now a new more urgent question occurs to me. Why did he send me here now, after all this time? He had known all along that Tamara and Naomi weren't here. He wanted to show me the truth, finally, a truth he had not ever wanted anyone to know, a truth he had perhaps denied even to himself. But why? And why now?

Sarah walks me out to my car, where that old dog still waits.

"Max —" she says.

"We can't apologize," I say. "Neither of us."

"No."

"We never know, do we? We just find our way. What else is there?" I hold her to me one last time, and then get into the car. I have started it and pulled it into gear when something else occurs to me.

"Sarah," I say, "earlier you said something about protecting my boys. How did you know I had sons?"

She smiles at me, that brilliant smile I loved for so long, and reaches in and touches my face.

Once I'm back on the interstate, I lift Bank's cell phone from the passenger seat where I had left it and see that it's been turned off. Almost as soon as I touch the power button, it rings.

"Mack," Peggy says, "I've been trying to reach you. You've been getting calls here all day."

"Sorry," I say. "Who called?"

"Katherine. Googie. Stu Marek just called. Something's wrong."

"Yes," I say. "Have you heard from Bank?"

"No. Mack, they won't tell me anything about Naomi. They say they still don't know."

"It's okay," I tell her, though I don't know if it is. "Just wait there."

I plug in my dash light and gear the car up to eighty. It's not long before a state cop tools up behind me and touches his lights. I pull over, and hang my badge and ID over the edge of the window.

"Got a hot one," I tell him.

He pulls out ahead then and gives me an escort almost to the Ulysses County line. We hit ninety most of the way.

Daytime homicide scenes are usually busy places in our city. Young detectives anxious to cut their teeth are brought out by the older guys training them; then when you add in the assigned Personal Crimes detectives actually investigating the case, the CSU techs, the coroner's investigator, and sometimes a doc from that office, too, you can easily have twenty or more people milling about, both inside and outside the perimeter, and this did not count onlookers, press, witnesses, and the like.

But the scene on Payco Street, a half a mile from the Shipley house on King's Court, is subdued. Patrol cars block the street at either corner, though the patrolmen let me pass without question. Only a few cars are parked in front of the address Stu gave me.

I called him when I reached the city.

"They found Father Hector," he told me. He was just headed out for the scene.

A patrol sergeant has been stationed on the front door to control access. As I approach him, I hear a voice from inside say, "He's okay."

A onetime Violent Crimes detective called Alphabet is running this scene.

Even before I step inside, I smell it. There is something about the odor of decaying human unlike any other rotting animal flesh, any sort of garbage or gas, that seems to penetrate directly from the sinuses to a gland at the center of the brain and to trigger a response there, an emotional reaction that in my experience is unique. I have heard soldiers speak of this, men who had to lie in jungles in Vietnam or the muddy hills of Korea as scores of bodies lying around them bloated and turned rancid. They speak still, decades later, of that haunting stench.

"Fuckin' new suit," Alphabet says, first off. This odor permeates everything, especially clothing, and does not wear off. I know wives of some of the old Homicide guys who make them keep spare clothes and a box of garbage bags in the garage, so when they come home from a bad scene they can change out there and bag the suit for dry cleaning.

The front room is low and dark, typical of many of the houses over here. Rusty water stains mark the ceiling, parts of which sag so badly it looks as if they might come down. Cheap wood-grain paneling covers the walls. Some of this has fallen away, too, revealing the broken and stained plaster beneath it. The carpet, a matted gold shag, looks moldy. The room holds no furniture but a couch and an old coffee table. Used crack stems and plastic vials litter the floor and table. A doper's flop, probably long abandoned by its last owner.

In the center of the floor, in the midst of the litter, the swelling body of Father Hector Morales lies facedown. One arm extends up over his head, the other is tucked beneath his belly. Beneath the surface of the skin faint streaks of blue-green mold point down along the arms toward the hands, which have just begun to shrivel and curl into dry claws. His head, turned to one side, rests on the black mat that formed where his blood soaked into the carpeting. His mouth has been pressed open by the swollen, protruding tongue. On the back of his head, just above the hairline, I make out a deep blood-crusted indentation several inches across. CSU has already bagged his hands and feet, and taped around the outline on the floor. They are apparently finished taking their pictures here, but someone with a camera works back farther in the house. Flashes reflect off the walls in the next room. I hear footsteps overhead as well.

"How'd we find him?"

"Kids," Alphabet says. "They been sneaking in to look at the body. It got around the 'hood, till somebody called it in. Pipe wrench in the kitchen. Hairs and some blood."

"Yeah?"

"CI says it's been four, five days, give or take. He's around here somewhere, you want to talk to him." The coroner's investigator, he means.

"That's all right."

"Woulda been quick. He didn't feel nothing."

We stand there a moment, contemplating this.

"Stu said to send you on up." Alphabet points at the ceiling.

The upstairs is in worse shape than down. Parts of the ceiling have actually fallen through. In one spot I can see clear into the attic, and beyond it to the roof, and through a small hole there to the sky above. The floor feels soggy beneath my feet in spots where it has rained in. The odor of putrefaction is muted up here, and mixed with the smell of mold. I come first to a bathroom. Beyond it, on either side of the dark, cramped hallway, are two bedrooms. Bright light and the sound of voices comes from the smaller one at the rear of the house.

Stu stands with his arms crossed while two CSU techs work. One of them is Bill Biner, who worked the LHS scene behind the Food King. They wear surgical masks and latex gloves. A portable halogen lamp has been set up above the bed, over which they both lean, their heads nearly touching. Bill lifts something invisible with a pair of tweezers while the other holds open a plastic evidence bag for him to drop it in.

"She was here," Stu says. "Tamara."

Biner looks up at me and says, "That's how it looks. Have to work this up, but I'm pretty sure. We got hairs off the pillows. Rope fibers from around the bedposts. Right-size latents. Strips of packing tape on the mattress and floor."

"They brought her here first," I say. "Back to the neighborhood."

Stu nods.

Father Hector dropped out of sight on Monday, the day after the abduction. And that's about how long he's been dead. So he found them, somehow, tried to get the girl back, and got clubbed in the head for his efforts. "Got an owner?" I say.

"Looking into it," Stu says. "Don't hold your breath."

"Any word from Bank?"

"Nope."

"I need to see him."

"Yeah, no shit."

"So," I say, "what about Naomi?"

"Oh," says Stu. "Googie radioed a few minutes ago. He wants to see you a-sap. He's downtown!" Stu has to yell after me because I'm already running.

"I kep' a guy on'a bus station," Googie says, in the conference room. " 'Cause she went there before, from what her friend tol' you, right? Man, you're a little ripe there, bud."

"Hey, thanks."

"Flashing her pic, right? Second trick janitor comes on 'nis afternoon, he says, yeah, he seen her the night before. Sittin'. She caught his eye, he says, way she looked. After while she made some calls. Then, just when he was gettin' off his shift, a car come round. He seen her get in."

"Who?"

"Couldn't make out the driver. But get this: He seen'a plate. Vanity deal. Easy to remember. *Par T.* Ninety-one Mustang registered to a Sherri Bell. Nineteen. Address is her mother's place, but Ma ain't seen her in weeks, says she don't stop at home much no more."

"Naomi got in her car?"

"Mack," Googie says, his voice dropping, "this bitch's got a sheet."

I look into Googie's watery old eyes and brace myself.

"Vice picked her up 'bout five months ago for solicitation. She pled it out. Suspended sentence."

"Fuck," I say. *"Fuck, fuck, fuck."* And with each word I slam my hand down onto the wooden table until I feel blood vessels rupturing.

Katherine's sitting on the wooden bench in the hallway when I come out. Waiting, I can see, for me.

"I talked to her, Mack," she says. "This afternoon." She looks around, making sure no one else can hear. "Sarah," she says.

I'm careful not to react. "Not now," I tell her.

"Yes, now," she says. "Where else are you going? What've you got?"

I shake my head.

"Then come on," she says. "Let's get out of here." As we're walking down the hallway to the elevators, she says, "Nice cologne, Mack."

At the center of the open concrete plaza called Government Center, where a green oxidized statue of one of the founding industrialists overlooks a misting fountain, Katherine sits on a cold concrete bench. A chilly wind rolls from the surface of the Ojibwa and is then amplified by the buildings of the downtown until it hits this square, making eavesdropping difficult.

Government Center has no overall design because these buildings were erected over a period of many decades, some beautifully ornate, dating back to the turn of the century. Before us, though, forming the center of the eastern border of the square, rises the Public Safety Building, a fifties utilitarian nightmare.

"I couldn't let the whole thing get blown," Katherine says, after I sit down next to her. "I'm sorry. I had to cover."

"For Sarah, you mean? Or the Sisters? Or yourself?"

"All the above, I suppose."

"So, what do you do?"

"Help funnel girls out of the city."

"Neatly bypassing the entire county social-services structure."

"Yeah, well, this way it gets done, you know? It hasn't happened often, but when

465

there's a kid who really needs help and who's in the right circumstance —"

"You call Father Hector."

"Well, I did."

"Did you call him for Jamie?"

"I wasn't in on it back then, Mack. I couldn't have done that, what Sarah did. I couldn't have played that charade."

"No?"

"No way."

"When did you cop to it, then? How'd you get into this?"

"I figured it out a year, year and a half later. You could have too. She set it up for both of us. You got a note from her after she left, with a phone number where she was staying in Indianapolis?"

"Right."

"Me too. All we had to do was go back and look at the Norke file. When he was busted in eighty-six for driving that girl from South Bend, that's where he'd been taking her — the safe house in Indianapolis. The address and phone number are buried there in all those reports. Same phone number Sarah sent us."

"So you called her then?"

"She wasn't there anymore. And they wouldn't tell me anything. I called Stamos back in Chi, asked him to run down these Sisters of Compassion. I drove up there and talked to one of them. And you know what? I liked her. I liked what she said. She was straight up with me. No bullshit. She couldn't tell me a lot, nothing about Sarah, but she said what she could. Six months later I ran across a girl here who I thought could use their help, so I called this woman. Next thing I know, I get a call from someone called Father Hector." She's quiet a moment. "Who was a good man. Anyway, it wasn't long after that that Sarah called me. I drove over there and saw her and Jamie. God, did we cry."

Dusk has begun to fall on the city.

"How long have you known Tamara?" I ask her.

"Four months. I picked her up on the street one afternoon around Christmastime. Bought her dinner, took her home. It wasn't hard to see she was cruising for trouble. But she had a great fear of the system, and her mother had no faith in it at all. So I called in Father Hector. And Rochelle liked him. I mean, he didn't go in with the angle of getting the girl out of here. His work for the Sisters was only occasional. Actually, pretty rare. But he did a lot of direct counseling; he helped run a battered women's shelter in the Near South. So, you know, he talked to them both, he listened to what was going on, he spent a lot of time with them. Eventually, though, he did start telling them about certain possibilities. It turned out that Hector had helped a friend of Tamara's a year or two ago, so she already knew something about it. And he told me a part of her was excited. She wanted to go.

"See, Tamara's not a bad kid. She's not some little doper whore hanging out on the street. I think this prostitution thing is a very recent development, the last month or so. That's why Hector decided it was time to get her away. Before that it was just her staying out partying, hanging with the homies. She might have been sexually active, but not selling.

"But like most kids, she's conflicted, so another part of her was fighting leaving. She had her friends, she told Hector. In the end, though, she agreed to go."

"She did?"

Katherine nods. "It was all arranged. Hector was going to pick her up on Monday morning, after the other two left for school."

"Why after the other two left?" I say. "Why hide it like that? It wasn't a custody fight. Her mother wanted her to go, right?"

"Yes. But that's how Hector wanted it. With this prostitution angle, who knew what her deal was? I'm pretty positive she was not out there alone, soliciting men. I think she just hung on the edges of the badness a little too long and it caught her up, in the form of a pimp or a crack dealer or a strong-arm boyfriend. Whoever it was, you know they wouldn't want her to go."

"And I guess they didn't let her. You think Hector knew who it was, from the start, I mean?"

"I don't know."

"He found where they had her. Something led him in there. Why wouldn't he call you in when he knew?"

She doesn't answer.

"Whoever took her," I say, "they knew it was set for that Monday."

"For all we know, she threw it up in their faces. It doesn't help us."

"But Hector knew."

We watch the night fall on the city, the streetlights flicking on, one after the other, down the avenues, the headlights on cars, the buildings. Soon I cannot make out Katherine's face.

"What does Bank know?" I ask her.

"Sarah said you figured he knows where she is, that he's known all along. I'd have never guessed that. I know he knows about the Sisters, and that Tamara was supposed to leave with them. I think he knows that I'm

469

involved with the Sisters, but he's never said anything to me or anyone else, as far as I can tell, about that. I suspect he knows that I know where Sarah and Jamie are, and if that's true, then he must think that I know something about what happened between him and Jamie. But he'd never ask me about that."

"What about that? You think anything really happened?"

"Don't you?"

"No. Maybe. I don't know."

She thinks for a moment, then says, "The truth is, I don't know, either, Mack. Really, I don't. There was a time when I was convinced he had. I went around fucking furious for months. I found out he'd started seeing someone. A professional. A shrink."

"Where'd you hear that?"

"I know people in the business. I sometimes share professional details with them I shouldn't. They do the same. At first, I figured, it proved he'd done something to Jamie. Why else get treatment? Then, later, after I'd gotten over the anger, I thought, you know, all the shit he went through, who wouldn't need to see a shrink? It didn't really prove anything."

"What if Sarah had come to you? Before, I mean."

"Yeah, well, you think about that, don't

you? But I didn't know her then. We met, I think, once when she was downtown for something. I got to know her really during the investigation into Jamie. That's the irony of it. And I think she saw that. I think she realized at some point that she and I together could have dealt with it. I could have intervened, handled Bank, kept a lid on it, worked it out differently. But, hey," she says, "she did what she felt she had to do. She did an amazing thing, if you think about it. She sacrificed everything. I know she loved him. I know she missed him, which I have never been able to get my head around, considering what she believes he did. But it's true. I've had a lot longer than you to think about all this.

"And then," she says, "you think — if it was true, if she was right, then it's possible that maybe she saved them all by doing it."

As we're walking back to the building, I say, "Katherine, I have to find Naomi tonight."

"What are you going to do?"

"I don't know. Will you —"

"I'm here, Mack. I'm looking. I'm not going home."

"Thanks," I say. She gives my arm a squeeze. I'm about to leave her there, at the front entrance, when another question occurs to me.

"Did the priest ever tell you how it really went down? Back then, with Jamie?"

"He did," she says.

36

Father Hector Morales did not know much about this new girl. He knew that she was eleven. He knew what she looked like because he'd been given a wallet-sized school photo taken the previous fall. He'd met the mother once, briefly. She'd impressed him as being very strong and clear-minded. And he knew that this was a messy case, involving the father and some possible sexual misconduct. Father Hector Morales knew also that this father was a cop, but beyond that he knew nothing about the man.

What Father Hector most certainly did not know was that the transportation of this girl would set off one of the largest manhunts in the history of the city and would make the national news. He did not understand, had not been warned, that it was going to be construed by the mother as a kidnapping. Had the Sisters themselves known this? Father Hector was never given a satisfactory answer to that question. What he did discover later was that this case had come accompanied by a very generous donation from a steel corporation. And that it had come in through unusual channels, via an attorney named Diane Norke, at the Chicago firm of Meeks, Gasset and Hunt, and with her strongest voicing of support. Diane Norke, Father Hector knew, was a great supporter of the Sisters, having given them, *pro bono publico,* many hours of her legal expertise. She had been behind them from the beginning, when the three original Sisters came together. Diane Norke, Father Hector had once heard, had been repeatedly molested herself as a young girl. Hence her vehement support and legal defense of this group.

And Diane Norke's son, Alan, Father Hector knew, had worked with the Sisters in the past, and had even been arrested once. Father Hector welcomed the day when he himself would be arrested for his work. He would consider it a high honor. Still, he was as careful as he needed to be. There was no sense in provoking the Fates, and the Sisters insisted upon the highest levels of prudence and discretion.

But Father Hector did not know that Alan Norke, Diane's son, was even living in this city, let alone the fact that he had become friends with, and an advisor of sorts to, Sarah Arbaugh, this girl's mother. If he had known that, perhaps he would have thought differently of this case, perhaps he would have taken a few extra precautions. Perhaps he would have refused the case altogether. Or perhaps not. It is impossible to tell.

In any case, on the morning of July 10, 1989, Father Hector awoke early in his simple room at the parish of St. Thomas Aquinas. He looked at himself in the small handheld mirror he propped on the back of the sink, at the wiry black hair he had to keep very short because it was so unruly, the wide jaw and nose, the long-lashed eyes. He washed and brushed, dressed in casual street clothes, and had a light breakfast of toast and tea.

At exactly a quarter to nine he entered the village of Heron Hills and headed toward the spot where two bridges crossed the Heron River. He did not drive down Detwiler Place, past the girl's house, though this led most directly to the rendezvous point. Instead he took a more circuitous route, coming finally down Riverview toward the two bridges at just the moment the girl herself was arriving. He smiled and waved at her. She waved back, a little flick of the hand. He checked the picture once more, just to be certain, then got out and opened the passenger door.

"Good morning, Jamie," he said.

"Morning, Father." So she'd been told he was a priest. She had also, unbeknownst to the Father, been given a detailed description of him by Sarah. Just to make sure, Sarah had said, she didn't end up with some stranger.

The priest looked around. No one would see them. The one house that was in view was closed up, window shades drawn.

Jamie paused a moment, then slid her baseball mitt from the bat and laid the bat on the ground. She tucked the mitt beneath her arm and got into the car.

"You can take the bat too," Father Hector said.

Jamie shook her head. Though Sarah had not told her much of what was going on, or why, Jamie must have sensed that she would not be seeing Bank again for a long time. She wanted to leave the bat behind, as a sign, maybe, or as a kind of good-bye. Though Father Hector did not know this, he inferred some special meaning, some importance, for the girl in leaving the bat, and so he did not protest. Still, even though he had no idea of the firestorm that would be ignited a few hours later, he felt uncomfortable just leaving it lying there at the edge of the road. That was asking for trouble. And so, without really thinking about it, he picked it up, took a few steps out onto the wooden walking bridge, and flung it out into the trees over the river.

He did not hear it come down, and he did not think of it again.

A few minutes later, in a dirt cul-de-sac deep in the forested end of Heron Park, they waited for another driver, who was running a little late. As they waited, Jamie wandered down to the banks of the river, which lay only a few yards away, and knelt there looking out over the rushing water.

A moment later another man, a man the priest knew only as Hansen, arrived in a ten-year-old faded gray Volvo. Father Hector made the introductions, he squeezed Jamie's shoulder, assured her everything would be fine, and backed his parish car up the dirt lane toward Morton Parkway. As he waited for the traffic on Morton to clear sufficiently to allow him to back out, he glanced once more down into the clearing. He saw that Jamie had already climbed into the Volvo. He saw Hansen walking around the front of the car. And then, at just that moment, he saw a runner emerge on a trail from out of the woods. Father Hector could see very clearly as the runner looked up at Hansen and the Volvo, as he slowed and watched them for a moment before continuing on his way. But, Hector saw, Hansen had seen the runner as well, and had paused, whether intentionally or by chance, in the center of the front of the car. His position was such that he blocked the license plate from the runner's view.

After Hansen started the car, Jamie jumped out, ran back to the river, removed her baseball cap, and flipped it out into the current. Hector did not know why she had done this, but as she walked back to the car, he knew from the sadness in her face that, even if she had been riding with him, he would not have asked.

Later, after news of the apparent kidnapping hit and the runner came forward with his description, which led to the discovery of the hat in the river, Father Hector reflected on these events. If the runner had seen that the car's plate was out-of-state, especially if he'd identified it as an Indiana plate, the whole course of events might have turned out very differently, the future of the Sisters might have been jeopardized.

Only through the granting by God of these small moments of grace are good works sometimes accomplished. Therein, believed Father Hector, lay the very proof of their goodness.

Some years later, with no thought of any possible connection between these two events, with no knowledge of the tragedies that were soon to occur, Father Hector knelt on the sidewalk in front of a house on King's Court on the East Side of the city. He had just spent an hour talking with a woman named Rochelle, and her daughter, Tamara, a troubled child, but not yet in trouble. Father Hector had determined not to let this girl slide any farther down that slippery slope. He had a strong feeling about her, that she was something special.

She walked outside with him when he left, and wheeled her bicycle from the front porch. When she tried to ride it, though, she found that the chain had fallen off.

"It's really messed up," she said, as he watched. "My brother says it needs a new chain."

"Let me help," said the priest. And so he knelt and slipped the greasy chain back onto its sprockets, utterly unaware of the perfect print his right index finger had left in the grease on the inside of the chain guard. This print would remain there undisturbed for more than another month, until the bike was taken in by the police department's Crime Scene Unit and disassembled by the crime lab. But by the time a tech had lifted the print and the AFIS computer had determined that it matched one left on Jamie Arbaugh's bat seven years ago, Father Hector had ascended, some forty hours earlier, to his eternal reward.

37

I drive once more into a corner of the night that is falling on the city. This time, though, I am alone, and I do not know where to go. I follow the routes Bank and I drove earlier this week. I watch the streets but see no one I recognize. I stop by Bank's apartment, wanting, needing desperately, to see him, but it is dark and his car is gone. I did not really think he would be here.

I end up finally at the Denny's on Alcore. I need to eat something and this is a place Bank might come, though I do not expect to see him here either.

I have trouble thinking clearly, sorting out what I need to. I could try to find Sleepy. He came through for Bank before. Maybe he's heard something new. Maybe Bank went to him again. Maybe he knows where Bank's looking. But I have no idea where to look for him. He moves around, and he probably won't even be on the street for another few hours.

Or Abel Jackson's woman, Kendra. It might be worth my going back there to talk to her again.

I think about Bank. I think about those first two nights when he was out here alone, muscling anybody he could get his hands on who might know something. I can see the shake-down scowl he always wears, theatrical as much as it is angry. Though in this case the anger would have been a large part of it. And how much he controlled himself after I started riding with him.

I put my fork down and look out the window across the Denny's parking lot. "This address," he said to me last night in the park, "I need to run it down." He knew the girls weren't there. But I took the bait so hard, he never even had to ask me to make that drive. In fact, he had to slow me down, warn me to go in the morning, after I got some rest. Because I was ready to leave then, and he knew it. He knew I'd be back too soon.

Bank, patient.

Until I could be gotten out of his way. That's why he sent me to Phillip's Landing. Maybe partly it was to show me the truth, finally — because on some level, in some bizarre twisting and merging of time and images, Tamara has become Jamie to him. But it was also to get rid of me. So he could stop the charade he'd been playing for my benefit. So he could unleash himself on the city. That is what he's doing now. Waging his war, a war that goes to his very core. A war against some lowlife pimps here, against the rage and helplessness he felt seven years ago, and, I suppose, against Ned and Frances Baxter themselves.

I have to find him. I do not know where to begin.

Begin where you left off, then, I tell myself. *That's just protocol. If you get lost, you go back to where you last had the trail.*

I throw a ten on the table and run for my car.

"Oh, no," Kendra says, her eyes locking fiercely onto mine. "Not this shit again." She tries to close the door but I shove the handle of my Maglite in, blocking it.

"Three fuckin' nights in a row!" she says. "Don't you guys have nothing else to do?"

I fight with her a moment, her beating on the end of the Maglite, me bracing the door with my shoulder, before I hear what she's said. "Three nights?"

"I talked to you guys enough already!"

"Detective Arbaugh came back last night?"

"What?" she says, pausing in her fight to shut the door on me. "Four goddamn times. Like you didn't know that."

"I wasn't sure," I say. "What'd you tell him?" I manage to move the door another inch, and insert my foot.

"Fuck you." She commences kicking my shoe with her furry slippers, and goes back to the shrieking. "You guys think you can just shove someone around. Who the *fuck* you think you are?"

My face is close to hers now, through the opening. I jam my shoulder harder against the door, pushing her back a little more, but still not far enough to get inside.

"What the *fuck!*" she says, shoving back, even angrier, grunting with the effort.

"What'd you tell him?"

"We made a deal, no one else would come around screwing with me."

"What deal?"

"He said not to tell no one else, not even no other cops." She's tiring, now, sagging against the door.

"Well, I'm telling you to tell. Then I'm gone."

"He said don't."

"Don't tell, I'm calling a squad to haul your ass downtown."

"I ain't done nothin'!"

"I give a shit? You go down, I got you for twenty-four hours. What'd you tell him?"

"I dunno."

"When was he here?"

"He wasn't. I made it up."

"You're lying."

"I ain't."

"You're lying."

"I ain't!" she screams, so close to me now, I can smell the beer on her breath. "Get outta here!"

"You close this door," I say, "I'm calling that squad."

"You're a prick," she says.

"What'd you tell Bank? Who Abel's hanging with? What's he doing? Give me something, Kendra, or I will fuck with you."

She pants heavily. "He told me not to say nothin'."

"He won't find out. I promise."

"Oh, that makes me feel better."

"What'd you tell him?"

And finally, then, she's had enough. Her rage dissipates, and along with it whatever loyalty Bank temporarily inspired in her. He either paid her or threatened her, I figure. Probably both. But she just does not care anymore. And who can blame her?

"This one guy," she says. "I remembered Abel called him after that old TV show. *The Addams Family* or whatever it is."

A beat. I say, "What?"

"That's all I told him."

We are both leaning against the door, sucking wind, two out-of-shape puppies. I

484

say, "You mean *The Munsters.*"

"Whatever."

"Eddie Munster." Tamara Shipley's brother.

Kendra looks out at me, knowing she's given it up, that the box is open now and there's no point in shutting it. She nods.

"Any others?" I say.

"I dunno no names. Bunch of 'em. And these trashy bitches they got. I followed Abel's ass one day. I seen 'em. When I called him on it, he tells me it's just business."

"Business?"

"Gives me this line of bullshit how he's gonna make big money off 'a girls, now. Like he's this big pimp. Like I'm supposed to believe that shit."

I do not thank her. She leans back from the door, so that I can remove my foot.

"Katherine," I say. I've reached her on Bank's cell phone, not the radio. I give her a quick synopsis of what I know about Abel Jackson, the history, and what Kendra told me tonight.

She says she'll meet me there, at the house on King's Court.

But she beats me there. When I pull up and kill my lights, her car is dark. She's inside already. I climb out of my own car, then pause in the night because some movement or noise at the side of the house catches my attention. As I watch, I make out a slight figure as it comes down from the back porch and rustles around in a different bush than the one where I found the pair of Ponies. Then it heads out into the night.

Eddie Munster, slipping out the back because the detective lady has stepped in the front. Or maybe his mother worked it so he could go. I see now what even Katherine missed — that Rochelle Shipley has been scamming everyone, caught as she was between two very different but urgent needs: to get her daughter back, and to protect her son from prosecution. Father Hector knew this, and was sympathetic. His trying to help her on both fronts got him killed. What Rochelle has not yet understood, or allowed herself to believe, what I am just beginning to realize, is that the two aims are mutually exclusive.

I think of that new TV and chair in there, the lack of any debt, and I wonder what Eddie told her to explain the money. I wonder what she allowed herself to believe to justify it.

Eddie makes his getaway. Down at the corner, under the streetlight, he sits and pulls off his old shoes and puts on the new pair of ball shoes he retrieved from the new bush, the ones he bought to replace the pair of Ponies Bank confiscated. Now he's a man. Now he's one of the crew. Now he's ready to deal.

I cannot alert Katherine without losing him or tipping him off.

I follow.

We walk a good distance from King's Court, through back streets and alleys, out onto Woodlawn Avenue at one point, then back into the dark streets. Until we pass alongside the edge of the fenced-in grounds of the sprawling Lloyd DuShane Homes, then across a street to a corner-lot four-story apartment house, before which Eddie stops. I know this place. Welfare digs. I was here once, years before, after a kid was spotted firing an air rifle from the roof at passing cars. Its bricks are painted an ugly yellow-green but I cannot see that now, in the night.

From the sidewalk Eddie checks out the street, up and down. As he does, a car pulls up. He leans in the window. Goods, cash, change hands. A little deal. This is where Eddie clocks. This building's his base. And, right on cue, as the car pulls away, Eddie heads inside.

I walk around the two sides of the building that front the streets, listening. It's quiet. Twelve, maybe sixteen, apartments, and there's no one hanging out, no party, no argu-ments. No noise but some faint music leaking through one of the windows. Nothing to draw attention or bring on the Man.

I finger Bank's phone on my belt. My radio's back in the car. I don't know the number at the Shipley house, where Kath-erine is. I don't feel like calling in backup until I know if this is something.

As I watch, another car pulls up and parks on the street. A man approaches the front door, presses a buzzer, answers the question that comes. The door opens. He enters.

At the front door I press the bell to Apt. 1A, then reach up and unscrew the lightbulb over my head. Nothing happens. I press 1B, then 1C. The buzzer sounds and the lock clicks open.

I find myself at the end of a long, musty hallway. Bare bulbs hang from either end of the ceiling. A plastic carpet guard runs down the center, but the carpeting beneath it looks stained and ruined anyway. I count four apartments on the first floor and a set of winding wooden stairs down at the far end. As I'm walking toward them, the door to one of the apartments opens and an old man in a bathrobe pokes his nose out.

I hold up my badge. He shuts the door, quick as he can.

It grows darker as I move up to the first landing. I brought the Maglite with me but do not turn it on. Sounds of the man who preceded me into the building waft down through the stairwell from the third or fourth floor. Knocking, a door opening, then closing again. The hallway immediately above me, the second floor, is lighted at either end, like the first floor, with bare bulbs. I hear crying. Or perhaps it's laughing. As I move up the steps it changes to a high-pitched, rapid monologue, an excited female voice babbling away.

"Hey, you bitch!" another woman says. Then more laughter, crazy and stoned. From the staircase I look down toward the end of the hallway and the voices. I creep toward the sound, reaching inside my jacket as I do and unsnapping the cross-draw holster to check the 9mm Colt Commander that rests there. In my left hand I shift the Maglite. And then my breath catches as I pass before another door and hear muted squeals and thumping coming from behind it. I open it.

It is a supply closet, long and narrow and suffused by a dim light. I make out three figures lying on the floor, the bodies of men. They are not dead, though. In fact, they look up at me. Duct tape seals their mouths and binds their feet. Their hands are riot cuffed behind their backs. One of them bucks, bouncing his head off the floor and making angry noises in an attempt to get me to undo him.

Bank is somewhere in the building, playing Spider-Man, catching the bad boys in his web, one at a time.

I'm about to slip back into the hallway when I hear footsteps in the stairwell. When they've passed, I go to the stairs and listen. Again I hear knocking, a door opening. The fourth floor, it sounds like.

At the other end of the hallway, outside the door to the last apartment, I can hear the voices clearly now, three of them, all female. "The son of a bitch!" one says. "That shit's wrong. He can't just do that."

"Shut the fuck up, Sherri," says another. Sherri. Sherri Bell. Par T girl. Little ghouls run across my back, their feet making me itch. I pull out the Commander and flip off the safety.

The third voice says, "Where in the fuck is he?" and then laughs that crazy laugh.

I look back down the hallway, then knock on the door with the butt of the Maglite. The laughter dies. I step aside so they cannot see me through the peephole, and listen to the footsteps.

"Why's he knocking?" one says. A voice

just inside the door says, "I don't see nothin'."

"Well, open it."

When she does, I step around and drive my right foot hard into the center of the door, which sends the girl sliding on her ass back across the kitchen linoleum. I point the Commander at her, then swing it quickly into the dim living room.

"Do not move," I say, as calmly as I can manage. The television is on. The two scaggy girls sitting on the ratty furniture stare at me with opened mouths, one still holding a pipe in one hand and a lit Bic in the other, frozen in front of her face, the flame leaping, lighting her features. The third, still on the kitchen floor, begins to say something nasty.

"Don't," I say, swinging the gun back to her. "Don't talk until I tell you to talk. Understand?" She does not nod, but she shuts up.

Now the smoker kills the flame and says, "Who —"

"I said shut up. No noise." I step inside and pull the door closed.

"Who else is here?"

They just look dumbly up at me. But I hear someone else coming out of one of the bedrooms in the back, approaching. I point the Commander into the darkened interior and find myself aiming at the face of a girl.

"Daddy," she says. Naomi.

"Oh, Jesus." I breathe. I breathe. I resist the urge to run to her, to take her in. I fight the tears I feel welling up. I shift the gun away. She looks amazed, more than anything, to see me. Her face looks red and swollen.

"Daddy?" one of the women in the living room says, the one who was not smoking. "That's sick."

"Shut *up*. You want me to thump you in your head?"

She looks up with the dim expression again, mouth hanging open.

"What's your name?"

"Sherri."

"You picked this girl up at the bus station?"

"Yeah. How'd you —"

"Kidnapping. Unlawful restraint. Major felonies."

"Felonies? All's I did —"

"I said shut up."

"Jesus."

"Who else is here?"

"No one —"

"Who're the assholes upstairs?"

"Upstairs?"

"In the apartment they're working out of. You want to tell me you don't know about that? You haven't been up there doing a little business yourself?"

She doesn't answer.

I motion Naomi out into the hallway, and follow her, keeping the door open a crack so I can watch the three beauties inside.

"Anyone else in here?" I ask her.

"No."

"Who else have you seen?"

"Just some guys."

"Naomi, did any of these guys do anything, you know?"

She looks at me.

"To you?"

"No, Dad. I've been in that room. I wanted to call. They wouldn't let me, so I locked myself in —"

I'm not sure what to do. I want her out of here, but I need to find Bank.

"You safe in that room?"

She shrugs.

"I want you to go back in there and lock the door again." I hand her my Maglite. "If anyone breaks in, stand by the door and use this on their head. Hard as you can swing."

Back inside the apartment I wait while Naomi gets herself a glass of water and uses the bathroom. When she's locked in again, I say to the three girls in the living room, "Where's Abel?"

Vacuous looks.

"Do you understand what I'll do to you if

anyone goes in after that girl? I come back and anything's happened to her? She's scratched. She's got a bruise. Anything, do you understand?"

They don't answer. I step over to Sherri Bell and press the muzzle of the Commander against her ratty, greasy hair.

"Do you understand?"

"Yeah," she says, in a whisper.

"Where's your phone?"

She points.

"Is that the only one?"

"Yeah."

I unplug it and carry it with me.

"Do not, girls," I say, "do anything to piss me off. Do not leave this apartment. Do not go in that room. Do not try to call for help. Do not do anything but sit and watch that TV until I come back here. You understand?"

They nod, slowly, finally.

"Believe me," I say. "It'll go very badly for you if you do."

On my way back to the stairs I toss the phone into the supply closet with the three bound young men.

On the fourth floor only a single bare bulb hangs down, at the head of the staircase. The far end of the hallway lies in deep shadow. As I stand at the top of these stairs, listening again, I feel something here.

And then it moves. From out of that darkness a shape forms itself. It is big and blond and it stares at me. It must have taken out the bulb to give itself some cover. It motions for me to leave, to get the hell out of here, back down the stairs, so I will not be detected.

I shake my head. Waves of telepathic profanity roll down the hallway because I have shown up here like this, interfering. Music seeps from the second apartment, and the sounds of men laughing. I hold the Commander in one hand. With the other I pull my jacket back to reveal the cell phone on my belt. Bank shakes his head and waves again for me to leave.

But I am going to call. I'm going to get Naomi out of here and call for every cop in the district to respond.

I hear voices just inside the door to the first apartment. The handle moves. I take a step backward, down the stairs. Bank's frantically waving me away. *Go. Run.*

Then the phone on my hip rings. Its shrill bleats cut into the gloom and silence of the hallway. I fumble with it, pulling it free and searching for the off button, and in the process dropping the Commander. The phone rings again. As I bend to retrieve my gun, the door to the first apartment flies open and two men run into the hallway.

"Hey!" yells one, a kid. The other, older, shirtless, simply points a gun at my face. He is Abel Jackson. I recognize him from an old mug. Abel motions toward me. The kid jumps forward and scoops up the Commander, then steps quickly back. The phone rings once more before it stops, finally.

"Who the *fuck* are you?" says Abel.

Now the door to the second apartment opens and others step out into the hallway, homies, East Side bangers. They all pause, looking from me to Abel with his gun pointed, trying to figure this scene, trying to know what to do. We all wait.

And then the hallway is filled with the huge, numbing blast of a twelve-gauge shotgun, and with clouds of dust as a portion of the ceiling collapses, raining down plaster and wood. Along with the ceiling, chaos descends. In the moment of this distraction I move down the steps farther, putting the heavy steel banister between me and Abel's gun.

But Abel turns and fires in the direction of the blast, of Bank, over the heads of his now panicked buddies. The window at the end of the hallway shatters. Bangers and johns are everywhere, breaking for the staircase, running like mad past me to get away from the bad shit they know is coming down fast. The kid who came out with Abel leads the way, still carrying my Commander. Then a couple girls run from the second apartment, and behind them the man who came into the building ahead of me. He carries his shirt and is buttoning his trousers as he runs.

Abel, though, does not run. He slips back inside the apartment and closes the door. Bank walks up and without so much as pausing fires the twelve gauge again, blowing the lock and handle, as well as a good portion of wood, from the door. It swings open. Then he looks at me.

"Got a gun?"

I shake my head.

He draws his sidearm, a 9mm Colt much like mine, tosses it to me, and follows Abel inside. The hallway is now empty but for me.

I retrieve the phone first and dial. Yells, shouted curses, sound inside the apartment, followed by a gunshot.

"Dispatch," I say. I'm yelling because I can't hear much except the flat ringing left by the concussions. "This is two two one. I'm code seven one at the corner of Balkan and McKinley. Fourth floor."

"Code seven one," the dispatcher is announcing already, into her mouthpiece.

"Notify Captain Marek," I say. I toss the phone away and follow Bank inside.

It's a big apartment, lots of rooms, though it is hard to make out because in the whole front of the place, the grimy kitchen, the living room to my left, the entrance to the hallway, there is not a light on. I try a wall switch, but it doesn't work.

As I pass into the hallway, I stumble on something. A man. A boy, really, I see, when I turn him. A boy called Eddie Munster. A boy who had already hooked his sister up with a North Side hustler and wannabe-pimp named Abel Jackson. A boy who knew exactly when the church people were supposed to come and take this sister away, and who then sold her out for a little crack business from this same North Side scumbag. Who maybe finally got a little respect on the street from the bangers he wanted so badly to emulate, who was maybe even able to toss them a little business, make them beholden to him. He's been hit once, from what I can tell, in the lower back. He will live or he will die. There's nothing I can do for him.

A gun blast sounds deeper inside the apartment. Another answers it.

I spin into the first bedroom I come to, pushing the Colt before me. It's hard to see in here, too, though the light is on. Someone put a red bulb in the overhead socket, which bathes the room in scarlet. A girl, late teens, cowers in a corner sobbing, a sheet wrapped around her body.

Then Bank, from another room farther back, shouts, "Leave her!"

"Get away! I'll kill her ass!"

"Let her go, Abel! Walk away from it."

"I swear I'll fucking kill her! Get away!"

Bank stands in the doorway to the last bedroom, the shotgun at his shoulder, trained into the room. I approach him.

"It's me," I say, so he doesn't have to glance. I peer around the door frame. The light in here is violet — what we used to call black light when I was a kid and we bought psychedelic posters that glowed in it. Though my eyes take a moment to adjust, I can make out a form sprawled on the single bed, and another behind it, crouched between the bed and the wall.

I remove Bank's Maglite from his belt, and hold it out in front of me with one hand, Bank's gun in the other, pressing them together with the gun sighted along the heavy barrel of the Maglite so that wherever I shine it, that's where the bullet will go. Bank himself taught me this many years ago.

It is Abel kneeling behind the bed, which he's pushed out away from the wall. His mulatto skin looks strangely luminescent in the purple light. His hair is so short, it looks shaved. He wears a goatee and no shirt. I can see a passing resemblance to the artist's sketch we got earlier in the week, one that I couldn't see from his mug shots. Abel bought the tape at the Southtown Food King.

A girl lies naked on the bed, her hands bound to the headboard above her. Her hair is snarled, her eyes huge with terror. But I know who she is.

Abel presses the muzzle of his gun, a large-bore revolver, a .45 maybe, against her left nipple.

Bank cannot fire the shotgun. There's no way he could hit Abel without hitting Tamara as well.

"Back off," I say to Bank, quietly. "It's over."

"He'll kill her. He doesn't give a shit."

"Come on, Bank. Don't give him a reason."

"Hold steady on him. Cover me."

I sense what is coming.

"Bank. Let it go."

"Partner," he says.

"Don't."

"No!" Abel yells. "I swear I'll kill her!"

Bank takes a slow step into the room. He moves to his right, away from the doorway and the bed, his cheek pressed against the butt of the shotgun, holding his aim steady on Abel.

"Get out!" Abel screams. I hold the light on his eyes. He whips the gun back and forth from me to Bank. "Get out!"

Bank moves slowly until he's a couple of steps in, and then he darts suddenly toward the far wall. Not at Abel and the girl, but away from them, and away from me, in an attempt to draw Abel's fire, to pull him off the girl. Which is exactly what happens.

Abel rises on his knees as he swings around toward Bank and fires almost simultaneously. I feel myself jump in shock at the flame his gun throws in the darkened room. The sound coming off the close plaster walls feels like a physical blow. My brain goes numb; time thickens and congeals.

But I find that I have somehow squeezed, too, fired in that same instant, at the circle of light painted on Abel's face. Nothing more than a reaction, really, a reflex.

Tamara screams.

It stops then, the thickness and the noise. The room grows still. Though the percussions in this small space have all but deafened me again, I can hear sirens. They sound like they're miles away, but I imagine they must be very near.

Abel lies folded awkwardly back on himself

behind the bed, one side of his neck blown open. Blood spurts for a few moments from the severed carotid, coating him. Though it's arterial, it looks like tar in the violet light. He shudders once, wheezes, then stops.

Tamara screams again. She sounds far away too.

"Shh," I say. It feels as if I'm talking underwater. "It's all over. It's all done."

It goes quiet again after her scream. Then, as if from a great distance, I hear Bank's harsh breathing. I point the light toward him. He lies on his back, propped against the far wall where he fell.

I cross the room and kneel next to him.

"Legs," he says.

"Your legs are hurt?"

"I can't feel 'em. Give me the gun."

"What?"

"My gun!"

I hold it out. Bank grabs it and begins wiping it with his shirt, but his hands are not steady and he drops it onto his belly and swears.

"What are you doing?"

"Shut up. Listen, I had this gun. I fired. The girl won't know the difference. You hear me?"

"Bank, it doesn't matter," I say. I press his hands against his body to steady them, and then I feel his own blood leaking upward, between our fingers. Too much of it.

I find a handkerchief in my pocket and press it into him, but it soaks through immediately. I pull one of the dirty sheets from the bed and wad it up and press it into Bank's middle.

"Hang on," I tell him.

He nods. His eyes do not leave my face now. He has stopped fussing with the gun.

There is so much I need to tell him. So much I want to ask. But he speaks first.

"You found her?" he says.

I nod. "She's beautiful. She's perfect."

I watch him for a moment, then say, "Do you want me to tell her anything?"

But I know in the moment of my asking that it is the wrong question. He would never send her a message of mere words. His message to her, his gift, is Tamara Shipley. I know this, though he never answers me.

I get home very late but find Naomi and Peggy sitting together at the kitchen table. They have been doing some crying, about a lot of things, I imagine.

Googie caught up with me at St. Jerome's and told me he'd found Naomi in that room and brought her out here himself.

I sit with the two of them. We do not speak.

Naomi is shaking still from her ordeal and from the news she heard before I got here — that Bank died just after midnight.

Peg holds her hand.

The next day, Easter Sunday, is a long, confusing blur. The calls come all day long, one after the other it seems, but I forget them almost as soon as I hang up. Many of the arrangements to be made have fallen to me, though Peg, I think, will end up handling them.

It is the morning I will remember. Though I wanted nothing but to stay asleep for days, to not think, to not remember, Peg and I crept from our bed and hid the two dozen eggs the boys had colored the day before, then slipped back upstairs.

Ben awoke not long after that, excitement filling his eyes as he danced in our bedroom, imploring us to hurry so he could rush downstairs and begin hunting. Jack played along for his brother's sake.

Before I let them start looking, though, I went down and woke Naomi. She, too, was groggy and cranky, but she slipped on her robe and followed me upstairs to join us in watching her brothers crawling madly across the floor in their search.

38

In the end I am left with far too many questions to ever find peace with any of this, questions that go to the heart not only of Bank's actions and motivations, but of my own self-recriminations.

Why did he provoke a gunfight in that room with Abel? Was it purely an action he saw as necessary to save the girl, done without thought of consequences? Or was it the burning car all over again, a reaction to his own despair and rage and shame at what had happened, and at my having finally discovered it?

Why did he send me to find Jamie? To get me out of the way so he could wage his one-man war, or to show me the truth, finally, of what had happened, to unburden himself in some apocalyptic revelation? Or was it to protect the secret, to keep me from stumbling on it in my investigations and so revealing it to the world?

And what really happened those years ago between Bank and Jamie? Had Sarah grossly overreacted to Bank's stalwart instinct to protect and love Jamie, and to her fears of the effects of his past? Or had that love, that need to embrace his daughter, warped in some way by his own horrible experiences, pushed him across a line I would never have believed him capable of crossing? Do the facts of his having found Jamie but not having gone after her, and his later psychiatric treatment, confirm this, or merely illuminate the depths of his despair?

Some mornings I awaken early and lie in bed next to Peggy and turn these questions yet again, or even find new ones, wrinkles, angles I had not quite considered. Once I convince myself of one interpretation or another, I carry it with me for days, feeling uplifted or crushed by its implications. Then, eventually but inexorably, my certainty fades and I am left again with little else but doubt.

The worst of it concerns my own actions, or rather inactions, across the course of my life and Bank's. The effects of my failures to act or speak haunt me, moments from a life of tentativeness, of thinking and wondering too long and acting too little, of looking but failing to see, of knowing but failing to confront. This is true not just of my dealings with Bank and Sarah, but with the others in my life, too, especially Naomi.

There is no doubt that Bank, through his

will and obstinance, instigated and compelled some of the hardest, most lasting decisions I have made — to support and stay with Gloria and help raise Naomi, to join the force and then to become a detective, even to investigate Tamara Shipley. He acted at times as my conscience and my spine.

And there is no doubt that his belief in the proximity of evil to all of our lives, and his vigil against it, were justified, more than I could ever have imagined.

And yet I am still little Maxie Steiner, who cannot help but wonder. What really drove Bank? Were his vehemence and strength the result of some remarkably clear-eyed view of the world, or of the demons that never stopped hounding him? Were the attributes we all so admired in him what led, ultimately, to his destruction? And, if so, does this somehow vindicate my more tentative approach to the world? Or do my inactions lie at the very root of all that happened; might it have been avoided if I had been more like Bank?

The answers to all of these, I have decided, lie somewhere between yes and no, this or that, somewhere in the gray middle, where we who have survived must live.

Bank was buried three days after Easter, on

as perfect a spring day as we ever see in our city. The forecasters had predicted showers but the weather held off until the evening, leaving the morning breezy but bright and almost warm. He had been a member of the parish of the Church of the Sacred Heart, in the central city, not too far to the north of Heron Park, so I spoke at some length with the priest there, who knew Bank well. He agreed in the end that it made sense to bury Bank in the old neighborhood, in the cemetery that Lourdes Church made out of the land at the corner of Liam Road and Pawtucket Street, the land we had once called the Wilderness.

Platoons of reporters and camera crews showed up. Even the national networks sent correspondents. HERO COP RESCUES GIRL IN MORTAL GUNFIGHT. COP DIES KILLING KIDNAPPER. LOCAL HERO TRADES LIFE FOR GIRL. It was a bit of a circus, but one I think Bank would have enjoyed. The cops were there en masse, too, in dress uniforms. There was a short procession from Lourdes Church, where the Mass was held, to the cemetery. The roads were blocked and the troops marched that half mile as a unit, if not in formation.

Tamara Shipley came and was photographed and interviewed ad nauseam. Her picture ended up on the cover of at least one magazine that I saw, and on endless broadcasts. She seemed in shock, as we all were. She had been repeatedly raped but not badly beaten during her week in captivity. The only outward sign of her ordeal was the cut above her eye that she got when she was initially dragged into the car.

A week after it all ended, Tamara was quietly slipped out of the city and driven by an undisclosed party to an undisclosed location. Her half-brother, Emilio Salano, Eddie Munster, did not die from his gunshot wound, which was fired, by the way, from Abel's gun, apparently as Abel was fleeing from Bank. Eddie was charged with several felonies relating to his sister, but not with the murder of Father Hector Morales, which was ascribed to Abel. After a quick plea bargain Eddie was sentenced to a juvenile facility near Columbus. He will be released in three years, when he turns eighteen.

We never discovered who accompanied Abel on the morning he kidnapped Tamara.

I gave statements to other detectives about the events that took place on the night of that Saturday, but for some reason I lied. Though I had actually killed Abel, I stood no chance of facing any kind of censure for this action. I was defending myself and Bank and the girl, and only did what would have been expected, what was called for. I confirmed, though, from the first, what everyone seemed to want to believe: that Bank had given me the shotgun, and that he had fired the final shot from the Colt. Silly, really. But somehow the story caught me up and I didn't want to deny it. I imagined and described for them the wild moment when Bank burst into that bedroom, firing at the same moment Abel was firing back. When the only readable prints the lab was able to lift off the gun belonged to Bank, the story hardened into fact.

On that Monday, after my questioning, Stu Marek pulled me into his office and shut the door. He opened a desk drawer and handed me a plastic evidence envelope, sealed and tagged. Inside were some bits of clear plastic and paint and mirrored glass. The label was dated July of 1989, the location as the Kestler Coil Factory.

"Lab report said those came from a Maglite," he said. "Black. Found inside the factory after Alan Norke's suicide. The rest of the flashlight wasn't found. Been bugging me for years."

"Hmm," I said, and put the bag into my pocket. Then I said, "Stu, I found out about some things that've been going on around here —"

"Do I wanna know about this?" he asked.

"I'm guessing you already do," I said. "That you've known all along."

He made a face and shook his head, but then the fingers started snapping. That night at the funeral home, at a small private viewing, I tucked the evidence envelope into the inside breast pocket of the jacket they had put on Bank.

Crowd Control estimated that there were a thousand people at the cemetery. I found it all a bit distracting, a little over the top, so it was hard for me to concentrate on anything. But then, I didn't have much to concentrate on anyway. At the graveside service I didn't really listen to what was said. I looked at the elementary school across the street, which had been closed and boarded up for years, and then off to the south, across those now groomed and planted fields, past the creek, to that stand of trees. It looked smaller now, thinned out and aged.

I wanted badly, then, to leave the crowds and the adulations and the hyperbole, to take my sons with me and walk across that grass to the creek, to follow it back to find the pool that I knew must still be there. I didn't, though it occurred to me as I stood there thinking about it that Bank probably would have.

The force has changed some, in the wake of all of this. The high Command has been reevaluating its decision to do away with most of the old detective squads. They've already reinstituted elements of some of the more specialized squads, including Katherine's Juvenile Sex Crimes Unit. Rumors have it that Violent Crimes and my old Juvenile Squad may not be far behind.

I tracked down, over in Akron, a woman named Angela Hall, who was born Angela Watson and lived for a time when she was a girl with a foster family near my house and was the object of my first crush. She told me, after we'd caught up and relaxed a little with each other, that she had in fact been regularly raped by Ned and fondled and penetrated by Frances as well. It had happened to Bank, too, she knew. She and Bank had never talked much to each other about what went on. She'd finally got some counseling in her late twenties, after she'd had two kids and a divorce. It helped her a great deal, she said.

At Angela's request I put out some feelers about Ned and Frances Baxter. Rick Simms, my FBI buddy, called me one afternoon to say that Ned had done some time in Michigan in the early eighties for statutory rape, but only a few months, and had died a few years later in a hospital in Kalamazoo. Frances moved after that, and had not shown up since then in the national crime computers. Rick said he'd keep looking if I wanted, but I told him no. I did not want to see her or talk to her or give her even the slim satisfaction of knowing that someone, somewhere, remembered her, or thought that her life, whether bad or good, had been worth recalling all these years later.

I am now a part of the Command. I took the exam this summer and was promoted to sergeant soon after. Googie's retiring after the new year and Stu tells me that I have the inside track to head Missing Persons once he's gone. I have mixed feelings about this. It is not a place I imagine myself staying for long, but it will be a beginning, as it was once before for me.

My kids are growing so quickly that I have trouble, sometimes, seeing them for what they are and not how I remember them. Naomi seems to be a part of us, now, though that does not mean we don't have rough patches. She is, after all, a teenager. Jack is as noisy and overly energetic as ever, and happy. Ben is quieter, like me, though not as moody or bookish. He seems already, at his age, anxious to embrace the world in ways I was not. In the morning preschool class he attends, he's become outright popular and tells us that he's received at least two proposals of marriage.

Not long after Bank died, Peggy started talking about wanting to go back to church. The idea didn't appeal to me, and she did not push, but she did begin taking the boys by herself to a Methodist church on Alcore. They go from time to time, often enough to have some continuity. The boys are enrolled in Sunday school classes. Naomi, believe it or not, goes sometimes as well, and has made some friends in the high school class.

Still, at times I do feel the need to find a quiet place to meditate or just sit. When I do, I usually park on Morris Hill, near the building where Bank once lived. It is at the opposite corner of the park from my destination, but I enjoy the walk and look forward to it. I pass beyond the section of picnic tables and grills, the pond near the clubhouse, to the first fairway. If it's a clear day and there are golfers out, I'll sometimes hike up north and east a little ways, to circle around the tenth green, and then cut back past the old shelter house. Or I'll just wait for a group to tee off and follow them up the first fairway, and find my way across the course in that manner.

Until I come to an especially heavily wooded spot that drops steeply away into a deep ravine, to an old band shell that still stands there. The graffiti is always new, always fresh, the language itself mutating with each new wave of artists. I hike down the slope, sometimes staying on the stone pathway, sometimes jumping from one tiered level to the next, until I reach the stage. There is never anyone around. The artists only come out at night. Night is the time I should come, too, but I have a family and so cannot. I do not go out much into the nights anymore.

Here in the daylight I sit on the stage, usually, my feet hanging over the edge, and look up into the high trees and listen to the city that lies beyond them — the sirens winding down as they approach City Med, the rumbling traffic on Andrew Jackson. And in what must be a form of homage, or remembrance, or perhaps even prayer, I suppose, I think about heroes, about what profound shortcomings all of them must have, what pits of rage or self-doubt or shame they harbor within them that they fight so mightily to fill, and about what it takes to become one.

I think about all of us who swirled around Bank in the vortex of his need and his compulsions, about Sarah and Jamie, my parents and my boys and Peggy. And about Naomi and how Bank gave her back to me. And then I think that, in a sense, by his dying, he gave to her, to all my family, a part of me they had never been able to claim.

I think that, from the time we were kids, I was afraid of losing him, or something in him I thought I needed. So that instead of facing him, naming what lay between us, forcing him out, all of which he needed me to do, I did the opposite. I went along; I played the good buddy. Though not, perhaps, the good friend. The irony, of course, is that this very fear begat the loss itself.

I see this now. I see it when I look at Naomi sulking in her room, or listen to the boys screaming, or grab Peggy for a stolen second during the day. And it is different between us. I face each of them in ways I did not, before. I am learning to name what I would once have left anonymous, whether it is fear or disappointment or simply joy. And I am trying to teach them the importance of this, of saying what they know, or feel, or wonder. Of opening themselves to those who love them best. Of the importance of daylight.

Still, it is hard sometimes to face what has gone before, and what will come. I ask for forgiveness, though Bank would say that it's an overrated commodity. Overrated because it doesn't change anything. So I ask, too, for courage. And in so asking, I sometimes find, as Bank would have known, that it is granted.

ACKNOWLEDGMENTS

My deepest gratitude to Gary Cook, Assistant Prosecuting Attorney, Lucas County, Ohio, for opening the door; Toledo Police Department Detective Phil Kulakoski for showing me the inside; and Detective Danny Navarre for taking me into the night. Each granted me nothing but generosity and patience.

Thanks also to Lucas County Deputy Coroner Dr. Diane Scala-Barnett; Toledo Police Department Senior Criminalist Ed. Franks; Jayne Waldron, for the use of her unpublished essay on gang graffiti; Alexander Holden for car-color-recognition research assistance; and Paul Weeman and Molly Behrmann, for editorial advice. A special thank you to my wife, Lisa, who believes implicitly, even when I am convinced that failure is certain. And once again, an acknowledgment of my debt to Leslie Schnur and Gail Hochman, whose collective tenacity, endurance, and perceptiveness continue to surprise me.

Though it is perhaps not necessary, I feel I must say here, finally, that no character, scenario, or institution in this book is based directly upon or meant to be representative in any way of any actual person, situation, or institution.

We hope you have enjoyed this Large Print book. Other Thorndike Press or Chivers Press Large Print books are available at your library or directly from the publishers.

For more information about current and upcoming titles, please call or write, without obligation, to:

Thorndike Press
P.O. Box 159
Thorndike, Maine 04986 USA
Tel. (800) 257-5157

OR

Chivers Press Limited
Windsor Bridge Road
Bath BA2 3AX
England
Tel. (0225) 335336

All our Large Print titles are designed for easy reading, and all our books are made to last.